Dive! Dive! Dive!
The Piracy of HMS Astute

by Brian Gregory

This book is dedicated to my dear wife Carol. A book widow for three years plus, bless her. She accepts that will carry on during phases of books two and three. I cherish her company for what time we do spend together.

A special thank you to Plymouth Central Library. The dedicated staff have been invaluable. The many hundreds of hours of research I have conducted there have been challenging. On the odd occasion when I have had a technical problem with a computer, someone has been there to help.

Chapter 1

Date: Tuesday 13th February 2018 Time 08.00hrs
Navy Command Headquarters (Northwood) Middlesex
Admiral of the Fleet (Chief of Staff) Simon Neilson's office

Assembled seven of the most senior and experienced members of the British armed forces. Also present the Defence Minister Lord Cunningham and Admiral Dexter Truman, American ambassador to the United Kingdom. In the anti-room to Admiral Neilson's office, Captain Blake Channing the admiral's adjutant had briefly laid out the format of the impending meeting.

The assembly consisting of Rear Admiral Stephen Jennings (Submarine Divisional Commander), Commodore Ayden James (AUWE weapons expert), Major General Andrew Arrowhead Horswell (S.A.S), Commodore Brian Toby Thomas (S.B.S). Also, present, Air vice Marshal Barry Symonds (Special adviser, black operations), Captain John Gould (MI6 security specialist) and Brigadier Rowland Blakelock (Finance director black operations).

"Gentlemen the Admiral will be with you shortly; he is just receiving the latest update of information from our people" said Blake Channing.

Jeff Cunningham sat stony faced while the rest of the

men chatted in hushed voices amongst themselves. The brief conversation was interrupted as the door opened and Admiral Neilson strolled into the room. Stern faced and holding a top-secret folder, he placed it neatly and precisely on his desk in front of him and sat down. Turning to his adjutant he barked,

"Blake, unless you deem it absolutely necessary no disturbance until this meeting is concluded."

"Understood, Sir." Blake left the room and closing the mahogany faced solid steel door behind him.

"Morning, forgive me if I dispense with the formalities, you all know me and small talk is not my forte." Admiral Neilson took a sip of iced water from his glass and opened the folder in front of him. "The seemingly impossible has become a reality. As of yesterday, at approximately 02.30hrs at Devonport Naval base, H.M.S. Astute, the first of the new class of hunter killer submarines was pirated away by persons unknown. The sub has recently completed a major refit, with weapons and systems upgrades. After extensive sea trials and with minor adjustments by the dockyard staff, they are now fully functional." The Admiral paused for effect, and looked at each man individually to gauge their reaction. As expected, there was very little. All were battle hardened veterans of various conflicts. "We need to come up with a plan to get my submarine and its crew back. The how it was pirated away later; the reason why it was stolen in the first instance seems apparent. From the information we have at hand, it would appear a ransom of £14 billion, the build value of the fleet of seven submarines, has been demanded by the instigator of this heinous crime." Admiral Neilson took another sip of his water and referred to his file again. Totally aware of the assembled team's expertise, he was glad no one wanted to ask a question the worst was still to come. "We know exactly where the submarine is, nineteen nautical miles off Plymouth sound in approximately 90 meters of water. We know they are there and they know we know. On-board are approximately a third of the full crew and that would normally amount to ninety sailors. The officer team consists of the Captain, Robert Southward, along with the Executive Officer, Lieutenant Commander Ray Lavis and Navigating Officer Lieutenant Jack Spalding. There is a team of senior and junior ratings, including the master at arms. The senior rate numbers are 13, while the junior rates are 14 that make up the complement. We are assuming all of those thirty are still with the submarine; at least we hope so. The two junior rate guards that were on the casing were left behind. The part crew are sufficient to operate the sub on a short-term basis. The rest of the assigned crew are in H.M.S. Drake at Devonport being debriefed. Not expected to glean much information from them. Thankfully no females are on board. I was instrumental in making sure the fairer sex never went to sea operationally on Nuke's, it just doesn't work for us. We have received information from the Pirate leader that he intends to ransom the submarine and crew to a foreign power if we do not co-operate. We have been given name, rank and numbers of all the British crew; this information has now been corroborated."

The Admiral paused once again and sighed. "There are eight tomahawk cruise missiles on board with a range of over twelve hundred miles. Also, six spearfish long range torpedoes, all with inert warheads, secured in the torpedo stowage compartment. We are dealing with a cunning individual who leads a very well-trained group of specialists, with considerable knowledge of the workings of our submarine. The numbers are unknown but my experts tell me at least twelve, with a maximum of twenty would have been required to take over the submarine."

"Admiral, why did we not have a full complement on board Astute when this piracy occurred?" The Defence Minister interjected.

The Admiral looked directly at the minister. "Well, Minister, you may or may not know our hunter killer submarines go out on patrol for up to six months at a time. Often in peace time and especially during theatres of war, that time can be considerably longer. It all depends on operational requirements, as in this case, trials of the new systems. Varying degrees of sea and dockside trials have taken place, hence the policy. It has been the Admiralty's policy on submarines, at the Captain's discretion to billet men ashore when possible. When base ported or visiting other naval dockyards, non-watch keeping and maintenance crew are allowed this privilege. It's good for morale. Watch keeping routine is exactly the same, there is no disruption to the submarine or welfare of the crew. As Astute was at waterfront state, approximately thirty crew members were required afloat at any one time. The submarine was due to come to ready for sea state and more trials in two days' time, when all the crew would be required."

"I see," said Jeff Cunningham, "and yes I did know that. Can I assume that adequate arrangements have been made to make sure all our remaining submarines are secure?"

The Admiral sensed the undertones in the Defence Minister's voice, but keeping his cool replied,

"Yes, Minister. My staff have revised and issued orders accordingly, to all base ported submarine Captains. In the first instance, our own marines and M.O.D. police have doubled patrols within appropriate exclusion areas."

Cunningham listened with a sense of annoyance. "Well, better late than never, I suppose."

Before the Defence Minister could say anymore, Admiral Neilson continued with his brief.

"Gentlemen we do have some facts regarding the pirate leader. At the moment his identity is unknown, however he has furnished us with a specific name, Red Fox. Our people are desperately trying to find out as much information as they can. The worrying facts are that he seems to know an awful lot about our submarine operations and our chain of command." The Admiral paused again, he knew these men would want to know the ins and outs of a cat's backside, but did not have the time to go into it all "This so-called Red Fox has made contact with his demands through flash traffic picked up at GCHQ. I am loath to call this pirate a mad man; however, it may come to pass that he lives up to that title. We do not have any facts regarding the state of the crew but must assume they are under duress or worse. It's probable the Captain has issued orders to co-operate with the pirates for the time being." The Admiral was intentionally withholding information he had at his disposal. To get a possible rescue / retrieval plan underway it was not necessary for the people assembled to know some information he was party to. Continuing "Gentlemen, we are faced with the worst possible scenario. We are dealing with a group of very skilled and ruthless people of foreign nationality, with definite navy background, and that certainly limits the options as to who they are. The Pirates know what they are doing and have a considerable shore based back up, that we are trying to penetrate. This is proving considerably difficult; they have covered their tracks extremely well. However, I am sure our security services are doing all they can and will eventually come up with some answers."

The Defence Minister commented that that may be wishful thinking.

Turning to Jeff Cunningham, Admiral Neilson said, "Minister, that is the bones of the problem we have. I assume you will need to brief the Prime Minister as soon as possible? I appreciate we need her approval to instigate negotiations with Red Fox. I will converse with you later as to the way ahead."

"Indeed, Admiral, the Prime Minister will insist on a meeting with you to go over some points at first hand, I will set this up with your people."

"Thank you for that, Minister"

Cunningham stood up, picked up his brief case and stowed the scant paperwork he had been given in the pre-brief. He nodded to the assembled men turned and left without another word. This situation had the highest level of security attached to it. Nothing of a sensitive nature would leave Northwood unless it was deemed absolutely necessary.

The Chief of Staff waited until the Minister left the room. "Okay people, we need to come up with a plan to cripple the Astute and if absolutely necessary, destroy it. We believe its capabilities are ahead of anything deployed by America or Russia. It will be a heavy price to pay but we simply cannot allow our submarine to leave British waters. It represents the stealthiest hunter killer submarine the British Navy has ever put to sea." The Admiral paused and gathered his thoughts. "You all have the next twenty four hours, and then I need you to get back to me with positive solutions. I appreciate it does not allow you very much of a window, but time is of the essence. At the very least, we have to incapacitate that submarine. I expect to authorise the infiltration of the sub regardless of casualties, friend or foe. Of course, this will need the Prime Minister's authority and I expect that to be a formality."

The First Sea Lord had at his disposal more potential destructive power than was dispensed during the Second World War. However, right now he was faced with a situation that was unique. Never in the history of the Navy had a British submarine been stolen. For that matter neither had there ever been a situation where a crew mutinied on a British submarine.

Black operations would need to fund this whole sorry mess from start to finish. Express authorisation would be needed from the cabinet; black ops was only budgeted with £1 billion at a time. If it was necessary the major part of the £14 billion would have to come from the war chest.

The Defence Minister was always at loggerheads with Rowland Blakelock who was responsible for allocating funds. Concerned about his ever shrinking budget, this would make things considerably worse.

"Gentlemen, this meeting is closed. I am sure you have plenty to think about." Admiral Neilson turned to Rear Admiral Stephen Jennings.

"I need to talk to you afterwards"

"Yes, Admiral, I think I know what's coming."

"We resume at 07.00hrs tomorrow morning."

Simon Neilson waited until all the others had left the room.

"Stephen what's the latest?"

"Well, Sir, previously to this meeting I spoke to Commander Lawrence, Exec Officer new projects. Jennings hesitated with concern in his voice. "The systems worked perfectly, with some minor adjustments, Trisonic imaging and Hovertrack are an incredible success. Furthermore, the submarine is stocked with enough supplies for a full crew for three months. With a skeleton crew and the pirates, it could circumnavigate the world's oceans without needing to surface."

The Commander in Chief leaned back and put his hands behind his head.

"Damn and blast. In a million years I could never have envisaged this situation. If these pirates succeed with their intentions, this could turn into a disaster. They must be stopped no matter what. Okay, keep me informed of all developments."

He returned to the file in front of him and poured over all the information page by page. Having a photographic memory was of great benefit but his mind was telling him he had missed something important.

He had requested the career and personal files on all the crew, captive or otherwise, associated with Astute. If there was the slightest hint that any one of his men had colluded in this heinous crime, then MI6 would have to act on that information immediately.

The Admiral had previously had two of his senior staff run all the checks and they had found nothing untoward. With the information at hand, he had to accept that all his sailors including the Captain were true to the cause. But how would they react under duress? Only those unfortunate sailors aboard Astute would know the answer to that. He imagined the situation was terrifying. Alone in his office he reflected on the state of affairs that confronted him. *'Well how the hell did this band of marauding pirates glean so much information to enact this crime? My God this is unimaginable and very frightening.'* The day to day administration would now be delegated to the next Admiral in the chain of command. The gravity of the situation and the planning of how to tackle it, would need all of the Chief of Staff's attention. He would remain in the Northwood complex along with his team until a satisfactory conclusion came about.

Chapter 2

Tuesday, February 6th 2001 early evening
Alicia's bar, adjacent to the Juliet restaurant, Rockingham,
South Australia

Alicia Juliet Harris was a beautiful woman; she scared some men off by her stunning beauty and elegance. Once she considered a career in modelling, but her mother had dissuaded her from doing it.

"That career is for those ladies less fortunate than you, my dear." she would say. Private schooling at Roedean College for girls in Brighton gave Alicia the grounding that her parents expected of a naval officers daughter. Being the only child, she was miserable in her formative years. She saw very little of Lionel, her father, who was busy carving out a name for himself while rapidly gaining promotion.

It was totally devastating when, at the age of 18, her mother was diagnosed with terminal cancer. Alicia gave up everything to be with her mother; during the two years, she saw her suffer and wither away. Alicia was with her constantly until the peaceful end came.

Despising her father for his lack of compassion and minimal physical presence, it was no surprise that three years later, he introduced a woman 20 years his junior who would become her stepmother. Julie Canning had been her father's wren secretary while shore-based at H.M.S. Raleigh, Torpoint in Cornwall. It was now quite obvious to Alicia that they had been having an affair for some considerable time.

This was the last straw, and she turned her back on the whole sorry episode even though she desperately craved family support. She decided to go to Australia and make a fresh start in life. She invested the sizable inheritance her mother had left her in a large waterside bar and restaurant close to the Naval Base H.M.A.S. Stirling, in Rockingham, South Australia.

Eighteen months later, it came as a complete shock when she heard of her father's death in a boating accident in the Bahamas. After retiring from the Navy, he along with Julie had decided to purchase a large yacht and sail around warmer waters. Evidently, late at night in choppy waters, he had fallen overboard while trying to secure some rigging. Copious amounts of wine had rendered his wife unconscious. She had eventually emerged from her drunken stupor and realised Lionel was missing. In the early hours when it was apparent he was lost overboard she tried to alert the local coastguard without success. Letting off flairs to attract attention was her only option left. Finally, a fishing boat came to her aid and the skipper took over.

The response from the authorities was slow, and it was not until late afternoon on the second day that his body was found washed up on a near-deserted beach by a local out walking. It had been dashed on rocks and was almost unrecognisable, and the crabs had started their grisly work.

It took a long time for the inquest and subsequent release of Alicia's father's body. There had been some doubt as to the circumstances relating to his death. The local police thoroughly investigated the case and interviewed Julie on several occasions. However, with a total lack of evidence other than her statement and that of the man who found the body, it was finally concluded that death was by drowning, an avoidable tragic accident.

Two fully functioning, unused life jackets were found stowed on-board the yacht. It was deduced that, although Lionel was a good swimmer he was not wearing one and had succumbed to the elements.

Alicia had contacted Julie to offer support and see if there was anything she could do. As expected, the response was negative; Lionel's wife having been labelled as something of a gold digger was not interested and was downright rude to her stepdaughter. Naturally, Julie's family had rallied around her; she had suddenly become a comparatively rich woman.

Retired Rear Admiral Lionel Harris's body was eventually flown back in a Hercules transport plane to Brize Norton military base, in Oxfordshire. Although he could not be afforded any greater military honours, his coffin was carried by ex-fellow naval officers to the waiting hearse. The Ministry of Defence had made all the arrangements to get his remains home; the military look after their own especially retired Admirals.

Alicia bravely attended her father's cremation, where she knew the reception would be hostile, only an elderly Aunt had bothered to make polite conversation. Feeling no sorrow over her father's death, she deemed best to leave the church service immediately after it concluded. To go to the wake would have just made things worse; after all, she had never been introduced to any of his naval colleagues or friends.

Deciding to have a few days in London until her long flight back to Australia she had contacted an old girlfriend from Roedean. Jenifer Baron had been her roommate, and they had developed a strong bond. The infrequent contact with her friend was now Alicia's only true link with the homeland, Australia and her business was her life now. It was great to spend some time with Jennifer, who had her own hairdressing and spa business. Having a husband, three children and her business meant life was hectic. Alicia envied Jenifer, who had always had great family support. On occasions while boarding at Roedean, during the non-term time she had been made welcome at Jenny's parent's sprawling farm in the Cotswolds. To Alicia, it represented true family life, and she really enjoyed it, they were like sisters and had great times together.

After a few days shopping, dining, and catching up on old times, it was time for both of them to get back to their normal lives. It was a tearful goodbye as they still enjoyed each other's company so much. Jenny promised when she could, to visit Alicia in Australia. It was an open invitation, and both of them assumed it would happen at some time. Little did they know events would overtake them both, and they would come to rely on each other again in the future.

The moment Alicia arrived back in her apartment at the waterside complex, she felt entirely at home. It was a safe haven, and the people who she employed were supportive and protective of her. Amongst others, American, Canadian and British officers frequented the place where Alicia and her female employees were the focus of the attention.

Very professional in her approach, she would not mix business with pleasure and kept the clientele at arm's length. That was until Lieutenant Robert John Southward walked in early one evening in April. He was on secondment to the Royal Australian Navy, having been a serving junior officer on H.M.S. Unseen. One of a class of diesel-electric submarines that after the end of the cold war, the Admiralty decided there was no longer a need for this type of sub. The four boats built, Upholder, Ursula, Unseen and Unicorn out of an intended fleet of 19 were subsequently leased and then sold to become an integral part of the Australia navy.

Unlike most of the men who walked into Alicia's restaurant, he did not initially acknowledge her presence. He was in civilian clothes, immaculate white cotton shirt and dark blue slacks and black patent leather shoes. She knew instantly he was a British Naval officer. He sat at a table near the front of the terrace bar, reading his paper and ordered a beer from one of the waitresses. She returned to the bar area and poured up an ice-cold lager.

"That's alright, Tracy, I will serve him."

"Dishy isn't he, boss? Not much of a conversationalist though."

"I would say certainly different and rather interesting." They both laughed, which attracted Robert's attention.

Alicia placed the beer on a mat with a paper napkin and bowl of peanuts on the tray. She strolled over to where he was sitting.

"Your beer, Sir, are you dining with us this evening?"

He folded his paper and looked at her. "Oh, thank you, that makes a nice change to hear a pleasant English voice, what are you doing out here?" He looked directly into her piercing blue eyes, God she was beautiful. Alicia matched his gaze, and he lowered his stare to his beer, he was blushing.

"Well a single girl has to make a living," she replied in her plumy English accent. "It's quiet, mind if I join you for a drink? It's my break."

"Please do." Robert rose and pulled the chair back for her to sit down. He could not help but notice her stunning form through the thin flowered cotton dress.

"Oh! A perfect Gentleman as well." They both laughed nervously. She sat, turned to the bar and waved to Petra, who was busy whispering to Tracy. Instantly a glass of iced soda water appeared on the table. Tracy beamed at Robert, turned and walked away with a wry smile on her face.

"Are they all as friendly here?"

"It is a requirement to look after the customers; our motto is bow low and charge high. You will find all waiters and waitresses are the same; tips mean everything here."

Alicia could tell Robert was shy around women, but she instantly liked him. He was different from her usual customers who in the main thought they were God's gift to women blinded by a naval uniform.

"Let me guess. British Naval officer on detachment to the Australian Navy not long arrived."

"Are you a Russian spy?" He jokingly blurted out, showing his perfect white teeth.

"Absolutely right, my orders are to seduce you and gain whatever useless information you are party too."

Robert looked away; he was nervous in her company and she sensed it.

Just then a party of Australian Naval officers walked in. Seeing Alicia, two of them approached her table, before they could say a word, she said,

"Good evening, gentlemen, usual cover?" Clicking her fingers, a waiter and waitress came rushing over. Tony, the head waiter chaperoned the officers into the restaurant. Southward was thrown off guard; he assumed this beautiful creature must be the head waitress, and those guys went like lambs to the slaughter.

"It's amazing here," said Robert. Do you stay open late?"

"We stay open until midnight weekdays, and 1am Saturdays; mind you, we do not tolerate any bad behaviour. Later you will see the discrete security guards, rather large characters with egos to match but their presence is enough to keep the few rowdy visitors in order. Infrequently the odd person having had too much to drink becomes rude or aggressive; they are escorted off the premises never to return. Sundays we close at 4pm." The small talk continued until Alicia said: "Right my break is over, did you say you were dining here this evening?"

He was taken off guard for a moment. "Oh yes I most definitely want to, is there any chance of you joining me? I can wait until your shift is complete if that's satisfactory."

It was Alicia's turn to be coy, "Let me think, this place will get busy now, but I do live above the premises and I finish at eight. I could get my friend the head chef to rustle up something interesting. Do you like Cantonese food?"

"Absolutely adore it, and I would certainly welcome your company, I hate dining alone."

Alicia was blushing now. "See you at eight then." She rose, pivoted and walked gracefully away.

When she got back to the bar, Tracy was there grinning like a Cheshire cat.

"Don't say a word, book me a restaurant cover and make sure my friend has a beer on the house. I will be having dinner with him at 8 o'clock. On second thoughts we will dine in my apartment. Oh! And don't tell him who I am or you will be looking for another job, I am off to see the chef."

"Yes, madam. Right away, madam! I knew it would happen one day, you have pulled." They both laughed again.

Alicia was extremely professional in her attitude towards customers and staff, and that's what made her such a success. The people she employed loved working for her, and there was a waiting list at the agency who supplied them. Alicia was a good boss and paying well meant she didn't need to keep an eye on the till. The ambience she had created in the bar and restaurant went down exceptionally well with all who frequented the establishment.

For naval and civilian clients alike it was known as the 'in place'. Alicia went about her business in the now very crowded restaurant and terrace bar. Occasionally she kept tabs on the stranger who sat on his own reading a book, totally engrossed. He seemed reluctant to join in any conversation with individuals who tried to engage him; he was certainly different from the run of the mill naval personnel. Most liked to let their hair down after a gruelling day, especially on a Friday. It was accepted that the officers who came into her bar worked hard and played hard. For the most part, they acted like gentlemen and were very welcome as they generally spent well. For those who were on call or doing late duties, alcohol was off the menu.

It seemed quite strange to Alicia that this particular British naval officer made no effort whatsoever to converse with two attractive young females dressed to kill. By their body language, it was plain to see they were very interested in him. Making the excuse of not being able to find an available table, they sat down at his. He smiled but remained distant, which they didn't much like. Eventually, when they realised they were getting nowhere, they politely left to take up residence on stools at the bar.

"What a boring fart, he must be English. Oh well, his loss. He could have had a good time tonight," said one of them. They weren't used to rejection. It came as no surprise that several predatory men instantly approached them.

Alicia found herself excited at the prospect of entertaining this mystery man. 'Oh God, I hope he is not married or gay,' she thought.

"Tony." said Tracy, "The boss wants you to show the British fellow to her apartment at eight-thirty, he's called Robert."

"I will have a job; he's gone."

"What? The only guy she has been interested in for ages, and he has done a runner, did he leave with a white stick?"

"Oh well, that's his problem. I had better tell the boss."

"No, give it a while I am sure he will be back, who in their right mind would pass up an offer of dinner with Alicia?"

Sure enough, just before 8 o'clock, Robert Southward appeared at the front steps with a huge bouquet of flowers.

"Christ! I will go and grab him before he trips over the ribbon," said Tony.

"Excuse me, Sir, are you dining with Miss Alicia Harris this evening?" Bob was embarrassed, he hadn't even asked her name, his throat was dry, and he felt like a lost schoolboy. I'm a leader, not a follower he thought, but for once in my life, I am not in charge of my own destiny.

"Oh yes I think I am, is she around?"

"Yes, indeed she is but has changed the arrangements as there isn't a cover available just now, so you will be dining privately. Follow me, Sir, she is expecting you. She finished a little earlier than normal."

Lieutenant Southward followed his chaperone across the bar without question. It was pretty evident by his mannerisms he was gay. Tony pressed the button to open the lift door, allowing Robert to enter first. Requesting the second floor, they rose in nervous silence. When they got there, the door opened to reveal a tastefully decorated corridor with lush carpet.

"Mr Robert, you are an invited guest to the Belvedere suite, third door on the left." With that, Tony turned around, entered the lift and descended with a smile on his face. Pacing the short distance, he gingerly knocked on the door then waited. As Alicia opened the door, his mouth fell open. She wore a pale blue dress cut from the top of her breasts to her thighs. He thrust the bouquet at her and made her step backwards. "Wow, what have I done to deserve these beautiful flowers? Please come in."

He was most impressed; the apartment was extensively decorated and complemented by expensive Japanese furniture.

"What would you like to drink, can I call you Bob? Please sit down."

"Oh, a beer please, yes that's fine."

She disappeared into the kitchen with the flowers. Southward sat down and took in the surroundings, 'Christ she must earn well to be able to afford a place like this,' he surmised.

Alicia appeared with a large beer and a glass of bubbly. She went back to get the flowers that were now in a beautifully decorated opal blue Japanese vase and placed them on the rattan table.

"The flowers are fantastic. Thank you so much."

"You are welcome. I hope you like the choice."

"Oh yes, I love lilies; such fragrance, my favourite."

"I can't remember the last time I bought someone flowers." They both laughed.

"So, tell me all about yourself, are you married?"

He smiled "No, still the gay bachelor; shall I rephrase that? Still a bachelor and certainly not interested in Tony, if you know what I mean?"

Alicia laughed "Yes, I know what you mean, he's a real gem around the place, and we don't know what we would do without him."

"What do you mean?"

"Oh! All the staff here, we are just one big happy family, and we accept Tony for what he is. Lives with his partner in a nice waterside apartment but never mixes business with pleasure, we never see Josh."

Bob looked around the place; it was pretty obvious this had the exclusive woman's touch; soft pastel colours and expensive ornaments adorned the place.

"Well, do you like what you see?"

"Sorry, you must think I'm rude I can't think of a more tastefully decorated apartment, your taste or the owner?"

"I have to say both, actually." Alarm bells rang in his mind, oh no surely she doesn't earn extra money entertaining male clientele here, he thought.

"You look puzzled," she said.

"Well I am, how can a waitress afford such luxury, are you sleeping with the owner?" "You could say that."

Bob looked directly at Alicia. "Is this how you supplement your income entertaining mugs like me for the right price? If it is then I'm not interested, you said you sleep with the owner, but obviously not just with him?"

Alicia lifted the champagne and took a hefty gulp. "Bob I'm teasing you. I am the owner, but I love working with my staff at the coal face, it's good entertainment most of the time."

He nearly choked on his beer, "Wow, you're the owner?" he blurted out.

"That's right; the whole complex is mine. I have worked hard to make the place a success. It was quite run down when I took it over five years ago. At that time, most of the grubby staff that worked here had their fingers in the till and it was losing money. The only honest one amongst them was Tracy; she has been with me from the start. The rest either got fired or left before they were — the sixteen staff I have now I trust implicitly. I pay them above the going rate, and they respect that, by not seeing me off. Over the years, I have expanded the business. The six spare bedrooms are nearly always reserved; mainly on short term lets, to selected service personnel." "Alicia, I am so sorry; I didn't mean to be rude. You certainly had me fooled." He went quiet and downed his beer.

There was a knock at the door.

"Ah good the food has arrived, you get it while I pour you another cold one, or would you prefer wine?"

"I'll stick with the beer please, heavy day tomorrow." They spent the rest of the evening in general conversation and the time passed enjoyably quickly. Robert looked at his watch.

"Wow, it's nearly midnight. I must go. I am starting trials at 06.00 hours. That meal was superb; could I return the compliment by taking you out to dinner on Friday?" "Well, yes, as it happens, it is my day off, and I would enjoy getting away for the evening. I expect you have been to Mark Rowland's restaurant in town?"

"No, I haven't yet."

"Well, in my opinion, they have the best-prepared steaks available anywhere, they are amazing."

"Okay, I will pick you up here at 7 o'clock if that suits."

"Certainly does. I will be waiting in the bar."

Alicia showed Robert to the door; he took her hand and held it gently looking directly into her eyes. "Thank you for a fantastic evening. I have enjoyed it immensely."

"You are welcome, Bob."

With that, he left and made his way to the lift. Alicia closed the door and sat down to finish her champagne. Surprising. He didn't even try to kiss me, she thought. Definitely different from the run of the mill guys I come across here. The trouble was, she had wanted him to make a pass at her, he was intriguing, and for some reason she fancied him. That hadn't happened for a long time; Alicia Juliet Harris wanted Friday to come around as quickly as possible.

Early the next morning she went down to the bar, opening time was not until 9 am, but a restless night had left her tired and confused. What was she doing getting involved with a British Naval officer? Had she not learned her lesson from her less than happy past instigated by her father?

As always, Tracy and Tony were already there preparing for the expected customers. "Hello boss, how did the date go? Did the dishy Bob end up in your bed?"

"Don't be stupid, Tracy; you know I would never do that on a first date if ever. The strange thing is we enjoyed a great evening together. At the end of it, we shook hands, and he left."

"What?"

"Yep, that's how it was, although he has invited me out Friday evening."

"Oh my God, I hope for your sake he doesn't bat for the other side? What a waste." "No, I don't think so; he just seems shy around women. Anyway, I will get to know more on Friday, he seems as deep as the ocean, but I will find out all I want to know for sure."

"No doubt you will, he won't know what's hit him."
They both chuckled at the prospect of chewing over the fat
again; they were more like sisters than work associates.

Chapter 3

Friday, February 9th 2001. Late afternoon
The Juliet restaurant, Rockingham, South Australia

Alicia had only had two serious relationships since being resident in Australia. The first was a short affair with James Stratton. He owned several car dealerships and lavished her with expensive gifts, including a beautiful red Ferrari. He took her to many top events associated with the motor trade where he paraded her as arm candy.

At any prestigious event, whenever a new model was launched, she was always invited to attend. He loved having her by his side as she researched the technical background to the car in question and became quite knowledgeable; his motor trade friends were very impressed. To Alicia, she though it all seemed a bit flash; his rich friends and colleagues with their partners or wives were not of the real world. Money was no object, and they took great delight in black catting one another. A bigger house, car or boat seemed more important than anything else; this was not what she wanted, and she was looking for a way of getting out of the relationship.

Finally, when he presented her with a large diamond engagement ring, the writing was on the wall. Letting him down gently was not easy; he worshipped Alicia; to him, she was not just arm candy but the woman he loved. James could not understand why she did not want the lavish life he could give her.

One evening after consuming far too much whisky he got into his Bugatti EB 110, super sports. It was raining, and he drove far too fast along the beach road for the conditions. Unable to negotiate a sharp bend, the car skidded off the road and ploughed into a tree killing him instantly.

It was hard for Alicia to come to terms with his death; she felt responsible even though she had no control over what had happened. It took a lot of consoling by her friends to get to grips with the guilt and awful depression she felt. He was a decent chap who treated her with respect, and now because of her rejection, he was dead. Not really loving him she knew she should have ended the relationship long ago and she wished she had.

The longest relationship Alicia had lasted for eighteen months. She had deep feelings for Guy Johnson, a local businessman who had made his money in real estate; he had social interests similar to her and endorsed charity work. He had made his money the hard way and was careful with it; he certainly didn't waste it on trinkets for her and that suited Alicia. It really hurt when she found out he had been seeing his ex-wife for sexual favours. No matter how much pleading and begging he did, he was unceremoniously dumped.

He hung around for a while, trying to put things right, but there was no forgiveness. Finally, he got the message and went to America to pursue business interests there.

She made up her mind that, for the time being, close male company was not important to her. Flirting with her clients in the bar was all she needed, and it worked well both ways.

Friday came, her day off, but two of her staff had called in sick, so she had to fill in for them. There was an awful flu virus going around, and she was in no doubt they were too ill to work. Anyway, spreading germs in the bar and restaurant was not good, especially for the clientele.

The agency was not able to supply anyone at such short notice, so it was down to Alicia to compensate. It was 6 pm when Tracy returned to the bar and looked at her boss.

"I thought you had a date this evening, leaving it a bit tight to get ready, aren't you?" "Oh, I don't think I'm going to bother; this place is packed and it's not going to slow any time soon. Anyway, it would be my excuse not to get involved with a British Naval officer."

"What? Don't throw up an offer like that, we can cope here. I like being rushed off my feet; the time goes by quicker; you go and enjoy yourself. I tell you, if it were me who had been asked out by that hunk, I wouldn't hesitate."

"Okay, you've convinced me, although I don't think it will go very far with him, dishy maybe but too much Naval baggage, it's his life."

Alicia went to her apartment, stripped out of her uniform and stepped into the welcoming hot shower. Having unloaded the rigours of the day, she had time to reflect on what was happening to her emotions. At least tonight would prove one way or another if there was going to be any sort of relationship between them. By the time she had dried her hair and put on her makeup, she realised it was gone seven, time to dress.

She phoned down to the bar and Tracy picked it up. "High love, is Bob there?"

"Oh yes, he was here by 6.30 and looks raring to go."

"Okay, would you let him know I'm running late, be about another 15 mins."

"No worries, I have already fixed him up with a drink and some nibbles. I told him you've been working your butt off when you should have been on a day off."

"What would I do without you, Tracy?"

"Perhaps allow me access to this gift to the male species sat at the bar?"

"Who knows; if this evening doesn't go well, I may throw him to you female predators, be down in a while." They both laughed. Bob turned and smiled at Tracy. "That was your date for tonight; she will be down shortly. Can I get you another drink?"

When Alicia arrived in the bar, Tracy was sat on a high chair chatting away to Robert who was smiling.

"Oh, I thought you were taking me out this evening?" He turned and drooled at what he saw. Dressed in a stunning black outfit that accentuated her totally fit body but left just enough to the imagination he could only blurt out the words,

"Well, the wait was certainly worthwhile, you look amazing."

"Thank you, kind Sir, I hope Tracy has been looking after you."

"Oh yes, no wonder she is so popular here, she has kept me entertained with some of her stories."

"Yes, bless her, that's why I employ her. Always bubbly and gets the customers to spend their money."

Tracy laughed, "Would you like a drink before you go, boss?"

"No thanks. I'm starving, shall we go and eat Bob?"

"Indeed, can't manage any more crisps and peanuts, I don't want to spoil a good steak."

Outside Bob hailed a taxi, and they both got in, it would take about twenty minutes to get to Rowland's restaurant.

"I understand you have been somewhat busy on your day off, so glad you could still make it."

"Yes, you could say that. I was tired but didn't want to pass up the chance of a great meal." The journey passed quickly. She found him so easy to talk to; in fact, most of the conversation came from her. He was a good listener. Although he didn't give much away as to his background, she wanted to know more about him. Alicia thought to herself, 'I'm going to have to work on that to glean information.'

When they entered the restaurant, Richard, the head waiter recognised Alicia straight away, he often frequented her bar.

"Good evening Sir, well hello, Madam, I didn't know I was going to be graced by your presence. Have you booked a table?"

"So formal, you usually call me sweet! Anyway, Bob booked it."

"Under what name did you book, Sir?"

"Southward."

Richard looked down the register for the evening bookings." Oh, I see they have allocated your table five.

Well, we can do much better than that. Table nine is not reserved and a much better option, follow me please."

He led them to a secluded booth generally reserved for four dinners, one of the best tables in the house.

"I think you will be more comfortable here, Champagne on the house, Sir?"

"Yes, that would be nice thank you." The menus were already on the table along with chilled bottled water.

"An old flame?" queried Bob.

"What makes you say that?" Alicia smiled. She could sense a note of envy in Bob's voice.

"Good looking guy who certainly lights up in your presence and seems to fall over himself to please."

She laughed, "Idiot, he comes to my restaurant with his friends and family. Happily married with no children. Often when he's not working, he visits my bar, likes his gin and tonic."

"Oh, sorry didn't mean to be insulting."

"No worries. Along with his wife, the manageress here, they dine in my restaurant and seem to enjoy the food. Not sure after running a place like this if they are just being polite."

"Not so, your food is excellent, and I suspect a darn site cheaper than here."

"Yep must look at that. Perhaps I will increase my prices, especially for you." They both laughed.

The champagne arrived, and Richard pulled the cork.

"Shall I pour?"

"Good idea."

"Are you both ready to order?"

"Certainly, I am I've heard a lot about your mouth-watering steaks."

"I hope it lives up to expectations. I recommend the rib eye steak; it's prime, and I don't have too many left. It comes with crunchy potato skins stuffed with blue cheese, olive and herb pate, Dauphinoise potatoes and vegetables of the day. Of course, Sir can have fries if preferred."

"Does that sound okay for you, Bob? Because that's what I'm having." Alicia said, authoritatively.

"Sounds delicious as it is, I'm salivating. Oh, and a bottle of your house red please." "That's already taken care of, Sir."

While nibbling on the appetisers and enjoying the champagne, they waited for the main course. The conversation was intriguing; she wanted to know all there was to know about Robert John Southward but knew it would be quite a challenge. He was such an introvert character and gave very little away; she put it down to his military training. After a while, she gave up on the idea and changed the subject. What was it about him that she found so interesting? Other guys had fallen at the first hurdle for being boring, but this one was different. The steaks arrived complemented by a bottle of good French wine.

Robert was confused; he only ordered the house red this was a 1998 Saint Emillion Pomerol. Alicia smiled.

"Richard and I know each other's tastes and respond accordingly, we are good friends and compare red wines often, hope you like this one."

"Oh yes certainly do, I must take the name of it for future reference."

"Oh, so you think there might be a future reference for us then?"

He was blushing again.

"Don't worry. I'm teasing you."

They sat and enjoyed what was an outstanding main course, probably the best he had ever had.

"Well, Bob, that was delicious how about a sweet?"

"After that superb main, the strawberries and ice cream sounds good."

Over coffee, he had to admit this restaurant and its food was marginally better than Alicia's although he would never tell her that.

At the end of a great evening, Robert asked for the bill.

"That's on the house, Sir. Alicia always looks after my wife and me when we dine at her restaurant and rarely takes payment."

"Well, thank you very much. This was my treat, but I might get the opportunity to take her out again, at least I hope so."

He looked at her nervously. She was smiling.

As the taxi drove them to her place, Robert was building up the courage to ask Alicia to dine with him again; when they arrived, he turned to her,

"As this evening was a freebie would you let me take you out to eat at my expense?" "Well yes I would enjoy that. There's lots I want to ask you about anyway."

"Great, I'm out on trials for a few days but will contact you early next week, if that's okay?"

Alicia leaned over and pecked him on the cheek. "You are so sweet; I'll look forward to it." With that, she left the taxi and walked to her private entrance. He followed her every move and when she turned and waved, he was beside himself and blew her a kiss. What is it about this guy? She thought. He didn't even make a move on me, am I losing my touch? Bless him. In her heart of hearts, she wanted to take it further but for once in her life felt nervous about that prospect.

Over the next few weeks, the two of them spend a good bit of time together alone or with friends. During those occasions, Robert was the perfect gentleman. This suited Alicia she had not had a sexual relationship since Guy. Bob seemed content to enjoy her company, and finally, when alone with him, he would open up somewhat. To an extent she was able to penetrate his hard exterior shell and gleaned important information, including the fact there was no wife or dependents at home. A good judge of character, her senses told her he was telling the truth. Light lunches in her bar, beach walks in the afternoon and evenings out, when the opportunities arose, became the norm.

It came as a bit of a surprise when Robert phoned Alicia to tell her he wanted to see her urgently. Well, of course, she was intrigued and asked him to come to her apartment that evening. She finished her shift and handed the reins over to Tracy.

"Go get him, Tiger, I know you want to."

"Oh, I don't know, he is such a strange fellow. I can't be sure he even fancies me sexually, or I'm just someone to hang out with."

"Oh yes he does I can see the body language between you two, it's electric, someone needs to make the first move."

"I wish he would flip the switch then, why has he not tried to bed me he's had ample opportunity?"

"Maybe this urgent meeting this evening is when he's going to ask your permission to go to bed with him?"

Alicia laughed out loud. "Don't be so stupid; he's not even got past the first stage of heavy petting yet."

"You wait and see," said Tracy "and if you need any help just phone down, I'll be there like a shot."

"My God, you're an animal."

"Well with him, I would like to be." They both laughed, and Alicia lightly punched Tracy's arm.

Surrounded by scented candles, Alicia had a long soak in her bath she relaxed and enjoyed her glass of red wine, dozing off for a while. By the time Robert arrived, she had put on a pair of tight-fitting blue jeans and a white blouse. A skimpy bra accentuated her pert bosoms with their taut nipples. After taking time with her makeup, she felt good. Putting on a lovely gold necklace and matching earrings, she looked at herself in the mirror and did a twirl. "Well if this doesn't do it, I don't know what will."

Robert entered the apartment with a beautiful bouquet.

"Well thank you, just like the first time we met. Help yourself to a drink, and I'll have a glass of red wine. I'll just put these in some water, they are lovely."

When she came back into the room, she thought Bob seemed a bit down. Putting the vase on the table, she sat down next to him.

"What's wrong?"

He picked up his glass of wine and took a hefty swig. "I've been given notice. I'm being called back to England; my twelve-month tour of duty here has been severely cut short."

"Can they do that?"

"I'm in the Navy, they can do what they like without explanation, orders and all that. The truth is I wanted to spend the remaining months working here and seeing you as often as possible."

Alicia took Bob's chin in her palm and kissed him gently on the lips. He responded and returned the kiss with enthusiasm. Wow, was this going to be the moment, she thought.

"Bring that bottle and let's go to the bedroom."

As they slowly undressed each other while caressing, Bob whispered, "Alicia, I'm not very good at this, but all I know is I love you."

"That's some statement to make; I've been waiting for this to happen, just relax and let's both enjoy it." When she took his semi-erect penis in her hands, she noticed he was well endowed.

Slowly masturbating him, it didn't take long for him to be fully aroused. She pushed him down; taking a condom from the bedside drawer, she gently rolled it on. She straddled him, and he entered her slowly while reaching up to caress her breasts. The gentle up and down motion of their naked bodies was driving them both to a crescendo as she used her index finger to play with her clitoris. He grasped her supple buttocks and held on as he climaxed.

"Alicia! Alicia, I love you," he blurted out.

As she went over the top, she leant down and kissed him passionately. "I love you too, Bob." Their immediate passion spent they lay entwined in each other's arms. During the night he was insatiable and desperately made love to her a second time trying to please her.

When morning came, Alicia got out of bed and went to the kitchen to make some breakfast. She sat on the bed while he ate some toast,

"When do you have to leave?"

"Not sure yet, there's nothing serious going on that any of my colleagues back home know about, they are probably an officer down on one of the fleet submarines. With all the cuts, experienced men are hard to find. I would assume I will have to go within a week. That's the norm with staff on detached duties. I expect to hear today or tomorrow. The placement here in Australia is always considered by the Admiralty to be a bit of a jolly."

"Well, we had better make the most of it then." Alicia turned and went to the bathroom, peeled off her robe and stepped into the shower. Bob was confused, what does she mean we had better make the most of it? Shit! Am I to be dismissed when my time with her is up? I don't like that idea.

He put his robe on, went into the lounge and turned the television on. Just then the phone rang; Alicia was still in the shower. He picked up the receiver.

"Hello."

"Oh! Hello Bob, this is Tracy. Sorry to disturb you so early, is the boss there?"

He could sense the sarcasm in her voice. Early, it was 9.15 for God's sake.

"Hello Tracy, she is in the shower, any message?"

"Well you can tell her we have enough staff in today if she wants to enjoy the time off elsewhere."

"Tracy, that's fantastic, I am not on call until late this evening and would love to take her out."

Alicia came out of the bathroom, towelling her wet hair. "Who was that?"

"It was Tracy, said you could have the day off, there is enough staff to cover for today."

"God, you wouldn't think I own this place and pay her wages. Still, bless her, that's good news."

Robert thought for a moment, "How do you fancy going out on a boat today? A friend of mine has a cabin cruiser in the harbour's marina. He lets me use it when he can't. I know he is busy for the week, so it's just sitting there. I'm not on a duty call until 19.00 hours."

"Well yes that would be great; I will contact Tony and have a hamper made up."

"You go and shower and shave, you look like you have had a night on the tiles."

He stood up and looked Alicia straight in the eyes.

"That was better than any night on the tiles, my darling, fancy another session?"

She smiled and pushed him away. "I think you have had enough practice for one night and it was perfect."

Kissing him gently on the lips, it was apparent he was getting aroused again. She slapped him on the buttocks and headed for the door before he could react.

As Alicia entered the breakfast bar, she could see her staff had silly grins on their faces. She made a beeline for Tracy.

"Don't say a word."

"No need to, boss, your radiant smile says it all."

"Christ, is it that obvious?"

Tracy wrapped her arms around her boss. "I am so pleased you have found some happiness at last. You deserve it."

"Still not sure if I am doing the right thing, what did I say about avoiding naval officers? The trouble is I am falling for him big time, am I stupid or what?"

"Enjoy all the time you can with him, babe who knows what the future holds."

"Do you fancy coming up this evening for some girly talk, Bob's on duty at seven." "Yes, I'll bring a couple of bottles of Prosecco."

"Okay, see you at seven, bring whatever food you want and put it on my tab."

"Wow might have the lobster thermidor in that case." They both laughed.

"Trace you can have whatever you like, my treat for being a good manageress and a great friend."

"So where are you going today?"

"Evidently, we are going out cruising on a boat somewhere, his friend owns it and keeps it in the harbour. We will be taking a hamper with us that Tony is preparing, bless him."

"Wow, you lucky thing there are some beautiful yachts down there, does it have a bed?"

"For God's sake, woman you're sex mad."

"Just give me a chance, never done it on a boat; I think they call it joining the two metre high club." Laughter erupted once again.

Chapter 4

Saturday, February 10th 2001 07.00 hrs
Rockingham Marina South Australia

Robert Southward went on ahead to the marina to prepare
the boat for sailing. When Alicia arrived and stepped out
of the taxi with the hamper and a small holdall she nearly
fell over. Bob stood there waving at her from what was a
beautiful gleaming white, six-berth Sunseeker cruiser. He
came down the walkway and took the hamper from her.

"Wow, what does your friend do to have a craft like
this?"

"His father is a multi-millionaire publisher. Ross is
a director and classes it as just a company asset, great for
entertaining clients."

She stood there in amazement completely absorbed
by its sleek and graceful lines. "Alicia let's get going, that
harbour attendant will cast us off, I want to catch the tide."
"Aye-aye captain, don't give me fifty lashes, or hang me
from the yardarm for being a bit slow."

Robert grinned like a Cheshire cat; he was in the
environment he knew best and loved being in charge on
the water. Taking the two flights of stairs to the upper open
bridge, he checked the instrument panel once again for any

malfunctions. All the systems were operating as they should; no red warning lights were flashing.

Alicia joined him and stood aghast at the array of switches and dials on the control panel.

"Wow, where do you start with this lot?"

"Not too difficult really, these yachts are so advanced they have a computer analysis programme built in that checks all the systems once you switch on the power. Then it's left hand down a bit, and off we go."

"Well I'm glad you are driving; it would scare the life out of me to operate this." "Well yes I am piloting to be precise, but this is absolute cutting edge technology. I sometimes think the private sector is well in advance of our Navy with regards to making life easier. Manoeuvring this beauty is as easy as driving a top of the range sports car."

"Well you would say that wouldn't you, but I am impressed."

They waited for the securing ropes fwd and aft to be released.

"Alicia, stow your change of clothes in the master cabin and put the hamper in the galley."

"Typical, now you're a Captain, I suppose I'm the galley slave."

"Do as you're told, or it's the scuppers in irons for you." They both laughed.

"Promises, can you keep them that's the question?"

He manoeuvred out of the harbour at the regulation 5 knots and increased the speed to 10 as soon as he was able. Shortly she joined him dressed in a pair of figure-hugging white shorts and a pink bikini top.

"Wow, that should awaken the natives."

"Where are we going, Bob?"

"Well as it's such a lovely calm sunny day, I thought we would go to a nice quiet inlet about 30 minutes cruising time. Of course, this beast would get there in a lot less than that if I went at top speed. It will be nice to cruise; we can have a fast run on the way back if you want."

"Yes, that sounds great, take as long as you like, I'm going to sunbathe on the fwd. deck yes I know some nautical terms as well."

"Bless you, where's Davy Jones locker then?"

"Erm, I think it's at the central railway station, Sidney."

With a grin, he said, "That's close enough, you will find a locker on the fwd deck with sunbeds and towels madam".

"Great."

He set the satnav coordinates for Darwin cove and engaged the autopilot. There was very little traffic around, and he could leave the bridge and join her if he wanted to. However, his naval training would not allow him to do that, minimal risk at all times. Being in his element, he sat back in the more than comfortable white leather pilots chair and studied the local charts. Looking out onto the deck, Alicia was preparing her sunbed. She peeled off her shorts to reveal the bottom half of her skimpy bikini. She tied her hair above her head with a bright red ribbon and removed her large hooped earrings.

Slowly applying suntan lotion, she was aware Bob was watching her every move. She spread herself on the sunbed and started to flick through the lady's mag she had bought with her. Without even looking up, she blew a kiss in the direction of the bridge.

"My God." mouthed Robert "She is so stunning."

As they approached the deserted cove, he dropped anchor about 100meters from the shore. Alicia was impressed with the incredible natural beauty of the area; she had no idea of its existence. There were no other people around. Accessibility by land was near impossible, due to the sheer cliff faces. Only the nesting gulls and those flying and squawking interrupted the total piece of this idyllic spot.

Joining her on the sun deck, he was pleased to see another sun lounger was laid out for him.

"We can take the small tender ashore if you like, can't risk taking this any closer to the beach, a bit rocky close in."

"No Bob, I'm happy here."

She had already got the hamper and spread out a superb buffet. Two bottles of white wine had been wrapped in ice packs.

"Wow, this looks great, so well prepared."

"All down to Tony I'm afraid all his input, he knows what I like. This place is amazing, how many other conquests have you brought here?"

"You are the first one actually; normally it's just us fellas out for a boozy bit of skinny dipping. We always draw straws as to who doesn't drink alcohol."

They both sat and enjoyed the excellent food while Alicia downed two glasses of wine; Robert stuck to chilled water. Even with the sunshade pulled out, it was hot, and they were both sweating.

"Can we go inboard for a while, Bob? I'm roasting."

"Good idea, I'm going to take a shower."

The air conditioning hit them like a cold blast, and he adjusted it to 20 degrees. Centrally locking the entry doors to the interior with the touch of a button was imperative. Although there was no other vessel around, he never took chances with Ross's boat.

He ran the shower and peeled off. Alicia was directly behind him and did the same. "Tracy said she has never had sex on a boat, and neither have I, but I want to."

They both stepped into the glass and marble veneer shower. Alicia took the scented soap and gently lathered Bob all over. He was fully aroused and could hardly contain himself. She allowed the warm water to remove the soap from them both, while passionately forcing her tongue into his mouth. He could taste the remnants of the sweet, refreshing wine. He wanted to enter Alicia in an instant, but she backed off and started to masturbate him.

"Turn the shower off, Bob." She sunk to her haunches and took his penis in her mouth. With gentle, rhythmic strokes of her fingers and the rolling motion of her tongue, he was in raptures.

"Alicia", he screamed, "I'm coming." He put both hands on her shoulders and expected some resistance from her, but there was none. Totally spent, he buckled at the knees and leant back against the shower wall. She raised herself, and he kissed her passionately.

"Wow that was fantastic, but I thought you wanted sex on the boat. What was in that for you?"

She turned on the shower, "Who says we are finished?"

"My God, I love you so much, I have never felt this way about any woman before."

"Well keep it coming; it has been a long time since I wanted to be passionate with anyone."

The master bedroom was tastefully fitted out in ornate Italian style. A sizeable sumptuous bed and thick cream carpet complimented the light wood panelling, and the whole compartment had a woman's touch to it. Bob had already made coffee for them both. Alicia arrived wrapped in a cerise coloured bath towel, sipping on another glass of wine. She raised it and saluted him.

"Well, love you're driving, so I'm drinking, I'll have the coffee later." Looking around at the opulence of the interior she said, "We could be in some top hotel room a lot of thought has gone into creating this, is Ross married?"

"He was, but she ran off with a rich business client. I was his best man that was a joke Sherrie even made a play for me early on in their relationship. Gently, I tried to tell him not to marry her; it lasted less than two years. She was a slapper, anything in trousers would do. Anyway, he wouldn't listen, said she had turned a corner, love was blind. It took a long time for him to get over her, but he has a nice girl now."

He was deep in thought, "Alicia, I have a confession to make."

"Oh, I thought this was too good to be true, you have someone back in England."

"No. No, that's not it at all."

"Well, what is it then."

"I forgot to bring any condoms." She laughed out loud, "Well, that's a relief, you fool, I brought some, you're not going back home and leaving me in the lurch."

It was his turn to laugh out loud. "The truth is I don't want to go back to England without you."

"Well I understand you have to, don't forget I grew up in a Naval environment, and I know how it works."

"Come with me".

Alicia looked stunned. "What? How can I do that? My business is here. What about if you resign your commission, and join the Australian navy?"

Bob looked stern "That's not possible, I am close to having my own command, it's all I have ever strived for."

"As I said, Bob, I know how it works."

They both fell silent, and the moment was gone. Bob got off the bed and went to a drawer in the dressing table. He pulled out a small black box and went and sat on the bed. Turning to Alicia, he said,

"Will you marry me?" She nearly choked on her wine and started coughing. He opened the box to reveal a sparkling single diamond engagement ring.

"This is ridiculous Bob we hardly know each other."

"I know that you are the woman I want to spend the rest of my life with." She took the ring out of the box and tried it on. It fitted perfectly.

"How did you know the size?"

"I measured one of your rings in your bedside drawer in your apartment. I had seen you wearing it before on your right hand."

Alicia sat there, admiring the beautiful ring. "Well, I don't know what to say."

"Please don't say no right now, think about it."

"I will." She took the ring off and placed it in the box.

"Bob, that's so sweet, and I don't know what to say. I need time to think."

"Yes, of course."

The rest of the afternoon was spent both on the sun deck and in the bedroom. Alicia was confused, was it the wine or the worry of what to do? This time the sex wasn't working for her. He climaxed again screaming her name. She held him close and for the first time in her life faked an orgasm.

The cruise back was quiet it had got a little choppy, so he didn't gun the engines in case she got seasick. Alicia was quite happy to watch the world go by. A pod of dolphins swam with them until they neared the harbour and then disappeared. After the boat was secured and everything was tidied away, Bob phoned for a taxi.

"I really enjoyed that, thanks for making it a great day out."

"You are welcome madam; wish we could do it more often."

Outside the restaurant, Bob kissed her passionately.

"I will contact you tomorrow morning please keep the ring for now, even if you don't wear it."

Alicia got out of the taxi and watched him as he waved goodbye. Why did she feel so sad? She rushed inside once again, needing the security of her surroundings.

Relaxing in her apartment, she felt tired. The knock on the door raised her from the deep sleep that had overwhelmed her. Looking at her watch, she saw it was 7 o'clock. She felt a mess, and had a hangover thanks to too much wine. She opened the door to Tracy.

"Well, you look like you had a good time."

"Trace, make me a strong coffee while I freshen up."

Alicia disappeared to the bathroom and showered; she dressed and felt a lot better. When she entered the lounge, she savoured the coffee made for her.

"Where's lover boy?"

"Late duty"

"You will never guess what happened today."

"Don't tell me you did it on the boat."

"Well of course we did, but that's not all. He asked me to marry him, look at this." Alicia showed Tracy the engagement ring.

"Bloody hell, things are moving at a pace."

"He is being recalled early; he will be gone by next week."

"Christ! That's something to chew on."

"Exactly. Evidently, he thinks he will be posted to a sub in Devonport, in the West Country; it's all a bit hush-hush. He owns a five-bedroom house in Derriford on the outskirts of Plymouth. It's let at the moment but becomes vacant in two months; he wants me to move in with him then."

"I don't know what to say, Alicia."

"That's a first, you lost for words! Not much you can say really."

Tracy thought long and hard, not wanting to say the wrong things to her boss and cherished friend.

"Do you love him?"

"Yes, I bloody well do, and that's the trouble. Never thought I would get serious with anyone again especially

Navy, but I could settle down with Bob."

"Then why don't you give it a go? You may regret it if you don't. You know Tony and I can run this place, and we would buy it in an instant if you wanted to sell."

They both sat there in silence, sipping the prosecco and picking at the food.

Robert Southward was nothing if not thorough. Naval training taught you to expect the unexpected. A British Airways flight home business class had been organised for 11.35 am on a Wednesday. He reserved a seat for Alicia but could cancel it at the last moment, if she didn't want to go; he so hoped she would. He always travelled light and knew he could tie up the loose ends of his detachment swiftly. However, there was one loose end that was playing on his mind. Would the woman he loved go with him to England, or would it be the end of their relationship? Although his naval career would always come first, he had every intention of trying to persuade her to become an important part of his life. The remaining few days went by in a flash. She insisted on having some space and did not change her work routine as he would have liked. She still had not given him an answer as to her intentions.

Alicia wanted the final evening to be a quiet affair in her apartment. She had arranged food and wine for 8 o'clock; succulent sirloin steak was on the menu, Bob's favourite. He arrived on the dot for the arranged time of 7.45 pm. He nervously rang the bell and waited for her to open the door.

Alicia had given him a key to the apartment, which he used frequently. She finally came to the door.

"Lost your key then?"

Bob kissed her tenderly on the lips. "No, of course not, here it is." He placed the key in the palm of her right hand and gently squeezed it.

"Silly boy, why didn't you use it?" He said nothing.

"Tony will be here with the food soon. I'm just going to the bedroom to put on my makeup. I didn't finish my shift on time; it's manic in the restaurant. You know where the drinks are."

"Oh, I will have just coffee, for now, thanks."

By the time he had made coffee and returned to the lounge, Alicia was standing there looking out of the window.

"I made you one as well, hope you want it". She turned and looked directly at him. "Thanks." She took the coffee and placed it on the table. Grasping both his hands in hers, she kissed him on the cheek. "I've come to a decision, just don't say anything until I have finished." Taking a deep breath and with a sigh, "Robert, I want you to go back to England on your own tomorrow." His heart sank. "If all works out, I will come over in a month and have a look at where you want me to live. I will spend a few days there and look up an old school friend. He knew better than to say anything. "You know I will be giving up so much here, but I want to see if it can work because I love you."

He smiled, "Well, that's what I really wanted to hear."

"I will be keeping the business on, if I do decide to move to England to be with you, Tracy and Tony will run it for me. I trust them implicitly and will be making flying visits to check that all is well." She turned on her heels and went to the bedroom. When she returned, she held up her left hand.

The sparkling engagement ring adorned her third finger.

"Darling that's fantastic, you have made my day. I will miss you terribly but would wait for you until hell freezes over."

"Will you come to the airport tomorrow to see me off?"

"No Bob, I don't think that's a good idea. I'm not very good at goodbyes, let's eat."

Alicia put some music on, and they dined without too much conversation. It was plain to both of them; the next few months would be crucial to their relationship. They went to bed early and made love passionately, and she climaxed, he fell into a deep sleep, but she was restless. Going into the bathroom she cried uncontrollably, she looked in the mirror and wiped away her tears.

"Pull yourself together for God's sake; it's not the end of the world unless you want it to be." She went back into the bedroom and saw him sleeping like a baby. It was 0600; he would be leaving soon. The alarm was set for 6.30. Quickly showering and dressing, Alicia wrote a goodbye note and left it on the lounge table near his coat. It just said,

Parting is such sweet sorrow; corny I know, but it does seem appropriate, take care, see you in England.

She had arranged to go to her supplier early knowing there was no point in having a tearful parting. That would not help either of them. A taxi would take him the fifty kilometres to catch his plane from Perth airport. Within thirty hours, Alicia Juliet Harris and Robert John Southward would be ten thousand miles apart.

Chapter 5

Saturday 14th April 2007 Midday
Location: The Florida Winds Grand Hotel Tampa Bay.

Robert Southward's career would be one of great changes. He had graduated from Dartmouth naval college as a Sub Lieutenant in 1988 aged 19, specialising in electrical engineering. His initial 30 weeks training would lead on to even more intensive training as a marine engineer. He served on H.M.S. Sovereign for two years, and then went onshore for a further eighteen months. Gaining the rank of Lieutenant, he then served a period on the submarine H.M.S. Sceptre. At this stage, most officers would choose to stay in the submarine service. Robert was not sure what route to take to advance his career. A captaincy was his ultimate goal, and whether it is skimmers or submarines at this stage, it was not an issue.

Requesting a posting to a surface ship, he was draughted to H.M.S. Broadsword a type 22 frigate. After a short period on Broadsword, he was restless. Frigates were interesting, and he gained a great deal of knowledge of how they operated. However, he now knew the silent service was in his blood, and he was itching to get back to the submarine branch.

On request, he was seconded to H.M.S. Trafalgar.

Taking all the exams he possibly could, would hopefully get him a further promotion. That would more or less allow him to seek his true aim, that of one day captaining his own vessel. The ultimate goal would be to take, and pass, the submarine command course (S.M.C.C), or perisher's course. He knew it would make or break him as to the possibility of becoming a commander of his own sub.

He was already marked out for rapid promotion by his seniors, who recognised his potential. He was assured a good post on a surface ship if he failed the course. To do so meant no more time at sea on a submarine. However, failure to Robert Southward was not an option, and he would eventually pass with flying colours.

A period of shore time saw him posted to the base H.M.S. Drake Plymouth and subsequently H.M.S, Raleigh, Torpoint Cornwall where he assisted with the staff training of new officers who had recently graduated from Dartmouth. He very much enjoyed his time there and was able to spend some lost time with his wife, Alicia.

He was offered the post of weapons electrical officer on H.M.S. Torbay, or the option to be part of the overseer team of the nearly completed Astute, pennant number S119. In his book, there was no contest. A new class of hunter-killer submarine, it was his preference.

Taking over from Lieutenant Commander Philip Brice, senior overseer was his next step. With his small team, he saw it evolve from the drawing board and be made ready for launch and subsequent long trials. To Robert, this was not just 7,000 tons of steel and nonferrous material. It was a living breathing instrument of war and peace that would be deployed to protect the realm. Brice would have liked to see the project through to completion, but he had to be content with handing the reins to Robert Southward for the last lap. Orders were orders, and as naval officers, they were accepted without question.

A period of leave was scheduled before the assignment. Southward was itching to get to grips with the challenge but knew Alicia would enjoy a relaxing holiday. America seemed a great idea, so it was booked, and their time together would commence shortly. Perhaps they could regain some of the old magic that they both yearned for; they had spent so much time apart.

Relaxing on the sun-soaked beach of the magnificent hotel in Tampa Bay, Florida, to Alicia, it was idyllic.

"Darling," she purred, "how wonderful to be together for a while. You spend so much time on your damn submarine. I feel we have missed out being apart for long periods. I know we can never get that back, but maybe we can try and make the future better. I would like you to seriously consider cutting your naval career short. You know money is not an issue, perhaps we could start a business together if you did not want to retire fully. Maybe spend some time in Australia again; you know I still have financial ties there that are very lucrative."

Bob laughed. "A business? What do I know about business? Anyway, I have worked so hard to obtain a captainship, and I think it's mean of you even to ask me to give it up."

Alicia turned on her side and continued reading her magazine.

"As expected, who's the one being mean?" Look what I gave up for you, she thought.

There was a long silence.

"I think I will go back to the room for a while," he said.

"Oh yes, and don't forget to check your emails. We might have declared war on some Polynesian Island," she retorted.

Walking back to the suite, he was confused. Although she didn't like it; Alicia had always seemed supportive of his time in the Navy and had appeared proud of his achievements. He mulled over the time they had been together. Perhaps if we had been blessed with a child, I would have looked at things differently. I guess I am selfish, but the Navy is my life, he reflected. Sitting at the computer screen, Bob accessed his emails. Going straight to the restricted emails, there it was.

With immediate effect, Lieutenant Robert Southwood is promoted to Lieutenant Commander. Well done, Bob, see you on your return from leave or sooner. Signed, Admiral Frost, (Submarine Officer Procurement)

Bob punched the air; this meant he was well on the way to getting his own command of a submarine. Any thoughts of leaving the senior service were now out of the question. He was somewhat puzzled though; the confirmation had not come from his own divisional Admiral. It could only mean one thing; he would be offered second in command of the latest hunter-killer sub to roll out of V.S.E.L... Astute.

Alicia walked into the suite, she put her hand on his shoulder and said,

"Sorry darling, I guess it is wrong of me to expect you

to give up your career at this stage. It's just that I miss you so much when you are away on long patrols. I saw how it affected my parents, it wrecked their marriage, and I don't want it to happen to us."

Bob beamed and nuzzled her hand with his chin. He held her hands and gently kissed her wedding ring.

"I have ordered two bottles of champagne and lobster salads. I thought we might celebrate here this evening."

"Celebrate what?"

Bob laughed, "Just read this email."

"Wow, promotion. Definitely cause for a party, well done. I'm going to shower and change into some evening wear."

That's just the news I didn't want to hear, she thought. She went into the bathroom and closed the door. Getting out of her brief bikini, she put the shower on full and stepped in. Soaping her tanned and superbly fit body, she suddenly began to cry uncontrollably. Oh, crap! Here we go again.

Alicia thought she knew what was coming. Another round of long lonely periods, while he is on patrol, is to be expected, I guess. I love him, but sometimes I hate him as well. Why did I get mixed up with someone who puts his career first? I should have known better.

The truth was he would be based in Faslane, Scotland, at least he thought he would be. No point in telling his wife as it was still very much up in the air. There would be a period in America for test-firing cruise missiles in the Gulf of Mexico, but he knew there was no way he could convince Alicia to move from Plymouth now she had established a social life.

She stepped out of the shower, dried her beautiful body and looked in the full-length mirror. She was still in great shape, and she turned heads. Adorning her body in the soft white robe hanging on the door, she decided this was not the time to let her true feelings be known.

Room service had brought their meal, and Bob had poured the champagne. Alicia lifted the glass and took a mouthful then a second; with the third, she drained it.

"Steady Tiger, that's £65 a bottle!"

"Who cares? I intend to spend your increase in pay!"

Refilling her glass, they both laughed. She picked at the lobster salad, but he devoured his with relish. Filling her glass once more, she let the robe part, to reveal curvaceous tanned thighs.

"You really are a pig with food," she hissed. Still, if you want some of this, you had better finish and go and shower."

Bob turned and stared mouth agape. He poured the last of the champagne from the first bottle, drank it and rushed to the shower. Alicia popped the cork of the second bottle and with the two glasses walked seductively to the bedroom. Feeling somewhat light-headed, she placed them on the bedside table. Tossing her still damp long blond locks over her shoulder, she peeled off her robe and let it fall to the floor. Hearing him singing in the shower, a wry smile came over her face. He would soon be back, joined at the hip to the Navy.

She murmured, "Robert Southwood, you are going to have a night to remember."

It didn't take him long, and he quickly returned in just a

large white towel. Sitting on the edge of the bed, he enjoyed some more of the champagne. Alicia ran her fingers up and down his spine and then gently massaged his shoulders.

"Bob, I think it is too late to have children now, but would you consider adoption?" He nearly choked on his champagne. After a long pause, he turned to face her, looking into her crystal eyes.

"Well, you do pick some strange times to ask me a question like that."

"When is it a good time then? You always seemed too busy when I want to discuss it." The moment had gone; she knew what his reaction would be. Turning over, she lifted the remote control for the television and tuned in to a film on Sky.

"I suppose you are going to be all sulky now, Alicia?" He was shocked to think it was too late to have a child of their own making. "Anyway, I didn't say no to your question." "That's true, but you didn't say yes or maybe either."

They made love, and after a short while, he climaxed. It is evident to her that no matter how hard he tried to make her come, she was not going to reach a crescendo. Their foreplay had become somewhat dull, and she blamed herself for that, but he was not as imaginative as he used to be. If she masturbated and fellated him, it was all over in seconds, and she was left frustrated. It was now a case of wham bam, thank you mam, and she hated it. Alicia wasn't in the mood for a long session even though he was aroused again, and she faked an orgasm.

Being the first one to fall asleep, Bob looked at her adoringly. She was still as beautiful as the first day he had set eyes on her. With all that lay ahead, he didn't want a child in his life to complicate matters, especially one that he had not sired. Knowing Alicia as he did, he knew the subject would crop up again; he would just have to bluff his way out of it and pretend to be considering the possibilities.

What was he supposed to do? She had known all along the Navy was his life. He considered a Commodore or even a rear Admiral's rank was within his long term reach. It had been her that had done most of the chasing back in Australia; he did not feel guilty about pursuing his lifetime ambition.

One thing he would change if he could was the fact she was not financially dependent on him. The truth was she had worked hard and amassed her own wealth. He admired her for that but did not like the fact he was not the sole breadwinner.

In their own way, they were both selfish. For his part, Robert did not truly comprehend why she could not understand his pursuance of a lifetime naval career and little else. She had all the trappings of success, a large house, with all the home comforts anyone could wish for. In what had been the stables, an indoor swimming pool had recently been constructed, along with a well kitted out gymnasium. The shiny new Mercedes cabriolet parked in the double garage was a dream car, but to her, this was all just a sham.

What she really craved was the attention of the man she had fallen in love with, long ago, back in Australia. The truth was, Bob and his wife were drifting apart, and neither of them seemed willing or able to rectify the situation. Although a very positive person she could come to terms with what was happening, the problem was depression was setting in and that would affect her reasoning.

To fill the time while he was away, Alicia had carved out some sort of social life at an exclusive club. The downside for her was most of the so-called friends she had made were so far up their own backsides it was unreal. Always trying to outdo one another with a bigger or better something or other, it was sickening. She had witnessed this before in Australia with James Stratton.

There was, of course, the conversation about children, this really grated on Alicia's nerves. It seemed that having had children, they were in most cases, just an inconvenience that had to be dealt with.

One of the so-called ladies was fond of bragging about having a toy boy on the side, as her husband did not fulfil her sexual needs. It was quite obvious she was not the only one at it either. This was particularly upsetting; Alicia had always been faithful to the few men she had had in her life.

So why did she feel envious of these people who seemed to live very shallow lives? Maybe they had it right, and perhaps she should have an extramarital affair. There were plenty of good looking suiters at the club. She had warned off one particular guy on more than one occasion, but he was persistent. It was true she enjoyed the banter and different sports activities, with the girls, especially tennis. Most of the time they all had a good laugh together, she needed that. Although some were so annoying, they were company for her during those long periods of isolation.

Robert thought it a bit strange that Alicia didn't want him to associate with the so-called 'in-crowd.' It was true that for the time he was home she devoted all her attention to him and he liked that.

On occasions he would ask if she wanted to invite some of them over for a meet, the answer was always the same. "Oh, you would find them boring, what interest have you got in tennis and that's all they talk about. To be honest, I find them a bit full-on sometimes, and it's nice to have a break, but it does fill my time when you are away for so long."

He did wonder if there was more in her affiliation to the club than she let on but trusted her implicitly. He was happy that during the time he was not on shore leave, Alicia was pursuing something she had an interest in, and by God, it kept her fit. It certainly seemed to make her more content with her life, if only he knew?

The truth was he did neglect her sometimes although with all that he had to focus on it was not surprising. It went with the job, and he assumed she accepted that. However, he could not possibly have envisaged the fate that awaited him, his crew and his submarine. Also, his marital status would be held up to scrutiny. Dark times were ahead.

Chapter 6

Friday 8th June 2007 p.m.
The Vickers Shipbuilders, Barrow. Cumbria, England

The naming ceremony had gone according to plan, and everything had run like clockwork. Dignitaries along with the top echelon of the Navy and other invited guests had watched in awe as this leviathan of the deep had been named H.M.S. Astute. Most had retired to the V.I.P. suite to enjoy the refreshments on offer. With immense pride, Captain Brooks had shown the handful of guests remaining on board, around the submarine. Of course, certain areas were restricted for security and health and safety reasons.

Those who were lucky enough to participate in this tour were extremely impressed by what they saw. Astute would soon become a living breathing powerful vessel able to wreak havoc wherever its footprint appeared in the oceans of the world. If policy dictated, she would unleash her awesome firepower on an enemy, without ever being seen. Able to circumnavigate the world without surfacing, the only restriction was the food supply.

Captain Brooks ascended the ladder, of the control room and appeared into the bright sunshine, accompanied by Lieutenant Commander Robert Southward. His wife was standing on the dockside, waiting for him.

"Alicia, sorry to have left you waiting here, I have just been showing a few people around my second home."

"Don't you mean your first home, Bob?" she retorted. Nervous laughter erupted from a junior officer, who had been trying to keep her attention, all be it with tedious details of the sub's ability.

"I have to pop back on-board for a short while I won't be too long."

For obvious reasons, he was enjoying himself far more than she was and had to make one more visit to the submarine. Brooks picked up the conversation.

"Sorry, Alicia, I probably do see more of your husband than you do. Being a naval wife is not the easiest job in the world."

"You can say that again."

In a foul mood, he put it down to the fact she was feeling unwell.

Back on-board, Southward continued with the guided tour. After 15 minutes, he was approached by Chief Petty Officer Jarvis, who whispered,

"Sir, you are requested to meet with your wife in the V.I.P. tent shore side."

"Very good, Chief, please relay the message I will be there shortly."

"I will do that, Sir."

Alicia always did have a terrible sense of timing, thought Robert. Some of the guests were very knowledgeable, and he was surprised by the technical questions they asked.

He could no longer ignore his wife's request to join her

and made his apologies. "Gentlemen, I have to attend to something ashore I will leave you in the capable hands of our weapons electrical officer Gary Miles, who will happily answer any questions he can."

Ashore in the V.I.P tent, he found his wife. He thought she looked a little pale.

"Bob, I have a visual migraine coming on, I am thinking of going back to the hotel." "That's fine darling; I will join you there. This will all be over in a few hours."

They pecked each other on the cheek, a bit different to some years ago when they couldn't keep their hands off each other.

Alicia Juliet Harris was still a strikingly attractive woman. With long blond hair, hazel blue eyes and a figure that a twenty-year-old would die for, she turned heads wherever she went. Was it a curse or a blessing in not having had children? Her figure was amazing. Regular visits to the gym allowed her workouts that kept her in trim. Other officers were in awe of Bob's ability to have nailed Alicia in the first place. They assumed their relationship was one made in heaven. Little did anyone know cracks were appearing in their marriage.

Ray Lavis had spent some time at the naval base in Australia and visited the bar and restaurant she owned as often as he possibly could. He tried his hardest to woo her to no avail; he was told in no uncertain terms she was off-limits to British Naval officers. What a joke that turned out to be.

Sitting in the staff car, Alicia could feel the tears welling up. They had not made love in the last three months.

'For God's sake, I have tried talking to him, but he is

either too busy or too tired to discuss our situation.' The tears were now running down her cheeks, and she sobbed uncontrollably. The driver purposely ignored his female passenger even though in the mirror, he could see her grief. Best left alone he thought, what went on behind closed doors stayed behind closed doors. 'Bob I still love you, but sometimes I hate you with a vengeance. I feel so neglected and long for a proper relationship, that damn submarine will be our nemesis.'

This masked her true feelings of abject guilt. Why did she not feel more supportive of her husband? After all, she knew from the beginning what was expected of her as a naval wife. Little did anyone know that sometime in the future, events would overtake Bob and Alicia Southward? Along with many others, their lives would never be the same again.

By the time the car got back to the hotel, she had composed herself. She thanked the driver and went up to her room. The visual migraines she had been having lately were quite nauseating, but she knew how to combat them. Lying down in a darkened room until it passed was usually the answer, and it worked on this occasion. After a short while, she felt much better. It was still quite early, and she knew Robert would not be back for some time. Now showered and dressed, the smart two-piece outfit she had worn for the ceremony had been replaced by a lovely summer dress which felt more comfortable. That made her feel so much better, and she wanted a walk. Not wanting to stay there on her own, she left a note to say she had gone to do some shopping at the local mall. 'Why should I wait around for him to arrive? I have been doing it all my married life.'

It was a lovely warm summer late afternoon, and as she left the hotel, it was obvious admiring glances were being given by, passing mail motorists. White man van and his two mates took great delight in wolf-whistling as they passed. It only took 10 minutes to get to the mall, and she spent the next two hours window shopping. Popping into the odd shop, she treated herself to a new perfume not seen before. Also, a lovely pair of white chino's that she had tried on and they fitted perfectly.

Alicia was thirsty and a bit peckish and went into what looked like a good quality establishment. A waitress was there to welcome her.

"Hello, Madam. Do you have a reservation?"

"Oh no sorry, I was just looking for somewhere to get a snack and a drink."

"Well that's fine we don't stand on ceremony here, please follow me."

Alicia was shown to a small table with two chairs.

"Will this be okay?"

"Absolutely fine. My goodness, you do remind me of someone. I have a place out in Australia and my head waitress Tracy is running it for me at the moment."

"I've been to Aussie; a great place would love to emigrate there sometime."

"Do you know what; I think I will have a bottle of white wine, a Chardonnay and bottled water please."

While the waitress was getting the drink, Alicia looked at the menu. The bottle was placed in an ice bucket on the table along with the water.

"Anything you fancy from the menu?"

"Yes, I will have the cheese and ham panini, and a side salad thank you."

"Okay, it won't be long. We are not very busy. This time of the day always goes quiet."

She poured a glass of the wine and savoured it while she waited for the food.

Suddenly she had a flashback to the time she had spent on the cabin cruiser with Robert. It had been an exciting part of a wonderful romance that had now seemed only a distant memory. What was to be done to rekindle the magic that they had enjoyed? She didn't know the answer to that; in truth, she wanted to escape to Australia. Alicia was quite happy to enjoy this respite from the stress of yesterday. Not intending to rush back and wait for her husband in the hotel room, she would savour the simple food and the Chardonnay.

As Bob got back to the hotel, he had a tinge of sadness. He pondered, 'Coming from the background she does, why does she not accept my one hundred per cent commitment to the Navy? I would have thought she would be more understanding about what I am trying to achieve, and back me all the way.'

So many intelligent young officers fail at the first or subsequent hurdles, quite often through family pressure but go on to have successful careers in civilian life. Of course, this is how the system has to operate. The process is rigged so that the Admiralty board end up with submarine Captains who are the cream of the Navy. Totally dependable, they will be in charge of multi-billion pound submarines, and men's lives.

'I don't know what to do to make her happy. Pointless trying to buy her something nice, she has everything.

Flowers don't seem to work anymore either. When I do attempt to make love to her, it seems such an effort on her part, almost like she's doing me a favour. Where did the magic go? Robert! Stop this; you have a job to do, be prepared to get on and do it.' He quickened his step as he approached the lobby and pressed the button for the lift to take him to the top floor suite. He thought he would take Alicia to a nice show; the Sound of Music was on at the local theatre. Not really his scene, but he thought she would enjoy it. 'I must try something to rekindle our marriage.' It came as a bit of a shock when he entered the hotel room and read the note. My God, she couldn't even wait for me. I told her I wouldn't be too long. He went to the drinks cabinet and took out two miniature red wines. The bag of nuts was all he wanted to go with the wine; he had eaten well at the buffet. Turning on the television, he settled down to watch some sport. Robert Southward got through two more bottles of wine before Alicia arrived back.

He had a great ability to structure his life accordingly, regardless of the situation at hand. Yes, this was a great opportunity to relax and enjoy time with the woman he loved, but his commitment to career was never very far from his thoughts.

First and foremost was his passion for attaining his own command. It was within his grasp, and nothing would detract him from achieving that goal. If in a reasonable amount of time he wasn't successful with an 'A' class submarine then if offered he would accept Captainship of one of the "T" class.

They had proved their worth and had been the

backbone of Britain's hunter-killer fleet for well over two decades. Covert operations and surveillance on eastern bloc countries, Russia, in particular, was their forte. Numbers were now limited as the Astute class was superseding them. They would be an absolute leap in submarine technology.

H.M.S. Talent had completed a major refit and weapons upgrade, and after extensive trials, was fleet ready. The Tomahawk cruise missile was now in its arsenal along with the latest torpedoes and mines. Southward knew Captain Garth Meadows well, and they kept in touch. At Dartmouth, he had been a year ahead in his training, it was obvious then he was going to be a formidable naval officer. Due for promotion and a shore appointment, the vacancy for a new Captain would occur. "Don't get ahead of yourself, Robert" he pondered, there would be more than one capable officer after that appointment, and you are still reliant on your extra half a stripe? There was no need to worry; he had been pencilled in for promotion and secondment to H.M.S. Astute.

He was sure of one thing, under no circumstances did he want to become a civilian; leaving the Navy would not be by choice, not even for Alicia. That was a problem; no matter where he was or what he was doing, his passion for command was constantly on his mind. He would achieve it, but at what cost?

Chapter 7

Saturday 9th June 2007, 8.30 am
The Royal Clarence Hotel, Berwick Street
Barrow in Furnace

When Alicia finally arrived back at the hotel the evening before, the ambience between the two of them was not good. While waiting for her, Robert had indulged himself with red wine. He had been reflecting on the previous day that had gone so well. Remembering every detail, he mulled over it with enthusiasm.

That previous day, he had welcomed the handful of dignitaries on board Astute to have a look at areas of this state of the art killing machine. Certain areas were off-limits even to these important persons and not just on health and safety grounds. History had proved the control room, galley and living accommodation were the most points of interest for a visiting public.

Captain Thomas Broady had requested the Lieutenant conduct the rounds with the party. Something Robert hated but was a necessary part of a naval officer's life. He could never be accused of being an after-dinner speaker but dealt with the situation to the best of his ability. Navy officers and especially Captains, had to remain aloof; it was a lonely position to hold. The day might come when orders had to be given to sink enemy ships or subs and waste lives without hesitation. It would be a question of kill or be killed.

At 7,800 tons submerged Astute was 30% bigger than the previous Trafalgar class of submarine and an absolute leap ahead in design and technology. The privileged personnel on the guided tour were in awe of what they saw; all be it in the confines of security and safety. The defence minister, Sir John Bingham and Admiral of the fleet Simon Nielson, held prime positions. Rear Admiral James Tovey submarine flotilla command, was also a very welcome guest.

Robert Southward's Uncle retired Commodore Daniel Southward and was one visiting V.I.P. that could hardly contain his pride. His nephew had worked hard and achieved the position of navigating officer on the first of this new class of nuclear submersible. The Lord Mayor of Barrow Keith White and the local conservative M.P Stanley Wallis made up the small assembly that was given a guided tour.

Prior to his nephew's achievements, Commodore Southward had carved out his own amazing naval career. He had graduated from Dartmouth Naval College in 1968. Specialising in navigation, after a brief episode on surface ships he joined the submarine service. He served in H.M.S. Warspite as a Sub Lieutenant, then a period on H.M.S. Churchill where he gained the rank of Lieutenant and subsequently Lieutenant Commander.

After a shore-based command, he was posted to H.M.S. Courageous. On recommendation, he took the perishers course. During the assessment at sea, all manner of problems were thrown at the candidate, to see how he could cope under extreme pressure.

Anything from marauding fishing boats, to simulated malfunctions and crew regulated indifference. Daniel Southward did not pass and knew his next appointment if any would be on a skimmer. In 1982 events overtook him when the Argentines invaded the Falkland Islands. As Courageous was having a docking and essential defects period, he was seconded to H.M.S. Conqueror.

He found himself heading thousands of miles south to take up station patrolling the 200-mile exclusion zone. His saving grace was that he was mentioned in dispatches for navigating skills that culminated in the sinking of their intended target. The Argentinean cruiser Belgrano was sunk with the loss of 323 lives. She posed a considerable threat to the British task force with her fifteen 6 inch guns and French helicopters. It was a course of action that had to be taken.

Daniel Southward's future was assured, and he rose through the ranks. As the retired warhorse stood in this futuristic control room, he could only marvel at the strides that had been made over more than three decades. Evolution means changes in all aspects of man's ability to build great things and that can undoubtedly be attributed to nuclear submarine design and build.

The Admiral had been instrumental in pushing Robert into taking the naval officer's entrance exam. A bright boy he had a troubled life as a teenager. His father had walked out of the marital home with no explanation at all. It was no surprise to the young man; he only remembered the constant rowing between his parents. That was a bad chapter in his life. It was only years later he learned they had both been having affairs. His uncle and aunt were very sympathetic, and he went to live with them. It turned out to be his saving grace.

Robert focused again on the previous day. The Captain was entertaining the remaining guests in the marquee on the dockside. Descending and ascending the fwd access ladder on the submarine to the control room was a challenge, to say the least. A superb array of food and drink prepared in the Portakabin galley was presented by the boat's leading chef and his aides. It was a great opportunity for the ship's crew and families to come together and learn more about submarine life. Both experienced submariners and new draughties were enjoying it, and the man in charge endeavoured to talk to as many of the guests as he could.

H.M.S. Astute, pennant number S119, was a complex war machine that had to evolve from the drawing board. Materials drawn from all corners of the globe were moulded and machined into intricate shapes for the various systems that were then set to work, to become an all-powerful submarine. To the Captain and crew, this near 8,000-ton marvel of engineering had become a living breathing monster of the deep.

This first build had been a trying time; all manner of problems had surfaced that had to be dealt with as the work progressed. Finally, after much determination and hard work, the skilled design staff, Naval and civilian engineers and skilled tradesmen were pleased with the end product.

Previously, while it had sat in its cradle having been

wheeled out of the building hall, the submarine looked menacing. Thirty nine thousand acoustic tiles covered the hull and coning tower to mask the white noise generated. It would only radiate the same as a small whale when traversing the oceans of the world. Now floating in the basin, two-thirds of this awesome beast was underwater.

A new standard for the Royal Navy in terms of improved communications facilities, stealth, weapons load and crew comfort would have been achieved. At 97metres long, 11.3mtrs in the beam and 10mtrs draught it was a big submarine. Submerged at sea and manned by a highly trained crew, it would pose a significant threat to any would-be aggressor.

At various dates in the future, it's sister submarines, Ambush, Artful, Audacious, Anson, Agamemnon and Agincourt would be following in Astute's footsteps. The intent by the Ministry of defence is to have these hunter-killer submarines operational well into the 2030s and beyond. Necessary essential dockings and refits would be programmed in accordingly.

It was anticipated at least seven submarines would be required by the Navy to carry out their worldwide commitments, as subsequently the ageing Trafalgar class would be withdrawn from service. The "A" class were a totally different concept with regards to their operational requirements.

The preceding "T" class were designed and built during the cold war, mainly as an anti-submarine warfare concept to counter the threat of the many Russian submarines deployed. This threat having somewhat evaporated meant that the new British class had to encapsulate a far greater commitment.

So, the emphasis was focused on 'Maritime contributions to joint operations,' this, in effect, meant being in direct support of surface forces. To this end, the armament to be carried would be formidable. Thirty eight spearfish torpedoes, UGM-84 sub harpoon, Tomahawk block four cruise missiles with a range of over 1000 miles. These missiles have a nuclear-tipped conversion capability. Navy mines could make up the arsenal in various combinations if required.

Sitting there in the lounge area of their bedroom, it was almost impossible for Robert to switch off. He had the day to himself after all that had been achieved the previous day. Alicia had gone for an early morning run, and he was waiting for her to come back. Nothing had been decided for the rest of the day.

His mind focused yet again; there wasn't anything the Captain and crew did not know about the functions of the submarine. The all-powerful Rolls Royce PWR2 reactor that would probably never need refuelling during the life of the submarine was its core source of power.

When submerged the submarine would be propelled at nearly 30 knots. The 1900 kilowatt diesel generator that sustained the life support systems would operate 24/7. The advanced 2076 sonar system, capable of identifying and tracking vessels across thousands of square miles of ocean was awesome. The two Thales optronics CM010 periscopes provided an instant panoramic view above the waves. The Captain looked forward to putting her through trials in the near future.

The door opened, and Alicia walked in.

"Bob, have you not showered yet?" she asked, bringing him sharply back into focus. She was back from her run and expected him to have shaved, showered and dressed. "Just going, I've been busy."

"Oh yes, it looks like it, thinking about that damn submarine again."

He raced to the bathroom, "I have something planned for this evening. I have tickets for The Sound of Music. I hope you want to go?"

She smiled, "Well, yes, that would be great."

Chapter 8

Tuesday 31st March 2015 Early afternoon
The Sunray Princess Hotel situated in Side (Turkey)

Red Fox (Dmitri Sparrov) was relaxing on the terrace, smoking his favourite Turkish cigarette and enjoying a decent glass of French brandy. Ivor Pushkin (Codin) came up with a local newspaper tucked under his arm and a long cool beer in his hand. He sat down on one of the comfortable loungers beside Dmitri.

"Ah Pushkin, you are up, at last, it is nearly midday."

"Yes Sir, I could not sleep, spent most of the night pouring over what you gave me, where on earth did you get such detailed plans? That is an incredible submarine the British have."

Red Fox looked sternly at his subordinate. "I assume those same plans are securely locked in the special wall safe reserved for you."

"Indeed, they are, Sir."

"Good, they must never be seen by anyone outside of our small circle who will eventually need to study them rigorously. The complete set was not too difficult to obtain really, dollars talk in mother Russia. The F.S.B, (Federal Security Service) holds a vast amount of foreign data relating to all manner of so-called top-secret projects throughout the western world. Still regarded by some as the old K.G.B under a different name, the committee is just as secretive and ruthless. Housed in the same building the newer organisation has access to all the data collected over the decades. Not only that, it is the focal point for all foreign intelligence that has been and will be, gathered. It has cost me a small fortune to get this far, but it will be worth it if everything comes to fruition. I still have ears in the top echelon of our Navy's build programme; we are years behind in developing this technology. I heard about the British plans when they first surfaced over three years ago; they grabbed my interest immediately."

Dmitri Sparrov, the ex-navy Captain, was now a successful industrialist who had built up considerable wealth, estimated to be over a two trillion Rouble. (24 million English pounds) For a second he had questioned his own ability, was it right to get involved with the Russian mafia to fulfil his dream? Yes, of course, it was; the only way a plan of this magnitude could be financed was to bring a heavyweight to the table. He took a decent sip of his brandy.

"Ivor with you and the other thirteen selected ex-submariners, we are going to steal a nuclear submarine from right under the noses of the British."

"What? That's not possible, is it?"

"Well yes I believe it; I have been considering the possibilities for some time and have conducted a lot of covert investigations. Enjoy your beer while I map out the basic details of what is proposed."

The plan would take some time to come together. All the other potential sailors that were needed to make up a working crew had to be vetted before they could be approached. If accepting the challenge, Red Fox knew he could rely on his trusted first officer to deliver; he would be a busy man.

"Having established weakness in the ability of the British military services to be on full alert all the time, there are windows of opportunity. Regarding a certain submarine, it is most vulnerable when in port and at various times not as secure as it should be. That's where I plan to let's say, borrow it for a while."

Ivor Pushkin was rendered speechless. With a huge grin on his face, he couldn't help but listen intently to what Sparrov had to say.

"You will have served with some of our intended comrades before. The rest I know and trust well enough to offer them the chance to join us. As I told you, this operation will be mainly financed by the Mafia and the F.S.B. My own investment will be sizable, so I have every intention of making it happen. Furthermore, it is fully backed by the President and his inner circle."

Codin could not believe what he was hearing, but was thrilled and delighted with the prospects of being part of this escapade.

"If we pull it off, all will be hailed as heroes to the motherland and will be forever remembered in our country's history. Of course, if things go wrong, we will be thrown to the wolves and portrayed as a band of mad unpatriotic Russian navy submariners, acting alone. For the time being this is privileged information and I want it going no further, do you understand?"

"Yes, of course, Sir, you know you can trust me implicitly." Captain Lieutenant Ivor Pushkin was in awe of his esteemed leader.

"Sir, sometimes I think you are a little mad, but I have followed you for most of my naval career without question, I will continue to do so for whatever time I have left on this planet. Our comrades will be extremely grateful for giving them some respectability. The naval establishment left us to rot on that obsolete submarine 'Minskiv,' in the Severomorsk shipyard years ago, our punishment for not in their opinion being up to the task set."

"Ivor you are absolutely right, but there is more to this, we must never forget our comrades on that ill-fated submarine Kirsk; it could have so easily have been us the Stb'd crew."

They both reflected on what had been a terrible tragedy.

"I'm sure you will recall as the primary crew; we were supposed to take Kirsk to sea on that fateful mission but were stood down at the last minute. Considered not fully conversant with the new weapon, that conclusion was unjustified, and I argued the case strongly but to no avail. Little did those poor souls of the Port crew know that when they left the base, it would be for the last time. All 118 enlisted officers and men perished when it foundered 135km off Severomorsk in the Barents Sea, in 108 meters of icy water. It was a terrible way to die."

The K141 an Oskar 1 class, nuclear cruise missile submarine had been lost with all hands on Saturday 12th

August 2000. It had put to sea with the intention of firing experimental torpedoes at the "Pyotr Velikiy" a redundant Kirov class battleship. Twenty four in the number of the new SS-N-19 shipwreck missiles were carried in silos, twelve in port tubes and twelve stb'd. These missiles were designed to take out NATO's aircraft carriers. Each unit primed with 740kg of high explosive, the equivalent of double the Hiroshima blasts, it could also be adapted to carry a nuclear warhead.

There is still speculation as to what happened, maybe a collision with an undetected WW2 mine, but more likely a torpedo malfunction. They were capable of speeds of 70 knots, with the advanced model able to reach an incredible 250 knots. To achieve this phenomenal speed, hydrogen peroxide was the chosen propellant. Highly volatile and very unstable under certain conditions, the Russian Navy were the only ones still using it. What is known is that after a series of explosions that propelled debris from the bow section backwards through the sub, she foundered.

"What fools we were to believe Admiral Korskov that the fateful mission was for the good of the nation. However, that is in the past. Let us hail to a glorious future and our lost comrades." Solemnly Red Fox carried on.

"Codin, on this undertaking we will have to spill blood that is inevitable. Conversely, it's conceivable some of it will be our own, if necessary are you prepared to pay that price?"

"Without question, I would be."

"I am convinced my plan can work, but there will be sacrifices' possibly the ultimate for all of us."

"Captain Dmitri Sparrov, you only call me Codin when something unbelievable is going to happen. I am excited and worried at the same time."

He laughed, "Relax Ivor, lots of time to get you excited and a little worried, maybe."

The two men had great respect for each other. Ivor believed that this man was the greatest sea Captain he had the privilege to serve under. His ability to read situations and stay calm under pressure was incredible. The most testing time, was when lying in wait near the mouth of the Garlock, Scotland, for a British submarine to leave its base at Faslane. A frigate and an American submarine out of Holy lock were in the vicinity to monitor movements and ward off any potential enemy. The game of cat and mouse went on for days. At one time Dmitri estimated the American sub was metres away. At a depth of nearly two hundred meters, it was a dangerous game to play as both submarines were drifting silently with the current; indeed, a collision seemed possible. Captain first-class Sparrov held his nerve. Finally, the American sub engaged secondary propulsion and left at four knots to search another area, did they know of each other's presence? Who knows? He was confident he had second-guessed the American submarine Captain, who had deemed there was no Russian sub there, how wrong he was.

This role was played out many times by the British, American and Russian navies. The American hunter-killer subs out of their Holy Lock base and the British out of Faslane and Devonport often laid in wait for Russian Nukes running out of Severomorsk on the Murmansk Oblast and especially Zapadnaya Litsa within the Litsa fjord. The latter had been extensively modernised in the late nineteen fifties to house the latest K3 class. Ill-fatedly, The Leninsky Komsomol, being the first to go to sea on active service. The base is situated 120 kilometres from Murmansk and 45 Kilometres from the Norwegian border. The long polar nights could last about 43 days. With changeable temperatures and strong winds, it is a very inhospitable place. The constant low cloud makes it an ideal location from which to conduct soviet submarine patrols and covert operations. Now their modern fleet of nuclear submarines is more than a match for the fleets of the western world.

At least they had been until Astute came along. The Sevmash shipyards in Severodvinsk are building incredible submarines. The Borel 11- Yury Dolgorukiy class SSBN's carries an impressive array of nuclear missiles and can dive to an incredible 400 meters. Also, the hunter-killer Yasen Severodvinsk class are state of the art technology and very formidable.

After the extensive refit and modernisation of the British submarine H.M.S. Astute, it is in a class of its own and a real challenge to any would-be aggressor. The imbalance that it has caused is the main reason Red Fox wants to steal it.

"Sir I have many questions I would like to ask as no doubt you are a party to a lot more information."

"You know me too well. For now, I have told you as much as you need to know. As everything comes together, I can brief you and the men accordingly on what more needs to be done. Walls have ears, and loose lips cost lives; I don't want it to be mine."

"No Sir, I totally understand." It was a heavy burden to carry.

Sitting here enjoying all the comforts that the Sunray Princess had to offer was a world away from the days as submariners in the Russian navy.

"We have been through a lot together Ivor, and you have never questioned my orders or reasoning. I commend you for that but this last phase of our sea time together will be the most challenging, who knows what lies ahead? The British are not fools, and security will be tight around the submarine, but there's a chink in their armour. Our agents have been watching developments, and after analysing all the information I truly believe in the not too distant future, the time will be right to strike. I intend to take advantage of that window of opportunity, with intensive training, we can gain the upper hand and land ourselves an enviable prize. My small band of agents and spies are gathering intelligence all the time. We will reach a point of no return, so you need to think very carefully if this challenge is for you. For the last time, do you fully understand the implications and want to take on the responsibilities of being my first officer?"

"Yes, Sir, I fully understand what's at stake and I am one hundred per cent up for the challenge no matter what it involves."

And so, the infancy of the master plan was put into place.

"I propose a toast, Good fortune and success." Captain First Class Dmitri Sparrov and Captain Lieutenant Ivor Pushkin chinked glasses.

"Nazdarovya, my Captain."

Chapter 9

Thursday, 10th March 2016. 4 p.m.
Appledore Shipbuilders and repair North Devon

The shipyard workforce had been assembled in the dining hall of the once-proud shipbuilding and repair yard. After the union member's cards had been vetted, the doors were closed. The area (Unite) union representative was there to brief them on what the management had divulged to him. The one covered dock and large lay apart area, making up the enclosed yard had lurched from owner to owner. They had all tried hard to make a profitable success of the business. In 1996 under a Swedish owner, a brilliant contract had been won against fierce competition from other private yards to build H.M.S Scott for M.O.D. It was designed and dedicated to spending most of its life in the Arctic or Antarctic waters. At the height of its build, over four hundred local tradesmen and women were employed on that project alone. The drawing office was very busy with computer-assisted drawings. (C.A.D.) That was the last major contract the yard managed to win; subsequently, only minimal orders were forthcoming sometimes at cost price to keep the yard going. Any significant contracts for the M.O.D. would be awarded to the larger dockyards, through the tendering process.

A rolling contract to overhaul the 16 landing craft carried by the Landing Platform ships Albion and Bulwark would be the last for the Navy. It was feared, that if Appledore failed, the Ministry of Defence would have to stump up considerable amounts of extra money to get them finished elsewhere, so small subsidies were in the contractual price for each craft. Odd bits of commercial work drifted in, fishing boats, dredgers; in fact, anything that could be built to float or refit would be tendered for. Of course, this was insufficient to sustain the total workforce, and the inevitable happened, the rundown began.

Malcolm Saunders, for Unite, stood up to talk. One thing he was good at was explaining to the members how things stood. Not one to mince his words, he went straight to the heart of the problem.

"Good afternoon lads, I have met the management, and the future could go one of two ways. Firstly, there is a Russian company that is showing interest in leasing the yard. They are in the dredging business; at the moment I don't know any more than that. Secondly, the whole kit and caboodle could be sold, dismantled and shipped to India just like Camel Laird on Merseyside was. The good news is I have a cast-iron guarantee from the management that for now we are not going into receivership. Wages will continue to be paid until lease, sale or closure. That's the best news I can give you I am afraid."

There were murmurs of unrest amongst the assembly.

"Do you trust the buggers, Malc?" It was Paul Bratton who did not trust the management or the union. Because of all that had gone on before, most employees were distrustful of information, either briefed or leaked.

"Well, in general, no I bloody well don't, but in this case, yes I want to. Any chance of saving the yard is welcome, don't you think?"

"Have you been bought off, Malc?" shouted someone from the back of the room. "Don't be bloody stupid. As most of you know, I started here as an apprentice. I consider myself to be a shipwright through and through. The best interests of this yard and the industrial workforce are my main concern." He scowled at the accusation. "It was my choice to go into the union side of things, and I have tried over the years to protect your jobs. You know I am a local councillor, I see at first hand what effect run down has on the Westward Ho and Tiverton areas, so don't chuck that shit at me."

The dining room went quiet. What Malcolm was saying was correct, and most of them knew it.

"As I said, the Russian interest at the moment is no more than that, as far as I know, no contract has been issued or signed. I don't want to be too optimistic, but the signs are encouraging. Ship build and repair is in decline all over Europe, there are lots of small yards like ours up for sale or closed. What we do have in our favour is the expertise that they are looking for. I have another meeting with the directors on Thursday; I assume they will give me something more as to our future. All I can say lads is keep your heads up and don't let your skills slip. The minimal amount of contracts still being worked on must be completed on time and to a good standard. We still have to prove we are the best at what we do and maybe, just maybe, we might keep the majority of jobs, that's it in a nutshell; I'm not going to take any questions because at the moment I don't know any more than what I've just told you. What I can promise is, when I glean any information from the directors, it will be cascaded to you all swiftly. For God's sake, read my web page, for those who don't have access to a computer Jane in my office will print off whatever I have posted. Go in your own time please; we can't let management think the time is being wasted on union business. That's it, for now, lads."

With that Malcolm Saunders picked up his papers, stuffed them into his briefcase and stern-faced, walked out. A few people tried to catch his eye for a private word, but he looked straight ahead and marched on. After all, what more could he tell them? The bullshit he had been fed over the last two months from the owners was something he could do without. He was straight down the middle man. Yes, he had been offered attractive inducements to flour up the situation with the workers. He had told the executive director in no uncertain terms where to get off. As far as Malcolm was concerned, the present management had sat on their hands when they should have been out chasing what little work there was to be had. Instead, they just talked about a run down and disposal. It was probably more lucrative for the owners to close and sell off the fourteen acres of land the yard covered. Situated on the banks of the Torridge River it would make a prime site for expensive housing development. More and more people from outside the area were retiring locally and pushing up prices; top-end property was in short supply.

What really pissed Malcolm off was that certain elements amongst the workforce were spreading malicious lies about him accepting bribes. Yes, he drove a nice car and lived in a nice house at Westward Ho. His wife was the principal of a top grammar school and that was the main reason they had the trappings of success. With regard to the union side of things, he could earn more on the shop floor, without all the hassle.

"Why do I fucking bother, the men don't trust me and the management try to stitch me up," he muttered. "Perhaps I'm getting too old for this bloody job."

He wanted to confide in someone as to all he did know about the yard but he couldn't.

Having been sworn to secrecy by the owners, because the term lease and possible purchase of the yard to a Russian consortium was imminent. The potential purchasers were very secretive and did concern themselves with how foreign ownership would be viewed locally. He had been told that the talks were at a critical stage and any pre-press release would probably delay or scupper the whole deal. If this happened, the yard would go into receivership.

An Indian buyer was waiting in the wings that would get the contents of the yard at a knockdown price. Eventually, it would be totally stripped out, and everything of value would be shipped abroad. The loss to the area would have far-reaching effects for years to come. To the detriment of the workforce, a chosen few would make small fortunes, whichever way it went; Saunders was between a rock and a hard place, he had known most of the skilled men and their families for a long time. If this all went pear-shaped, he would be derided along with the management.

The men were reluctant to leave the dining hall and stood around discussing the situation with grave concerns. They had been allocated an hour for the meeting but were in no hurry to get back to their respective jobs after just 30 minutes. The future had never looked so bleak, and they all knew it. Ryan Taylor turned to Tom Miller, the old shipwright and whispered,

"I reckon we've been sold down the river, stitched up like bloody kippers. I don't trust any of the twats. The management and the union are just looking after their own interests. We'll all be down the dole office before long, and I expect Saunders will get a nice fat cheque for letting it happen."

"You are talking out of your ass as normal," said Tom. "I served my apprenticeship with Malc; he is honest and trustworthy and does his best. I wouldn't want his job for all the tea in china; I remember when times were good, and he started attending union branch meetings. No other bugger wanted to know, rather be out playing football or down the pub. We would always get briefed about what was happening, and it quickly got around that he had the ear of the management. Whatever he has achieved as district divisional organiser, he has earned on merit."

"Yeah I know he is a good negotiator; I am just scared shitless about the future."

"My missus has just been laid off from the laundry; this crap could not have come at a worse time."

Without further discussion, the downhearted assembly started to disperse and go back to their respective workplaces.

They all wondered for how long their skills would be needed, and they would retain a job.

It was common knowledge of the wealth of experience in ship build and repair these people had, was second to none. But because of the downturn generally, there would not be much employment available elsewhere.

At the end of the working day, the men and women clocked off and trudged home. Only essential services managed to get a little bit of overtime. It was pouring with rain, and that added to the generally sombre mood. Ryan Taylor turned the key in the lock of the door to his small terraced house. His two kids would be home from school, and his wife would be getting a meal ready for them all. Ryan's wife, Sally, tried to put a brave face on it all but was just as worried as he was. For the next three days, the routine was the same. However, on Thursday as he was leaving the yard early, having worked a continuous-time (C.T.) to finish a job, there was an air of excitement. Jason Mackie, who had also finished early came rushing over.

"Have you heard? The Russians are coming."

"What?"

"Yeah, evidently it's all on the telly, their buying the bloody lease." Ryan took off like a greyhound and ran all the way home.

As he entered the lounge, the television was blaring. Ryan's wife threw her arms around him, and blurted out,

"The Russian consortium has made a commitment to run the yard, watch the telly." Ryan sat down and listened intently to the local broadcast. Sally skipped into the kitchen and reappeared with two cans of cold lager in her hands.

"Here I think it's time to celebrate."

"Don't be too eager Sal the inks not dry yet."

"According to the news, it is, shut up and just focus on the broadcast."

For the first time that week, they were laughing and joking.

The newsreader read the following statement.

"It has been announced that Appledore shipbuilder and repair facility has had a reprieve from closure. A Russian consortium, subject to terms to be agreed with the current owners, and the local council, will lease the yard on a short term basis with the option to buy. An immediate injection of four million pounds will be advanced. This will be for refurbishment and update of machinery to cope with the major refit of a large commercial vessel. Subject to options it is hoped the intended leaseholder would want to extend the lease or purchase the facility for future expected contracts. Our roving reporter managed to get the reaction from some of the workers leaving the yard at the end of their shift."

"Hello, Sir, can you spare a moment to let us know what you think of the news? A lifeline being thrown to the yard with a guarantee of work to come."

"Yes hello, well I'm Bob, a ship fitter and I think its great news. Don't care if it's the Russians, Chinese, French or whoever, if it saves the yard and jobs then that's great. Let's face it; the government hasn't helped much. To the politicians, it's sink or swim so yes bring it on."

"Thank you, Bob. Madam, what do you think of the news?"

"Fantastic, I'm the canteen manageress, and I've been

working here for fourteen years and love it. My husband works in the yard as well, so to lose two jobs would be terrible. With three children and a mortgage to pay this announcement is very welcome not just for us but for everyone involved. I will personally run up their flag in the back garden if it keeps us employed. Other than the tourist trade, there isn't much else around."

They both laughed. "Thank you for your comments; I think you speak for a lot of relieved workers."

Various people scuttled by without comment, not having heard or were not sure of what it truly meant.

"And you, Sir, what do you think about the proposed rescue?"

"Don't know too much about it, really." "What do you do in the yard, Sir?" "Oh, I'm a general labourer, not been here very long but the best job I've ever had — good pay and up until recently plenty of overtime. Trouble is I'm one of the last ones in and expect to be the first one out, so a bit worried really. We have already been told when the Caissons and liberty tenders for the Navy are finished, there's little on the horizon."

"Thank you for your time. Well, there you have it. In general, a positive reaction to the news just announced, back to you in the studio."

"That was Jack Trevaskis, our roving reporter; let's now have a word with our political correspondent, James Cooper. How does this look for the immediate and possible long-term future?"

"In the short term, it looks very good. It seems very encouraging for this substantial refit on a large dredger. A quick turnaround means the work will be progressed night and day to meet the finishing deadline, like most contracts, there are heavy financial penalties for late delivery. Of course, past that, the order book is empty. However, the Russian consortium is making all the right noises about bidding and winning future work. Very unlikely they will be awarded any military contracts, especially Navy, that would be too political." James looked at his notes and rubbed his chin.

"It is very difficult to predict where any other work might come from. Still, with an initial investment of four million pounds, it seems the new consortium is determined to try and make it work. Who would invest that sort of money if they weren't in it for the longer term?"

"What do you make of that then, Ryan?"

"Bloody good news Sal, never thought it would happen; I could see me travelling again. I know with my skills, I would get another job elsewhere, but I like being at home on my time off. Remember when I worked on the rigs in the North Sea, fantastic money but I hated it, being away from you and the kids. Don't really want to think about working away again. Anyway, I can't see anyone investing all that money and possibly more in the yard to walk away after one refit."

Sally smiled and kissed him. "I love you, you old bugger, let's drink to the good times. Err the kids are at my mum's for tea; let's go upstairs for a while."

"Suits me, I forgot they were going there after school." Ryan switched the T.V. off and ran up the stairs. "I'm going to get in the shower."

It was as though a huge black cloud had been lifted

from the area of North Devon. In particular, the town of Bideford would now see a stream of steady spending. For the workers and their families of the yard, the last eighteen months had been troubling. On flat time with little or no overtime, living standards had been cut to the bone. For the people who had overstretched themselves and relied on the overtime, it was particularly tough; more than one family had downsized or renegotiated their mortgage. Everyone associated directly or indirectly was hoping and praying the Russian consortium would be in for an extended stay; it looked like the good times were coming back. This would be the case while the big refit took place, in reality, however; this would be short-lived.

The leasing company had been set up in such a way that, with offshore accounts and almost no traceability to the various contacts involved, virtually everyone with their fingers in the pie would disappear without a trace. When the shit hit the fan, only the London based intermediaries would be left holding the baby. They would have been paid substantial amounts of money for their services. However, this would never cover the cost of litigation; they would be sued for millions, and some would go to the wall. Dmitri Sparrov and all his willing associates would never be held to account; they had become the untouchables. It would be impossible to prove that his scheming and marauding antics had anything to do with the demise of Appledore shipbuilders Ltd. That's how it worked, no room for sentiment. The deed was done, and Red Fox had pulled off a masterly plan. Much to the annoyance of all those affected, they could only wish for retribution.

Eventually, MI6, along with the other intelligence agencies, would piece everything together and compile a dossier. The background of a lot of the people involved in the piracy of H.M.S. Astute would be fully investigated. M.I.5 agents would secure related files on memory sticks, and external hard drives and all other evidence wiped from military and private computers. No trace of the disastrous events that took place would exist. The substantial amount of detailed information would be gathered, and a final report would be written by "S" from M.I.6, listed Top Secret. This would be secured in government vaults for eternity. It would probably never be released for public consumption. Only the Prime Minister and those with a vested interest would be a party to its content.

Chapter 10

Friday 8th April 2016 20.00 hrs
Penthouse Suite, the Casal Matre Hotel Funchal Madeira

Dmitri Sparrov sat looking out of the panoramic window at the beautiful sapphire blue sea. He wondered to himself just how much time he had spent under the oceans of the world during the progression through the ranks of the Russian Federation Navy. The son of a Senior Michman (Junior Officer), he had graduated from the St Petersburg formally Leningrad University having obtained a degree in Marine engineering. It's location on the Neva River at the head of the Gulf of Finland, allowed Dmitri to see the comings and goings of many great ships. He dreamed of one day being able to navigate the earth's watery passage. The sea was in his blood. It would have been unthinkable to pursue a career in anything other than the motherland's Navy.

He had been accepted as a junior Lieutenant (equivalent to a Midshipman in the British Navy) at the age of twenty. His family were extremely proud of his achievements, especially his father, who Dmitri hardly saw during his formative years. The family had minimalistic but well-kept accommodation on the second floor of a functionalist apartment block in central Pavlovsky. It was in the Oblast district near the Volga River. The young Dmitri had his mother and aunt to care for him. They made sure he was brought up and educated in the best possible manner. Irina, a beautiful woman with long dark hair, sacrificed much to ensure her son had all he needed. From an early age it was apparent he was well ahead of his classmates and excelled at whatever subject took his fancy.

Irina could remember many chilly wintry mornings standing on the railway platform when Dmitri was seven years old. He would wave goodbye to his father as he boarded the train to take him to the naval shipyard, there to join his missile cruiser. On one occasion, Dmitri had tears in his eyes.

"Mother, one day, I will follow in my father's footsteps and be a great sea captain." Irina had laughed and hugged him tightly.

"Your father is not a captain but does a very important job in keeping us all safe. Anyway, Son, I do hope you change your mind and become a scientist or academic; maybe, you are bright enough."

She thought to herself; it is such a lonely life without the man I love to keep me warm in bed at night and to talk over life's hardships. With the ever-present danger of being a sailor, she really didn't want that for her beloved son.

"But Mother, it is all I dream about, I believe it is my destiny."

She hugged him even closer, scary! Even at a tender age he already purported to know what his future would be and she had to accept it. Or did she? After all, she was a grown woman and a doting mother; he was just a boy with a dream. The next few years would see Irina do everything in her power to turn her son's head and heart away from the federation navy. Even hiding away the precious artefacts Dmitri had been given by his father on home leave, it made no difference. By the time her son was 12 years old, they both knew where the future was going. The Russian navy was all her boy would focus on. Every waking moment that he wasn't doing schoolwork; he had his nose in books concerning the federation.

After the cold war ended, like so many of the Russian Federation ranks, Senior Michman Nikolay Sparrov was pensioned off to live the rest of his life in relative obscurity. Although he still commanded respect from all who knew him, he had not been able to find work that amounted to very much. His pension was adequate for him and his family to get by on, but that was about all. There were few treats. He drifted into an endless round of consuming large amounts of cheap Vodka while living the past with ex-naval comrades. On the few occasions that Dmitri managed to get home, he could hardly believe the rapid deterioration of his father. He had become an old man very quickly. So, it was with no surprise when he learned of his death.

Nikolay had suddenly passed away at the age of sixty-one. Irina had taken him a cup of coffee while he was lying in bed and discovered him prostrate. The doctor diagnosed a massive heart attack but concluded he had gone in a relatively peaceful manner. What the doctor had not listed on the death certificate was the fact that his patient had underlying ailments as a result of his past working environment. It had undoubtedly contributed to his state of health and early demise. A deadly cocktail of asbestos fibres, diesel fumes, and cadmium and lead oxides had been ingested over many years on Russian Naval ships. Never having been one to rush to his doctor at the first sign of a problem was the very reason there were scant medical records to refer to.

It was Dmitri Sparrov's wake up call. He had seen at first-hand what loyalty and devotion to duty bought by way of reward. As he stood at his father's graveside with his mother a broken woman, a few relatives and the remnants of Papa's friends and naval colleagues, he made a promise.

"Father, one day I will be rich and famous, and Mother will want for nothing. But I must follow my chosen career first and be a great sea captain. You gave me the vision to work hard and achieve success, and I will not let you down."

He could shed no tears; he had learned the hard way to be strong in body and soul. Spending some time with his mother was good, but he was itching to get back to what he did best. It was her that insisted he go with the words,

"Son, I am so proud of you." He loved his mamma dearly and understood her heartache, leaving her was hard. Depositing sufficient roubles in her account to live comfortably for the next year eased his conscience.

For the first time, here alone, in this palatial suite in the Casal Matre Hotel, Dmitri felt a pang of conscience. His mother was in a residential home, suffering the advanced stages of dementia. She was comfortable and received the best treatment money could buy. Dmitri's sadness lasted a fleeting moment; he had a mission that carried a heavy burden. Dependence and expectance of the people involved rested on his shoulders. His sponsors, the Russian Mafiosi, would not accept failure and the likelihood was he would be pursued and held to account if things went wrong. He knew roughly the structure of the organisation and a few names and their input. Conversely, the only thing that his financiers wanted was a good return on their investment and perhaps some national pride to reflect on.

Dmitri had purposely kept the game plan to the chosen few. There had been covert meetings with a second or third party; this was where Ivor Pushkin, (Codin) came in. Years earlier he had been a KGB case officer, Spetsnaz field operative and F.S.B, an intelligence officer in tandem with his naval career. He was the most reliable but ruthless person Dmitri knew and was the only one he could trust to negotiate the funding required. Of course, the people who were putting up the money had looked into his background and knew Ivor Pushkin would deliver or die trying.

Red Fox savoured the fine Lagavulin whisky, one of the best things to come out of Scotland. He recalled the fact that at one stage on patrol; he had been just a few miles off the coast of the Islay Island where it was distilled. During the cold war, American nuclear submarines were running out of Holy lock. They were considered to be undetectable when they disappeared into the North Atlantic. The truth was, while in command of a nuclear hunter-killer sub, Captain Dmitri Sparrov with his well-trained crew would lie in wait to pick up the signature trail of any western submarine going out on patrol. They had tracked one skipjack class heading to the Barents Sea and monitored it for days. Over hundreds of miles playing the game of cat and mouse without being detected was formidable. He knew the waters of the British Isles like the back of his hand. To his knowledge, he had been the only Russian Captain to navigate the Irish Sea from north to south without detection. Or had he been detected? Listening devices on the sea bed should have given away the fact; a foreign submarine was lurking in territorial waters. The captain and crew were on tenterhooks until they were once again safe in the North Atlantic. The truth was the submarine had not been spotted.

A knock on the door brought Captain Dmitri Sparrov back to his senses. The tumbler with the remnants of his whisky was secreted in the drawer and a bottle of water substituted. He opened the door and welcomed in the first two visitors.

"Good to see you comrades, come in and make yourself comfortable. Over the next 15 minutes, we will be joined by others, some of whom you will know."

To all intents and purposes, this would be an arranged card school, one of many. The various palms had been greased to make sure no prying eyes or interruptions would occur while business was conducted, two fishing trips had also been arranged. Once the seven men were assembled and the formalities over, Sparrov started his address.

"Comrades, you all know who I am and what I represent. The scant information you received when individually meeting with Ivor has tempered your curiosity, otherwise you would not be here. You represent almost half of the skilled technical people I need to fulfil my mission; the others will receive the same address as you. You have all been vetted with regard to your financial position and likelihood of wanting to join me. I make no apology for that because if any man here does not want to follow me, then he will leave 200,000 roubles richer. Of course, I will be buying your silence, and I mean silence, Red Fox glared at every man individually. If you decide to join in this adventure, then the sum each man will receive is 50,000,000 roubles."

The men were excited at the prospect but stunned into silence. Most were eking out an existence while supporting their families. Having never known anything but a naval career, their pensions through inflation had been reduced in purchasing value. Working for one of Dmitri's companies had been a Godsend for some of them. They knew that he had taken them on as a favour, as their worth to the company was minimal. The truth was they were extremely grateful for the chance of a better life for themselves and their families and worked hard for him.

In his early years of building a business, Sparrov was not one to share his ever-increasing wealth with too many people. He had been mercenary with clients and competitors to accumulate what he had. However, he never forgot people who had been loyal to him and repaid that loyalty to the chosen few who had been.

Captain Dmitri Sparrov continued his brief.

"What I propose is highly dangerous, and I do expect casualties, possibly fatalities. If we succeed, history will be written. The financial rewards will be beyond comprehension, and we will be held in high esteem by many of our ex comrades. It may be necessary for you all and your chosen family members to relocate to a country with new identities for several years, maybe indefinitely. If this becomes a necessity, I can tell you; these arrangements will be in place before we undertake our challenge. You and your families will be relocated and have the best facilities money can buy. Gentlemen, you must have many questions I can only answer some?"

The men remained silent and pensive. Sat before Dmitri Sparrow were some of the creams of the Old Russian Navy. They were all specialists in their respective fields, and he needed each and every one of them. Lieutenant Sergey Gikalov was the first to speak.

"Captain, obviously because of the people I have the great honour of sitting with; this operation is of a naval structure. Can you expand on this and what the chances of success are?"

"Sergey, you are correct; it is a great naval adventure and will be full of excitement and danger. We will be secreted to a foreign country, and I would expect to be away in total a matter of weeks. Having researched the feasibility of this undertaking for the last two years, I consider our chances of success at greater than 50%."

Senior Lieutenant Nikolay Popov spoke next.

"Captain, where will we be expected to relocate with our families?"

"It will be a country with no extradition treaty with our own. The location will be a brand new complex of luxury four-bedroom apartments with every comfort available, overlooking the South Pacific Ocean. All infrastructures will be there, including a school for the children. This is only a contingency measure, and I hope it will not be required. If it is, I believe you will all be able to return home eventually. However, security will be paramount, and it is not possible to say how long we would be expected to be away from our motherland. What you should be totally aware of, we may not all survive. The worst-case scenario is we all perish." Red Fox paused to let the enormity of what they were undertaking, sink in. "In that eventuality, your families will be looked after financially for the rest of their lives. Instead of a lump sum, a monthly income of 25,000 roubles will be made available to them individually."

Minds were racing; having circumnavigated most of the world the men had a good geographical background. They knew there were only two or three countries that would fit the bill for repatriation if it came to that.

"Well, how bad would it be to escape the Russian winter's comrades?" said Starshina 1st stage (OR-6) Stepan Aleksandrov.

Laughter erupted.

"Good point Stepan, Ok gentlemen keep it down. I know this is a suspected card school, but I don't want to attract any more attention than is necessary." The room fell silent again.

"Captain, how long do we have to make a decision, about our individual course of action," said Chief Ship Starshina, Mikhail Somov.

"Well Mikhail, you know you are all booked into this hotel for two nights. In that time, you are not to discuss the situation with one another outside of this room. I expect you to come to me individually, with your decision as soon as you have made up your mind."

He looked at the assembly with intent.

"For those of you, who wish to leave, arrangements will be made, and you will be compensated for your silence. However, be very aware you will be under surveillance, any loose talk or misdemeanour will result in punishment."

"Captain, can you expand a little on what this mission is and likely to entail?" said Starshina 1st class Aleksey Petrovskii.

"Aleksey, we have been subject to secrecy and security all our federation lives while protecting the Motherland. I will be treating this mission in exactly the same way. Hence for all those who sign up, sufficient information will be furnished to allow you to hone the tasks you will be assigned. For those of you who decide to bow out, it is better you know no more."

What a decision for each individual to have to make; or it would have been for lesser men. It was apparent whatever Captain Dmitri Sparrov had in mind, it would be highly dangerous and extremely controversial. The men sat at the table, looking at one another to gauge any reaction. Aleksey Petrovskii, Starshina 1st class, was the first to break the silence.

"Captain, I would be privileged to follow you on whatever crusade you have in mind. I have served under you on two of your commissioned submarines and look forward to the challenge ahead."

This was the flood gates for every man to speak up. One by one they stood up, saluted and pledged their allegiance to Dmitri Sparrov. Red Fox smiled; it was the outcome he had expected.

"Well, my chosen comrades we will be embarking on an extraordinary journey that will show the world what our motherland can achieve. There will more individuals joining our crew to make up the numbers required, and, as I said, some will be familiar faces."

He looked at each man individually. He was a good judge of character, and there was no doubt in his mind these were the men he needed.

"This is a big commitment, and for some, possibly the ultimate sacrifice will be the outcome. For that very reason in the next 36 hours, anyone who changes his mind can come to me and relinquish any further involvement."

He allowed time for anyone with doubts about their ability to take on this mammoth challenge to voice their concerns. Looking around the room, there appeared to be none.

"If as I suspect you are all fully committed, then you will return to your families for a week. All that you are allowed to tell them is you have landed a good job working away for a period of up to three months. The 400,000 roubles that will be deposited in your individual bank accounts should convince them of your worth. Do not raise any suspicion by spending irrationally; all your financial affairs will be monitored. You will be contacted by a member of my organisation and told of your destination a day before departure; there will be no paper trail. You will be supplied with all clothing and footwear needed and your travel arrangements made, so travel light. That is all, comrades."

There was silence as the men stood up, ready to troop out; it was no surprise that Red Fox knew so much about them. While in the Russian Federation Navy, this was how the state monitored their daily lives. It was obvious to all that this would continue for some time, possibly indefinitely.

"We go fishing tomorrow where I can furnish a little more sensitive information."

After the assembled men had left, Dmitri sat back in his chair. He was fairly confident the remaining seven coming to the hotel next week would be recruited. The total of fourteen sailors that would make up his crew were known for their reliability and commitment, also for their technical and practical ability.

It was amazing how much information could be bought, doctors reports, bank statements, and just about everything relevant was known about each individual. Most importantly was the state of mind and family stability of all recruits, many good men had been rejected. Out of over two hundred potential ex submariners; the numbers had been whittled down to the crème de la crème. There was still a long way to go, but this part of the jigsaw puzzle was slotting into place.

Captain First Rank Dmitri Sparrov had spent a considerable amount of his own money and so much had already been achieved. However, as the Mafia were the chief financiers, they expected significant returns on the vast sums committed. Everything had to be meticulously planned and executed, and the most difficult challenges lay ahead. An old friend who had been a senior member of the K.G.B. was now deputy head of the F.S.B; this was a great help. Codin (Ivor Pushkin), being the go-between was privileged to sensitive information about the financial backers. Dmitri knew whatever he requested was supplied without question. A number of untraceable bank accounts had been set up for his personal use. He knew these tranches of money were by no means gifts and were expected to be repaid. His life was on the line if they were not although it didn't bother him too much; it would be glory or death for Red Fox.

Chapter 11

The eight men Dmitri Sparrov, Ivan Petrovich, Oleg Ivanov, Nikolay Popov, Boris Maklakov, Vasiliy Baskov, Sergey Gikalov and Leonid Kuzlow were milling around the lobby of the hotel. They were waiting for the taxis to take them to the port for the days fishing trip. The catch would be good; Dmitri had hired the Santa Maria, with a small crew before. The skipper Carlos Hosta knew all the best marks, to catch Sea Bream, Bass, Scabbard and the great Marlin. The eight Russians, who spoke respectable English, knew only to engage in small talk until they were safely out to sea and never refer to any individual by name.

The taxis arrived, and the waiting men quietly and patiently gathered up what they would need for the day's excursion. For some of them, it was exciting to go fishing; for others it was just an unenviable chore to get away and discuss whatever lay ahead and find out what they were expected to do. Of these seven men that Dmitri had in his company, he would have put money on the fact that each and every one of them would not change their minds about following him. It was not just the financial reward that would convince them of the validity of this dangerous and maybe life-threatening adventure, but also the fact they were the chosen few.

Each man considered he had a debt to settle with regard to the way he had been treated in previous years by the higher echelon of the Russian military machine. Subsequently, if Red Fox had formulated a master plan, then it had to be in all their interests and would complement the modern government.

Orchestrated by Sparrov, the ten-minute ride to the dock was in silence. Once they were on-board the boat, there would be plenty of time to voice concerns and opinions. As they vacated the taxis and headed for the Santa Maria, a sense of foreboding entered Oleg Ivanov's mind. In all the time he had served in the Russian Navy, he had never been a good sailor. The hatred of confined spaces and experiencing seasickness were things that made his sea time uncomfortable. However, he had trained as a professional marine engineer and knew no other way of life. For that reason, Oleg was able to overcome his inner fears and take medication for his seasickness. That allowed him to function as well as the others.

Carlos welcomed each man on board with a nod and helped load their personal effects. In Portuguese, he muttered under his breath,

"To discuss laundering money or whatever you do, keep using my boat, my friends, I am happy, no questions asked."

The crew, his two adult sons, were busy checking the supplies for the trip. Once everyone has settled, the skipper made the final checks ready to go to sea.

"Release the mooring ropes fwd and aft he bellowed in his broken English."

Did he assume Sparrov, (an alias used Alexi Fedorov), was a rich businessman entertaining some of his clients along with trusted staff maybe? His air of authority certainly led to the assumption he was the head honcho.

Carlos sensed these men had only come for the fishing and drinking and did not want to engage in conversation with him or his boys. They could have helped the party to land a better catch but ha-ha! Good money.

Hosta could not speak Russian, and he was sure they didn't speak Portuguese. Little did he know these people could all speak good English. Sons Carlos junior and Filipe had learned how to keep out of the way for most of the trip. When they got to the fishing grounds, their job was to make sure rods, bate and drinks were available and deal with the fish that were caught. These outings would be charter booking; they had much better-earning potential than just landing fish to sell. The agreement was payment in cash at the end of the two-day hire. Charging the equivalent of a two weeks wage, he was highly delighted when it was accepted without question. A substantial retainer had already changed hands for the hire of the boat, Alexi was a generous man, and the crew liked him very much. Cash in euros was always a welcome sight; it was getting ever more difficult to make a living from commercial fishing.

Proceeding out of the harbour, the skipper took a south-easterly direction on the way to the first fishing spot, twenty minutes steaming at fifteen knots. The eight men sat on the less than comfortable bench seats exchanging idle chatter.

It was considered their own mother tongue would be harder to interpret by anyone listening to their conversation. What Carlos did not know was that Dmitri Sparrov's contact had thoroughly investigated the Santa Maria, its owner and sons. His information was that they were a respectable commercial and charter fishing business. They were solvent and had never been in trouble with the authorities. Prone to sell the odd basket of fish to the highest bidder, they would also consider anything nearly legal that would produce the non-taxable euros. Just the sort of people to accept good remuneration, no questions asked. It suited both sides very well.

The skipper called to his sons to make ready to drop anchor and get the rods ready for the first try of the day. It was a hot, fairly calm day with a slight sea breeze. The boat was built so that no fisherman had to sit in the full glare of the sun for hours on end. The men settled down to fish,

"Okay" said Dmitri, "Down to business. I have in place all that is needed to provide the platform for an adventure."

He laughed on purpose, and the men followed suit. In the wheelhouse skipper, Carlos laughed as well. He did not understand what on earth they were laughing about, but if his clients were happy, there would be a good tip at the end of the day. Within minutes the first nice fat bream was hauled to the surface, followed by a healthy bass. Filipe rushed to deal with the catch; re-bated the hooks and retreated to an inconspicuous distance. This was how the day would go.

Dmitri continued, "Ivor sends his apologies he is very busy dealing with the complexities. I only intend to sketch out the rudiments of what I want to achieve, I want no questions here, and they can wait until this evening when we are in the comfort of my suite. Dragging the light anchor, the skipper will drift the boat and hopefully, today's catch will be rewarding. We will stay over this fishing ground; I am assured it's the best for rod and line."

Spasmodically, during the day, the basic details of what he required from the men were mapped out. It was all from memory; he did not want any paper trail whatsoever, a name or place scribbled on a piece of paper could spell disaster.

During their time in the Russian navy these men had been subject to a strict regime, secrecy and security was second nature to them all. Naturally, there was the odd eyebrow raised, and sometimes a blank expression was in evidence. Between them, they had a vast amount of knowledge and experience, and the proposal that had been put to them seemed feasible; a well-orchestrated but totally ruthless plan that had death and destruction in its content.

On purpose, Red Fox supplied just enough information to whet their appetites. For these hardened warriors, it was more intriguing than worrying, to say the least. Some of them, since leaving the Russian Navy had settled into quite dull and boring lives. Civilian life was hard to come to terms with, and they had considered re-enlisting. Their skills would be welcomed, and at the very least, they would be engaged in a training role for new recruits. Now this proposition of getting back into what they were experienced and good at seemed like a dream.

At approximately 1600 hours Dmitri considered he had briefed the men sufficiently to allow them to ponder. Staying on the same mark suited Oleg Ivanov; he was actually enjoying catching fish and had not experienced any seasickness. The skipper knew that the fishing party wanted to pack up and go home as no more bait was requested, and the rods were laid on the deck. He called on his boys to secure everything and make ready for home. It was in silence that they made their way back; Carlos imagined it was because everyone was tired after fishing and heavy drinking. Little did he know that most of the alcohol had gone over the side, and the sailors were stone-cold sober?

When the Santa Maria got to Port, Carlos junior and Filipe went about their business of securing the boat, the fishing party all but Dmitri got off. It was common practice for them to have the first choice with regard to keeping the best fish, and the skipper could have the rest. To his delight, he had been told to keep the catch as they had only come for the sport. When he had a fat, brown envelope stuffed with Euro notes pushed into his palm, he shook Dmitri's hand profusely. In broken English, he repeated,

"Senor, see again, comes again."

"Danka, yes, same time on Friday," replied Dmitri, he jumped off the boat and headed to the waiting taxi. The Hosta family waved ecstatically to the departing men; they knew this would be the best payday of the year. Strange people these Russians thought Carlos senior, don't take any fish and pay over the odds for the hire of my boat, I love big spenders. He kissed the brown envelope and turned to his sons,

"Boys, we drink big time tonight."

It was fair to say that Red Fox had mapped out only the briefest of information to this first fishing party; it would also apply to the subsequent one. It had been flowered up to some extent, but that was all part of his plan to keep their interest. He needed time to gauge the reaction of all the men he wanted on his team and Dmitri was happy with the progress so far. They all knew from past experience not to probe too deeply as to what lay ahead. Including Ivor Pushkin, these and the seven others were the very best he could recruit for the mission. He knew a minimum of twelve would suffice, but two more would provide a level of wastage if any were rendered incapacitated. With a contingency plan of a further four that could be approached, the team leader felt confident things were going according to plan.

All in good time, the men would have progressive and sufficient briefings conducted by Codin. It could not be emphasised enough about secrecy and security; it was of the utmost importance. What these men didn't know was they were constantly under surveillance by a small, highly skilled team of Sparrov's henchmen. Anyone deemed not to have the best interests regarding what they were a party to, would be removed from public life. They would be confined or worse until it was considered they were no longer a threat to the mission. Red Fox was confident the men were trustworthy, but he could take no risks. Regarding this planned mammoth undertaking, no one was above the watchful eye of his inner circle.

Chapter 12

Wednesday, 8th February 2017.
Appledore Shipbuilder and repair yard.
Bideford in North Devon, England

It was nearly 16.00 hours, high tide. John Banfield, chief shipwright responsible for the docking of any vessel in the covered dry dock, looked at the "Thor Variant" an ocean-going dredger.

"Big mother fucker," he proclaimed to the docking party assembled.

"Yes, sure is," said Matt Cummings, senior planner. "Big and ugly, nothing like the beautiful vessels we've built in the past. Still, that's all gone now. I just see it as a great opportunity to pay my mortgage for as long as possible."

They all laughed. The good times had returned thanks to their new Russian owners.

True to his word, the Executive Director Keith White, with the prompting of the union rep Malcolm Saunders, had kept the men informed of all the developments as they had evolved over the last twelve months. It had been a traumatic time, and it really looked as though the Russian negotiator would walk away when there was a serious problem over the lease of the yard. However, the local council leaders had got their heads together, intervened and coerced the site owner to conclude a suitable lease of tenure. It had suited the Russian negotiating team and the unknown bogus purchaser. As promised, once the contract was signed, steady streams of finances were made available. They would cover the service and running of the dockyard and the payment of wages.

Suppliers of raw materials insisted on being paid on delivery; they were still not sure of the long term financial prospects of the company. Everything required to get the refit started was ready in the stores and on the docksides. The design team had instigated the programs for the CNC machines that would shape the required steel and nonferrous components for the refit. The welders would be the busiest of the workforce and would be on six-day twelve-hour shifts. For the time being, a steady workload was pencilled in to get the dredger ready for sea by the completion date. That was paramount.

Keith White was very sceptical about the London based company, negotiating on behalf of the Russian consortium. Every time he tried to glean any information, regarding the principal financial backers, he was met with a wall of silence. He was reminded on more than one occasion that other yards that would jump at the chance of securing the intended work. Keith knew the managing director of the now-defunct Torpoint slipping company. A small docking and repair facility on the river Tamar it was a minnow in an ever-competitive industry. Set up with good intentions to secure work from the government it had failed miserably although work could be done at a much lesser cost than the main yards, the initial outlay was crippling. The banks were reluctant to loan ever more tranches of money without secured contracts, and it went into receivership. With no buyer coming forward it closed completely and was asset stripped. The council who owned the land sold the 3-acre plot to a developer who built executive townhouses that encompassed amazing views across the Tamar River.

Keith had to toe the line; he knew his head would be on the block if he did not wholeheartedly embrace the people with whom he had to negotiate. For the time being, he would be subservient and not let his workforce down. However, he did have a deep routed suspicion about the long term prospects of Appledore shipbuilders and repair facility under the new management structure imposed. He would be kept on by the consortium to oversee the start of the refit, but he hated the short time he was there. It was obvious from the start; corners would be cut, and safety put at risk. Finally, after six weeks he resigned and abruptly left, having been sworn to secrecy. He had been offered a position in Dubai in the UAE overseeing maritime construction. An agent of Dmitri Sparrow would monitor his movements and woe betide if he made public the present state of Appledore Shipbuilding and repair facility. For his own safety and that of his family he complied.

Jim Mayer, ship fitter, scratched his forehead, "It may be the frigin Russians who own us, but as long as they provide work like this, who gives a shit. There is the talk of a small Russian cruise liner being tendered for, wouldn't it be great if we got that for refit. I'm calling in at the off licence on the way home, to get a bottle of vodka to celebrate with the missus, no more gin for her."

They all laughed again. The situation at Appledore reflected Naval and private shipyards throughout Britain. Once the greatest nation, able to build anything and everything that could and did sail the oceans of the world. Over the decades, the industry had been undermined by subsidised cheaper foreign competition. Coupled with the fact, successive governments had run down and even shut naval dockyards and some of the remaining civilian yards, they had been starved of funds to survive.

So here we were, a small shipyard paramount to the local economy, struggling to exist, but having had a lifeline thrown to them by way of a foreign investor.

The "Thor Variant" was in for a major upgrade. Millions of pounds were involved, and day and night shift working and overtime was a must to make the completion. Nearly all the men had signed the opting-out clause of the working time directive that limited working hours. Standing on the dockside, Forman painter Mike Dobson, piped up,

"God! Even my missus is off my back and actually allows me in the bed again. Amazing what happens when there's a few bob around to buy a new dress. The winceyette pyjamas have been changed for a red negligee."

"Lucky bugger." said Fitter Paul Cox, "Lovely looking woman married to a fat twat like you, where did I go wrong?" Mike laughed out loud.

"You can't help it if your mother threw out the baby and kept the afterbirth."

Everyone began to chuckle; good times were to be had again.

The village of Appledore and the town of Bideford three miles away, relied heavily on the tourist trade. In the summer months with all the visitors to this attractive north Devon area, things were vibrant. A lot of walkers came to enjoy the Northam Burrows country park, a really pretty area popular with the locals as well. In the winter months, a lot of the shops that catered for the visitors temporarily closed. Only the two pubs and the conservative and the working men's clubs managed to carve out a reasonable existence. In the workies club, for the nightshift team, it was regarded that the all-day breakfast was the best value for money in the whole town. For those who wanted it, a late breakfast was something to look forward to. A plateful of hot succulent food washed down with a couple of decent pints, allowed the boys a good sleep during the day.

Little did any of the dockies know there were two spies, working for Sparrov's organisation. They had made their temporary home here while pretending to be doing contract work on the Pylon cable replacement that was going on all over Devon. They were the eyes and ears of what went on, so much information could be gathered to pass on to Red Fox's team. The workies club was regarded as having a loose lips canteen, but that would change abruptly. Once the dredger refit started, conversations were monitored by agents planted by the new owners. If any of the workers were overheard bragging about what they were doing on the dredger, they would be hauled in to see the human resources manager. Given a dressing down and told to keep their mouths shut or face being sacked.

Fitter and turner William Fox and Tom Nancekivell

were talking in whispers about what was going on.

"Fucking Hell, security is tighter than a duck's arse. You would think we were back contracting for the Mod again."

"Yes, Bill, I bet they have even put listening devices in the crapper."

"Not sure about that but either way we must be careful about what we say. John Frederick got his cards the other day; he was mouthing off about being the best welder put on a special job. He was only working in the bilge tanks for fuck sake; anyway, they got rid of him."

"Yeah, I heard, this new management are ruthless and expect their pound of flesh, but they pay well. From now on in this place its football only, Bideford Association or Liverpool, I can't afford to lose this friggin job."

"No mate me neither."

And so it was that the whole town came alive. The shops were well stocked, and the pubs did a brisk trade. That's the trouble with dockyardies, in good times they and their families live and spend well and sod tomorrow. No one could guess that when the Thor Variant was complete and ready to leave, there would be no more Russian investment. When the web of lies unfolded, the police and government officials would be involved interviewing people about what they knew. Of course, the two spies were long gone, the stable door was open, and the horse had bolted. To the people they had befriended the story was, the local contract had finished, and they were going to Scotland to work there. They even had the audacity to have a leaving do at the workies, with food and barrels of beer laid on. As they said,

"For the great people of this town that had made them so welcome."

Now once again, when all this unravelled the skilled staff would be laid off. It hit everyone hard because it had all looked so good. The union representatives would be given assurances from a government minister and the local MPs that all would be done to secure the future of the yard. Some chance, the defence budget was under pressure to save more billions, and the Navy would be expected to burden its share. The refit work Appledore might have secured on older small vessels would be taken out of the equation; they would now be placed in reserve. In Naval terms, that generally meant layup, and subsequently cannibalisation to keep similar vessels going. In the end what was left, usually ended up as scrap. Any ships worthy of sale had already been sold to foreign navies, Brazil and Chile being the main buyers. Romania was more than willing to buy the type 22's London and Coventry to become the capital ships of their Navy. There are frigates and destroyers of 30 years vintage, still very much sea-going warships protecting those countries that purchased them. Subsequently, ships thought to be surplus to requirements by the British government, are considered to be very good investments for third world countries.

When Babcock International bought the Devonport facility from the government under privatisation rules, it was deemed a good purchase. Only the infrastructure, with all that went with it, was released by the M.O.D. For all intents and purposes, the base was still a naval asset. For a private company with shareholders, one major consideration was making a profit. Their global network was vast, and they were considered a prime operator at what they did, so it came as no surprise when they bid and secured the Devonport complex. The government considered Babcock to be the best company to take on the massive task of turning around an ailing facility. Over the years reducing the poorly structured workforce and hiving off unprofitable sections, proved to be the dockyards survival. Babcock was now established as the quality front runner for build, refit and repair of the British Naval fleet.

Contracts of a military nature are normally bid for and secured years ahead of planned start dates. All government work would be much sort after ahead of any commercial work that was up for grabs. Hence when it became necessary again to dredge the Tamar estuary, it was put out to tender. The European consortium that owned the dredging company was chosen to carry out the work. As the Thor Variant would be based in Millbay docks it was considered there would be no security risk to the naval base. Other than emergencies, there would be no need for any ships staff to enter dockyard premises. The M.O.D. police on launches would be monitoring movements of the dredger anyway. The silted up channel would be the working platform for the vessel. Working on a twenty-four-hour basis, it was considered the four to six weeks would see the work carried out to a conclusion. The only downtime would be for ships movements or repairs. That time would be spent in Millbay where there was no military presence.

What could never have been envisaged was the involvement of the Thor Variant in the plan to steal a submarine from Devonport Naval base. When everything unravelled, and MI5 got involved, traceability back to the Russians was almost impossible. In the main, their input could only be surmised. A deep web of lies and intrigue, coupled with offshore accounts that financed everything, led to dead ends. Everything had been very cleverly set up and would be just as cleverly dissolved when the time came.

Chapter 13

Wednesday 15th February 2017. 9.30 am
Dr Cherkesov, s office Russian hospital

Dmitri Sparrov sat in the private waiting room, waiting to see the specialist. He hated consultants, especially those who had in-depth knowledge of his medical condition. Trying to avoid this one, in particular, it was now deemed necessary to have the face to face meeting after numerous requests to do so. Having picked up a virus; he had felt under the weather for the last few months, his daily visits to the gym were becoming increasingly tiresome. He thought, maybe it's just the stress of the mammoth task about to be undertaken. In Russia, like most countries, if you have the money, access to the very best medical treatment was instantly available. Hence, he found himself a patient of Cherkesov's in the private Moscow Medical facility. Situated in the very expensive and the fashionable district of Tverskoy Moscow, it was only available to very wealthy Russians. Over the years, the consultant had advised Dmitri as to what treatment was considered necessary. Not at all a good recipient, the drugs prescribed were taken sporadically or quite often ignored altogether.

His thoughts were interrupted by the attractive

receptionist. "Mr Babachencko, you can go through to the Doctor's office now, Sir, he is waiting for you." "Thank you." Looking directly at the attractive beaming female, he thought, 'Not seen her before.' He had sensed a spark when he first walked in. Alina had noticed his sharp good looking angular face, broad shoulders and authoritative stance. His piercing blue eyes made her blush. Under normal circumstances, he would have taken this encounter further, but on this occasion decided against it.

On entering the Doctor's office, a loud voice barked out, "Come in and take a seat." Accessing the computer, the Doctor had Dmitri's file, containing past and present records. He was studying the four radiographs that had been taken on the last visit. He paused for a while removed his horn-rimmed glasses and looked directly at Sparrov. "What the hell have you been up to, as if I didn't know?" Over the previous years that Cherkesov had been Dmitri's consultant, he had never known such a healthy male considering the lifestyle he led. However, there were disturbing signs that all was not as it should be. Looking again at the x-rays, he selected one and projected it onto the large monitor on the wall. Sitting there tutting really irritated Dmitri; 'The bastard could be a little more reticent with his synopsis considering the exorbitant fees he charges me.' No point in arguing with him, 'Just take it on the chin and get out of here as soon as possible.'

"You are obviously still smoking those strong cigarettes and drinking too much whisky. I have told you on more than one occasion if you carry on like that you would not make old bones and you continue to ignore me." "Not all the time." Sparrov was annoyed. The Doctor put his glasses back on and studied the graph, ignoring his patient. "Well just take a look at this x-ray the darker areas around your upper chest area that is what I'm worried about." Dmitri made a cursory glance at the graph, looked away and sat stony silent. He knew Cherkesov didn't flower up bad news.

Well aware of the harmful effects, especially exposure to asbestos and radiation that Dmitri had endured, it was of concern to the Doctor. Considering the facts, lesser men would have succumbed to a rapid downward spiral of ill health.

Pushing his glasses back onto the top of his balding head, he turned and glared at Dmitri. His staring eyes told the Russian naval captain all he needed to know. "How long Doctor?" The Doctor paused and rubbed his chin. "Well if you cut down on the cigarettes and alcohol maybe four to five years. You must also religiously take the medication I prescribe if you do not heed my advice then less than half that time. You are one of the most interesting patients I have, and I would like to give you a thorough examination and progressive treatments. Seeing you on a regular basis to monitor progress would benefit us both. New treatments are evolving all the time. I believe one, in particular, would help immensely; it is experimental and not readily available. With it, I am treating other patients with similar conditions to yours, so far in most cases; it has greatly improved and extended their quality of life." He took a box out of the top drawer of his desk and read the label.

"I can obtain a full course of this drug if you wish me to; it's expensive but in trials has proved its worth." The

Doctor poured over the notes in front of him while Dmitri pondered the way ahead. "It's difficult to make a completely accurate assessment of your medical condition. On the few occasions you decide to visit my consulting rooms, I never quite know what to expect." "Thank you, Doctor, for now, that's all I need to know." Dmitri pushed his chair back, turned and left the room without another word. He knew already that his state of health was deteriorating. He needed time to fulfil his ambitious dream but did not intend to become an experimental Guinee pig. Certainly, wouldn't be the case at Cherkesov's exorbitant prices.

As he strolled back into the waiting room, he looked directly at Alina and cheekily winked at her. She smiled, blushed and fiddled with her long auburn hair. He had not truly realised how beautiful she was. Spotting there was no ring on her wedding finger; he changed his mind and would chance his arm. Walking over to her desk, he placed his large curled knuckled hands directly in front of her. "I'm sorry if I was a bit abrupt with you when I walked in, too much on my mind. Your good Doctor has managed to allay my worst fears." Lying bastard, he thought to himself.

"Oh, that's all right, you have to get used to it in this job. Some of his patients come in, sit and wait with not so much as an acknowledgement of the person attending to them. Fortunately, I am just juggling two jobs, while our receptionist has her day off." "Well I find it hard to believe they would ignore you; I would have thought any male patient coming through that door would be only too pleased to pass the time with a lovely lady." "That's nice of u to say that, I'm flattered. I have my own office through there and deal with all the administration for the Doctor. He's a busy man, being a self-employed consultant, he tries to keep costs down, and we all have to muck in when necessary; hence, I'm on the front line today."

Dmitri paused for a while and then looked deep into her amassing brown eyes.

"I just had a thought; I will be in town for the rest of this week and wondered if you would have dinner with me, maybe this evening?" Before she could answer, he interjected, "Of course if you have a husband or fiancé, I would understand your refusal." Alina looked away, "Well, oh! No, I don't have anyone in my life at the moment, divorced and well rid of the bastard, cheated on me with my younger sister. I will never forgive the both of them, not acceptable. Oh sorry, didn't mean to blurt that out, it's still raw."

"Luckily, I have this job to keep me going, as I said; I do all the administrative work, and the Doctor pays quite well. Being on my own I need all the income I can get, renting in Moscow is so expensive."

Just then another patient walked in, Dmitri took a few steps back while Alina dealt very professionally with the smartly dressed elderly gent with a walking stick. He was grumpy and said very little, finally parking himself on a deep high back leather chair, adjacent to Cherkesov's office. Dmitri observed a rich man, who by the looks of him, would soon be parted from his money, life's a bitch he thought. Turning his attention to Alina once more and biting the bullet, Dmitri said "So how about dinner this evening. I'm staying at the Hotel Marrishuge International."

He reached into his top pocket and brought out a business card and passed it to her. Alina took the card and read the name, Nadim Babachencko, Industrialist. "Yes, that would be nice, it's been a while since I've wanted male company, just don't trust them anymore. "Well, I hope you will trust me enough to treat you to an excellent meal? I will book a table in the restaurant for seven o'clock; if you make your way to the reception, I will wait for you there." Before she could change her mind, he flashed a smile, turned and walked out of the door.

He waved to the driver of his waiting car that was parked across the road. He wanted to go directly back to the hotel; he knew whatever happened between himself and Alina would be short-lived but most enjoyable. His focus was on the task ahead, and nothing would distract him from it. His true identity could not be traced; he had several aliases set up by naval intelligence and recently by the Russian Mafia. He did not doubt in his mind that a surveillance team was following his every move. They had to cut him some slack; otherwise, he could not function as they wanted him too. The powers that be kept a discreet distance.

Alina finished her days' work and hurried home on the Moscow Metro, it was always busy, and she was relieved when she got home. She took off her coat and kicked off her shoes. Traversing the bathroom, she lit some aromatic candles and stripped off, leaving a trail of discarded clothes behind her. Then she went to the adjacent kitchen diner, poured a glass of white wine and took a generous sip. "Why? Am I excited about meeting a man I don't know, who stays in a five-star hotel full of the bourgeoisie? Not really my scene. Going back to the bathroom, she turned on the vibrant shower. Indulging herself by looking at her reflection in the full-length mirror, Alina was pleased with what she saw. "Not bad for a forty-one-year-old." Stepping into the steaming shower, she felt so relaxed. Exploring her body came naturally, and she allowed herself the pleasures that came with it.

Dmitri Sparrov sat in the reception area of his hotel. He was enjoying a superb single, single malt whisky on pure ice, both imported from the Isle of Sky, Scotland, so much for the Doctor's advice. He wasn't sure Alina would turn up and expected to be dining alone. He was reading the Moskovskaya Pravda when the concierge approached. "Mr Babachencko, this young lady has requested to see you." Dmitri folded his paper and looked at the transformed goddess that stood in front of him. Her daily crisp white attire had given way to a figure-hugging red dress that accentuated her previously hidden figure. The short tan leather jacket complimented her ample bosom; she looked like a trillion roubles.

He stood up, dropped the paper and almost knocked over his remaining scotch. "Alina, great to see you, what would you like to drink?" "I will have white wine please." "I will attend to that Sir, when you are ready, your table is waiting." acknowledged the concierge. "Thank you, Igor; we will be there in about five minutes." The wine appeared in an instant, wow! Thought Alina, this man has some influence.

She removed her leather jacket and draped it over the adjacent chair. When she sat down and crossed her legs, her dress rose up slightly, Dmitri could only drool at her shapely legs. "How has your day been?" "Oh, same old boring stuff, but it pays the bills. Actually, I have booked two days off. I thought I might do some shopping. There is a good mall not too far away; I can lose myself for a whole day bit of a shopaholic really." The nervous small talk went on for a few more minutes. "Shall we eat?" "Absolutely, I'm ravenous in expectation of the meal you promised me, not had much to eat all day." "Well let's hope you won't be disappointed, although I have to say the food here is excellent." They both rose from their comfy seats, and the concierge was there instantly. "May I take madam's jacket? Please, follow me?" As they walked across the vast reception area, heads turned. There were many businessmen sat enjoying their early evening drinks. As Dmitri and Alina passed, some were thinking the same thing. Another Russian Oligarch with his expensive hooker, lucky bastard.

The head waiter was there to greet them and showed them to a beautifully presented table. Flowers, scented candles and bottles of plain and flavoured still waters in a large bowl of strawberry ice, adorned the gold and purple table cloth. Alina stood there and took in the spectacular view of the Kremlin from the large panoramic floor to ceiling window. "Wow, what a view, it looks totally different from here, it's absolutely spectacular." "Yes, said Georgiou, I would actually say a beautiful example of Russian architecture madam." Dmitri thought to himself; you don't know the half of it. Over the years it has been the centre of planning for some terrible acts of barbarism.

Georgiou drew back the chair for Alina, and she

gracefully sat down. Black leather-bound menus were placed in front of them both. "Oh my god, what do I choose?" "If you like seafood, can I suggest the Lobster; it's one of my favourites. The way they prepare it is second to none. In my opinion, the Canadian lobsters they serve, are the best in the world, this hotel is famous for them." "Yes fantastic, I love Lobster; but it's been a long time since I sampled one. Not an every week occurrence on my salary." Dmitri smiled; he could afford one whenever he wanted. "Okay, what about an antipasto platter to start? They are large portions and compliment the lobster perfectly. I suggest we share one." "Oh, my lord, how the other half live, yes please, sounds great."

Georgiou retrieved both menus folded them and tucked them neatly under his arm. "Are you having Champagne Sir? "Ah, yes! Of course, we will have Saint Gall 2002 and a bottle of Didier Daguen Sancerre, if you have it in your cellar." "Excellent choice Sir, yes we have a case, it will go well with the food." It should do thought Dmitri at 12,000 Roubles (£150) a bottle. Alina sat there, staring out of the window, amazed at the incredible Moscow skyline ablaze with coloured lights. Coupled with the constant flow of traffic in the street, it was like a magnetic merry go round. Dmitri could not take his eyes off her. "Can I offer a few Roubles for your thoughts?"

"You don't want to know."

All her adult life, she had struggled to make ends meet. When her parents had passed away within a year of each other things became difficult. They had always rented the apartment in a pleasant and trouble-free neighbourhood.

It was where Alina and her younger sister had grown up, and it held many fond memories. Her mother had kept the apartment going from the small amount of savings in the joint account. When she died, there was very little left. Subsequently, it became necessary to move to a smaller, less expensive apartment for her and her sister Anastasia to rent. They muddled through financially from month to month, but it was a happy time for them both.

Alina had studied and worked hard to get a good job. When she got married, she believed it was for life, and all her dreams would be fulfilled, how wrong she was. That chapter in her life made her shudder, she dismissed it instantly, and it wasn't going to ruin this fantastic evening one iota. "My God, this is like something out of a fairy tale, I could sit here for a week and just watch the world go by." "Yes, I suppose it is, I shouldn't take it for granted, but I am fortunate to travel the world and stay in some amazing places, although this is certainly one of my favourites." She looked back and purposely made accusing eye contact. "You know I don't really feel at ease here; I am not sure whether to call you Nadim or Mr Babachenko, God knows what Dr Cherkesov would say. Do you have someone in your life who doesn't know what you are up too?"

He laughed, "Well, you can call me whatever you like it's not really that important, and no, I do not have someone special in my life female or otherwise. Well, that's not strictly true, my mother bless her, is still alive but in poor health. I visit her as often as I can, but she doesn't recognise me anymore." "Oh, I am so sorry to hear that, I'm an orphan both my parents died quite young. Anyway, why have you invited me to this incredibly wonderful and expensive place, do you expect something in return?" He hesitated for a while, "Well it's quite simple, I travel a lot, and it's a lonely life if I can enjoy the company of a beautiful lady to dine with me sometimes that's great. It's nothing more than that."

The food arrived, and it gave both of them the chance to reflect on what had been said. Alina had to admit this was one of the best experiences she had ever known. 'Oh crap' she though he's good company and I'm not paying. Not just that he is so knowledgeable and pleasant to talk and listen too. I really do hope he doesn't expect more than just my company for dinner. She had never seen such a well-dressed or a delicious tasting Lobster. The wine that Dmitri had chosen complimented the meal exquisitely. "Look if you feel uncomfortable, I can get Georgiou to box up another meal and you can take it home." "No! The ambience in my little apartment would hardly be the same, and I would not insult you by doing that." He smiled the evening would not be entirely wasted although he knew there was no chance of her gracing his suite. Alina continued to enjoy her meal but was perplexed, 'Who is this man, and why is he so interested in me?'

Chapter 14

Wednesday 15th February 2017, 23.00hrs
Hotel Marrishuge International, Moscow

Both Alina Petrenko and Dmitri Sparrov alias Nadim Babachenko enjoyed a superb meal. She had been very wary about his intentions and made it quite plain from the start she was not there for his sexual gratification. He respected that, even though she looked amazingly attractive and he would have loved to have taken it further. The conversation between the two of them flowed like a good red wine. Dmitri looked at his watch.

"Wow, it is eleven o'clock, where has the time gone?" He looked over to the head waiter, and he was there in an instant. "Georgiou, would you order my car to the front of the foyer, brief the driver to get the lady home safely."

"Yes, Sir, for about five minutes?"

"That will be fine."

Alina's heart sunk; she was having such a good time and didn't want it to end.

"Oh, that's alright, I will get a taxi." She blurted out.

"Nonsense I won't hear of it at this time of night."

"I'm sorry to be a bore, but I have an important meeting early in the morning. However, I did wonder if you could meet me for lunch somewhere of your choosing?"

"Oh yes I can fit that in my diary," she said nervously. "As I said, I have two days off."

"Of course, how could I forget? Wait! I've got a better idea, what if you come here for mid-day and then show me the sights of Moscow?"

"Okay, I can do that, I mean, I would enjoy that, maybe take you to the place I like to go for lunch occasionally. It's a great place where you can get a nourishing meal for 400 Roubles (£5)."

Nadim laughed "Right that's set then, lunch is on you. My car will pick you up at midday tomorrow. We can then have a cocktail here and cruise or walk the suburbs for the rest of the day; I will see you to the car."

Alina's head was spinning, was it the wine or the whole experience of a male company she had purposely avoided for a long time? The limousine was waiting outside. The chauffeur held the door open and as gracefully as her dress would allow, she climbed in.

"Thank you so much. I have had a very enjoyable evening Nadim."

He kissed her gently on the cheek; she smelled of expensive intoxicating perfume. "So, have I until tomorrow then."

Nadim Babachenko slept like a baby; Alina hardly slept at all. Her mind was in turmoil, why had he shown her so much interest? She was a poor working girl who had rarely ventured far from Moscow. In fact, she had only left Russia once, for her honeymoon to Paris. He was a wealthy industrialist who travelled the world. More importantly, why had he not tried to seduce her with his charm, even though she had warned him off? The few men she had been out with since her divorce had not taken no as meaning no. Demanding a kiss or trying to grope her after an evening out was the norm. A slap around the face or swift kick in the nether regions had seen them on their way. Alina could look after herself; the martial arts she had practised for years often came in handy. How would she have reacted if Dmitri had tried it on? She was glad he hadn't. Finally, sleep came to her, a deep sleep.

Usually, the morning rush hour traffic would wake her around seven o'clock. It was nine o'clock when she slipped out of bed, went to the kitchen and made a cup of strong black coffee. She turned on the radio and listened to the usual boring commentaries from a local station. By eleven-thirty, Alina was showered and dressed in a nice pair of figure-hugging blue jeans and a white tailored top. The pink underwear, especially her bra, gave a hint of naughtiness. Her long silky hair had been brushed and tied back in a ponytail. Paying particular attention to her makeup, Alina tried the new peach lipstick. Looking in the mirror, she felt good. Putting on her black leather knee-length boots, a powder blue full-length coat and matching gloves, she was ready.

There was a knock at the door; the chauffeur was there. When she got to the limousine, to her surprise, Nadim was waiting in the back. As she got in, he was dazzled and delighted by her appearance.

"You look nice, love the hair, it makes you look twenty years younger." Alina smiled, "Nadim, flattery will get you nowhere. Anyway, I thought we were going to meet at your hotel."

"Couldn't wait that long, I'm hoping you will show me some of the sights before this expensive lunch."

"Yes of course, have you been to the Fersman Mineralogical museum?"

"As an industrialist, I have been quite a few times, but not for a while. I would love to go again."

"That's great. I love going there, looking at all the wonderful crystals and artefacts on display. Until I went there for the first time in my teens, I never realised there was so much mineral wealth in mother Russia."

"Yes," replied Nadim, "135,000 items at that venue alone. Among them, natural crystals, Geodes (hollow rocks with cavities lined with crystals) and Druses (calcium oxalate crystals). God knows how much there is still to be dug from the mines. I would hazard a guess, precious new gemstones that haven't even been discovered yet."

"Wow, you know more than I do."

"Well as an industrialist I have to. I buy and sell many expensive items. It wouldn't do for one of my clients to pay much Rouble for a worthless piece of rock."

He directed his driver to head for the museum. On the way, Nadim impressed Alina even more with his wealth of knowledge regarding the venue. Of course, she had read about Alexander Yevgenyevich Fersman, who founded the museum, back in 1716. What she wasn't aware of, he actually set it up originally in Sankt-Petersburg. The collection, along with everything from the Russian academy of science, was moved to its present location in 1934. It took 30 railway carriages to move it all.

They spent two hours going around the museum; he was

charmed by Alina's excitement. She was like a schoolgirl on her first outing, bubbly with a thirst for knowledge.

"I don't know about you, but I'm ready for some lunch, I skipped breakfast in anticipation," he said.

"So am I. I totally forgot about eating; this place is just so absorbing."

"Absolutely but let's go and get some nourishment before I faint." Smiling, a gentle punch on his arm was his reward.

"That will be the day - you going without!"

They left the warm comfort of the museum and emerged into a cold but sunny Moscow day.

"Right take me to this Reestaram (cafe) of yours."

Alina laughed "Are you sure you want to go to my eatery? You will see all manner of characters there; you won't believe what some people can eat for 400 Roubles."

It was his turn to laugh, "You haven't seen what I can put away when I'm hungry. Yes, I'm looking forward to it; let's go. Give my driver directions."

Alina wasn't wrong; the Stolovaya 57, Krasnaya Square, was just as she described. The place was well patronised, and the welcoming staff were smart and attentive. The food smelt delicious and turned out to be good and wholesome. The place was packed, some people in smart office clothes others in drab outfits, this place catered for all. Moscow was like most other capital cities, bursting at the seams with people from all walks of life. This certainly reminded Dmitri (Nadim) of his days back home when he was a boy. On occasions, his mother would take him to a local Reestaram. At the time, he never realised how much she had sacrificed to give him these treats. Saving the odd Rouble here and there, meant she quite often had to go without herself. Money was always tight, but she did her best to make sure her son was okay. Irina would never use money that was allocated for other bills, so the visits were very infrequent.

When they had finished at the Reesteram he got his wallet out to pay. With a look of admonishment, Alina grabbed his hand and squeezed it.

"No, this is my treat; I just hope you enjoyed the food, By the amount you consumed I think you did?"

He laughed, "Thank you, certainly was good value for money, couldn't possibly eat any more."

"No, I expect they have needed to send out for more supplies." They both laughed. "Do you fancy a walk around Red square? I need to walk off some of that delicious meal?"

"Good idea, Nadim, Moscow is an enchanting place, but I think especially so at this time of the year."

"You are absolutely right; I don't spend anywhere near as much time here as I would like too. Maybe that will change, the present company accepted." Alina gave Nadim a warm, welcoming smile. They left the Reesteram and crossed the road to the waiting car. (Nadim) instructed his driver to go back to the hotel and be back for 5oclock and wait near the entrance to Gorky Park. They walked across Red Square to the end of the Kremlin. From here it was a short walk to Volkhonka, passed the Pushkin museum. Then over a footbridge, the views were absolutely stunning.

The rest of the afternoon was spent in pleasant chit chat while walking the park. Stopping at a small venue with quaint rustic furniture, they both enjoyed a Raf coffee and a slice of sour cream cake (Keks). Sitting watching the people go by, he noticed she was deep in thought.

"Is something troubling you?"

"Oh, I just can't believe this is happening to me. I keep thinking I'm having a dream and will wake up at any moment."

He leaned over, pecked her on the cheek and pinched her arm. "Is that a dream? When you are in Moscow, you are allowed to dream; sometimes dreams come true, if you really want them to."

"I did make the mistake of dreaming here once, and it turned out to be a nightmare. I trusted my husband and believed in all that he promised me, and it turned out to be just a pack of lies for his own gratification. He swore his undying love and then bedded my younger sister behind my back." He noticed Alina was spitting feathers at the thought.

"I'm sure," said Nadim, "that his loss is my gain, Ying Yang I believe."

"Do you really believe that? I wouldn't have thought that was your philosophy?" "Well, I guess we all have to believe in something." He smiled and looked away. My God, this woman is good at sizing people up. She may have made that one awful mistake with her ex-husband, but I bet that won't happen again. Be on your guard, Sparrov, keep focused, he thought.

"Would you mind taking me home now, I'm tired and would like to take a shower."

He looked at his watch. "Yes, of course, the car will be waiting across the square. I guess you do not want to join me for dinner again this evening?"

"Nadim, why do you want to spend so much time with me? I'm confused. Our lives are worlds apart; you can see how humdrum my existence is. There is one thing you need to know. I'm not an easy lay. I haven't slept with a man since I kicked my husband out."

"Hold on Alina, nothing is further from my mind. You are a beautiful, intelligent woman and I enjoy your company. That's it, I have to leave tomorrow, and we will go our separate ways."

Not the truth, he would be around for another couple of days at least. Although this hotel was his favourite, and the suite he had was exclusively his, it would soon be time to move on. A change of venue and some time would allow him to tie up loose ends. She was becoming a big distraction, most enjoyable, but he had to stay focused on the way ahead.

He could see tears welling up in Alina's eyes.

"I'm so sorry, Nadim, what do you think of me. It's just a few men I have been out with, were only after one thing, I don't need that."

He put his powerful arm around her shoulders. "Come on. I'll take you home." The journey to her apartment was in silence. Dmitri's conscience was pricking him. He was a hard man, and most of the time treated women with contempt, Alina was different; she was not out for all she could get.

At the apartment, Alina opened the rear door of the limousine before the driver could and got out.

"Is that offer of dinner still on?" She asked.

"Well, yes, of course, if you are sure you want to."

She just nodded, closed the door and turned away. Nadim pressed the button for the window to slide down.

"My driver will call for you at 7 o'clock."

"No, I will get a taxi, thank you." And without looking back, she marched back to the safety of her humble apartment.

Dmitri Sparrov, alias Nadim Babachencko was sure that would be the last time he saw Alina Petrenko. Maybe a good thing, I really like her, but it can go nowhere, he thought.

Back at the hotel, he dismissed his driver.

"Thank you, Alexi, have the rest of the evening off."

"Thank you, Sir; I will be at your disposal in the morning."

Dmitri was tired and went straight to his suite. He peeled off his jacket and turned on the television. He went to the drinks bar and into a crystal cut tumbler, poured himself a large Talisker over ice, sat down and savoured his favourite whisky. He suddenly thought, while I was with Alina, I never had one cigarette. He drained his glass, lay back on the sumptuous lounger and fell into a deep sleep.

He was startled by the phone ringing. It was the reception.

"Hello, Sir there's a lady Alina Petrenko here, requesting your company." He looked at his watch. Christ, it's 7.15! I have been asleep for ages.

"Okay. Would you tell her I'm a bit behind, would she mind waiting or if she wants to come up to my room?" There was a short pause.

"At her request, I will escort the lady to your suite, Sir." Dmitri opened the door to the penthouse, and Alina stepped inside.

"My God, this KOMHaTe (lounge) is bigger than the whole of my apartment." She wanted to take her shoes off as she did every time she entered her own small but well-kept home.

"Wow, you certainly showed me the sites today. I got back here and fell asleep, hence my appearance. Please pour yourself a drink from the bar while I shower and change."

"Okay thank you. I do love a glass about now, normally when I get home from work and prepare an evening meal, I have one then. A bit of a bad habit, I suppose?" Nonsense everyone has to relax at some time, I do the same."

Still bleary-eyed, he suddenly noticed her appearance. A black full-length figure well-tailored dress zipped from her neck to just above her knees. Her small shapely ankles were complimented by 5-inch stiletto heels.

"Wow, you look like a billion Roubles, and I look like garbage."

"Go and shower lightweight while I relax in this amazing place." Dmitri was overwhelmed; he expected to be dining alone but was delighted to have Alina's company. She turned off the television, went to the drinks cabinet and poured a large glass of white wine. Returning to the enormous marble table, she picked up a glossy magazine. The Royal Report-Viling was the world's most expensive read. The magazine was full of all the latest information on the rich and famous. Top-quality products that she could only dream about started in a price range of more than her yearly salary. She sank into the sumptuous leather upholstered lounger and engrossed herself in the magazine.

Dmitri appeared from the bathroom in tailored black slacks and a crisp white shirt. Alina looked at him.

"You look and smell so much better than when I walked in. What is that eau de toilette?"

"Oh, Clive Cristian No1, I only wear it on special occasions."

"I'm not surprised; I have just been reading about it, 22,000 Roubles a bottle."

"Yes, well we all like our little treats, shall we go and eat?"

"I would rather have something here, it's so cosy and in the restaurant, people just stare."

"Of course, they do, but it's not me they are looking at. Anyway, that sounds good to me; the menu is here, what would you like?"

"Something light, a Caesar salad please." Good thinking, that lunch today was a banquet." Dmitri phoned down to reception and placed the order. It was there in record time. The waiter wheeled in the food accompanied by two bottles of champagne in silver buckets topped with ice.

"I took the liberty of including the seafood platter of the day Sir if that's okay?"

"Yes Georgiou, good thinking, I am feeling quite peckish at the sight of the food displayed.

"Shall I open the champagne, Sir?"

"No that's fine, thank you." The head waiter turned acknowledged Alina with a bow and left. He could only imagine what the goddess looked like out of that stunning dress.

"Would you like Champagne, Alina?"

"Oh okay, when in Rome." They both enjoyed the meal and champagne. Dmitri was aware Alina was staring at him.

"Nadim, who are you?" Dmitri laughed nervously.

"What do you mean?"

"Well, I have access to most of Doctor Cherkesov's patients, but there is no file on you. I am aware that some are military and their files are locked securely in his safe. You say you are not the military federation, so who are you? More importantly, are you married with a family just looking for a bit on the side?"

"A reasonable assumption I guess, but no I've never been married, and I don't have children." Well at least he was telling the truth about that part of his life. While with her, the rest had to be a sham, he wouldn't let anything jeopardise his master plan, especially a beautiful, intelligent woman. Of guard, it would have been so easy to allow her to realise he was not the person she thought he was.

"I admit to having had my share of women in my life, but none I wanted to settle down with." For a fleeting moment, Dmitri Sparrov felt a pang of conscience, and it showed. Alina held his hand and caressed it gently.

"Well I'm a grown woman and I would desperately like to meet a man to have a child with, but time is running out."

"Nonsense, there is someone out there who will fulfil your wish."

"I would love that person to be you, Nadim; I don't care about your wealth and all the things it can buy, it's just not me."

"I know Alina, but it's difficult at the moment, I cannot commit to anyone."

"Does that mean never?" Dmitri thought for a long time. "Well it's very difficult, but who knows."

He was shocked and taken aback; he hadn't expected her to come on so strong. She had made it quite plain from the outset that there would be no sexual encounter.

Nadim looked directly into her beautiful but sad eyes.

"I am an industrialist, and frequently I am engaged by rich clients to act as an agent. I negotiate with third world countries in securing jewels and precious metals."

"Blood diamonds?"

He laughed. "Well if that's what you like to call them then, yes. I have to keep a low profile, hence the absolute secrecy with the likes of Cherkesov. I demand it for the exorbitant amount of Roubles he charges me. Coming into contact with rich Russian Oligarchs, in general, they are ruthless people, but they pay extremely well. Naturally, they don't want their business made public. Well there you have it, Alina."

She put her half-empty glass on the table, got up and went to the Vannaya (bathroom) without a word. Nadim guessed she would come back, give her excuses and leave.

He went to the bar and poured himself a Talisker on ice. Oh well, nice while it lasted, he thought.

"Mine's a white wine please, I'm not that keen on Champagne, really." He turned and could not believe what he saw before him. Alina was draped in his fluffy cream bathrobe. Before he could say anything, she flung her arms around his neck and kissed him passionately. He smelled her heady perfume and tasted her sweet orange lipstick, and his passion went into overdrive.

"Steady tiger" Alina looked into his piercing blue eyes. "Don't you want me, Nadim?" He stared back into her large sparkling brown eyes with a passion he had never experienced before. "Of course, I do you are a beautiful woman but as I said won't be around for a long time, that's just how it is."

"I don't care, I want you to make love to me, and I don't care about tomorrow or the consequences."

Nadim wrapped one arm around her waist and kissed her on the neck. His hand wandered under the robe and cupped one of her breasts, her skin was silky soft, and it was obvious she was completely naked.

"Let's go to the spal'nya (bedroom). Don't forget my wine."

Alina lay on the huge bed still in the robe but with one long silky leg protruding. She had turned the main lighting out. Only the soft glow of the bedside table lamps were left on, Nadim placed both drinks within easy reach. While he undressed, he was conscious of her propped up on one arm, sipping her wine, watching his every move. She noticed he had some nasty scars on his back, fingering one, about five centimetres long he shuddered with bad memories.

"An encounter long ago, the other feller came off much worse." He joked.

Slipping onto the bed, she admired his toned body.

"You have looked after yourself, Nadim"

"I have to, no one else will."

She smiled nervously at him. He slowly parted the robe

that smelt of his eau de toilette and her enchanting perfume.

"You are beautiful Alina." He nuzzled her ear and kissed her neck. His tongue traced a path all the way to her breasts. In turn, he took each nipple between his lips and used a gentle circular motion to enlarge them. Alina put both hands around his neck and gently played with his hair. Nadim slowly followed a line with his tongue to her naval. She was wearing a sparkling crystal there that was a real turn-on for him. His tongue eventually found her shaven vulvar. He gently parted the lips and tongued her clitoris. This sent Alina into raptures she grasped his head with both hands and held him tight. After a while, she felt an orgasm was building.

She purred, "Nadim, that's fantastic, but I don't want to come just yet."

He raised himself and kissed her passionately, and her tongue drove deep into his mouth. She peeled off the robe and then sipped some of her white wine; likewise, Nadim enjoyed his whisky.

"Lay back" she whispered.

She knelt between his parted legs and gently stroked his manhood. Taking his now erect penis in her mouth, she sucked the bell end while masturbating him; her long silky dark hair brushed against his belly.

"God, it's my turn to be near an orgasm." Alina licked and kissed his manhood, rose and wiped her chin on the back of her hand; she once again thrust her tongue deep into his mouth. Propping herself up on one arm she savoured some more wine.

"You know I have only done that to one other man,

my ex-husband, I can only assume my sister did it better."

Nadim held her chin in the palm of his hand and gazed into her eyes. "That was amazing for me. Nobody could do it better." They kissed passionately.

"Nadim I'm so aroused, please make love to me now."

Her lovely long legs parted as he gently entered her. Soft thrusting strokes built to a crescendo as he nuzzled her ear. She dug her fingernails into his back as she passionately held onto him. As Nadim exploded, they climaxed together; it was earth-shattering for both of them. She resisted the urge to scream the place down by gently biting his shoulder.

They lay spent in each other's arms and dosed for a while. She untangled herself from him, got off the bed and donned his robe. It was only when she returned from the bathroom that Dmitri stirred. As she sat at the dressing room table brushing her long wet locks, he realised she had showered.

"What time are you leaving tomorrow, Nadim?" Caught off guard, he blurted out "Oh! I have a plane to catch at 11am."

"Well, I had better get dressed and get home then."

After a short pause, he said, "You can stay till the morning if you like."

"No! I feel guilty enough as it is. I've never done anything like this before. It was so enjoyable, but I must go."

Nadim slipped on his boxers and stood behind her caressing her shoulders. "I understand."

He left the bedroom while Alina got dressed and went to the lounge. He walked over to a large mirror, touched the top right-hand side, and it slid sideways to reveal a wall safe. He tapped in a six-digit code, and it opened. Taking out a small strong jiffy bag, he locked the safe, and within seconds the bulletproof mirror slid back into place. It held not just valuables but secret plans as well.

Alina walked into the lounge, and they looked at each other nervously.

"I want you to take this with you." He handed her the bag.

"What is it?"

"Something of interest, at least I hope you find it so."

She frowned and looked puzzled but put the item in her clutch bag. Dmitri looked directly into Alina's eyes,

"You are not to open it until I have left tomorrow. Promise me."

"Okay! If it's that important to you, I promise."

He called reception to order a taxi for her. He smiled. "I gave my driver the evening off I thought I would be dining alone. It was such a fantastic surprise that I wasn't." She put her coat on and walked to the door; he followed and stood close by her.

"I will wait for the taxi in reception."

He went to speak; Alina put her index finger to his mouth.

"No please don't say anything, Nadim."

With that, she turned and left without a second glance and Dmitri Sparrov (Red Fox), alias Nadim Babachenko was alone with his thoughts.

Chapter 15

18th February 2017. 6.45 pm.
Flat 14 Block 6 Nekrasovka, East Moscow District.

Inna Petrov had just left Alina Petrenko's apartment and
walked the short distance to the main street. It had started
to rain, and the wind was fierce. Well, it's been a long day
she mused, think I will make tracks for my local Gastobar.
Have a bottle of Clairette Blanche and a Pork Pelmeni.
There isn't much I can add to my report that won't wait
until the morning. Sticking her hand out to hail a cab, a
familiar black and red car stopped, and the driver lowered
his window.

"The Birog Bestroi Gastrobar, Lyubertsy, 400 roubles,
(£4.68p)"

The driver rubbed his chin "Okay jump in."

Strange occurrences in Moscow and elsewhere, the
taxis don't have illuminated signs to show whether they are
available or not. More to the point of passengers' safety, if
indeed they are a proper cab or not. Many private cars give
lifts for some remuneration or even as favours. The practice
is literally to stick out one's arm as if requesting a bus. Tell
the driver what you are prepared to pay for the journey
and that's it. Of course, if the driver thinks the offer is too

cheap, he will say so or drive off. The state is desperately looking to stamp this out.

Petrov relaxed in the back seat thinking about the day's events, looking forward to a nice meal when suddenly her mobile rang. Noticing it was Konstantin Abramov, her boss, she answered,

"Yes, Sir."

"Where are you?" His tone was sharp.

"I am on my way home having just left Petrenko's place."

"Okay, I want you here in my office, post-haste. You are not to make any further enquiries regarding this case whatsoever, is that understood."

"Yes Sir, of course, I will be with you in about 15 minutes."

The line went dead.

"What the hell? Driver, take me to Lubianka state-building instead."

The driver knew instinctively she was Cheka, (secret police). Trying to make conversation was a complete waste of time. She sat there in stony silence. They were all the same, not to be messed with. He didn't care that the fair had been agreed. Where she wanted to go now was a lot nearer. The sooner he got rid of Scary Mary, the better.

The driver pulled up at the main entrance to the foreboding looking building. It always gave him the shivers. During the cold war, many suspected spies or subversives arrived under duress and were interrogated in the basement cells. Most of them left in wooden overcoats, never to be heard of again. Inna got out of the taxi in a hurry, Sergei wound down the window, took the 400 roubles and smiled, and there was no response. Sour faced old cow he thought; wouldn't want to be her husband. Nice body, though. Wouldn't mind her handcuffing me to the bed for a session, I bet she's wild.

Inna entered the building went through the security checks and hurried to her boss's office and knocked on the door.

"Come in."

Walking into the office to her amazement she saw Gregor Amatov the director-general sat at her desk. Standing to attention and saluting reminded her of the lowly position she held in this organisation of thousands of staff.

"Ah Inna, good, you know of the director, you now have the privilege of meeting him in person."

"Hello Sir." She didn't know whether to shake his hand or salute again.

"Ms Petrov, please take a seat, you must be wondering why I am here? Firstly, do you have your work iPad and notebook?"

"Yes, I have them here."

She took them both out of her satchel and placed them on the table. Amatov opened the notebook to the relevant page that recorded the start of the investigation and subsequent information gathered. He read the four pages of entries then ripped them out and stuffed them in his coat pocket. Inna sat there speechless and looked at Konstantin for some guidance. He just shook his head and slowly rolled his eyes. She really didn't understand what had just happened but knew better than to say anything. The directors' attention turned to the iPad. He handed it to Inna.

"Please flag up the relevant contents you have in connection with this case."

She was nervous, was she under investigation for something, what had she done wrong? Fumbling to enter her password she looked at the director.

"Is there something amiss, Sir?"

"Let's hope not, Ms Petrov."

He held out his hand, and she handed over the computer. He looked at the four entries that were available and selected the one that was titled Dr C Investigation, doc1. Opening it, he read all the contents that had been loaded. After some minutes he looked at Konstantin and then Inna.

"Your recordings and assessment regarding this case are very good, precise with all the relevant facts contained, good work."

She let out a sigh of relief.

"Is this all you have stored concerning Dr Cherkesov's untimely death?"

"Yes, Sir, it is. The other three documents are places times and dates. I have some other intelligence that has been gathered, not yet logged but you now have that information in your pocket."

"Oh yes, explain to me what other evidence that is?"

"Well, the cleaner who found the doctor hanging drives a top of the range car. I believe she can't have bought it and run the thing on her meagre salary. Not just that her residential address is non-existent, she's a fraud. I have every intention of following that up tomorrow."

"Good work, that could be of significant interest."

The director-general put the iPad down, sat back and

folded his arms. He thought for a while.

"Is this absolutely all the remaining evidence regarding the case?"

"Yes, Sir, it definitely is."

"Right then, I will be retaining it to be destroyed; Mr Abramov will issue you with a new one."

"But Sir" Inna protested. "I have information appertaining to months of intelligence on other cases stored on my computer."

"May I remind you this is state property and as such you have no permanent right to it? However, I will have that information retained for you on a memory stick."

Inna Petrov sat there dumbfounded. In the 15 years, she had worked for the department, nothing like this had ever happened. Through hard work, she had gained promotion from a secretary to intelligence gathering operative to an investigator and now a senior investigator. The scenario she found herself in now was unprecedented. "Right Ms Petrov the situation is this, from now on I will be taking personal responsibility for this whole sorry saga. You are not to mention or discuss anything whatsoever regarding the events; do I make myself clear?"

"Well, yes, Sir of course you do. I will not mention another word about it."

"Mr Abramov has briefed whoever else has been involved to forget the whole thing." With that Gregor Amatov picked up the iPad and left the office without another word. Konstantin was smiling, "Starchy old bastard, is he not?"

"Okay, Inna after that encounter I could do with a

drink, will you join me?" "Certainly will, and something to eat, I'm starving. I was on my way to a Gastobar when you phoned."

"Good my treat you have earned it."

He grabbed his coat, Inna suddenly realised she hadn't even taken hers off. There would be no further conversation regarding Dr Cherkesov; walls have ears, no one was above surveillance.

What they would never know, was Amatov had set up a six-man surveillance team to watch over Alina Petrenko 24/7. Her very existence was threatened by her involvement with Dimitry Sparrov, a very influential man. The tentacles of Red Fox's organisation spread far and wide.

The ride in the taxi was sombre; both of them had a myriad of questions but knew better than to ask each other anything. After the mauling she'd had by that bully Amatov, an early night in her own company seemed a better idea; she was exhausted. The trouble was her boss didn't like refusals, and he was paying so not all bad. They got to the Gastobar, and he paid the agreed 450 Rouble fare. A black car stopped some distance away, and a man and women got out of the back before the car sped off. Oh yes, thought Konstantin we are being followed. His training had taught him to be continually looking over his shoulder. He was head of a senior department and was now being tailed like a common criminal. That's how the FSB organisation works, and he accepted it, both of them had nothing to hide.

The place was busy, but they found a table by a window looking out onto the main street.

"What do you fancy to eat then, Inna?"

"I had made up my mind to have the Pork Pelini, and I'll pay for the bottle of Clairette Blanche."

"No, you won't this is on me. Anyway, that sounds delicious. I'm going to have the same."

When he ordered at the bar, Konstantin asked how long it would be.

"No more than 15 minutes, Sir"

"That's good, and we will have the wine now please."

"Right away, Sir, I will bring it to your table."

On his way back, he was sure the couple sat at an adjacent table were the same ones who got out of the black car. He certainly didn't recognise either one but would have bet the cost of their meal they were Federal Security Service (FSB). Another department, another building perhaps, it was thought 22 thousand people operated under the state umbrella.

"The food will be about 15minutes and here comes the wine."

The waiter arrived and popped the cork filling the two fluted glasses. Inna sniffed the delicate floral aroma and tasted the fruity liquor; it always reminded her of vermouth. At last, she relaxed a bit,

"What a day."

"Yes, certainly interesting, look you can have tomorrow off or start later if you like. I want you to look at a case that has just come in. Two young people fished out of the Moskva River. It looks like they were sleeping rough and high on drugs. Anyway, that can wait. How is your mother?"

"Oh, she's okay under the circumstances. She never stops

moaning, but at her age and with her ailments that's to be expected. I believe it's only the vodka that keeps her going."

Konstantin chuckled. He knew they both lived in a big house together in a nice Moscow district, with a carer come housekeeper. Inna's marriage had broken up a while ago. The commitment to her job had proved too much for her husband to contend with, and the inevitable happened. He was a department head of rural planning in the local state department. Starting an affair with his secretary spelt the end of what was a strained marriage. When Inna found out, it came as no surprise to her; there hadn't been any sex between them for ages.

They finished the excellent meal, and he picked up the tab.

"Come on. I will walk you home."

"That's not necessary; I only live ten minutes away."

"I insist, after that, I need a walk anyway."

"Okay, let's go I'm tired."

As they walked the short distance to her house, there was very little conversation. Abramov wanted to check out his theory.

Seductively she said, "Right then would you like a coffee?"

"No Inna I will pass on that thanks, it's been a long and eventful day."

"Certainly has, I will be in for the afternoon if that's okay, spend a morning with mother, bless her, can't wait for all the boring local gossip."

"Okay, see you then."

He turned and walked to the corner. Sure enough,

there was the female member of the surveillance duo hanging about talking on her mobile. He smiled to himself what would they have made of it, if he had accepted Inna's offer and stayed a lot longer than just for a coffee. He had suspicions there was always more to her than meets the eye? Who knows? Maybe that's how she got to be a senior Praporschik, bloody good at her job though.

The plain fact was she was not his type, and he had a very supportive wife whom he loved dearly. He didn't think Petrov had a male companion at the moment, although she was quite attractive and darn fit. Often to be found in the well fitted out gym, either lunchtime or after her shift, she trained hard. Never having to go further than the basement of the Lubianka building where it was, it suited her needs. Haling a cab, the fair was agreed, and he got in. A black car stopped to pick up the operative tailing him, and it sped off.

Konstantin Abramov sat in the cab, pondering all that had happened in the last 24 hours. Whatever shit was going down, it was heavy. You didn't get a visit from the Director-General unless it was a very serious matter. His instructions had been specific, and he would follow them to the letter. Was there anything he had inadvertently done to cause suspicion in the hierarchy? No, with regard to the Cherkesov case, all had been conducted in the correct manner. My staff and I do not need to worry about retribution. He would sleep well tonight. Somewhat differently for Inna Petrov, she was tossing and turning and couldn't sleep. Finally, at four in the morning, she got herself a large vodka and tonic and turned on the television. No worries, she wasn't going in until midday and mother never stirred until gone ten anyway.

What on earth were we under surveillance for when we left Lubyanka? The duo were crap at their job; they may as well have had illuminated signs on their foreheads. She thought the woman was familiar but could not remember where their paths had crossed. No doubt her boss had picked up on the situation before she had. If he didn't consider it enough of a threat to mention it, then it wasn't. Suddenly she blurted out,

"Of course, we were supposed to know we had a tail, very clever."

Inna downed the last of her Vodka and instantly fell asleep.

Chapter 16

Friday 3rd March 2017 Time 04.15 hrs Friday nightshift
Submarine Refit Complex, Babcock Marine, Devonport.
(England)

Mike Grayling was sitting on his toolbox having his snack,
halfway through the nightshift. He suddenly put his head in
his hands and cried uncontrollably. "Why did the fucking
bitch do that to me he sobbed?" Mike was a loaner and a
looser, but was a first-class electrical fitter, with an ability
to spot and highlight problems as they occurred. While
working at V.SE.L, in Barrow, he was the man who
years ago had discovered a section of the rolled hull of the
nuclear submarine Tribute, had been lined up 180 degrees
out of sync. Preheating had earlier been engaged, and the
continuous welding process to the previous section was just
about complete. The removal of the heating mats would
begin the slow cool down to prevent serious cracking.

Mike had gone to his boss's office and in a calm manner
and had explained what was wrong. His chargeman had
almost fallen off his chair with laughter. However, checks
were made, and the problem confirmed, which had worried
Vickers top brass were running around like headless
chickens. Leave cards were paraded like lottery scratch cards

by the production engineers who should have spotted and prevented the severe error. For his keen observation, Mike Grayling was eventually given a financial reward of £500 by the management's suggestion box award scheme. He had saved the company much embarrassment and a considerable amount of money. A reclaim plan for the problem would be formulated and agreed with the customer the M.O.D. who was not best pleased.

Grayling had been offered promotion again, as he had been on more than one occasion before. Although he took great pride in his work, he did not like responsibility and was not popular with the men he worked with. They all found him a bit sly, always willing to let the young apprentices make silly mistakes and get a rollicking from the boss, before passing on his wealth of experience in a begrudging fashion. Although he was acknowledged as the best electrical fitter in the gang, his working colleagues would take great delight in making his life a misery if he was ever made up to a boss's position.

Moving to Plymouth, his skills were welcomed by the naval dockyard employers, and he was immediately seconded to hunter-killer submarine refits. He had moved to be with the love of his life, Sharron, who came from the town and had a yearning to return. Little did he know she would turn out to be the Bain of his life. Always the selfish cow, previously, and with little warning she had up stumps and returned to her home town, leaving Mike in the lurch.

"That fucking bitch" Mike repeated, she's really done for me" The bitch he was referring to was his wife. He had dotted on her and spent every penny of his hard-earned cash endeavouring to keep her happy. His reward, while working all manner of unsocial shifts was that his so-called pal Mark Johnson was having a passionate affair with Sharron. While Mike was busy on whatever shift, Mark would eagerly spend all the time he could wining and dining her.

His reward was sexual favours, whenever and wherever it could be had. The marital bed where he always felt nervous was an option but out on Dartmoor in her car was his favourite.

Both of them were exhibitionists, and he loved the foreplay that Sharron was particularly good at. With the other cars parked up, it was obvious they were being spied on; this heightened the sexual experience for them both. On one occasion she suggested a bit of dogging, but he was not prepared to share her with anyone else, he certainly didn't want to watch while she gave another man a blow job. He even hated the idea that Mike spent more time with her than he did, even though she said her husband was crap in bed and she did not like doing it with him. The truth was she had the best of both worlds; she wasn't prepared to give up her security with Mike but wanted the attention and risk that Mark gave her. He was a mechanical fitter in the main factory at Devonport, who still lived at home with his mother. He never saw his mate while working, and that was a good thing. God knows what he would do if he found out he was knocking off his missus.

Because Mark's outgoings were minimal, he only worked a straight five-day shift and an occasional Saturday morning. His father had died of an asbestosis related disease ten years ago at the age of fifty-four, having spent all his working life as a labourer, in the shipyards. He was a casualty of the aircraft carrier refits in the early sixties. Then, it was not regarded as a too serious problem to be working with the asbestos insulation. He had inhaled the dust while brooming up after the laggers.' The health and safety rules were lacking under crown immunity, and personal protective equipment was just that. What was available was your responsibility to request and use, or not, unlike today where strict rules in their use, are in place.

William, Mark's dad, was immensely proud of him when he passed the entrance exam to become a journeyman apprentice mechanical fitter. In the local working man's club, "Bill" Johnson had bought all his mates a drink to celebrate his lad's achievements. They considered him a bit of a simpleton but were quite happy to take his hospitality. He knew by then he was under a sentence of death with Mesothelioma of the lungs. Sometime after litigation, his wife Ruth had received £46,000 as compensation for her husband's incapacity and eventual death. A much lesser sum than it should have been because he was a heavy smoker and this was deemed to have aggravated his condition. She had been advised by the trade union's appointed solicitor, not to accept this as total compensation, but to go for a lesser interim payment. For most of the previous claimants, this had proved more fruitful with an ongoing claim base. However, to Ruth, this was a life-changing sum of money, and she probably did make the right decision to accept the offer.

As a result of washing out William's clothes in the early years, she herself was under a slow death sentence, due to ingesting the asbestos fibres. She doted on her son Mark, and all she could see by accepting this money was an opportunity to buy him all the things he had never had. Little did she know he would waste a lot of it on the little grabber who was married to Mike Grayling.

It seemed so simple; Mike had been befriended by a guy in the Prince Albert pub, not far from the dockyard main gate. It was a local watering hole for dockyardies, who stopped off for a quick pint after finishing a late dayshift. The regular darts competition was always held on a Friday evening. Mike would play when his shifts allowed; he was a tidy player and often took a pint off his opponent from a visiting team. Indeed, it was the only sport in which he had any interest.

Strangely enough, this character John Balfour was always willing to play Mike for a pint. Well, the outcome ran a similar pattern, John the poor sod, was not much of a player and nearly always lost. He was never a bad loser though and seemed flush, always flashing the cash.

Mike liked his new friend, he did not have many, and this guy was good company. For a while, he was worried about him being an ass bandit. That thought was soon dispensed when one Friday evening after a serious bout of drinking John latched on to one of the local good-time girls. After lashing her up with lots of Vodka and tonics, he took her back to her flat and gave her good seeing to. It was the talk of the pub, how Marie had found the man of her dreams and she wanted to settle down and have babies with him. Stupid bitch, he poked her for about a month and then dropped her like a hot potato.

"So," John said, do you want this loan of £400 or not?"

"Fucking right I do; I will pay you back £50 a week every payday."

That's how it started. He remembered one evening over a game of darts and a pint saying to John.

"I'm really in the shit; just found a letter from the building society, threatening to foreclose on the house if we do not come up with the six months of arrears on the mortgage. I really didn't know she had missed payments."

Right from the beginning of their twelve years of marriage, Mike had allowed Sharron to deal with all the financial arrangements. It seemed she was bloody good at it, as the house was always immaculate, with the latest gadgets on show. If anything needed to be done, she would sort it and pay the relevant tradesman accordingly, sometimes in kind. Mike wondered why a particular bathroom fitter seemed to take an age on the total refurbishment. Whenever he was confronted, he got the same response.

"A lot to sort out with the pipework, boss and that particular bathroom suite your misses ordered had defects and had to go back. It's a six-week delay for the replacement."

Yeah! The plumber had created the defects himself.

"Don't worry you have a downstairs loo and shower, and Sharron seems happy to wait and get a good job done. I'm not a cowboy Guv, leave it to me, you will be happy with the end result."

Mike though the bastard was spending time on other jobs and he was just a fill-in for cash. The truth was he was spending more time in the bedroom than the bathroom. Finally, she got tired of him; after one early morning session on the couch, where he just satisfied himself, his time was up. Sharron put her dressing gown on and headed for the kitchen. Always expecting a good fry up after a sex session, he laid back and yawned. She shouted at him,

"I want you to finish the job now and get the fuck out of my house; there's no more of anything for you mate."

He thought to himself, oh well it was good why it lasted; she's turned into a boring shag anyway. In just two more days, the bathroom was completed to her satisfaction while hardly a word was spoken between them. As agreed, she paid the fitter in cash after demanding a good bit off the bill.

When it came to changing the car every year, she negotiated everything; Mike really did not know how she did it. The truth was Sharron had saddled them with huge debts. She was a complete waster and had run up bills on credit cards from banks and building societies. Even with the money she coerced out of poor Mark, by opening her legs or giving him the odd blow job, it could not keep pace with her spending habits. If Mike had found out about her indiscretion, he might have done something about it, but she was cute and had both of them wrapped around her little finger.

Back in the transit shed, sat on his toolbox, he was scared shitless. The solution had seemed easy, good old John had come to his rescue financially, on lots of occasions, Mike's debt was now £9,600, and his so-called new friend was putting the pressure on to pay the money back. He remembered the cold rainy evening when he was on the way home from the end of a twelve-hour shift. Deliberately avoiding the Prince Albert pub, out of the shadows, stepped two huge ugly men. First of all, Mike thought it was a mugging, but it wasn't. They lifted him bodily off the ground and held him against the slimy wet wall. It was only after one thug grunted at him, "I understand you owe a good friend of ours some money and his debt is our debt, meet him and sort it or else." After kneeing him in the bollocks, they left him lying in the gully writhing in agony and walked off.

What the fuck was he to do; he had considered selling the only real asset they had, the nearly new car. After badgering Sharron, she burst into tears and told him only two payments had been paid off the balance, and this did not even cover the interest owed, the truth was it was better to let the finance company snatch it back. After tossing and turning all Sunday night, Mike was up early and ready for work the next day. Worried all the morning about his predicament, he made silly mistakes, and this made the situation even worse.

"Oh, fuck it; I am going to report to the surgery I cannot carry on like this."

After checking him over, he was sent home by the duty nurse. Noticing he had bloodshot eyes and looked completely wrecked, he was not fit for work. The nurse wrote on his sick chit, high temperature and bouts of shaking due to suspected virus. After giving the sick chit to his chargeman, Mike picked up his snack bag and walked to the main gate.

I must find John and try and sort this out, home for a couple of hours shut-eye and then see what can be done.

When Mike got home, Sharron was out, thank God for that he thought. He was getting to hate their time together; even though he loved her dearly, the rows over money were getting him down. He didn't like to think about where she was, probably trying to negotiate another credit card loan. Well, good luck with that then he thought, her credit rating was just about zero. She had nagged and nagged him to take out a card himself, but he had always stayed shy of them, he was adamant over that one and wouldn't back down. Sharron had tried everything; good meals, seduction, and generally being a good partner. In the end, she gave up calling him a tight selfish bastard and turned her full attention to Mark, who always came up with the readies.

He must have fallen asleep on the settee because the next thing he remembered was the key in the front door and Sharron appeared.

"What are you doing home?" She demanded as she plonked herself down on the armchair.

"Oh, I was feeling unwell at work, and they sent me home."

"You look fine to me; I suppose you have lost the dayshift bonus and overtime for today."

"Don't fucking start, there is method in my madness, I am going to see someone soon anyway to get us out of the shit."

"Oh yes you will come up with some master plan, I don't think! You have always been better than fucking useless at providing for me." She snarled at him and turned on the waterworks.

"That's not true, and you bloody well know it."

He said no more and just took it on the chin, he allowed himself to be manipulated all the time, but what could he do, love was blind. He picked up his jacket and headed for the door.

"Look, I have to see someone about a loan, I will be a couple of hours, and I will bring a Chinese in."

Sharron just waved him away and buried her head in the cushion.

Mike marched straight to the pub, Prince Albert. He entered the lounge and looked around. There he was sitting in the corner of the pub reading his paper. John Balfour looked up, smiled and waved Mike over.

"Well hello stranger, fancy a pint?"

"Yeah cheers, I will have a lager."

John pulled out a roll of £20 notes and peeled one-off.

"Here he said, "I will have a Jack Daniels on ice, you get a chaser as well if you want it."

He was hooked once again; he returned with the drinks and sat down.

"I believe you had a visit from a couple of so-called friends of mine?"

Yeah! How could you do that to me, mate?"

"Well, it's like this Mike, I owe them money, and if you don't pay me, I can't pay them. For sure, I am going to make certain it's not my legs that are broken."

"John! I can't pay you the money I owe, my fucking bitch of a wife has really done for me."

John pondered for a while, "Okay, believe it or not, there is a way out. These people I deal with are a nasty bunch, but they can also be very generous when I help them out."

"How do you mean?"

"Right, this is the way you can write off your existing debt and earn yourself another twenty grand as well."

Mike was all ears.

"What the hell have I got to do to get that then?"

Chapter 17

Friday 6th October 2017 06.30 hrs
Control Room H.M.S. Astute

The Captain stepped on-board and descended the fwd control room ladder of the newly refitted and virtually rebuilt killing machine. At 7,800 tons submerged it was 30% bigger than the previous Trafalgar class of submarine and an absolute leap ahead in submarine technology and ability. The refit with Trisonic imaging and Hovertrack now incorporated had added another 1000 tons to the overall weight. Any defects in the sub, especially the hull, had been detected by non-destructive examination methods and painstakingly put right. Weld design highly trained engineers poured over every feature to ensure when it went to sea, it was fit for purpose, a costly process but very effective.

To accommodate the new stealth systems, the sub had spent three years in dock and seen some major changes internally. Parts of the hull had been removed to allow access for the fitting of new machinery and electrical components. Extra segmented frames had been welded in to facilitate a deeper diving depth, trim tanks had been altered, and new pipework installed. It was thought the latest stealth systems would be ahead of anything the Americans or Russians were developing. At the research facility (AWRE), it had taken a decade to design, build and perfect. The top secret facilities at Southwell and Portland were the nerve centres of underwater specialist projects.

The Trisonic imaging allowed the submarine to create a virtual electronic-mechanical image while hovering just above the sea bed or at a depth of up to 400 metres. The Hovertrack would enable the sub to creep away from its known position at up to ten knots by a system of silent water-ram jets. The depth of the submarine could be adjusted to keep the display constant; it would be miles away before Triso was switched off. In effect, the submarine would have disappeared from its known location. An enemy who thought they knew where it was would be tracking a ghost image thinking it was contained. They would not have a clue as to why the submarine had vanished when the profile disappeared from their sonar screens. If by chance the shine path of the beam was detected, the onboard computers would diffract it just like a straw in a glass of water.

In number five basin at Devonport, naval base Astute sat alongside the jetty. As well as the skeleton naval crew, key dockyard technicians were honing the various hydraulic and pneumatic systems. Small leaks, typically nothing more than a badly fitting O ring on a coupling or a pinhole in a non-ferrous fitting was dealt with until everything worked perfectly. The hydraulic Telemotor controls for driving the sub had been upgraded; one-man control was as responsive as flying an aeroplane. The planes man would be able to manoeuvre the submarine with ease as the Captain dictated.

Every now and again the submarine though stationary lurched a little. The trials on each of the six torpedo tubes were conducted over four days. Water shots or dummy firings allowed the technicians to gauge and set the correct pressure needed to eject a torpedo in the quietest way possible. Torpedo overflow tanks would gather the spent water to leave no visible trace on the surface when dived. All electronic and navigation systems were new and the latest available. What the Captain and crew could not possibly know, there were bugs in the system. Mike Grayling had done his job well the components he had swapped would not be discovered until it was too late.

Devonport was the only remaining refits /refuels facility available to Her Majesty's submarine fleet. Managed and run by Babcock Marine the dockyard was the biggest and best in Europe. The Navy was totally reliant on the expertise of its workforce to keep the British deterrents maintained and fit for purpose. To this end, the best naval and civilian submarine experts had been seconded or migrated there. During successive governments, Chatham dockyard had been run down and closed, Faslane had a limited capacity with the enclosed synchro lift system, able to dock subs for minor repairs. Portsmouth would be the home of the new aircraft carriers and destroyers but would have no provision for nuclear submarines.

The Plymouth base frigate complex built in the late sixties had been continuously upgraded, and it provided an all-weather capability. Able to house for repair or complete refit, frigates and destroyers it was a mainstay for the Royal

Navy's surface warships. On and off, Captain Southward had spent many years here and had built up a good circle of friends and colleagues. He knew that government proposals were to transfer the ocean-going submarine fleet to Scotland in about 2020. Over one billion pounds would be spent on upgrading the facilities in Faslane. Seven hunter-killer and four trident missile-carrying submarines would eventually be based in the Scottish complex; no one knew how this would work out. It was a government decision to have the entire nuclear fleet base ported there. It would appear the Russian threat was as big as ever and growing; our submarines would be nearer to the expected theatre of operations. The defence budget was always overspent, and the Navy had to incorporate its share of cuts.

The Falkland Islands had to be continuously patrolled and protected; a submarine would be in a state of readiness to head south or be on patrol there. Whenever the need arose, more than one unit would be dispatched to contain any threat. After the Falklands war, the Argentine Navy re-equipped with modern diesel-electric submarines, and they are considered a threat within the confines of their operating range. It is deemed that the Royal Navy nuclear fleet could contain and deal with them if necessary. H.M.S. Astute and the rest of the class are a perfect example of the latest design and build of British hunter-killer submarines. They are capable of conducting long extensive patrols, far beyond diesel-electric boat capabilities.

Full Commander Southward was ready for the next challenge as Captain. His mandate was to trial and evaluate all the systems at sea, contained within or associated with the vessel. It was only then when everything was in full working order that it would re-join the fleet as a capable deterrent.

He was immensely proud of his keep and especially his crew who ran it. On deployment, having played a significant role in the submarines ability to become a front line warship, it would be the ultimate challenge for him. There wasn't much he did not know about the functions of the submarine.

The all-powerful Rolls Royce PWR2 reactor that would never need refuelling during the life of the submarine was its powerhouse. It would provide the energy when above the waves or more importantly submerged, to propel it at nearly 30 knots. The 1900 kilowatt diesel generators that sustained the life support systems were the latest available. The advanced 2076 sonar system was capable of identifying and tracking vessels across thousands of square miles of Ocean. The 2 Thales optronics CM010 periscopes, gave an instant panoramic view above the waves. All the mechanical, electric and electronic functions were second to none. He looked forward to putting her through trials in the near future. It gave Captain Southward immense satisfaction to know he had been chosen to be the master of this incredible ocean-going leviathan of the deep.

An impressive array of armaments would be carried, in the torpedo stowage compartment. A combination of Spearfish torpedoes, UGM-84 sub harpoon and Tomahawk block four cruise missiles made up thirty-eight potential firings. The cruise missiles had a range of over 1000 miles. These missiles have a nuclear-tipped conversion capability. Navy mines could also be incorporated when deemed necessary.

Robert Southward pondered the thought, throughout the world 500 plus subs are operated by various Navies'. Russia and America have the biggest sub fleets, although China is catching up fast. Evolution marches ahead at a competitive pace.

The first-ever purpose-built submarine named "Resurgam" was built in 1879 at Cockram & Co shipyard of Birkenhead. Designed by George Garret, the sub was to incorporate the first effective torpedo designed by Robert Whitehead in 1866. This was the start of a long history of evolving technology that has led to today's incredible submarines. In fact, it is thought that boats of the future would put to sea totally unmanned and controlled from satellite and shore base communications. With the advent and development of composite materials, it is not beyond the realms of feasibility, that remotely controlled submarines could become a reality. For now, evolution dictates that nuclear submarines will get more complicated and ever more evasive. Governments will continue to direct vast amounts of money to design and build them to keep up with potential enemy developments.

Today, well over 200 submarines are on patrol at any one time, and the missile-carrying subs have awesome power. Their destructive arsenal far outweighs the combined total of all weapons used during both world wars. All types have a role to play; the hunter killers like Astute are designed to seek out and destroy the enemy without being detected.

War games are enacted regularly between friendly countries and in times of war N.A.T.O, would be responsible for safeguarding commercial interests at sea. It would be impossible to predict the outcome of a conflict between the East and the West. If war came, as a Royal Navy submarine captain, Commander Robert John Southward would not concern himself with the politics of it all. His job was to keep his submarine and 120 crew members in a state of readiness for any task they were instructed to undertake. To this end, he was one of the best in the service and was regarded as such by his superiors. He would be groomed for ascent into the Navy board's hierarchy. At least that was the intention until events beyond his control would change that perspective forever.

Chapter 18

Wednesday 3rd January 2018 (am)
The Albert Gate, Devonport naval base, Plymouth Devon, England

Chris, the security guard, stood at the barrier entrance to Albert gate. He was flanked for his own protection by the M.O.D policeman who carried an A10 assault rifle. The private security guards carried no weapons themselves and had limited powers. They were responsible for the control of service and civilian personnel entering and leaving the base. "How much more bloody scrap metal are they going to dredge from the river? It's unbelievable the amount they've recovered," said Chris "Yep, years of neglect and waste, the poor old taxpayer has to foot the bill once again. Mainly stuff lost overboard by the dockies and matelots, but contractors can be just as bad. A lot of it is from the aircraft carrier refits, back then the yard was bustling with over 12,000 workers. For the scrap metal merchant, there's a new car out of that lot for sure."

Few people knew the true purpose of the regular visits; it was all just a front.

The eight-wheeler lorry that trundled back and forward to the yard had been rigged with secret compartments to smuggle all the equipment the pirates would need. Over many weeks secured items including guns, grenades, shackles and heavy lifting equipment had been transported. In Red Fox's arsenal, the most important of all would be the warheads; they had been adapted to fit the latest British Spearfish torpedoes. The block-4 tomahawk cruise missile that Astute would be carrying he didn't have a need for. Everything would be previously crated. Marked Electrical and Mechanical spares they would be ferried to the dredger by its tender without raising any suspicion. The implication of using a nuclear weapon was something Sparrov knew would be an incredible bargaining chip. It would be a bluff, and it would later be confirmed none were missing from the Russian arsenal. The hope was that the British government would negotiate to avoid a catastrophic loss of life.

Time after time, the security guard would waive the lorry through without stopping it. Vladimir, who spoke perfect English, had an impressive fake passport and relevant security documents in the name of a Ukrainian heavy goods vehicle driver. That's all that was needed. Passes had been checked on the first day weeks ago and found to be in order. The most important pass was required to be visible when entering the dockyard. The driver had taped it to the visor and would display it on entry, during and exit from the yard. Hundreds of passes for cars, taxis and lorries during the day and night meant the guards sometimes became complacent. As long as the driver had his personal photographic pass on a lanyard around his neck, and the vehicle pass in evidence, all was assumed to be in order. The continual checking of entry and exit went on night and day in a three-shift system. It was imperative to know who and where people and vehicles were at all times. Considered to be a fool proof system, at a later date this would turn out to be not the case. More stringent checks would be put in place, but on this occasion, it had been a case of locking the stable door after the horse had bolted.

Any new or unrecognised vehicle was subject to scrutiny and thorough search. The base was at black alert, the lowest security classification. If paramount security was implemented, it meant virtual lockdown. Movement of staff and equipment would be contained, and armed M.O.D police would patrol the yard with dogs. Rapid reaction Royal Marines from the nearby Stonehouse barracks could be called upon if deemed necessary. A stroke of luck for Red Fox's team the status quo was as it was. If amber alert had been in operation, vehicle access would be restricted. If a red alert was in place, almost all transport would be denied entry and the Russian captain would have to review contingency plans, perhaps necessitating a delay in the planned piracy date.

Moored at slip jetty the tender had the same routine, food, water and spare parts for the dredger in and container scrap out. The designated berth was part of the dockyard waterfront; it had its own high-security fence topped with electrified intruder alert. When required, the integral locked gate would be manned by a security guard. The large tender with its deck-mounted lifting crane had a crew of four. It was constantly ready to offload dredged scrap and on load the various wooden crated items. Sometimes, this included Russian sailors and their weapons. The practice for the constant workings had been agreed with the naval base security office. The dredging company's negotiator had persuaded them there was insufficient craneage in Milbay docks for their needs, and that part was true. Oblivious to what was actually going on, the arrangement was considered secure enough.

The lorry would drive through the gate to the dockside and the gate secured. The men from the tender would never enter the main dockyard as such. They would conduct their business, then ferry whatever to the Thor Variant, working in the middle of the Tamar. All the inbound stock, including the smuggled Russians, would be handled by the tender crew, (Sparrov's men). While Vladimir was in the adjacent office going through the permit to work and the health and safety literature, human trafficking would take place. Over a period of time, all would be secreted aboard the dredger. There was a satellite canteen nearby if time allowed, he would go there to have his lunch in the dockie's canteen. Having got to know one of the canteen ladies, he thought he had a good chance of forming a relationship with her. She was a bit on the lumpy side but had a beautiful smile and was always joking. When she was serving his plate was always piled high, wedding ring or not I must try and pull that one he thought, any port in a storm.

As subsequent delivery and collections were concluded, Vladimir Koscho would exit Albert gate and trundle up the road in his eight-wheel vehicle chuckling to himself. He was paid weekly and had been promised a handsome bonus at the end of the contract. His brief was, 'Simple just to maintain simplicity,' and if things worked out, he could enjoy a comfortable life, instead of grubbing around trying to eke out a living. No need to let his handler know all was well; the agreement was little or no communication while all went according to plan. Through the grapevine, Red Fox would know if the operation was compromised. Vladimir was followed wherever he went by car or on foot; if he got things wrong, he would be eliminated without question. Over a period of time, 14 men would be secreted on-board the dredger. Smuggled from the tender two at a time the whole operation went like clockwork. The jigsaw puzzle was building all the time.

Subsequently, Sparrov's team were now fully ensconced and out of sight in the large converted training facility below deck. With express orders never to venture from their enclosures, this handpicked crew would await orders to enact the audacious plan. It came easy to them, having previously spent up to six months or longer below the waves on patrol in Russian submarines, the comfort they had now was so much better.

They also knew the confinement would be considerably less.

The M.O.D. police had the right to inspect the dredger at any time. This took place a couple of times when random searches were carried out. The river police did not really know what they should be looking for. A brief by the sergeant to the two constables consisted simply of letting the dredger crew know an eye was being kept on them. Their visits usually coincide with lunch, where they were treated to slap-up meals with a bottle of wine each to enjoy later. Little did they know below decks, fit, and seasoned Russian ex sub-mariners busied themselves honing plans to steal a nuclear submarine?

What a shit job the constables thought, the smell of dredged silt in the holding tanks was fierce. The crew's only respite was when the vessel traversed the channel and went out well past Rame Head to dump its contents of muddy silt. Having to live amongst it all the time was not for the faint-hearted.

"Not for us, mate," John Rodgers said.

"No, you're right, the food's good, and I expect the poor buggers working the dredger are glad to have a job."

To the Russians, (Sparrov's men) the harsh conditions were nothing they had not experienced during their time in the Navy. At that time, the submarines they served on were not known for their creature comforts. While the pirate team were confined, the thrill of what was to come kept their interest high. All the equipment and information they needed to practise for the boarding of Astute was readily at hand. They would take the opportunity to make sure all would go as smoothly as possible when the time came.

If they survived, the Russian sailors that made up Red Fox's team would be rich men. They trusted Dmitri Sparrov to keep his word that his organisation would look after their families if any one of them succumbed. Of course, there were niggling worries about the eventual outcome, injury or even death was a real possibility. The topic was never discussed between individuals; they all knew loose talk would render their positions null and void. It was a known fact that on Russian submarines at least one KGB operative then subsequently F.S.B would be secreted on board. They could be masquerading as the ships cook, doctor or any officer or rating. Their task was to monitor the crew and report back to headquarters anything they considered suspicious regarding individual crew members. It wasn't beyond the realms of possibility the same scenario was operating here.

The fact that the captain had handpicked all the men meant there was very little chance of a week team member. Even the few who had been chosen as backup had little idea of what was at stake. They had each been paid a retainer and told their knowledge may be required for a special project at a later date. The truth was they wouldn't be needed; the initial fourteen would be able to capture Astute and sail it along with the few British crew members on-board to then dive 19 miles off Plymouth sound. As the time grew nearer to anticipated day, every aspect was repeatedly gone over until perfection was achieved.

From the expected weather conditions through to any change in the subs operational expectancies was taken into consideration. Only minor adjustments were needed, and the date of 12th February 2018 was set for the piracy to be enacted. This date would be kept a secret from the crew until the last few hours. Only Captain Dmitri Sparrov and his second in command Ivor Pushkin (Codin) would know the exact time and date, secrecy at all times was paramount.

Chapter 19

Friday, 9th February 2018. 04.25hours.
Submarine refit complex tool shed, Babcock Marine, Plymouth (England)

For Mike Grayling, it had seemed the only way out of his predicament. John Balfour had mapped out exactly what would happen if he did not comply. A long spell in hospital or worse would be forthcoming if he refused to do exactly as he was told and the debt would still be in place. So, what other option did he have? Maybe go to the authorities and explain to them what he had got himself involved with. Once again, he had been reminded his every move was being watched and he would be dealt with in a very unpleasant manner if need be. The best he could expect was broken legs the worst, ending up splattered in the bottom of a dry dock, so he had made up his mind to comply.

All that was required of him was to replace certain items of electrical furniture on-board Astute. Six in number items, three in the torpedo stowage compartment one in the control room and two in the coning tower. The smallest was the size of a cigarette packet, and the largest was the size of a shoebox. These components were identical on the exterior to the existing ones already fitted by the electricians. It would take minutes to exchange the smaller ones and approximately an hour for the largest. There was some simple wiring to adapt, that would not prove too difficult for a tradesman such as Mike. It was put to him that everything would be verified electronically by a third person. He did wonder how this was possible but was too scared to ask questions and mess with these people.

Balfour had pictures on his mobile phone of all the six components and where they were located. He had also drilled Mike as to how to carry out the changes and the tools needed, second nature for him. During a week of nightshifts, the task would be easy to achieve, along with completing his allocated work. Except for the reactor compartment, he had access to all other areas of the submarine. Fortunately, he was the only electrician on nights working aboard along with three fitter's two coppersmiths, a slinger and some labourers. A lot of the major work was completed, so the larger gangs had been moved elsewhere. There were about another dozen working in the shore side workshop. He knew precisely when the navy did their rounds and could adapt the changes he was ordered to do accordingly. Mike was on good terms with the junior rates that wouldn't know what he was doing but enjoyed a chat, to break the monotony of their 4 hours on, 4 hours off shifts.

Everything would be smuggled on-board in his tool bag, item by item. The redundant components would be dumped in the corner of the basin, outside the dining hall. This was where the dockies went for a smoke and to dispose of redundant rabbits. (Anything of a personal nature made in dockyard time, surplus to requirements).

Little did Mike know that in the near future this area was to be dredged and some of the larger components he had ditched would be discovered. John assured him there was no way he could be found out as being the culprit. That was so wrong; the game was up, spooks in suits and dockyard Ministry of Defence senior detectives were crawling all over the dockyard, especially the S.R.C...

Sat on his toolbox Mike Grayling took a large swig of the whisky he had smuggled in his drinks flask.

"Fuck, that's harsh should have put ice in with it! What a fool I have been," he sighed. "Because of Sharron I will lose my job. Not just that, I have compromised a submarine and will end up with a prison sentence and never be able to hold my head high again. I cannot live with the shame of it."

He took another swig of whisky and grimaced at the harsh attack to his throat. He stood up, opened the toolbox and took out a long lanyard, woven from a thick chalk line. He had been taught by an old shipwright how to tie knots properly and weave anything from a ships bell pull to a decorative lanyard. He looked at the noose he had completed recently and without hesitation, threw it over one of the horizontal metal beams that formed the roof trusses. The other end, he secured to the eye plate on the adjacent wall. He reached for the stool that stood in the corner and positioned it directly below the noose. Mike stood on the stool and put the noose around his neck. He drained the last mouthful of whisky from his flask and threw it at the cream-painted brick wall. He restrained both hands with strong tie wraps to his thick leather belt, there was no going back.

"Thank God, my mum and dad are not alive to deal with the aftermath of this. They told me not to have anything to do with that gold-digging cow, but she got me in her clutches, and that was that."

Kicking the stool away, he dangled there, legs flaying, his life drifting away. "Fucking bitch see you in hell."

Thirty minutes later, the rest of the gang from the workshops had finished their lunch break and were transiting through the toolbox shed to their workplaces. Mike Grayling's lifeless body dangled, swinging gently in the draught from the open door.

Jack Saunders was the first one on the scene and desperately tried to hold Mike's lifeless body up, taking the tension off the noose.

"Shit, somebody get a knife or something to cut him down."

Jeff Truscott kicked open his toolbox and got a hand saw out. In no time at all, he cut through the noose, the lifeless body slumped to the floor. The first aider, Chris Rowlands ran over and checked the pulse and breath with a pocket mirror.

"Poor bastard, he's dead."

"Are you sure?" Jack didn't want to believe what he was seeing.

"Well for fuck sake, I'm not a doctor, but I know when someone has snuffed it. Quick contact the surgery and tells them to get an ambulance here and let Mod Plod know. He must have hung himself within minutes of the lunch break starting."

Throughout the complex, the news spread like wildfire,

with mixed reactions. Mike had been a loaner and didn't have any real friends amongst his work associates. None the more for that it was an awful situation, especially for those who found him.

The whole of the Submarine Refit Complex went into lockdown. Armed M.O.D. police would man the entry/exit gates. Over the tannoy, workers were instructed to proceed at once to the dining hall. Only health physics personnel would remain at their stations to ensure nuclear safety was maintained. The S.R.C. duty manager, the supervisors and the rest of the staff on the nightshift would be detained and interviewed. As everyone had signed the official secrets act, they would be told not to discuss anything they knew about what had happened. This was a top security nuclear submarine refit and repair facility; all staff were well aware of the consequences of adopting loose lips. It was drilled into them, for anyone silly enough to discuss the event, the cost would be dire. Loss of employment and probable prosecution

The incident would be hushed up; it would be a long time before the press was informed of the demise of Michael Grayling due to a tragic accident.

For the sad soul, it was the end of a generally miserable life since his love and infatuation for Sharron. For his money-grabbing cheating wife, it would be the beginning of a nightmare. No! She wouldn't shed a tear for the loser that had died in mysterious circumstances that's for sure, plenty more fish in the sea. It would be different when the basin was drained, and the components found that Mike had removed and substituted on-board Astute. Things would really get nasty for Sharron who was believed to be implicit in what he had done.

Agents from MI5 would arrest her, take her into custody and go through her house with a fine-tooth comb. What they would find was incriminating evidence that had been secreted on purpose by her husband. To the criminal investigators it proved beyond doubt she had been compliant, a willing accomplice in his treasonable acts, all for financial gain.

Under the circumstances, a trial and subsequent prison sentence were deemed out of the question. It was not possible to trace all of her previous movements. There was evidence that Sharron had at one stage had an affair with a Russian fisherman. Apart from one month back in Russia each year, his trawler was permanently fishing off the West Country coast in international waters. Whenever it entered British territorial waters, it was covertly shadowed by fishery protection and M.O.D police vessels. It would often spend time in Sutton harbour docks Plymouth, for maintenance, re-stocking and allowing crew leave. It was more than likely the mother ship cruising in the western approaches, was a spy ship. Eves dropping on the garrison town of Plymouth, where information would be gathered to aid foreign intelligence services, that was its prime task. Moreover, it would definitely be monitoring the comings and goings of ships and subs base ported at the naval dockyard.

Was it a coincidence that both Russian ships left for home two months before H.M.S. Astute was pirated away? The evidence suggested otherwise. National security was at stake, and for that reason; it was paramount to get Sharron off the streets. She would be dealt with; time was on the authority's side. The few remaining relatives turned their backs on her and assumed she had absconded to some faraway place with the latest conquest and Mike had trailed after her. She was a disgrace to the otherwise honest hardworking family members.

It was impossible to establish completely what part Sharron had played in this heinous crime against the state where people had died. In truth, it was difficult for her to comprehend the seriousness of what her husband had done. Pleading her innocence, she was totally uncooperative with whoever conducted the long interviews blaming it all on her worthless husband. Yes, she admitted having an affair with a Russian fisherman but swore she had not passed on any information about what Mike did at work. Frequent ranting and raving about her human rights did not help her case. Finally, an assault with a knife on one of her guards played right into the authority's hands. It was not difficult to have her certified as criminally insane and humanely detained indefinitely.

Chapter 20

All items were stowed ready on the covered deck walkway of the Thor Variant. The engine had been run up earlier to make sure all was in working order, and it was now at idling state. Loaded with ballast, at this time of the morning it would be assumed it was catching the tide to dump another load of dredged silt. The dockyard and especially the river police were used to the vessel going about its business at all times of day and night. The harbour master would have the weekly movements sheet, with intended times of arrivals and departures.

Red Fox had gone over the plans again and again; every one of his men knew exactly what they had to do and in what order to do it. It needed split-second timing, and there would only be one chance to get it right. The securing ropes were let go, and the dredger left its mooring at a leisurely five knots. It needed to move less than a mile to be adjacent to the intended target. Silhouetted by the glow of the dockside tower lights, a menacingly large black shape was visible. The silhouette of H.M.S. Astute sat motionless secured by ropes to the capstans fwd and aft of her port side. The dredger trundled slowly getting ever closer to the submarine. Until the last minute, the duty guards on the casings took absolutely no interest in what was going on. As the dredger inched ever nearer to Astute, it became evident that something was very wrong.

When the stun grenades were lobbed in their direction, they were taken entirely by surprise and incapacitated. The afterguard, junior rate James McNally just had time to raise his A10 assault rifle, before he was knocked overboard and rendered unconscious. That would be the last he would ever see of the submarine and his mates. The fwd guard also ended up in the water between the wharf and the sub but was conscious. He swam to the nearest set of dockside steps and clambered up the slimy surface to the walkway. Having ingested mouthfuls of the dank river he sat there coughing and spluttering, his situation was hopeless. The radio and gun were lost, and he felt totally helpless and alone as he sat watching his friend James float past, face down in the oily water. Dumbfounded he could do nothing but watch the unbelievable scenario unfold in front of him, what the hell was going on?

Grappling irons were swung over from the dredger and coupled to the conning tower handrails of Astute. Shear legs hoisted onto casings were quickly chained to the fwd and aft submarine capstans by the two burly invaders. The shear legs were required to get the guns, heavy weaponry and other equipment slung from the dredger. While this was happening, the other Russian sailors led by Ivor Pushkin (Codin), quickly slid down rope ladders and headed for the open hatches. Stun and gas grenades were dropped into the submarines confined spaces, and all hell broke loose as Sparrov's men went about their allotted tasks. Donning his lightweight breathing apparatus Codin quickly climbed down the fwd access ladder and as the captain's cabin door slid open, pointed the barrel of the Russian made PSS Vul silent pistol, directly at Robert Southward's head. He had been resting on his bunk, but as soon as he heard the commotion headed for the cabin door. Too late, the pistol in his face was enough to throw him off balance.

"What the hell is going on?" he stormed. The Russian captain, Lieutenant Pushkin, said nothing but beckoned the British captain to get back on his bunk. There he was secured by handcuffs to the tubular metal frame, and his watch was forcibly removed. The subs intercom mic was unplugged and secured in the pirate's rucksack. He quickly searched for any weapons that may be in the captain's possession, though it was thought highly unlikely. Information was that the tradition of having all firearms safely secured in a locked steel cabinet was how naval vessels operated. When in port, the officer of the watch would issue guns and live ammunition to the duty guards that patrolled the outboard casings. Signed in and out in the weapons log on duty changeovers, it was thought to be full proof. While on patrol, the captain and the master at arms were the only people to have keys to the arms locker.

"Is this some sort of exercise I'm supposed to know about?"

Codin just grinned and slid the door shut. He waited for a short while until the din of the attack died down.

Requesting sit-reps from the control and manoeuvring rooms, it was judged the submarine was now in Russian hands. The British sailors on watch in the various compartments did not have time to get their Drager anti-gas masks on; they have them on now. Quickly overpowered by the pirates, the officers' quarters, senior and junior rates bunk spaces were overrun. The compartment fans were started to vent the air.

Dmitri Sparrov slid down the rope ladder onto the fwd casing. Giving his men time to contain the situation and mop up, he calmly lit a cigarette and deeply inhaled. It was a beautiful early morning, and the Tamar estuary looked particularly attractive in the soft glow of the dockside lights. He scanned the surrounding area for any sign of enemy movement; there wasn't any. Straining to listen for inboard sounds, apart from some raised voices all seemed as it should be. Red Fox knew his men would be doing all that was necessary to secure the submarine totally; there had been no gunshots that had to be good news.

After a short while Codin ascended the control room ladder and out through the hatch, removed his oxygen mask and with a wry smile, he announced Astute was secure. "Good work, any causalities?"

"Not counting the casing guards, just a few sore heads sustained by the British, and some superficial bumps and scrapes by our men."

"That's great news, where's the captain?"

"He is handcuffed to his bunk with an armed guard outside the cabin door."

"Right, get everything slung inboard, then get ready

to uncouple the sheer legs and ditch them overboard. Give the order to slip the moorings as soon as we are ready. We are an hour after high tide and our passage downriver will be helped by the outgoing tide. Place two of our men on the casings and two up on the coning tower platform with Kalashnikovs, RPG's and hand grenades. Issue orders to use whatever force is necessary to dissuade any possible rescue attempt."

Codin was ecstatic. He expected some serious casualties, even deaths amongst the opposition and his men. It was sad for the two British sailors whose fate was unclear, but it could have been a lot worse if resistance had been heavy.

"Are the engineers confident about handling the boat?"

Red Fox was a little worried about things going wrong at this stage; the immediate situation was critical to the whole operation.

"Too early to say, but whatever coercion is required will be used, so the Brits cooperate."

"Okay but tell the men to try and gain their trust rather than beating them to death." "They will be treated like lambs, Sir."

"Not to the slaughter, I hope?"

Relieved at the swift progress that had been made they both laughed, the initial act of piracy had gone like clockwork.

The torpedo loading hatch that had been the main focus for slinging and stowing the heavy equipment was finally secured shut. Captain Lieutenant Ivor Pushkin gave the order to release the grappling irons and manoeuvre the Thor Variant to proceed to its final resting position; straddling the entrance to No 4 basin. Here the seacocks would be opened, and the dredger would sink, trapping the duty frigate H.M.S, Cumberland. It was an incredible stroke of luck that the warship had been in the basin. Expected it to be on the sea wall south of the basin entrance, the intention was to ram the aft end and severely damage the steering gear. With a light collision, it was expected the watertight bulkhead would buckle as designed but the frigate would not sink. The men on the dredger would board the lowered speed boat and high tail it to Moon cove, there to be picked up and disappear into the night.

The M.O.D police launch, Calibre, with three police on board were busy checking the secured ammunition barges in Ernesettle creek when they heard the commotion going on further down the Tamar. It was muffled slightly by the bend in the river, but at that time of the morning when it was reasonably quiet, the sound reverberated intensely. Reflected off the tree-lined riverbank on the Cornish side, it sounded like a distant earthquake.

"What the hell was that?" said Constable Dick Dreyfus.

"Not an f-ing clue," replied Sergeant Jim Walker. He picked up the ship to shore radio mic,

"Launch CA.1, to Porterhouse base come back?"

After what seemed like an eternal wait. Duty inspector, Roy Hanwell responded, "Base to launch, hallo Jim. Yeah, I know what you're going to say, sounded here like a ship's boiler exploding. We think it's the Thor Variant. The security camera in that area has relayed pictures of it colliding with a submarine, think it's the Astute. I am dispatching a mobile unit to the area, but they are on patrol in South yard at the moment. Fire brigade alerted from Camel's head. They are on their way. Look, Jim, you are the nearest, so stop what you are doing and high tail it to the scene." "Message received, over and out."

"Right lads, let's crank this thing up always wanted to see what it could do," Jim said with a laugh.

The speed limit was normally 5 knots for all vessels except in emergencies. The Calibre was fairly new and had just been given its licence to operate for the river police. It was designed and built with twin Paxman diesel and could reach speeds in excess of 25 knots. With blue lights flashing and sirens bellowing, it thundered under the Tamar Bridge towards the bend in the river.

"This should wake the natives up," said Dick.

They all laughed; little did they know what was waiting for them.

On the fwd casing, the Russian sailor noticed a white van slowly heading towards the brow with its lights on full. He cocked his Kalashnikov and gave two short bursts at the glare, glass splintered and plastic melted. The wharf master and his rigger crapped themselves.

"What the fuck was that?" shouted Peter "I've been hit in the leg with something. "Yeah! And somethings hit me in the guts," replied Brian. "Quick, run for it."

They both jumped out and ran for all their worth in the opposite direction, not realising they were both bleeding. Stopping behind the waterside fitter's workshop where they thought they were safe, Pete said:

"Ring the fucking police, I'm hurt."

"Yeah and so am I, anyway I can't, I left my mobile and

the walky-talky in the van." "You twat, what are we going to do now?"

"There's a dockside telephone just over there by the wheelie bins."

"Just hold on a minute I'm bleeding like a stuck pig."

Tutting, Brian mumbled,

"Always fucking moaning, what the hell you think this is?"

Blood was seeping through his overalls and into his cupped hand,

"This fucking hurts, mate."

"Wait here, and I'll go."

Just then, the door of the fitter's workshop opened.

"Please ring for an ambulance we're hurt."

"Okay mate no worries."

How fortunate the guy was a first-aider? They would survive.

Using the two-way radio Nikolay Popov contacted Red Fox inboard.

"No 3 to leader come in."

"Leader receiving go ahead."

"Enemy dockside activity neutralised, the white van has been stopped in its tracks, no assistance needed, over and out."

Calibre navigated the turn in the river and headed past Camel's head creek. They were just in time to see the muzzle flashes from the Kalashnikov and the exploding headlights.

"Quick break out the guns, there's some heavy shit happening here."

They were now within three hundred yards off Astute and could see the armed Russian sailors on the casings. Before the Calibre crew could react, they were hit by a hail of bullets that shattered the wheelhouse. Sergeant James Walker died instantly. Constable Richard Dreyfus sustained three wounds in the neck and chest, from which he would die before reaching a hospital. Constable Barry Davis sustained a severe bullet wound in the right arm but would survive. He was able to manoeuvre the launch away from the scene to safety. He grabbed the radio and screamed into it "Emergency, emergency, this is police motor launch Calibre, C.A.1, middle of Tamar, adjacent to a mooring buoy, opposite Sub refit complex. We need urgent medical assistance; repeat we need urgent medical help."

He was trembling trying to keep the launch stable while it drifted. There was no way with his one functioning arm he could do anything but wait for rescue.

Looking at his colleagues, he was violently sick. James was flopped in the driving seat like a rag doll, blood oozing from numerous wounds. Richard had half his neck hanging in a mess and was rasping and gurgling on the cabin floor. Barry dropped the mic and likewise slumped to the cabin floor and passed out.

"This is Tug Grateful receiving, come back?"

No answer.

"This is Porterhouse base receiving come back?"

No answer. The skipper of Grateful, the duty tug knew something was very wrong. He had heard what was going on and had aroused the crew with instructions to fire up the powerful engines. Within five minutes, they could be underway.

In the control room of Astute, Dmitri Sparrov spoke into his two-way radio,

"Team leader to dockside and casing crew. Release gangway and securing ropes and make your way inboard, secure all hatches."

They sprang into action; within three minutes, all was ready to get underway. The gangway would fall into the river as they moved from the dockside.

"No 4, as soon as we are closed up, engage secondary propulsion for six knots."

In the dimmed lighting of the control room, Boris Maklakov looked at the panels in front of him with the numerous controls at his disposal. Two red lights turned to green, indicating the fwd and aft hatches were shut tight. Only the conning tower upper and lower hatches remained on red. He had read the manuals until he knew them parrot-fashion. On the computer simulator back in Russia, he had honed his skills for just this scenario.

Red Fox was ready for any problems that might arise and had one of the British helmsmen handcuffed to the adjacent metal and leather swivelling chair. He was sure that if Boris could not cope with the subs manoeuvre, for his own survival the Brit would co-operate. The display on the monitors of the fwd and aft-facing inferred cameras gave a panoramic view of the Tamar River. Built into the coning tower, they could transmit even when the submarine was submerged. Extremely robust with powerful sidelights, they could relay underwater images, at considerable depths.

"Right No 1, you have control of the sub, I'm going

to the conning tower platform." "Captain confirmed I have control of the submarine."

Dmitri Sparrov ascended the ladder and joined his two men on the coning tower's cramped platform. He could see the Thor Variant was now sinking fast by the bow. His men had literally managed to scrape the granite walls either side of the basin entrance with the port side of the dredger. Not even a rigid raider from the duty frigate would get out. The speed boat with the four-man crew from the dredger was hastily making the short journey to Moon cove. The tug Grateful had got underway and was heading north as fast as she could towards the drifting Calibre.

"Wait a minute, that's Astute heading down river with no pilot boat or escorting tugs, what the hell?"

The skipper quickly turned slightly to stb'd to investigate.

"There's no way we should have a nuclear submarine loose in the Tamar."

At the top of the conning town, Red Fox saw the impending danger. Calmly, he said to Vadim Borowski (No9),

"When in range, give them two rocket-propelled grenades at the waterline that should stop them."

At 12 knots unaware of the danger the tug headed directly towards what they thought was a drifting nuclear submarine. To the tug master's surprise and horror, part of the bow of his vessel exploded into steel fragments as two holes were punched through by the shaped grenade charges. He immediately cut the engines, and the tug slowed and wallowed helplessly. It was plainly evident it was starting to go down by the bow. Shouting into the intercom,

"Shut the watertight doors, all hands on deck, get the tender over the side, we are sinking."

He punched a button to start the pumps; nothing happened, in the fwd compartment, the circuit board had been knocked out by shrapnel.

Chapter 21

Monday, 12th February 2018. Time 03.45hrs
H.M.S. Astute, Conning tower

As Astute passed the lifeless tug Grateful, Dmitri Sparrov was pleased to see the tender had been lowered into the water and the crew were scrambling aboard. Minimal injuries and loss of life were an important factor in his plan; it was paramount for his crew but also for the enemy. He turned to Vadim Borowski No 9. "This is all too easy, where's the opposition we anticipated?"

He laughed, "Maybe we have caught them napping, you know the Brits, love their shut-eye."

"Maybe, but don't underestimate them, there's a Special Forces base close by and we really don't want them on the scene any time soon."

Red Fox raised his night vision binoculars and scoured the river and coastline. Onshore to his port side, he could see blue lights flashing and hear sirens blaring. All the services that had been alerted were now in full swing. He managed a wry smile, whoever they were; it was too late to stop him here in the middle of the Tamar. The thought of sinking a nuclear submarine with all that implied would be out of the question for the British armed forces. The duty frigate had been neutralised, and ships movements had indicated there was no significant vessel available at short notice to stop their escape, he was confident that no relent attack was likely soon. The sub continued its journey down the river, passing the surface fleet complex. It was obvious work was being carried out within, as all the lights were on and the massive door to the middle dock was in the raised position. He could recognise the upper silhouette of a type 45 destroyer behind the caisson.

Almost adjacent, he could see the Torpoint ferry. On both the Devon and Cornwall sides, each ferry was being readied to cope with the early morning commuter rush. With one in reserve, it was always a busy place. For those who lived in Torpoint and the surrounding area, it saved the long road trip to the Tamar Bridge to make the crossing. From Plymouth, naval and civilian staff would be commuting to H.M.S Raleigh the primary training base for new recruits. From the Cornish side, the same would be happening to feed H.M.S. Drake and Devonport the largest dockyard in Western Europe. Plymouth, in general, was a significant employer of the people in south-west Cornwall and further afield. As they left the ferries behind, he could see the operating crews were all stood, gaping at Astute. Further up the river, the mayhem the Russians had instigated was focusing the most interest. It would be quite a while before it was established what was going on.

H.M.S.Westminster, a type 23 frigate was on the dockside wharf by 3 basin. With scaffolding and thick plastic tenting covering the flight deck area, it was obviously undergoing maintenance work. The bridge was in darkness, no threat from that ship.

Astute steered around the bend in the river; strong currents were always a threat here. In the control room, the planes man worked hard to keep the submarine in the middle of the deep channel; to run aground now would not be good. Although either side was mud and silt, a metre or so down would be jagged bedrock. No fear of penetrating the hull but severe damage could be done to the manoeuvring props.

R.F.A. Wave Ruler, a fast fleet replenishment tanker was on slip jetty. It carried ammunition, freshwater and general supplies for the fleet at sea. Only walkway, masthead lights and the bridge were illuminated. Dimitri Sparrov could see the duty officer of the watch on the darkened bridge wing with his infrared binoculars; he was scanning the scene of Astute passing. As the officer of the watch, he would undoubtedly be aware of all local ships' movements for today, and this submarine should certainly not be on the move. For fear of collision in the narrow channel, only in emergencies would the movements be changed. The officer was confused, time to wake the captain of the R.F.A; however, Wave Ruler was without engine power and posed no threat whatsoever.

Passing the Silhouetted statue of King Billy, (William of Orange) all was calm, In Mutton cove, a few fishermen were mucking about with their small inshore fishing boats. Another slight manoeuvre to port and they were passing Millbay Docks, the Brittany ferry, (Pont Avent), was getting ready to sail to Roscoff, France.

Now the channel had to be navigated past Plymouth

Hoe. Probably the trickiest test for Red Fox's planes man, but he had every confidence in him. As they approached the breakwater, Dimitri said:

"Look No 8, the towed array buoy, if we had time we would stop and steal that as a souvenir." Mikhail Somov laughed; "I think we have enough British hardware in our possession captain."

The Russian sailors knew that once past the breakwater, the task of escape was within their grasp. Within ten minutes, they could dive and be hidden from view. Suddenly No.9 whispered,

"Two rigid raiders coming out from Whitsand Bay."

Red Fox raised his binoculars, two teams of six men. With their blacked-out faces, camouflaged clothing, and heavily armed, they had to be Special Forces. It was a threat.

"Get ready to blow them out of the water when they get within a two hundred metres range. Vadim and Mikhail readied their rocket-propelled grenade launchers. With no navigation lights on display, the rubber inflatable boats, (R.I.Bs) were moving fast. The Russian sailors had itchy fingers; they would not hesitate to waste the British lives if necessary.

Suddenly the R.I.B.s slowed to a crawl and turned hard to port. It was obvious they were going to pass west of Drakes Island and navigate the shallow channel there.

"I reckon they are on a night exercise and playing games. Taking that route is a risky business I've studied the charts, its shallow even at a near high tide." said No 8.

"Well they obviously know these waters like the back of their hands."

"Yes, and they will never know how close they came to ending their exercise prematurely."

Red Fox and his two man team on the fin platform breathed a sigh of relief.

The submarine continued its course to the west of the Eddystone lighthouse 13 miles South West of Plymouth sound. The depth of the channel increased sufficiently for them to disappear to a safe depth.

"Fin to control room."

Captain Lieutenant Pushkin answered, "Yes, Captain?"

"Dive to 30meters, increase revolutions to 15 knots and disengage secondary propulsion."

"Dive to 30meters, increasing speed to 15 knots, secondary propulsion disengaging, Sir."

"Right Vadim, time to disappear, the two of you take your weapons inboard now" They both sprang into action with Borowski descended the internal ladder in an instant, quickly followed by Somov.

The relevant controls were set, and within seconds high-pressure air was released from the tanks that controlled water ballast ingress. The submarine started a controlled dive into the inky black waters. Controlled fuel rods were lowered in the Pressure Water Reactor, and the process of advanced nuclear fusion increased. The circulating water system coupled to the port and stb'd pressure vessels produced super-heated steam. The steam activated the turbine that turned the propulsor. H.M.S. Astute gained speed as the propeller gathered momentum.

Red Fox lifted his night vision binoculars and took one last look at the spectacular panoramic view. In the dull glow of pending dawn, the lights of Plymouth, especially the Citadel, breakwater and the Mountbatten peninsular were a magnificent sight. He wondered if and when he would walk on dry land again. Closing the outer hatch and quickly descending to the control room, the lower hatch was shut and secured tightly. Having got this far, he was under no illusion as to the possible fate of the submarine and all aboard. They had just purloined the most advanced submarine in the British fleet and would be hunted relentlessly.

Dismissing all negative thoughts, he calmly strolled to the periscope area. Captain Lieutenant Ivor Pushkin saluted Captain Dimitri Sparrov. Returning the salute with a wry smile, he authoritatively barked,

"I have control."

"You have control, Sir."

Red Fox studied the map on the chart table.

"No2 set the course for south-south-west, and increase speed to 25 knots we want to be 19 miles out from Plymouth as soon as possible."

"Course set south, south, west, speed 25 knots, Sir." In the short time it took to travel the six nautical miles there was silence. Amongst Sparrov's crew, the enormity of what had just been achieved was on everyone's mind. High on their adrenalin rush, the excitement of what had happened in the last hour was overwhelming.

"Reduce speed to stop and secure."

"Speed reducing to stop and securing Sir."

"What's displayed on the sonar No 2?"

"The Roscoff ferry is just passing the breakwater. There is a large tanker 10 miles to the South East. There are five trawlers and two smaller fishing boats heading into Plymouth. Other commercial traffic is passing 45 miles to the south, in the main shipping channel Sir."

"Okay, take her up to periscope depth." The order was carried out, and the submarine rose to just under the surface. The days of the direct view device were long gone. Having to assess the situation through the lenses of the raised periscope, by the submarine commander could be long and laborious. Totally dependent on the Mk1 eyeball, details could be missed. Now with the push of a button on the consul, the optronics CM010 device could instantly be deployed. In three seconds the (QLR) quick look round facility, gives a 360-degree sweep above the waves and then retracts into its housing, external of the pressure hull in the fin. The thermal imaging is transmitted to the internal monitor displays and recorded on the computer. Red fox looked at the total recordings almost in real-time. He was pleased there was no military traffic on display.

"The Brits have certainly got one up on us with this equipment. Shame Thales UK cannot sell the packages to mother Russia for our submarines."

The control room echoed to the sound of muffled laughter.

"Okay, take her down to the sea bed."

The submarine slowly descended the 90 metres and came to rest in the silt.

"No2, check all departments are functioning as they should be, especially the main machinery space. We will need the trisonic imaging and hovertrack at a moment's notice. Get the men to make sure the restrained British crew, especially the captain, are behaving themselves. They will be wondering why we have stopped and not put as much distance as possible from their base. We will be going to periscope depth again in 15 minutes with our demands.

"Yes, Captain." Along with Red Fox, only the planesman and one sonar operator remained at their stations. The time was fast approaching for the ransom demand to be sent, it would be brief and to the point. The radio mast would be raised to send the transmission; it would be picked up immediately by Northwood and GCHQ Cheltenham. For Dimitri Sparrov and his piratical band, the ball would then be squarely in the enemy's court.

Sitting in his cabin Captain Robert Southward had been straining hard to glean anything that would help him understand his predicament. He knew they had been travelling South West and not deviated from that course since they left Plymouth. Having taken this route many times before, it would have been almost possible to navigate it in his sleep. Known as the quickest way to get to the western approaches and relative obscurity, it was the chosen route by most submarine commanders. Having been left alone since forced to conform and address his crew, he could only wonder at what was happening now. Why had the sub come to rest on the sea bed? Was there a problem that had to be rectified before they could continue to wherever? Had members of his crew caused some sort of problem to negate the ability to carry on? No! His instructions had been explicit, and he was sure they would have been carried out to the letter. The time passed very slowly as he tried to make some sense of it all. He was becoming more and more frustrated.

The stainless steel restraint had proved impossible to remove; his wrist was red raw with the effort of trying. The movement and sometimes hushed conversation between the armed guard and others passing his door was further evidence of this hopeless situation. It would have been so easy to slip into a negative mindset. However, to keep his brain active, he went through every aspect of the sub department by department. With various sounds, mechanical and electrical, he could identify them and know if all was well. Such a complex build with millions of components would challenge the crew twenty-four seven. The first-class naval training for them oversaw almost every challenge. With the submarine now on the sea bed Captain Southward could only guess as to what the pirates were up to. He knew there was an armed guard outside the cabin door. He was extremely silent but for comfort reasons, from time to time made some movement in the restricted space he had. It was very disconcerting when there were sounds of footsteps, probably a change of guard. In most cases, no one entered the cabin, other than to bring him some food.

Back in the control room, it had now become a waiting game. It was evident that sea traffic was on the move, but what was the British enemy up to?

"We can now only wait and see how the authorities react, No2. In the first instance, the best we can expect is an acknowledgement of our demands."

For the next 48 hours, this submarine would become a silent resting place for all entombed. An answer to the Pirate leader's demand was slow in coming. Initially, only the briefest of a formal signal had been received by the radio operator on the submarine; it was time to up the stakes. There was no point in staying in the present location.

Red Fox gave the order to engage trisonic imaging and hovertrack.

"I want a course set for Hurds Deep."

"Yes, Captain setting course for Hurds Deep."

This was the deepest part of the English Channel and at high tide would register a depth of over 170 metres. During the late 1950s, 28,000 containers of low-level radioactive waste had been secretly dumped there by both Belgium and Britain. It is continuously monitored and not considered a threat due to the dissipation of the sea. With all the ferrous material littering the deep, it would be almost impossible to find a submarine.

Red Fox turned to Codin.

"That should be a good place to hide and wait for a while; we might find out if we are rich men or poor sailors destined for Davy Jones' locker."

The Russian sailors, although concerned, were beaming in adulation for their captain. They were on the move, the further they could get away from the naval base the better. Not the same thoughts for the unfortunate shackled seamen. Unaware of their fate and still smarting from their demise, would they ever see the British Isles and their families again?

Chapter 22

Monday 12th February 2018 11.00hrs
Captain's cabin on-board H.M.S Astute

"Commander, I want you to address your crew with this statement."

Red Fox handed the shackled Robert Southward the English transcript along with the ship's log. Dmitri Sparrov stood back and allowed the Captain to digest the contents. He read it twice and then took a deep breath.

"This is ridiculous. You are on a British warship, and this is sheer lunacy. How do you expect to get away with this?"

"That is not the point, for now, my men and I have control of this submarine. We can function with or without your crew's help. We may need assistance at times to maintain the integrity and safety of this vessel. I need to know if you are compliant with my orders for your wellbeing and more importantly, that of your crew. For the time we are on board you will be confined to your cabin with washing facilities and a chemical toilet and of course you will be fed. After your brief, there will be no further contact with your men whatsoever. This is non-negotiable. I will return in ten minutes, and I expect an answer to my demands."

With that Sparrov turned and left the cabin, taking the Captain's log with him.

Robert Southward did not need to read again what had been placed in front of him. He sensed the armed black-clad figure outside his cabin door, a menacing-looking character, would shoot him without hesitation if ordered to do so. At the very least a sore head would be forthcoming if he attempted anything untoward. Muttering to himself,

"Well, Bob, your options are somewhat limited." He felt strangely calm now; at least he knew what was expected of him. Of course, he and his crew had been trained in how to repel boarders. However, this situation could never have been envisaged. Top security naval base, well trained M.O.D. police, river and shore patrols, twenty-four seven. With his two armed sailors on the casing fwd and aft, the submarine should have been secure. How on earth did these people pull this off, he mused. What was to be done, that's the question, for the moment there was no feasible answer. Looking around the sparse cabin to all intents and purpose, it was now his prison. He hoped it would not become his death cell.

The cabin door slid open, and Sparrov entered with the Russian guard with pistol drawn.

"Well, Captain, what is your decision?"

Robert Southward looked at both men then directly at Dmitri Sparrov.

"How can I be sure my men will be safe once you have achieved whatever it is you have planned? That's if you manage to achieve it."

"Well, as one naval Captain to another, I can only give

you my word with regards to the situation at hand. What your superiors and government decide to do is beyond my control. We may all be blown to kingdom come, but honestly, I don't think that will happen."

"Well, I think you and your men are completely mad and destined to fail. However, for the safety of my crew and the integrity of my submarine, I will comply for the time being. Will you countersign my entry into the ships log, guaranteeing the safety of my crew?"

"Captain, I am unable to sign anything, but I will allow you to record your comments. There will be no further entries of any sort otherwise it will be destroyed. As long as your men do nothing counterproductive to this operation, they will be safe."

Both men knew it was futile to conduct any further conversation. Red Fox plugged in the ships address mic and handed it to the Captain. As the guard levelled the gun at his head, it was obvious a swift end would be forthcoming if he deviated from the script. This would be the hardest thing the British Captain had ever done. Effectively handing over control of his limited crew to a renegade bunch of marauding pirates about whom he knew very little. Clearing his throat, he prepared to make his address.

"Do you here there, this is the Captain speaking. Firstly, the welfare of you all and the safety of this vessel are paramount. To this end, you are instructed to co-operate with our captors. When ordered, you are to assist in the operational running of Astute; no sabotage is to take place whatsoever. The information I have been given is that at some stage this submarine and all its crew will be back in

British hands. Until that time carry on with your normal routine. That is all."

"Thank you, Captain; you have made the right decision."

Sparrov retrieved the mic, and the two Russians exited without any further conversation. As the door slid back, Captain Southward glimpsed the burly guard with a menacing stare take up his station, Robert felt very alone. From what he could glean, these people were very professional. They mainly communicated in nods and whispers. He was convinced they were highly skilled military trained personnel.

Being the Captain of a nuclear submarine carried huge responsibilities. His training had been progressively long and costly, it had to be that way, and he was now one of the chosen few. To become a submarine Captain required certain qualities far and above that of regular naval officers. The training course of capture and confinement related to the unlikely event of the submarine foundering in a hostile environment and the crew being imprisoned. His mind wandered back to the training facility at Gosport. After a very short brief of what to expect, two muscular guys dressed in black, took his watch, hooded him, and dumped him unceremoniously in a dank room. The balaclavas his guards wore with cut-outs made it seem all the more sinister. There was no conversation as the heavy steel door was shut and bolted behind him; he was entombed.

Removing the hood, his eyes adjusted to the accommodation; it was a dark, cold cell with a tiny window. A hard wooden litter with a rough blanket and straw-filled pillow made up the sleeping arrangements. His ablutions amounted to a hole in the floor and an adjacent cold water tap. During his stay with little food and water and hardly any human contact, it was his worst nightmare. Sleep came spasmodically when his body needed it. Robert did not know how long his confinement would be for. Human comforts were almost zero and time passed extremely slowly. He put himself into a daily routine of exercise. Press-ups and anything he could think of to keep body and soul going seemed the right thing to do even if bloody boring. Counting the measured paces between walls was the only thing he enjoyed, but it made him hungry and thirsty. He had to remind himself this was only an exercise, but it seemed so surreal.

After a week he thought he was going mad. He was shocked when an extra blanket was passed through to him, with the words,

"Don't soil it." He found himself actually saying, "thank you." Wrapping himself in the warm freshly laundered item, reminded him of home comforts. The only respite from his overwhelming sense of boredom was when his food or water was passed to him through a small hinged trap door. Whoever his captives were they timed everything to the minute. Early morning cold bowl of greasy soup and a stale bread roll. Midday; limited drinking water, never enough to quench his thirst. He would supplement it from the water tap, but it tasted foul.

When eventually the basic evening meal came, it never looked very appetising but was consumed with relish. This was the set routine, and he so looked forward to each occasion. If you are in a constant state of hunger, it's amazing what even the poorest of nourishment is something to look forward to. He expected to be dragged from his cell at any time and be physically abused, but it never happened.

By now, Southward knew within minutes what time of the day it was. He actually looked forward to the odd grunt from his jailors. Trying to make conversation was a waste of time, there was never any positive response. Keeping up a fitness regime got harder and harder as time progressed. Lying on his tiny bed with his knees draw under his chin, he would often wake in the middle of the night.

It would have been so easy to end his nightmare by triggering the alarm on the wall near the door.

The course was to test his metal, and by God, it certainly did. On more than one occasion, he approached the alarm with intent, what stopped him was the thought of failing the course. During the arduous process to become a commander of one of Her Majesties mightiest warships, he had not failed at anything that had been thrown at him. His movements were monitored by infrared camera 24/7. Should his condition deteriorate to such an extent his handlers were concerned, the incarceration would be suspended immediately. Finally, after 16 days, the door was opened, and two training officers entered the cell and shook his hand.

"Well done, Sir," was his greeting. In total shock, Captain Southward was unable to offer up any response other than demanding a hug and a strong cup of tea.

After a hot shower a change of clothes and a light meal, Southward was taken to be checked over by the doctor. He was then escorted to the debrief room by an Army Sergeant Major and a Corporal.

"Please follow me, Sir," were the only words spoken. He had no idea if they were the same burly guards that had been watching over him from the beginning. They opened the door, saluted, turned on their heels and marched back up the corridor. On entering the room, he noticed three officers sat at a large square table. One was Army, one Navy and one Royal Air Force.

"Come in, Captain Southward. Please be seated,"

The Major began, "I am Major Mark Johnson, this is Surgeon Lieutenant Commander Brian Cooper who you have already met and to my left Group Captain Tom Buckingham."

"Well, I bet you are glad that ordeal is over." said the Army Captain.

Still, in a somewhat dazed state, Robert replied, "Well, it certainly wasn't the best experience I have ever had."

He wasn't in much of a mind to engage in a lengthy conversation and let the Major do most of the talking. He went on,

"It may be of some comfort to know, this particular course is mainly reserved for Special Forces, and some of them fail. Good people but not good enough for the likes of the S.A.S, or S.B.S. You have distinguished yourself by your endurance; can I offer you a job in the Army?"

This broke the ice and Robert Southward drained of emotion with tears in his eyes along with the three officers chuckling, had a good belly laugh.

"You have earned a special week's leave to adjust before

you go back to your naval duties. I suggest you take full advantage of it. We have gathered a lot of information during the time this course has been running. One reoccurring factor shows itself often, some gung-ho candidates have gone straight back to other gruelling challenges and found it hard going."

Looking directly at Captain Robert Southward, it was he who avoided eye contact.

"Captain," said, Brian Cooper. "I have checked you over, and under the circumstances, all seems well enough. As expected, you have lost weight and are a little anaemic, but your urine shows no cause for concern. Your blood samples will be analysed, and you will be notified of the results. I will put you on a short course of tablets that will allow you to feel a lot less lethargic and get your wellbeing back on track. Try not to do too much running until your body has adjusted to having a lot more freedom of movement. You will feel cramps at times, so keep your body temperature just above normal at all times."

"So, these uppers, will I become addicted to them?"

The surgeon lieutenant kept a straight face, "Oh, I do hope not, they cost an arm and a leg, and the navy can't afford to turn you into a drug addict."

Robert smiled.

"Do you have any questions?"

"Just one, I expected to be roughed up while in captivity that didn't happen. Why not?"

The three officers looked at each other "Well, perhaps I am best equipped to answer that."

It was Group Captain Buckingham's turn. "This

establishment, like all others is constantly under review by the bean counters. Special Services, R.A.F. and Navy pilots along with Army and Navy specialists, undergo psychological, verbal and physical abuse training. This involves greater health and safety issues and costs considerably more money to administer. It is deemed unnecessary for most naval staff to be subject to, as the prospect of capture and confinement by a hostile power is considered a very low risk."

In the confines of his cabin that training seemed a lifetime ago and the words "Very low risk," seemed woefully inadequate to his situation at hand. The relative comfort he had here was something to dwell on. He had not been physically or mentally abused and was being treated with some respect. As far as he knew, his men were safe, although the pirate leader was unwilling to furnish any information regarding casualties. The confinement training, he had experienced would prove to be of great benefit over the coming weeks. It was anybody's guess as to how long he would be detained but assumed it would not end anytime soon. Captain Robert Southward was a professional naval officer and would carry out his duties to the best of his ability, regardless of the outcome.

Chapter 23

Monday, 12th February 2018. 12.00 hrs
Control room on-board H.M.S Astute.

"This is the control room ship's address Red Fox speaking.
For your information, this submarine is now totally under
my command. This is not an exercise, so for your own
safety and that of your Captain, obey all orders given to you
by my men." He paused.

"If any of you are intent on making audible mechanical
noise to give our position away, don't. You will be found,
eliminated and body bagged for the deep freeze. This is
now a hunted submarine, not just by the armed forces of
the United Kingdom but probably the Americans as well.
Rest assured the recapture or destruction of this sub will
be paramount to your government, the former will never
happen." He paused again to let his instructions sink in.
"You have my word that if co-operation is maintained
with my crew while we are here, all R.N. personnel will be
released unharmed. Failure of this mission is not an option
and discipline will be maintained at all times, comply with
the instructions given to you."

The British sailors listened to every word with horror
and bewilderment.

"For exercise, for exercise" had not been broadcast, had that been a mistake? That's certainly what most of the crew were hoping to be the case.

Confined to their mess, Fleet Chief Les Macdonald, (Mac) turned to Charge Chief Stu Baker,

"If I didn't know better, I would swear this was an S.B.S. exercise."

Mac had been in submarines for most of his naval career since finishing training at H.M.S.Raleigh and Fisguard in Torpoint Cornwall. Drafted to the submarine H.M.S. Courageous, he had fought tooth and nail to be assigned to a surface ship. However, he quickly adapted to submarine life, the camaraderie and the extra pay made it worthwhile. He excelled in his training as ships engineer and gained promotion rapidly. Mac was known for his cool approach to all situations and had been recommended for officer training. After making fleet chief, he felt content in that role; he considered it his comfort zone. Enjoying the banter with both the senior and junior ratings made the job all the more interesting; he was still one of the lads at heart that suited him.

"Stu, pass the word to the boys. No heroics until we have a better idea of what's going on. God knows what these people intend to do."

The Russian guard at the door spoke and understood perfect English. Stu's instructions would spread through the crew rapidly, no need to introduce any strong-arm tactics at this moment in time. The fact that Captain Southward had not been allowed to address his crew further meant he must be now under duress or worse. All the R.N personnel were confined to their respective messes or bunk spaces. They would only be allowed access to the heads (toilets), or assigned duties at their work stations when required. Handcuffs would be used by the guards when individuals were transited through the boat.

Mac whispered,

"Russians almost sure of it"

Stu nodded. Mac had been on an exchange visit to a Soviet Naval base at Ostrovnoy Murmansk years ago. After the thawing of the cold war, arrangements were made for America and the U.K to conduct exchange visits. At the time, Chief Macdonald was surprised to be allowed access to a Victor 3 class submarine. Although old technology, he was impressed with the condition and good working order of the vessel. Amazed at the areas he was allowed to visit, he could only imagine how formidable the modern Russian submarines at sea, now were. It had been assumed the Soviet navy was behind the west in technology and build capability, and it proved not to be so.

The exchanges with the Russian federation petered out when a new hard-line president was elected. Final reports were written, and the Admiralty hierarchy digested the information gained. In the first instance, they were keen but became increasingly worried about what could be gained by a potential enemy. A sigh of relief came over the Admirals when the exchange visits were stopped.

Dmitri Sparrov continued his address,

"I can assure you your Captain is perfectly safe in his cabin; he is unharmed but will be restricted there for the rest of the time we are on-board."

No amount of training had prepared them for this situation. It was totally unique. They lip read or talked in whispers. Silence was the golden rule.

"Stu, pinch me to let me know this is all a bad dream."

"Mate I don't need to, what the fuck is going on is anyone's guess, but I certainly have bad vibes about it. We have to hope the Captain has a handle on the situation and saves our bacon."

The mood was sombre; their fate hung in the balance, could this so-called Red Fox be trusted to keep his word? Or were they all going to die?

Both of Southward's subordinate naval officers had been confined to their quarters, effectively surplus to requirements. Handcuffed to their bunks, their only exercise would be an occasional escorted walk to the heads. The control and manoeuvring rooms were the main focus of the Pirate force. All aspects of the boat could be monitored and maintained from these compartments. There was no need for anyone to be in the torpedo space until required. For the senior rates left to their own devices but heavily guarded, it was important to instil confidence in the junior ratings. Inwardly the chiefs were alarmed and worried at the situation but totally helpless and could only comply with the orders they were given. These men were highly disciplined and would do whatever it took to keep morale at a high level; survival was paramount. In the hopeless situation they found themselves in for the time being it seemed appropriate to comply with their captors. At least the British sailors were being treated reasonably well. However, they were left in no doubt as to the outcome if they did not play ball.

So, the submarine functioned as normal as conditions would allow. All systems were monitored and adjusted accordingly, the Pirates were quick learners, and obviously had a good working knowledge of Astute. The computer systems were so good at controlling the submarine, and in this mode, they would make any adjustments necessary unless overridden. To the watchful eyes of the pirates, it seemed incredible that things were going so well. Their orders from Red Fox were to take whatever measures were deemed necessary to maintain the boat's integrity. This would include coercion and brute force if necessary, for the time being, this was not a requirement.

Back in the senior rates mess, you could cut the air with a knife. There wasn't much appetite for bravery, and one guard outside the door was all that was required to keep the peace.

Mac Phillips whispered to Stu Baker,

"What do you think the chances are of us surviving?"

"I wish I knew mate, two of the junior rates are missing, just hope they managed to get ashore. There was an awful lot of gunfire when these pirates stormed on-board, so it's anybody's guess as to the fate of some of our boys. You know these bastards won't answer any questions; I got a jab in the ribs from the butt of his gun for just asking what the hell they thought they were up to. Drawing a line across his throat was enough for me not to pursue the matter; his menacing eyes told it all. Wearing those black balaclavas, the entire time makes their appearance even more menacing."

"Yeah, tough bunch all right and they seem to know what they are doing. The only thing they are a bit wary of is engaging the Triso. They headed straight for the manuals, and it won't be too long before they have learned how to operate the systems."

"Well I'm bloody sure they won't get any help from me"

"No, me neither, they can go fuck spiders. This so-called Red Fox, who runs the show, is an elusive character; we never see him."

"No, I wonder if the Captain gets that privilege; after all, his entire cabin is so small, conversations, no should I say orders could be given from outside the door."

"You're right I bet the boss has a gun at his temple from one of the buggers when that happens, they have some fearsome-looking weapons."

"Do you think we should do something?"

"Oh yeah, what do you suggest? With these bloody handcuffs on most of the time, it's useless. The Ruskies are burly, and their guns aren't toys, I have no doubt they will shoot anyone who tries something on."

"What about sabotage then?"

"Good thinking but what? Are you going to head-butt the control panel or throw a toilet roll at the guard during ablutions? They haven't even left a spanner lying around its bloody hopeless. We are up shit creek. Stuart, we must bide our time and see what unfolds, the junior rates are our priority try and keep their spirits up."

In the junior rates mess, the concerns were great; they were all rendered surplus to requirements and had little or no part to play. Handcuffed and only allowed to the heads occasionally their plight seemed hopeless. Two of their mates were missing; God knows where they had ended up. And so, it was the pirate crew was gaining more and more knowledge about running the submarine and the British ever more fearful as to their future, or the lack of it. This was a handpicked selection of officers and ratings with a wealth of knowledge between them. Under normal circumstances, they would carry out their orders without question. Whoever or whatever was considered a threat would be dealt with, no matter what. The trouble was the threat was from within, and there appeared to be no solution to it.

Chapter 24

Tuesday, 13th February 2018. 010.00hrs
On-board in the senior rating's mess (dining room).

Charge Chief Stuart Baker sat handcuffed and shackled to the steel leg of the dining table. In front of him were the operating manuals for Trisonic imaging and Hovertrack Ivor Pushkin and Nikolay Popov were intently studying the contents. Stu was so nervous his hands were shaking with fear. In the whole of his naval career, he had never experienced anything like this, and he was a worried man. Ivor was the first to speak,

"Can I get you a cup of your excellent coffee, Chief Baker?"

"How do you know my name and no, I would not like a cup."

"Come on Stuart your subs manifest has all we need to know about who and what is on board. That's one thing you Brits are good at, keeping records, especially at sea. You know your submarines and ours are very much alike, oh! Yes, and the fact that we steal secrets from one another keeps it that way."

The two Russian's chuckled, Nikolay made two cups of coffee and placed them on the table.

Stuart so wanted a cup of coffee; they had only been given water since becoming captives on their own submarine. It was obvious to him why he was being softened up but would not willingly take part in their mind games. He sat there in silence.

Looking directly at the chief, Ivor said, "So you are the operator of this amazing technology."

"What technology are you talking about? I am an engineer, and with my team, we maintain and run the machinery on the submarine, that's all."

Nikolay rubbed his chin, "Do you want to see your family again? I certainly want to see mine. I have a wife and two sons."

Chief Stuart Baker had a vivid image of his loving wife Jenny and their beautiful twin daughters Ella and Katrina. Living in their family home in Higher Compton, not more than 30 miles away, they were never far from his thoughts, going about their daily routine the girls would have been dropped off at school in Eggbuckland and his wife would be busy at her job in the local post office. Completely oblivious as to her husband's fate, it was a life she had adapted to and got on with it, always looking forward to his next round of leave.

"You know Chief, my engineers will eventually master the equipment anyway, but you can operate it quickly and more efficiently, that's initially what we want."

With those words ringing in his ears, it brought Stuart sharply back into focus.

"You are a dedicated chief P.O, who would never betray his country; however, you are now in a situation that you have no control over. Your Captain has issued orders that you and the rest of the crew are to co-operate with us." Ivor Pushkin waved his hand across the manual to express what was expected. "We will leave you for a short while to ponder your fate."

With that, the 2 Russians picked up their coffee and left the mess sliding the door tightly shut.

Now sat there in silence not able to move more than a few inches, the chief could not contemplate what was about to happen.

"Oh, shit they want me to run the systems, how stupid to put the operator's name in the daily ship's log, that's how they know I'm trained in their use." But then who would have envisaged the present circumstances. The operative and the times had been recorded while they were on the training exercise.

The first reaction was that he would not comply in a million years, no Sir. He thought about his wife and children, what would these morons do if he did not co-operate? He did not doubt that the men who had just left him to ponder his fate, were committed, tough and brutal if need be. He now wished he had accepted a coffee to steady his nerves a bit. The wait for them to return seemed an age but was only ten minutes. The mess door slid open, and the two burly pirates entered, he looked at both of them the signs were not good. One of them had replaced his industrial work gloves with thick leather ones; they were going to beat him into submission.

"Now Charge Chief Baker you have had enough time to consider our demands, what is your answer?"

"I will not do your dirty work for you." he snarled.

"Oh, that's a pity, if you are going to sacrifice your life, remember it will have been for nothing, we know Fleet Chief Macdonald can also operate the systems." Popov was holding a roll of 2-inch wide black gaff tape; he tore off a strip and placed it over Stuart's mouth and wound it several times around his head. They were going to beat the shit out of him for sure; he began to feel nauseous as he tried to control his breathing through his nose. He could feel his heart racing and his blood pressure rising.

Pushkin placed a small long thin box on the table and removed a syringe that contained a purple looking liquid. He took the plastic protective cover off the needle and ejected a small amount onto a tissue that instantly stained it a dark brown. Popov had now positioned himself behind the victim and roughly rolled up his right sleeve. Grasping his arm in a vice-like grip, he waited for Pushkin to use the syringe with its evil-looking contents.

"Stuart, you have one chance and one chance only to save yourself. This is a particularly nasty substance that will slowly devour your internal organs as it travels around your bloodstream. It will be a slow and excruciating death, and you will have plenty of time to reflect on your decision. When we drag Macdonald in here, he will witness you lying on the floor writhing in agony in your death throes. I am confident he will not wish to share the same fate as you." Pushkin searched for a vein in the crook of the elbow and pressed the tip of the needle against the skin.

"Now for the last time will you run the stealth systems and stay alive? Your Captain will need you when we leave and hand back the submarine. Nod your head if you agree," was all he said. He placed his thumb over the plunger, ready to administer the deadly virus. Violently nodding his head, Chief P.O. Baker passed out, slumped forward and wet himself.

"Nikolay, make some coffee. I am sure our friend will be glad of a mug when he comes to." Ivor removed the tape from around the prostrate figure's head. "He made the right choice. I didn't want to kill him; he has a family, as we all do. In his position, I probably would have made the same choice, live to fight another day." They sat in silence, enjoying the coffee. When Chief Baker finally came around, he was relieved to find he was still in the land of the living.

"Ah Stuart, you are awake there's a coffee for you."

On this occasion, he grasped it between his cuffed shaking hands and sipped it with relish.

"Now, when you go back to your bunk space, I want you to tell Fleet Chief Macdonald of your harrowing experience. We will need him for back up if you become incapacitated. You can tell him if his services are required, we expect the same co-operation on pain of death, do I make myself clear?"

Stuart just nodded, these people had the upper hand, and he did not doubt their ruthlessness. He would tell his colleague word for how it is.

Back in the confines of the Chief P.O's bunk space, there was an air of hopelessness. "My God, you look awful, Stu what did they want?" asked Mac.

"They want us to run the Triso and Hovertrack."

"Well, they can go fuck spiders we're not doing that."

"Oh, you think not? I have just come within a few seconds of an awful death, and you would have been dragged in to watch me go."

Stuart went on to explain the treatment he had been subjected too. Mac sat there listening fearfully of what he was being told about his own fate if he didn't comply. "Is there nothing we can do to stop this madness?"

"Other than commit Hari Kari somehow, no I don't think we can, we are up shit creek without a paddle. Remember we are the hunted now by our own side, they won't let this sub leave territorial waters."

"If only we had some guidance from the Captain."

"Well you can't reason with these people; they are in control and have made it quite clear he is off-limits. What the Russian leader has in mind is anyone's guess; the whole lot of them are not to be underestimated. I think they would be able to master the systems fairly quickly without us, so, for the time being, we co-operate, Stu."

"It might be better to be destroyed by our own side; at least we take these bastards with us." Fleet Chief Les Macdonald went back to pretending to read his book. What more could be done?

Chapter 25

Wednesday 14th February 2018 Admiral Neilson's office
Naval Command centre
Time 06-30hrs

Admiral Simon Neilson, stood with his back to the
polished mahogany table, hands clasped behind his back.
He was studying a map of the world on a large flat plasma
screen. He moved forward to a consul that housed the
latest computer hardware.

Earlier, he had entered a code known only to himself
and his adjutant to activate the system. With a wireless
mouse, he moved the pointer on the map to an area of
the British Isles. With a click, he zoomed in to his area of
interest. Once he had an overview of the Plymouth area,
the Hoe and breakwater he zoomed out slightly to enhance
the channel at a distance of twenty nautical miles.

Suddenly a small green dot appeared with reference
points and a data hologram on the screen. This indicated
the last known position of the submarine H.M.S. Astute.
This latest technology from America allowed the top brass
to know exactly where the surface ship and to a much
lesser degree the submarine fleet were at any given time.
Because of the covert nature of submarines, they were

monitored as being in 200 square mile boxes; these were grid mapped across the oceans of the world. Because Astute had not left coastal waters, her exact location was known. It was updated, by links to military satellite and GCHQ Cheltenham, constantly. Ship to shore communications from and to the naval headquarters was instant. The system had been designed to resist all efforts to hack into it.

Because of the clandestine nature of the submarine service, exact locations were usually never known. In peacetime, the sub would report in on a pre-arranged date and time with coded flash traffic. At periscope depth, the onboard W.T office would transmit or receive any messages coming their way. Decoding by computer was instantaneous, and the Captain could respond accordingly. This would allow the brief monitoring of the location of the sub by Northwood and GCHQ Cheltenham, through a frequency reserved strictly for them.

Of course, any submarine would only linger long enough to transmit or receive information. Technology moved at a quickening pace, and the Russians were always eager to listen in to any high or low-frequency transmissions. Their spy ships scattered around the oceans of the world, were particularly good at what they did, gathering information. The west truly did not know what the enemy would deploy next and how sophisticated it would be, but the game of hide and seek was conducted 24/7. In wartime, our nuclear submarines would conduct operations on their own. The Captain could respond or not according to the situation. Only life-threatening emergencies or serious mechanical failure would force the officer in charge to seek assistance;

in truth, this would be an extraordinary occurrence. Submariners are a breed apart from the crews of surface ships. A greater degree of secrecy has to be maintained at all times. The clandestine operations that the underwater vessels undertake are one of the many roles they perform.

In Northwood, the mainframe package was five floors below in a bomb-proof shelter that was sealed from the rest of the complex. In times of hostilities, this would be from where operations would be directed. Only the electrical and mechanical umbilical cords needed to run the system penetrated the entombment. A suite of computer terminals was installed and would be manned twenty-four hours a day, every day. The constantly changing information with regards to the whereabouts of the whole British fleet would be funnelled here. The readiness of combat vessels including missile and general weapon status, downtime forecasts and a whole range of information would be gathered.

The naval computer operators would sift the data coming in. The Admiral and his team, plus civilian advisors, would be able to make on the spot decisions as to what needed to be done. Titanium blast-proof doors provided the only way in and out of this space-age technical marvel. It could stand all but a direct hit by a nuclear blast. The building of this facility was sanctioned by Margret Thatcher, prime minister at the time. Having been advised by the defence minister of the woefully inadequate communications network highlighted by the Falklands war, things had to improve. It was nothing short of a miracle that during the excursion to the South Atlantic to retake the Falkland Islands we actually succeeded. At times with the thin line of military traffic stretched between here, Gibraltar, the Azores and the Falkland Islands, communications, at times were sketchy. After the war ended, the funding was agreed to centralise the whole Navy operations, Northwood was the obvious choice. Subsequently, over the years, communications were regularly upgraded. Today's network was second to none throughout the western world.

The Admiral in charge had experienced a chequered naval career. In the cold war, he had been involved in many culvert operations involving the submarines under his command. Once he had run silently near a Russian Naval base, monitoring the comings and goings of various vessels while staying out of the way of a menacing enemy.

His thoughts were focused on what might be happening within the confines of Astute. The tension must be unbelievable, was all his men still alive, probably at the very least incapacitated. How was Robert Southward, the Captain dealing with the situation? If only he knew more about the enemy. Intelligence gathering was at full stretch but what had been uncovered so far was sparse. This situation was unprecedented. Not in 91 years had there been piracy or a mutiny on one of the Royal Navy's warships. Could there have been some collusion by crew members? He dismissed this thought; the crew had been handpicked for the trials of the latest underwater technological marvel.

The Chief of Staff's thoughts were interrupted by a light rap on the door. Blake Channing walked in with a folder in his hand. He placed it on the table adjacent to the Admirals chair.

"The latest sit-rep Sir, as formulated by rear Admiral

Stephen Jennings. His team had interviewed the shore billeted crew and all civilians that had been involved with Astute's capture. The one overriding fact that had emerged, whenever the enemy conversed with each other, it was by way of very good if sometimes broken English. It was difficult to obtain factual evidence to the supposed nationality of the raiders. At the time of the piracy just by chance, there was a senior rating on the dockside, having a smoke; he was convinced the mother language could be Russian, certainly Eastern Bock. The senior rate had been engaged in a correspondence course and picked up some of the vowels from the orders being given by the pirates."

"Okay Blake that could be of value."

"The team are ready when you want to convene the meeting, Sir."

"Very good. Show them in at 0700 as planned."

The Admiral returned to his chair and opened the folder. Sipping his coffee, he read the report that contained the latest factual information regarding the demise of Astute.

Chapter 1 The Crew of Astute aboard and billeted ashore
Surviving British Officers and Ratings are known to be on board, as listed.
Officers and Ratings not on-board billeted in H.M.S.Drake barracks.
Debrief of those crew members continuing.

Evidence obtained from dockside
Considerable small arms and rifle fire in evidence, casualties external of submarine known.

The submarine Astute, overrun by an estimated force of 12-20 black-clad people, the crew were overwhelmed by the use of stun grenades and instantaneous gas inhalation. Origin and status of chemicals used, as yet unknown. Most crew probably unable to initialise the Drager oxygen breathing system. Extent and condition of causalities on-board unable to assess, considered highly likely.

Casualties (Naval)
Sub Lieutenant Chris Barker, a bullet wound to the leg, not life-threatening.
Charge Chief Brian Foster, facial injuries not life-threatening.
Petty Officer Arthur Squires, fractured leg.
Leading Seaman Ryan Hawes, back injuries and broken bones, serious but not life-threatening.
Junior Rating, James McNally death by drowning

Casualties Ministry of Defence Police (River)
Sargent James Walker, died from bullet wounds sustained.
Constable Richard Dreyfus, died from bullet wounds sustained.
Constable Barry Davis shot and wounded. Plus, superficial injuries not thought to be life-threatening.

Casualties (Civilian)
Wharf Master Peter Shepard, presumed drowned, body not yet recovered.
Rigger Brian Davis, superficial gunshot wound not life-threatening.
Ocean-going tug 'Grateful,' damaged at the waterline by R.P.G's subsequently sunk.
M.O.D. police launch, Calibre, wheelhouse wrecked by machine gunfire.

Possibilities of enemy personnel being shot and injured by M.O.D. River police no relevant evidence available.

Strength of enemy opposition estimated to be four teams of five men. Fwd torpedo loading hatch, control room and engine room hatches used for forced entry. Some machinery of a heavy nature transferred to the submarine by barge or boat.

Dredger, Thor Valiant sunk at the entrance to 4 basin trapping duty frigate H.M.S Cumberland.

Admiral Neilson took a sharp intake of breath. "Bastards, these pirates are ruthless killers." The Admiral read the list of the on-board crew who were effectively now prisoners. He knew some of the officers and ratings personally. "Poor souls what must they be going through?"

Chapter 2 Ordinance: Intelligence

Confirmed, 2 in number nuclear warheads unaccounted for from the Russian arsenal.

Semi-automatic rifles used during assault quantity unknown, assessed as considerable. Handguns in evidence, assessed as considerable.

R.P.G launchers quantity unknown, assessed as at least two.

'Well, I'm amazed our people have gleaned that information already. What the hell are the intentions of these madmen?' He continued reading the report.

Coded information picked up by GCHQ transmitted from Astute's W.T. office suggests nuclear devices are on board. Intelligence suggests the enemy are of Russian or Ukrainian origin. No individual as yet identified, shortlist of over one hundred suspects formulated.

Chapter 3: Containment

H.M.S. Somerset, (type 22 frigate), positioned 30 nautical miles South East of Astute on a training exercise. Captain briefed as to the situation, status top secret. Ordered to monitor subs movements by dipping sonar only, from the ship's helicopter.

H.M.S. Talent (Trafalgar class submarine). Southwestern approaches, Captain briefed as to the situation, status top secret. Ordered to silent running, stealth position within 10 nautical miles, south-west of Astute's known position. Three Merlin Mk2 sub-hunting helicopters out of Culdrose on standby. Roborough airport, Plymouth, Devon, north of the city can provide refuelling facilities. Self-supporting Naval teams in situ at this location.

The Admiral read and digested the information. Well, the sub is effectively boxed in, or is it? I have all this military power at my disposal, and it could be rendered unusable by the actions of the pirates. Very clever indeed, he thought, is it just piracy for financial gain or something else? These men are more than just thieves, the secrecy and planning involved in an operation like this, must mean they have some sinister ulterior plan. He was deep in thought, trying to imagine the scenario being acted out on board the boat.

His thoughts were interrupted by his adjutant. He looked at his watch, 07.00hrs on the dot. Admiral Neilson continued to read the report as the elite of the armed forces were shown to their seats by Captain Channing.

"Blake any updated information I need to know about?"

"No Sir nothing of importance, as per your instructions, exclusion zone now in operation. Civilian commercial and military briefed accordingly. Instructions had been given to effectively avoid the exclusion zone in the vicinity of Astute. Small fishery protection vessels are patrolling, unarmed. They pose no threat to the submarine."

The press had been told a quantity of ordinance of an explosive nature had been found. Unstable and in a dangerous state, it was probably World War 2 munitions. It was a plan that had been hastily put together in Whitehall and was considered the best option in response to the imposed restricted area. A navy diving team trained in underwater hazards was being assembled in Devonport. Reporters would soon see the weather proven Dutch barge heading out to address the supposed problem

"Why was our duty frigate in the basin and not on the dockside?"

"Well Sir, it would appear some minor repairs were being made to one of the communication masts on the ship. The basin crane was the best option to carry out the work. The estimated time to complete the job was three hours it took four."

"Where and what was the ships Lynx helicopter doing all this time?"

"Sir, it was in the hanger for routine maintenance, it took two hours to get her airborne. Not apparent what it could have done other than assist in the rescue of the injured personnel. The Frigate's Captain had no authority to attack the submarine, the pirates got lucky."

The Admiral looked away, not best pleased.

At 07.02 the Admiral looked up,

"Good morning gentlemen, please be seated, before I ask you where we are with a rescue/retrieval plan for my submarine and crew, I need to cascade some information. We now face a grave danger; any thoughts of destroying the submarine in its present location cannot be justified. GCHQ has told us via communication from Astute; nuclear devices have been placed aboard. I assume the radio operator has been coerced into sending this information, it cannot be confirmed, and they could be bluffing. However! If true, we have to believe they have been adapted to fit our torpedoes or cruise missiles."

The assembled team realised this was a different situation now than the one for which they had planned.

"Our submarine is within twenty nautical miles of Plymouth. With a population of over 260.000, we cannot risk a disaster. With a main Cornish town, villages and hamlets that come within the effective area, we are probably talking 500,000 possible evacuees. What these people on board my sub have in mind is anybody's guess, but we must plan for the worst scenario. Evacuation may become necessary, but at the moment we are trying to deal covertly with this and not alert the press or alarm the public. It's unimaginable that anyone would use such devices to kill and maim so many people. But then it seemed unimaginable the submarine could be stolen in the first place. We are still not totally clear about who the terrorists are and what they intend to do." The Admiral hesitated and took a deep breath,

"To our knowledge, there have been four fatalities and

six wounded outboard of the submarine, and they are all our people. We have absolutely no idea what has happened inboard and can only speculate as to the wellbeing of the crew. There is no medical specialist of our own onboard, some of them can administer basic first aid, but that's about it. I would hazard a guess; the pirates have at least one medical operative, in case their own men need treatment."

The Admiral removed his glasses and carefully placed them on the desk.

"Well, people that's the latest situation as we know it."

Chapter 26

Wednesday, 14th February 2018. 4.40 pm.
Doctor Ivan Cherkesov's office, Medical Centre, Moscow

Cherkesov was sat at his desk in his private office.

"How the hell did I let things get into this state," he muttered. He read again the list of spiralling debt that he could no longer ignore. Creditors, some of them not very nice people who wanted payment, were chasing him. Especially his gambling debtors. He had been robbing Peter to pay Paul for some time, but now bank of Peter was empty. Pressing the intercom, Alina answered right away,

"Yes, Doctor?"

"Has Ms Resnetnikov arrived yet? He barked.

"No, she is 25 minutes late."

"Yes, I know that. Have you tried to get hold of her?"

"Yes, indeed three times since her appointment time expired, but it just goes to her answerphone."

"Well try one more time. If she doesn't answer, leave a message that the clinic is closing and she must make another appointment tomorrow. I have matters to attend to elsewhere."

The line went dead. Rude old bugger Alina thought, probably thinking of the consultation fee he has lost. She dialled the number once more and got the same response. Leaving a polite message for Valeriya Resnetnikov was all she could do. She pressed the intercom,

"Sorry Doctor, I could not get a response from your last patient of the day."

"Okay well you might as well go home; I will deal with her personally — what a waste of my time. I could have seen another paying client. This clinic doesn't pay for itself; you know."

"No Doctor I am well aware of that, but it's not my fault."

Alina thought to herself, on one of these occasions I will tell Cherkesov where he can stick his job. She knew this was not the time, he did pay well and it allowed her to live without fear of being evicted from her apartment, the rent was always paid on time, and she had enough left for food and clothes. The wealth that she had recently acquired was a worry, and she did not want to rely on it. Could it be snatched away by the authorities if Nadim Babachenko her benefactor turned out to be a crook? Her meagre savings could replace the small amounts she had used. Alina logged off her computer, tidied her desk and locked the drawers. She put on her coat. There was no point trying to engage in conversation with the Doctor. Her instructions had been explicit as they always were at the end of the day.

Walking out into the early evening, twilight Alina buttoned up her thick coat. It was beginning to snow, and the biting chilly wind made her gasp. It was just above freezing which wasn't bad for this time of the year. Sometimes the temperature went down to minus 10. As she hurried home, she recalled some of the unpleasant memories encountered since she had worked for Cherkesov. On occasions, he had made innuendoes that she had found abhorrent. Naively she had thought the expensive gifts he had given her was as a thank you for the excellent work she was doing, in keeping his practice running smoothly. It was only when he made it quite plain, he expected to get into her knickers in return that she politely refused any more. There had been young female assistants who had come and gone. She suspected at least one or more had succumbed to his charming and generous ways. No doubt paid off handsomely for their silence.

"I hate that man, I should report him for sexual harassment but who would believe me, he's an eminent specialist. Thank God it's Wednesday only two more days in that pig's presence."

She would not allow herself to get upset at the way he treated her. Craftily Alina had become invaluable to Cherkesov; he relied on her to do just about everything. The fact was she could easily steal roubles from the business accounts without detection, but her moral upbringing would not allow her to do that. It was obvious to her that the Doctor was creaming off quite a lot for whatever purposes. That was his problem if confronted by the Federal Tax Service; her records were perfectly in order. If uncovered, his secret dealings that Alina knew nothing about would bankrupt the business.

Cherkesov retired to his inner sanctum and locked the door. Again, he poured over his troubling debt mountain. He went to his private cabinet and took a litre bottle of Vodka out. Pouring a generous glass with a small tonic top-up, he drank. The soothing liquor had a calming effect. What to do, what to do? Unbeknown to his wife the large house that had been the family retreat for her and the three children was mortgaged up to the hilt. Catherine Cherkesov had never worked since they got married. Devoted to looking after their beautiful home and bringing up their three daughters was what she enjoyed doing. She doted on her hardworking husband, who never questioned her spending habits. Private schooling, nice cars and expensive holidays were what she had come to expect. Shopping expeditions and endless rounds of lunches within her ladies' circle was the norm; they were all married to high flying professional men. Charitable work gave the ladies the satisfying comfort of knowing they were helping the less fortunate members of society. In reality, they were all selfish bitches who didn't give a hoot for the working classes.

The Doctor was on his second glass of Vodka when the phone rang.

"Hello, Ivan. So sorry I couldn't make my appointment, how are you?"

"Val why didn't you ring my secretary and tell her you were not coming; I could have squeezed another client in who pays?"

"I completely forgot about it darling until I heard my voicemail, by then it was too late, are you really mad at me?" she purred. "Come over, and I will make it up to you. I have just stepped out of the bath, just wrapped in a large towel."

Cherkesov smirked, "Well, I am very busy, but I could

take time out, I suppose." "That's a good boy I will order your favourite Beef Stroganoff and Blini, and I will have the Coulibiac salmon loaf. Get here within the hour, and I will have a steaming bath ready and lots more besides."

"You are incorrigible," he said laughingly "I should be going to my youngest daughter's school play but what the heck. That's what I pay my wife for. I will ring and tell her I have an emergency distressed patient to see, quite near the truth actually." They both chuckled.

Ivan Cherkesov's financial problems would have to wait; the thought of having wild sex with his mistress was uppermost in his mind. He had set her up in a cosy apartment in the expensive Khamovniki district of Moscow. Divorced with one son who lived with his father, it was an ideal situation. Valeria was very discreet but made financial demands on him all the time. It cost him a small fortune, but he wrote most of it off as business expenses. At one stage, she had worked for him as an assistant in his practice and flounced her femininity right from the start.

After having worked there for a month, she was called into his private office for her job appraisal. It was not at all good, and she ended up in tears when he told her she had to go. Not willing to accept that, she grabbed his bottom and suggested she could be useful in other ways.

For Cherkesov, that was the beginning of amazing sexual encounters, including oral where she would fellate him to ejaculation, something his wife would never do. Alina was getting suspicious, and the thought of his spouse finding out was a real concern. Valeria didn't want to be stuck in the clinic anyway. Living with her mother was bad enough. They argued all the time, so when it was suggested she would be set up in a nice apartment, she jumped at the chance and became a kept woman.

In the taxi to his mistress, Ivan was excited at the thought of what was to come. Sex with his wife had never been anything other than the occasional favour on her part, or to produce their offspring. After the birth of their third daughter, it was just high days or holidays. The thought of leaving his wife never entered his head, for her sake and that of the children things would remain as they were. However, what Valeria had awakened in him sexually was a new lease of life; the trouble was he was deeply in love with her. She had introduced him to things that heightened the experience that he had only read about in magazines. While watching a porn film and not at all shy, she would use sex toys to make herself come when he had climaxed before her. Quite often watching her in raptures would get him aroused and he would enter her and have a second orgasm. In the taxi, his male hormones were in overdrive, and for the moment, it allowed him to forget his problems. He smirked, and muttered,

"I really do have the best of both worlds if only I can sort out the financial side of things? I will get to grips with that soon."

Lying in the arms of Valeria Resnetnikov totally spent, Ivan Cherkesov slept like a baby. The food, wine and sex had been exhausting for him. She gently untwined herself, put on her red silk linen-lined dressing gown and silently crept onto the balcony and lit a cigarette. It was a beautiful if somewhat chilly evening; she pulled her thick dressing gown around her and inhaled deeply. The smell of tobacco smoke drifted into the bedroom and awakened him.

"Val, how many times do I have to tell you smoking is very bad for your health?"

"I know darling but other than you I have no other pleasures in life."

What more could he say he didn't want an argument, looking at his watch it was nearly 9.30 pm he would have to go soon.

"I'm just going to take a shower and get dressed; I need to talk to you about something when I come out."

"Okay, darling, you know I will wait for you forever."

She felt nauseous at what she had just said but needed to keep him sweet.

"There is no easy way of saying this Val; you have to move out of this apartment, I cannot afford it anymore."

"What? You must be joking, where do you expect me to go?"

"Well I own two very nice modern apartments in Nekrasovka; I bought them a few years ago as an investment."

"Well sell one of those then," she retorted.

"No, you don't understand they have lost value since I bought them and they are heavily mortgaged. I have tenants in both, but the rent just about covers the mortgage repayments. Any repairs or alterations, the money comes out of my pocket."

"But that place is over 30 kilometres away. I will never see you."

She sat beside him and started to cry crocodile tears.

"Don't be silly, of course, you will. I will never give you up."

Taking his hand in hers, she said: "I have an idea, you could charge your wealthy patients more roubles for their treatments."

Ivan shook his head violently "No, no I already charge most of them exorbitant amounts for what is in the main worthless treatments. Luckily, I have a free reign, but if the medical board ever investigated, I would be struck off without a penny and probably prosecuted, and what then? As it is, I have to tell my wife we have to give up the house and move, through constant loans the banks own most of it anyway."

Valeria was in shock; this was the first time he had told her of his financial mess. "Why didn't you tell me before, I would have got a job or something to help you?" She was lying through her back teeth; he would be dropped like a hot potato if he stopped financing her good life. Building a nice nest egg at the expense of the doctor was all she was interested in; he certainly wouldn't be getting any of that back. He got hot sex on demand, and she thought she deserved the spoils.

The doctor sat there with his head in his hands, but she felt no pity. He got what he wanted in return for her security, that's how it worked. Valeria went to the balcony and lit another cigarette; her mind was racing as to how she could turn this situation to her advantage. No, she didn't want to give up this fabulous apartment but was not prepared to lose everything either. She hadn't told Cherkesov, on previous occasions she had visited her sister who lived in Volskaya Street, near a huge new shopping mall. The Russian government had pumped trillions of roubles into what had been a large, almost derelict industrial estate. Stubbing out her smoke, she went back to Ivan with a purposeful idea.

"Okay, darling, anything for you. I will move to Nekrasovka, but I want the best one, and I want it redecorated with new carpets and curtains before I move in. I will also need a car to come and see you at a discreet location with you being so busy with work. I can't live without seeing you."

The doctor was ecstatic; he beamed "Of course, of course, anything you want. Apartment 30 on the 1st floor is the best one, it's on the corner of the block, and it has the two largest bedrooms. I will give the tenant three months to quit; it's in her contract." He picked up his coat and readied to leave. Valeria kissed him gently on the lips,

"Don't worry, everything will be alright. I know it will."

"Val, I love you so much you are so understanding, thank you." With that, he left a much happier man.

Once again stepping onto the balcony in the dim light, she stood there admiring the view across the main road to the park, Madam Resnetnikov reviewed her situation. She had a healthy bank balance from her professional clients that she entertained without Ivan's knowledge. One, in particular, was getting too close and swore his undying love for her. He was boring, and she always faked orgasms when having sex with him. The good thing was it would all be over in about half an hour and then feeling guilty he would hurry on home to his loyal wife, having given Valeria 16,000 roubles (£200) in cash. She thought, yes, it's certainly right to move. I will not inform the perverse idiots I am going. I know the discreet clients I can tolerate will travel the distance to enjoy my favours. Building a new clientele in Nekrasovka will be fun; it's so easy to attract the right men in expensive clubs and restaurants. Smiling, she whispered,

"Men are such fools. They think they can buy love, but in the end, it's just sex." Lifting her glass of Vodka and tonic, she proposed a toast,

"Here's to the next chapter of your life Valeria, God bless Ivan Cherkesov, not a bad old soul really."

Chapter 27

Wednesday, 14th February 2018. 09.00hours
Cabinet Office, 10 Downing Street,

Sat at the table where the Prime Minister was, the Defence Minister, Admiral Nielson and his adjutant. Also present the D.P.M, Lord Claremont. The American Ambassador Dexter Truman was in attendance as a matter of protocol.

"Well, Admiral this situation is unprecedented, what do you propose we do about it?"

"There are several options we have, Prime Minister. Special Forces teams are being assembled and briefed to act at short notice in whatever course of action we take. Available fleet resources are and have been directed to take up station in and around the area Astute is in or expected to head. Our aim is to incapacitate the submarine and deal with it accordingly."

"When you say incapacitate, what does that mean?"

"In the first instance, we will attempt to spike the propeller. The secondary propulsion system used mainly for manoeuvring would only allow the sub to generate about 5 knots, not much use for escape."

"I see, and how do you propose to retake the submarine?"

"SBS teams would blow the torpedo loading and engine

room hatches, to gain entry. We have assessed the ability of parking one of our mini-subs on the after casing above the engine room hatch to gain entry. It is considered a near impossibility to gain access without internal assistance." The Admiral removed his spectacles and waited for a response.

The Prime Minister thought for a moment. "What do you think the chances of success are?"

"Difficult to say, but not greater than 50%. Men will die, and the sub will founder, however, at that depth some of the surviving crew members could use the after escape hatch. This so-called Red Fox has pulled off an act of piracy that could never have been envisaged. I do not underestimate his ability and determination; I believe it is a death or glory mission, it's possible no one would survive, friend or foe."

"So, it is a scenario of a 14 billion pounds ransom to be paid or the loss of our stealth submarine and its crew."

"Yes, Prime Minister that's it in its entirety, we have limited options." The mood was sombre. The Admiral continued, "In the unlikely event of Astute evading our forces and escaping there is a second plan. H.M.S. Victorious has just finished a four year extended refit in Devonport. She has been made ready for trials in the North Sea prior to inert missile firings in the Gulf of Mexico. She would then be joining our ballistic submarine fleet in Faslane. I propose to have a Trident 11.D5 transported in an armoured vehicle under armed escort from Coulport, Scotland to the naval base in Plymouth. It will be carrying a limited nuclear warhead, and placement would be in one of the silos on the submarine. All sixteen tubes have been gas ejection tested so we know the launch would be successful. A hardened nose cone and a delayed fuse would ensure a prescribed depth detonation. The warhead has a limited destructive radial area of about a mile. Subsurface, everything in that zoned circle would be obliterated. Of course, our success would rely on the fact the near approximate location of the sub is known. This operation would not detract from our commitment to having a Trident submarine deterrent at sea, at all times."

The Admiral looked directly at the Ambassador.

"I do not think the Russians would respond if we took this course of action. As you know in the Barents Sea, they conduct test firings with live warheads attached to their sub-launched missiles; we monitor them they monitor us. They have 1.4 million square kilometres to operate in; we have a fraction of that. My proposal can only work in our own back yard, so to speak. If Astute manages to make international waters, we will have to reassess the situation."

"So, you think that's a possibility then?"

"Dexter, we have a nuclear submarine with devastating weapons power onboard, controlled by a rogue band led by a fanatical Captain. I do not underestimate his ability to evade my forces."

The Prime Minister was out of her depth. There wasn't much she could add. Turning to the Ambassador, she expected some response to the brief so far. He sat there stony-faced, contemplating the seriousness of firing a limited Trident weapon.

"Well that damn submarine must not at any cost fall under the control of the Soviets, pirates on board accepted.

The thought of it ending up in an Eastern bloc naval dockyard scares me." He rubbed his chin and thought for a while. "I think you are right Admiral, although the Russians would make political noises, there's not much they could do about it. The missiles you have are under your control and considering the situation we are in, there would be no objection from our government to one being used as described. I consider it somewhat different from the option of starting world war three. That would be far more serious."

The Prime Minister and Admiral Neilson had met on previous occasions; they had great respect for one other. He had been instrumental in briefing the first minister of what action would be needed if an aggressor ever declared war and nuclear weapons were used. In that situation, the head of the government had the unenviable task of releasing the launch codes to the submarine Captain. He in turn with his second in command would authenticate them and unleash the awesome arsenal. If for any reason the PM was incapacitated, then it would fall to Lord Stephen Claremont to take control and issue the codes. The Trident weapon systems are manufactured in America but stored and maintained at Coulport as the British deterrent. The true purpose for which they are deployed will hopefully never be used; their destructive power is immense.

"Admiral, my President is somewhat dismayed at the fact your naval designers and engineers have managed to perfect and put to work a stealth system that makes a submarine almost impossible to track. Yes, we have been following the same lines for some time but with limited success, would it not have been prudent to share your success with us?"

"Not my decision Ambassador and anyway trials have only recently finished, I am sure that at some stage you will have our technology."

The Defence Minister interjected, "Well, we are all agreed our submarine must not end up in some eastern bloc shipyard, it must be retaken or destroyed at any cost."

Vice Admiral Raymond Spruance interjected. "Our top Navy seals have conducted trials to retake a submarine at various depths. The scenario was a rebel faction of the crew had mutinied and taken over, no matter how our boys went about the task, the end result was the same. In all simulated exercises, the loss of the sub and most of the crew members, and some of the navy seals was the outcome."

The Chief of Staff listened with interest, "Yes, thank you for that information, Admiral. However, it is my decision to proceed as planned and assess options as they develop. We need to resolve the problem as quickly as possible."

"Does anyone have any more to add?" asked the Prime Minister. The assembly shook their heads, what more could be said.

"Admiral, I do not want to detain you any longer than necessary. You have my full approval to implement either of the two plans outlined; we must have a successful outcome to this preposterous situation."

"Thank you, Prime Minister; I will keep you informed of progress."

Chapter 28

Thursday 15th February 2018 01.30 hrs
The Captain's cabin HMS Triumph, 90 miles South West
of Lands' End

There was a knock on the Captain's cabin door.

"Enter."

"Sir, Signal just received top-secret communication urgent."

"Thank you sparks, did you acknowledge receipt?"

"Yes, Sir."

"Okay, stand by for any further communique from me."

The radio operator touched his forelock, left the cabin and slid the door tightly shut. The wireless transmission was coded and encrypted; all top-secret ones were. In the unlikely event it was intercepted by any other receiver it would be meaningless. The Captain was the only member of the crew who had the relevant codebook locked in his safe. The radio operator's computer would decode normal flash traffic for instant action by the officer of the watch. Commander Stephens dialled the four settings required to open the small wall mounted safely. Withdrawing the codebook, he deciphered the message.

It read, 'Proceed with caution to position longitude 0

degrees 42 minutes west, latitude 48 degrees 30 minutes north. There to take on-board three naval service personnel, including divisional Admiral, by way of the Merlin Helo. Further! Monitor and track the rogue target at co-ordinates given. Only passive sonar to be used, adopt silent running. Hostile target to be engaged only if considered a threat. Hover and await further instructions. This is not an exercise, message end.

Captain Stephens read his brief for the second time; dispatched from Command Headquarters.

"Christ'! It must mean a Russian submarine has been detected near our territorial waters approaching our sub base at Devonport. That has not happened for a long time."

Recently the Russians had been operating more spy trawlers that had similar operational capabilities as a Nuke's. Great at gathering intelligence but without the firepower of a submarine, it was a much cheaper option. Reaching for his intercom, he communicated,

"This is the Captain speaking, XO to my cabin, immediate."

The Executive Officer Lieutenant Commander Colin Barratt was in the control room as the officer of the day. He turned to his next in command, Lieutenant Clive Smart. "Lieutenant, you have control."

"Yes, Sir, I have control."

The Executive Officer left the control room and hurried to the Captain's cabin. He knocked on the door and was greeted with "Enter."

"Come in Colin, shut the door and take the other seat."

The Captain's cabin, on the port side, was extremely

small. He enjoyed a few basic creature comforts that the rest of the crew had to share elsewhere on the boat. Perhaps, the most important features were his writing desk and the computer. The bunk was the regulation size and when in the upright position allowed a little more seating space. A codebook, along with any top-secret items was housed in the admiralty safe, bolted to the steel partition, forward of the diesel filling station. Every submarine Captain preferred to be at the helm in the control room and only spent brief amounts of time in their cabin. To sleep and deal with anything of a secret nature that was about it.

"Colin, we will not be docking at Devonport in the next twenty-four hours. I have received instructions to take on board three specialist navy personnel and then proceed to shadow a target. In fact, we have the coordinates for it so will listen on passive sonar while proceeding to the rendezvous point. Northwood has instructed me this is not an exercise; we will come to action stations soon. Just between the two of us, I can tell you; rear Admiral Stephen Jennings, our divisional commander, is orchestrating this and my orders come directly from him. Referring to the sea chart on his desk, he ringed the intended rendezvous point. He and two others will be joining us here, transfer by Merlin helicopter."

"Wow that's a new one an Admiral joining us at sea, transferred by helicopter. Will you be addressing the crew, Captain?"

"No, for the time being, this is on a need to know basis. I will brief them as soon as I have formulated a plan, though what that plan is, at the moment I have no idea. It is more

267

than likely Admiral Jennings will be running the show. It must be paramount otherwise why go to all the trouble of flying in specialists. In the meantime, bring us to action stations, reduce speed to 12 knots and order silent running, make for the coordinates to meet the Helo. I will be in the control room within 10 minutes" "Understood Sir. I will go to the bridge."

The Executive Officer returned to the control room to carry out his orders.

"Lieutenant, I have control."

"You have control, Sir."

"Do you here there, this is the XO speaking, submarine to come to action stations, reduce speed to 12 knots implement silent running throughout the boat. Helmsman, take us up to 150 feet."

"Yes, Sir, trimming to 150 feet."

The co-ordinates to give them a course directed by the Captain were typed into the navigational computer. To the well-trained crew, this seemed just another exercise. Constant practice not only kept them on their toes but improved their efficiency to respond to any situation at a moment's notice. Silent running meant just that. All machinery that could be would be switched off. The washer/driers fell silent, and the showers were off the menu. There would be no hot food while the sub was on high alert. The crew went about their business with a minimum of noise.

H.M.S. Triumph was the seventh of the Trafalgar class submarines; launched in 1988 displacement 5,200 tons submerged she had recently undergone an extended docking and essential defect programme. She could circumnavigate the globe and was now capable of firing the TLAC-M cruise missiles. She had recently returned from trials in the Gulf of Mexico where dived, a success rate of 95% was achieved on test firings. Spearfish torpedoes with inert warheads, for engaging surface and subsurface targets, were also trialled. (Siren) active decoy rounds gave her an extensive survivable capability. Over the last six months, Bernard Stephens R.N had honed the submarine and crew, to become one of the most efficient underwater war machines on active service. It was just coming to the end of a three-month patrol, and the men were looking forward to some shore time. Not for the first time, it would not happen now. The crew accepted this as part of their job description; never a nine to five job.

The Captain sat back and put his hands behind his head. Christ this is a new one on me, what the hell is going on? It must be very serious to have the Rear Admiral piloted on board. Naturally, I will billet him in my cabin, he thought. It took him eight minutes to formulate a plan of action and then proceed to the control room.

"Attention. Captain on the bridge."

The officers and duty men came to attention. Only the sonar operators carried on with their tasks of listening to the many sounds, animal and manmade that was generated in the vast expanse of water.

"As you were gentlemen, report please."

"Well Sir, reactor functioning well to give us 12 knots, manoeuvring propulsion shut down, all secondary machinery required okay, no reported defects. The Port T.O.T (Torpedo overflow tank), main discharge pump inoperable, the main bearing has gone, it's noisy. I have spoken to Fleet Chief Gerry Burne Sir; it is beyond repair and will have to be replaced. Of course, this means a job for the dockyard."

This was a major problem; the demise of the pump meant that torpedo tubes 2 and 4 were not safe to operate. With the bow cap doors shut after firing of a torpedo or missile, the water in either tube could not be pumped into the T.O.T. To drain them manually by opening the discharge valves would be noisy and give their position away to any listening enemy. Torpedo tubes 1, 3 and 5 able to operate normally. "Sonar has picked up several faint contacts within our box, recognition incomplete, probably of animal origin, Sir."

The truth was, Astute had such a quiet profile, and the rest of the Fleet could not be expected to recognise her. More akin to a dolphin in the water and certainly not much louder, it would be a hard task to locate the submarine. For Red Fox, this was a known fact. It was what he was relying on to make his escape.

"Very well, XO, I will brief the crew before we take our passengers on board."

The Merlin ASW (Anti-submarine warfare) transport Helo skipped over the waves at 200 feet, at a speed of 150 knots. Rear Admiral Stephen Jennings and his two associates, Commander Dean Richards and Lieutenant Commander Glyn Barratt, sat in the rear catching up with the latest communiqué from Admiral Neilson's office. They had been flown by fixed-wing aircraft from R.A.F. Northolt to Culdrose helicopter base in Cornwall, then transfer to the Helo.

Designed and built by Agusta Westland, the Helo could be adapted to many roles. This particular naval version had the latest Blue Kestrel radar and sonar system. On anti-submarine warfare operations, it had an effective dipping range of up to 50 nautical miles. It could hover on the station for over 3 hours while searching for targets. In times of hostilities, surveillance and the tracking of hostile ships and submarines was its forte. It could relay information instantly to the allied command ship for assessment. It now had three very important passengers that would be winched onto the catchment area of Triumph's deck aft of the fin.

Vice Admiral Jennings pushed the button and spoke into his mic.

"Navigator, Jennings speaking, how long to our E.T.A?"

"Nine minutes arriving at 06.31 hrs, Sir. We have the submarine beacon on our radar; they are hovering below until they have visual contact with us."

The rendezvous point had been chosen so as not to be in the shine path of Astute's big ears. It could be changed at any time to avoid the prying eyes of any surface contact. From time to time at periscope depth, the Captain of Triumph had eyeballed any surface traffic that could pose a threat. Content in the fact there was none he would not issue further orders to alter their position.

The deck party were instructed to make ready to assist the transfer of personnel from the Helo. This had been rehearsed on previous occasions so all should go according to plan.

The Merlin had hovered 30 miles off the coast and had

picked up Triumph on its first sonar dip, an easy task as the Sub was in hover mode, with its distinctive tracking beacon on. Only recognisable to blue on blue, any foreign vessel would not hear it. The frequency was only akin to the Merlin; Astute would be deaf to the pulse. The trained crew of the Helo knew it would be a totally different scenario if the Sub did not want to be found. In fact, on a recent exercise in the Irish Sea, H.M.S Talent had evaded entirely all efforts to locate her. It had landed its contingent of SBS for a covert training exercise and retrieved all of them 10 hours later and then disappeared without a trace. Surfaced near the Clyde submarine base two days later, the mission was appraised as having been a complete success.

The Admiral double-checked the instructions from the winch team. Neither of the two with him had been in a harness before, let alone be jettisoned onto a submarine deck in the choppy waters of the western approaches. Thankfully all three men were extremely fit and looking forward to the experience. In the Triumph control room, the Captain took another look at what was above the waves. During the last extended docking, both her periscopes had been upgraded. The old hull penetrating types had been removed and replaced by a mast topped with 2 Ultra-sharp Thales optronics CM010 periscopes. The main scope would be raised for a 360-degree scan that would only take 3 seconds. In that time a complete picture would be recorded and transmitted by fibre optics for the Captain to assess. Fortunately, the visibility on the surface was fair with occasional rain and a three-foot swell. The ordinarily busy sea lanes were relatively quiet. The nearest vessel being tracked on passive sonar was a large fishing vessel 17 nautical miles away. There were various commercial merchant vessels and a cruise liner 30 nautical miles distant. Going about their business in the shipping lanes, they were completely unaware of the Sub's presence.

All submarine Captains hated to be on the surface for longer than was really necessary; it was akin to being naked. Apart from any spy in the sky that might be passing; today's advanced radar fitted to commercial vessels, might indicate a static object on the surface. However, Triumph provided a small radar reflection due to her coating of acoustic tiles. Bernard Stephens lifted the intercom mic from its cradle, "This is the Captain speaking, deck party to control room hatch, prepare to secure three V.I.P. passengers. E.T.A... Eight minutes, prepare to surface."

The four sailors in the deck party were already kitted out with survival suits and all the lightweight ancillary equipment necessary, should any passenger or crew member go overboard. They made their way from the chief's mess to await the opening of the control room hatch. This was a scenario that had been practised many times. The arrester ring was kept in the fin and was rigged in a matter of minutes. The slippery deck was not an ideal place to be, so to have containment for the deck party and any passengers taken on board was certainly a help. It took less than five minutes to conduct the retrieval operation, after which time the lanyards were uncoupled, and the arrester ring was stowed. All crew and the passengers were now safely secure in the confines of the submarine. The Helo made for its base, and with the watertight hatch closed, the Sub dived to four hundred feet and resumed its planned course.

The three men were shown to the officer's mess by the Sub-Lieutenant. As he assisted them out of their survival suits, he was speechless to see the epaulettes of an Admiral and two commanders on the shoulders of their woolly pullies. "OKAY sub," said the Admiral with a smile,

"We could be here just to see how good you all are. Please request the Captain's presence."

"Yes, Admiral, right away, Sir, please make yourself comfortable."

Sub-Lieutenant Banfield hastily made his way to the control room.

"Sir, the Admiral and two other officers await your company in the mess."

"Very good Sub, show him to my cabin in five and make sure they are all provided with hot drinks. Get their names put on the list for immediate access to the sonar cab space and wireless transmitting office. Other than the reactor compartment, they have my authority to all other compartments requested. Oh! And make sure they have a junior rate escort, for their own safety."

"Yes, Sir."

For all those within earshot, this was a real eye-opener, the assembly of officers and ratings were somewhat dumbstruck. Why the hell had an Admiral and two senior officers been airlifted to their sub? It had to be a special exercise that was for sure. The whole crew trusted the Captain implicitly and knew he would pass on whatever information he could; in the meantime, there would be much speculation as to the reason for this unprecedented visit.

Captain Bernard Stephens turned to his executive officer,

"XO, I am going to my cabin to liaise with Admiral Harris, I will brief the crew after that you have control."

"Aye-aye, Sir, I have control."

In trepidation, the Captain made his way to his cabin. Even he was somewhat in the dark as to what was happening. Admiral Jennings waited until he had been informed that the Captain was there. A navy tradition, the Captain, was in charge and remained so; regardless of the fact, a more senior officer was on-board. He was shown to the cabin by the Sub-Lieutenant. The door was open. The Captain rose from his chair and greeted the Admiral with a salute and a firm handshake. "Welcome to my humble abode Sir, take a seat."

"Thank you, Bernie, I had forgotten just how confined these things are, still a bit better than the old Valiant class that I commanded."

"Indeed, Admiral."

Bernard Stephens slid shut the aluminium door and sat down at his desk.

As Captain of H.M.S. Triumph, the three stripes on his epaulettes denoted a full commander. As an Admiral and two other officers of the same rank to him were now on-board, the situation was unprecedented. There had been scant information passed by radio traffic from Northwood, so whatever was going down was top secret.

Chapter 29

Thursday 15th February 2018 01-55hrs
The Captain's cabin HMS Triumph, 90 miles South West of Lands' End.

Rear Admiral Stephen Jennings wrapped his huge hands around the steaming mug of black coffee and took a comforting swig,

"You remembered Bernie, just the way I like it."

They had met many times before, and the Admiral knew Captain Bernard Stephens very well. He knew from the body language; this was not the time for small talk and remained silent, awaiting the Admiral's brief. He placed his mug on the small shelf adjacent and produced an A4 folder from his waterproof zip-up black leather briefcase. Marked top-secret, he opened it to the first page of four.

"Bernie, this information and directive are straight from the war cabinet, authorised by the prime minister. We face an unprecedented situation that is grave in the extreme. Three days ago, H.M.S. Astute was pirated away from Devonport Dockyard by a party of, we believe, trained soviet sailors' strength up to twenty. We assume our crew are under duress or worse and there have been casualty's military and civilian, including fatalities. With the mayhem left behind, we know the pirates are heavily armed and prepared to be ruthless. As far as we can ascertain the submarine is functioning normally. The people, who have carried out this extreme act, are very professional; their full intentions are unknown. Our intelligence tells us they are most likely of Russian or Crimean origin not linked to any terrorist organisation that we know of. A large ransom has been demanded for the return of Astute with its crew. The powers that be think this might be a red herring and their true intent is to take the submarine to a northern docking facility. It would not take too long for engineers and technicians to understand and copy the workings of our most advanced submarine." The Admiral paused to let the Captain digest what he had just been told.

"Unfortunately, it gets worse. We have been reliably informed that there are two nuclear warheads not from our arsenal I might add taken on-board we have to assume they have been adapted to fit our cruise missiles or torpedoes."

"Wow this is sheer lunacy, how on earth could it have happened? The logistics to carry out such a raid seem incomprehensible."

"Well, Bernard the truth is, Astute is out there somewhere being controlled by a rogue band of, I hate to say it, highly-trained specialists. Commanded by a very experienced Captain who certainly knows what he is doing, our task is to find the sub and neutralise it. The co-ordinates you have been directed to aim for should see us on an interception course with our designated target. Commander Dean Richards will now be in the sonar suite with your authority directing operations. He is one of the few people who knows Astute's signature. Unlike Triumph, the A boat is still not fully functional in terms of battle readiness, at least we hope not. Your sub is the only one on station that has the remotest chance of finding and engaging what we must now call the enemy. The Tireless is in the Irish Sea, having left Faslane. She is steaming at 28 knots submerged but will take another 15 hours to be anywhere near the search area. Having the older sonar suite; it would only be by chance that she picked up Astute on active sweeps, and not very likely. Our American friends have the U.S.S. Iowa searching as well. She is approximately 100 nautical miles south-west of us. A very able submarine built to hunt the Russian Typhoon and Akula class subs. If Astute is within range, I think the Americans could locate her. With instructions to relay the position and shadow if possible, that could be our best chance. I do not give the skimmers with their Helos much of a possibility if our target runs silent and deep. Astute will undoubtedly hear our three frigates and a destroyer with her big ears. If she runs at flank speed, I very much doubt she could be caught anyway. Short of one of our crew members making some mechanical noise and giving her position away, our options are limited."

The Admiral looked concerned. The task to find the submarine weighed heavily on his shoulders. Knowing what he did about this particular quarry, in his heart of hearts, he thought the task was hopeless.

"Well, Sir, never in a million years would I have guessed this scenario. Pirates on a British warship, a submarine at that, how on earth could it happen?"

"I imagine that question has been asked at the highest

level. Heads will roll over this, possibly mine. Anyway, positive thinking, that's why Dean, Glyn and I are here, to evaluate what can be done, Bernard, how are you with this?"

"Well Sir, I find it incomprehensible that myself and my crew are tasked to find and destroy one of our own. Is it possible the British submariners have already been eliminated?"

"It's possible, but I believe not practical, not easy to store 30 odd rotting bodies. To surface and dispose of them or as discharges from the torpedo tubes would invite detection."

"Well perhaps that's good news, but I would rather have the option of dispatching a bunch of marauding pirates to a watery grave. However, I am in charge of this submarine, and you are my divisional chief. I will carry out whatever orders I am given, without hesitation."

The Admiral stretched and put his hands behind his head.

"Captain Stephens that's the response I expected. This is a very sad business, but I know all my submarine Commanders very well. I would hazard a guess that every one of them, including Robert Southward, would make the same decision. Because of the nature of this operation, where your crew is concerned, it must be conducted on a need to know basis. It will get very lonely in the control room if you are commanded to destroy Astute; I will be at arm's length to give that order. As I said, we have the express permission of the Prime Minister to take that action if the opportunity presents itself."

Admiral Jennings looked directly at the Captain, "Any questions?"

"How the hell will they explain this one, if the boat is destroyed?"

"A very good question, one I can't really answer."

"I am sure as we are hunting our quarry and the Defence Minister's team are working on a possible press release should it be needed. 'British submarine lost with all hands due to a terrible accident.' World War 2 mine possibly, there are still a lot of them out there gradually rotting away, who knows? Not our remit. We will do the job we are paid to do in the knowledge that our efforts will never be made public, but if we get a result, we will be applauded in private."

Both men reflected on the gravity of the situation.

"Any other questions, Bernard?"

"Was there any attempt to cripple or board Astute before she left territorial waters?" "Plans were put in place, but she disappeared before anything could be tried."

"Well in that case, Admiral I have no further questions, my instructions are perfectly clear."

"That's what I expected to hear, good luck and good hunting I will be in the officer's mess if you need me."

The Admiral finished his coffee, doffed his cap and exited the Captain's cabin. He picked up his escort and descended the ladder down to two decks and the officer's mess, now his office and accommodation space. He had no intention of taking over the Captain's cabin.

All the naval training in the world could not have prepared the Commander of this submarine for the task he had been handed. With an element of luck, he could find Astute and engage it to effect with the spearfish torpedoes he had on board. After all, his was a fully operational submarine with a highly trained crew. Unfortunately, his quarry was a friendly submarine, all be it with a hostile element on board. The fact that he knew Robert Southward and some of the other sailors he would have to dispatch to a watery grave, would not detract him from what he had to do. One worry troubled him though; all aspects of Astute's technical build would have been copied and enhanced from the 'T' boat build like his, was his submarine disadvantaged?

The Captain allowed himself a few seconds to reflect on what this operation with a successful conclusion really meant something he would have to live with for the rest of his life. Submarine Commanders were a breed apart, and very few men had the aptitude or ability to make it. He knew he had very little time to ponder his thoughts. He had one ear to the ships tannoy and expected to be interrupted at any time to be called to the control room. Okay, he mused to himself. The way ahead is set. For the next 10 minutes, he poured over the charts and concluded a plan that would allow engagement with the enemy. He made rough notes as to his intentions and was totally focused on the best course of action. As they raced South West at 27 knots' 250 feet below the cruel North Atlantic Ocean, this Captain had no doubts whatsoever as to what could be his destiny.

"Captain, Control room"

"Control room"

"XO to my cabin and the Admiral is requested to join us"

"Aye Sir," said the officer of the watch.

The Executive Officer Colin Barratt left the control

room and made his way aft to the Captain's cabin there to be joined by the Admiral. The XO knocked and entered on request with the Admiral. When they were seated, the Captain outlined his plan. "Gentlemen, I have been studying the area of operation, and I believe I know how our target will try and evade detection. Unless we have a definite contact conveyed by another unit, we will continue on the set course. I want to be actioned for the next eight hours. At that time, we will be 200 miles North West of the Azores. We will reduce speed to 5 knots and wait for our quarry to come to us."

"With all the listening devices the west has on the sea bed, I do not believe the pirate Captain will risk the Med all the way to the Gibraltar Straits. Heading for a Black seaport would be very risky indeed. The busy sea lanes east of the Azores are his best option, hiding under a super tanker maybe; I believe our search needs to be in that direction. If I were in his shoes, I would then head North West and use the Mid Ocean Canyon with its deep water and saline changes to hide for a while and then continue to run north to a Crimean port."

"If his course were to be directly south, it would be impossible to catch him as we are matched for speed. It would have to be left to the surface units to locate the submarine; however, I do not think that is his intention. It's unlikely he would sail the boat to China. It would be a massive undertaking upwards of 16,000 sea miles. Yes, Astute can circumnavigate the world underwater, but would he want to? The longer he keeps a captive crew, the more likely someone will find a way to retaliate and harm the integrity of the boat or give their position away."

"Bernard, we could be as close as one hundred miles to our quarry, or a lot less if she has turned north. I think we should go active on the next sweep."

"That's all very well Sir, but with Astute's big ears we could immediately give our position away."

"Yes, Captain I concur we most certainly will highlight what we are and where we are. But if as I suspect she takes retaliatory action; the other units might pinpoint her position and destroy her."

"So, Admiral, you want to use my submarine and crew as bate?"

He thought for a long time. "Well, yes, that's exactly it. I cannot reiterate enough how important it is to negate this problem. I do believe this unit is perfectly able to avoid an attack by our own torpedoes; you have had enough training for God's sake."

That much was true; the use of decoys was practised frequently.

The Admiral was agitated. "Look, Bernard, I am your divisional chief, and as such I know how good you and the crew are. You have the only submarine in the vicinity that can take on the challenge. That's why you have been chosen to go up against Astute, believe me, this is the last chance saloon to get a satisfactory result."

"Okay, Sir, I need to get to the control room, we will go active on the next sweep, but I will log my objections in the Captain's log."

"Okay Captain, how sure are you that Astute will emerge west of the Azores? Would it be just as likely that he hugged the coast of the Canary Islands and with stealth circumnavigated our forces?"

"Admiral, I have considered that the problem and it does not allow him an opportunity to fast cruise. He would have assumed we have ships and submarines on patrol there to interrupt his progress. I do not consider it worthwhile to chase our tail across the Ocean and achieve zero results, hence my observations. I stand by my conviction as Captain of this submarine."

"Very well, Captain, this is your command, and I certainly have no better plan, we will see what happens in the next sweep."

He stood up, doffed his cap and opened the sliding door,

"I need to talk to Commander Richards."

Chapter 30

Thursday 15th February 2018 04-10hrs
Control room submarine HMS Triumph

The submarine had been heading on a southerly course in the western approaches. The whereabouts of their intended target was still unknown. It was very perplexing to be chasing a shadow, but this is what submariners were trained for. Hour after hour, four on four off, the sonar operators would watch their screens patiently waited for the opportunity to track their prey. The last communication from naval headquarters was transmitted at the prearranged time. At periscope depth, the coded information was gathered by computer and deciphered immediately.

Co-ordinates were given for the box area of the North Sea where it was suspected Astute would be. It was the best possible guess as to her location formulated by the experts naval and civilian in Northwood. The surface ships in the hunt had gathered no data that was relevant to the search. The sonar dipping Helos had also drawn a blank.

"One would have thought a contact would have been made by now, especially by the destroyer. Christ, the type 45 is supposed to have the best location and tracking systems in the world."

"Yes Colin (X.O), they most definitely have, but our 'A' class subs are so stealthy, needle in haystack springs to mind. The co-ordinates we have been given include Hurds Deep; it is possible the rogue pirate Captain has the submarine lying on the sea bed, biding his time."

"Indeed, that's a strong possibility; the deepest part is 180metres with a very undulating channel. It could stay there for weeks, and we would never find it."

"Ok, but why would the cunning devil idle there knowing our forces would be waiting for him to come out?"

Captain Simmons unhooked the ships mic. "Do you here there? In four minutes, we will be reducing speed to 5 knots for our next active sweep. Remain at action stations with all watertight doors secured, that is all."

The submarine slowed, and the active sonar was engaged.

The operators at their screens waited in anticipation for a reflected return that would reveal what they were looking for. Both experienced commanders intensely concentrated for the 10-second duration, after which time the pinging stopped.

"Well is there anything of significance, asked the Captain?"

Commander Dean Richards responded. "Not a thing that would represent a submarine least of all the one we are looking for."

Bernard Simmons looked at the charts. "Okay time to try a new strategy, make a new heading, 49 degrees 30 minutes north, 3 degrees 34 minutes west."

"Yes, Sir dialling in the co-ordinates now 49 degrees 30 minutes north, 3 degrees 34 minutes west."

The computer responded immediately to the command, and the sub lurched slightly to port and steadied on a straight run. The computer would calculate a series of zigzag manoeuvres. No submarine Captain liked to travel in a straight line, sudden death in a war situation. If necessary, the computer could be overridden and a calculated manual course adopted.

Triumph was running at 20 knots submerged. The Captain was convinced they were on an interception course with Astute. He concluded the information that had been relayed from Northwood was dated. As the commander in the field, it was always his prerogative to take whatever course of action he deemed fit. They would run at this speed for 15 minutes, stop and hover while listening to the mouth of the English Channel and the Atlantic, with the towed array deployed. As its name suggests, it is a passive sonar listening device, towed well away from the submarine. It has a 360-degree hearing capacity, able to be spooled up to 500 meters. When deployed from its normal housed position on the aft casing, it would relay information to the sonar operators instantly. That information would be stored on a computer for immediate and future analysis.

The worth of towed array to the sonar operators was in its simplicity, generating very little noise while gathering information. In fact, the noisiest task was in deployment and retrieval from the submarine.

Time ticked by, and the submarine had slowed and was ready for the next 10-second active sweep. As the first seconds ticked by Commanders Dean Richards and Glyn Barratt watched their monitors with renewed vigour. A faint trace appeared on both their screens. With headphones on, they strained to make sense of the strange very faint sound coming through.

"That's her," whispered Dean.

"Yes, I concur that is the signature alright," replied Glyn excitedly. The X.O. interjected.

"Range 42 miles speed 18 knots, green 9 degrees stb'd".

"Increase speed for 28 knots bring her on a heading to intercept. We must close the range. Control to Torpedo room?"

"Torpedo room Aye, Sir."

"Load spearfish, tubes 1, 3 and 5."

"Loading spearfish 1, 3 and 5 Sir."

At 21 inch diameter, 16 ft. long and 4,080 lbs dead weight the wire-guided weapon was awesome. Able to reach a speed of 80 knots it would have a limited range of 14 miles. Reducing the speed would give a target range of 30 miles. On impact, the 660-pound warhead could penetrate double-hulled vessels. When nearing the specific target, the internal guidance system would take over and make a covert passive search, trying to ignore decoys. Maintained at Beith Ordinance in North Ayrshire an upgrade was planned for 2020. Amongst other things, the copper wire guidance would be given over to fibre optics.

The Captain had a grin on his face, "I knew this was the right place to be looking; now the serious work begins."

In the officer's mess through his headset, the Admiral was listening to the conversation. He mused, 'Well done, Bernie, I certainly had doubts about deviating from the planned co-ordinates.'

And so, the game of cat and mouse began. The most important aspect for Triumph was to get near enough to loose off a salvo of torpedoes. It had to be achieved by patience and cunning. Did Astute know she was being stalked by another British submarine with hostile intentions? The Admiral was on edge; he knew the submarine he was on would have its work cut out to compete with the much stealthier quarry they were after.

As they raced towards Astute, the passive sonar was able to identify far more indications. The ship's operators were good but couldn't distinguish all that was coming in. The two experienced commanders could.

"Captain we have her on passive, she's dead in the water 34 miles away, depth 300ft " "That's strange. Why has the decision to stop and linger been taken? It doesn't make sense. It's quite obvious to me we have been spotted."

That was indeed the case. On-board Astute, Red Fox, had decided to use Trisonic Imaging and hover track to manoeuvre his escape. He would wait until the approaching submarine was in range and if necessary, dispatch it to the bottom. His own sonar operator had quickly established it was a Trafalgar class travelling to intercept.

"Ok No 1 put the stealth systems to work and let's move; it could get rather hot around here."

"Yes, Sir engaging stealth systems."

Sergey Gikalov and Leonid Kuzlow had become expert in the use of them in a very short space of time. The two British sailors who would usually be in control were shackled in the senior rates bunk space with no idea as too what was happening.

Dmitri Sparrov looked at the screen and the approaching menace. He passed the order to his men in the torpedo tube space.

"Ok load inert torpedo and flood 5 tube, load live spearfish into 2 and 4 tubes, open bow cap doors, stand bye."

"The order was acknowledged, all was ready.

On Triumph, all was calm as the submarine catlike stalked its prey.

"Captain Control to Torpedo room flood tubes 1, 3 and 5, stand by to open bow cap doors."

"Yes, Sir flooding tubes 1, 3 and 5."

Commanders Richards and Barratt were explaining to the less experienced men how to distinguish Astute's trace as opposed to all the other blips on their screens.

"Reduce speed to 6 knots we will go for a shot. What is our distance from the enemy?"

"18 miles Sir we are just out of range for a maximum speed of our fish."

"Ok, Colin set the running speed appropriate for an intercept."

The information was fed into the computer that would, in turn, direct the torpedoes as to speed direction and maximum depth to run at.

Alarmingly the chief sonar operator let out a gasp. "Christ, she's gone."

On all the computer screens the image they had been tracking simply vanished.

"What reboot the computer?"

The backup computer took over while this happened, and there was a millisecond interruption to the images portrayed. Richards and Barratt sat there, stony-faced in silence; they were well aware of what had happened. Just then, an alarm sounded.

"One torpedo in the water, Sir 28,000 yards at speed and closing us fast."

The Captain acted in seconds.

"Increase speed for 27 knots, angle down 10 degrees turn 30 degrees to port." The helmsman acknowledged the order. "Prepare the release of decoys."

The control room went into overdrive as evasive action was taken. Captain Stephens knew he couldn't outrun the torpedo but had a good chance of survival with the use of decoys; they had practised it many times.

"Do we have an ascertained target yet?" The senior operator was confused as were the rest. "No Sir, I cannot understand it. She just isn't in the last known position anymore."

"Any answers, Dean?"

Both Dean and Glyn just shook their heads, resigned to their fate.

"Where is the torpedo now for God's sake?"

"19,000 yards, Sir it has acquired our position."

Captain Dmitri Sparrov waited until the loosed torpedo was within 12,000 yards and then gave orders to blow it up. The signal travelled down the wire guidance system in an instant, and the 2-ton weapon self-destructed. Smiling, he turned to Codin, before he could say anything a message from Starshina 1st class came through.

"Sir the enemy has opened their bow cap doors."

"Ok Discharge tube 2."

The deadly cargo released from its confinement gathered speed towards its intended target.

The relief on the Triumph was overwhelming but short-lived.

"The second torpedo is in the water, Sir, heading straight towards us, range 26,000 yards.

The Captain reacted. "Has any operator acquired a target yet?"

There was no positive reply. The whole of the control room staff waited with dread as their fate appeared sealed. The Captain kept his nerve as he accepted the reports of the torpedo getting ever nearer. At 6,000 yards the decoys started to be released, it was their last hope.

Red Fox watched the scenario unfold; at 3,000 yards, he gave the order to destruct the spearfish. Milliseconds later a huge explosion was heard as the torpedo evaporated. "Let's hope that will be enough for them to give up the chase; their position is hopeless. If required the next and last one we fire, will not be neutralised."

It was a sobering prospect to kill 120 men, but they were the enemy, hell-bent on his destruction. It was a simple equation, kill or be killed.

"Admiral Jennings to Captain Control room, Come in."

"Yes, Sir."

"Direct order, break off the attack and secure bow cap doors. Set a course for Devonport."

"Would you repeat that please, Admiral?"

"I repeat, break off the attack and secure bow cap doors. Set a course for Devonport, out."

Perplexed Bernard Stephens barked out an order to

do just that. Looking at his X.O and rolled his eyes. The control room went very silent. Both Commanders looked at each other well aware of what was going on.

The Senior and Junior ratings had no idea, was it just an exercise after all. No, it couldn't be surly with live torpedoes, crazy? From time to time, while the Captain was busy, his X.O no relation to Commander Barratt had been watching his namesake. It was apparent to Colin Barrett they had not been surprised by the Admiral's command.

"The bow cap doors on the enemy vessel have been closed, Sir, and they are turning away."

Captain Dimitri Sparrow managed a broad grin. "Very sensible I think, I would not have been bluffing with the third torpedo. Whether their decoys would have dealt with it or not, we will never know, thank goodness. Set a new course, our journey continues."

Onboard Triumph the mood was sombre. In the control room, there was an air of relief but also bewilderment.

"X.O. you have control I am going to see the Admiral."

"I have control, Sir."

The Captain made his way to the officer's mess and saw the door was open. The Admiral was busy writing some notes.

"Come in, Bernie, you must be wondering what is going on?"

"With respect, Sir, that's a complete understatement."

"What I am about to tell must not be discussed with anyone else. I am not the least surprised we lost track of Astute. She carries some hardware that no other submarine does. The surface fleet would have monitored the torpedoes she fired. It's over to them now; it would have been a suicide mission to carry on with the attack. I consider we did our job."

"I understand Admiral, that being the case it was the proper course of action to have taken. I am somewhat disappointed we were not successful in dealing with the problem. However, I am happy my men and submarine have been spared. I don't know about you, Sir but I could do with a coffee."

The Admiral smiled "Excellent idea, Captain. I will make it."

Chapter 31

The seven men sat around the table were considering the way ahead with regard to the present situation. Admiral Neilson had been called from the room by his adjutant Captain Blake Channing; they knew it must be very important for the meeting to be interrupted. He re-emerged ten minutes later and took his chair at the head of the table.

"Gentlemen, GCHQ have picked up flash traffic from Astute and patched it to my network immediately. We requested Astute's code and that has now been verified."

(This is a four-digit number given to the Captain that only he knows and is changed and memorised for each patrol). The Admiral looked concerned.

"That's worrying; we can only assume the pirate leader has gained knowledge of the code through coercion. It may be that Captain Southward has complied for the safety of his men. When we make prearranged contacts, we can ask for the code from any patrolling sub, to verify the Captain is still in charge and no mutiny has taken place. In most circumstances the code would never be passed on to any other crew member, this situation is unique."

The last recorded act of mutiny in the British Royal Navy was in September1931. It had started in the British Atlantic fleet. Based at Invergordon on the Cromarty Firth in Scotland, it took the Admiralty and the government by surprise. The talk of mutiny had spread like wildfire after newspaper reports had suggested a 10% cut in pay was imminent. It was planned to be introduced without consultation. This was to match the general cut in the private sector due to the state of the economy.

The Admiral continued, "My people have tried to glean information from the duty radio operator on Astute but have been met with a wall of silence. He is obviously under duress and only allowed to transmit when and what Red Fox allows him to. I am confident that the findings in the first report are good. English was communicated amongst the boarding team during the initial assault. That may well have been to confuse us as too their identity. The fact remains the pirates are able to closely monitoring what our own people on-board are discussing. From what we do know, all the signs suggest Russian or Ukrainian sailors. It's plain they have a wealth of knowledge of the submarine that is now under their control."

The Admiral turned to Commodore Brian Toby Thomas,

"Well Brian what have you come up with?"

"Well Sir, before I get to that, you might be interested in some information I have regarding Astute's movement from Devonport. We had Special Forces in two rigid raiders exercising around the Rame peninsula. Naturally, they were unaware of the sub's demise. After hearing the gunfire and commotion, the senior officer radioed base. At that time of the morning, no one was completely sure of what was happening. They were instructed to investigate and came across the mayhem in the river, left behind by the pirates."

Previously to that fortunately or otherwise, they had changed course and cut through the shallow channel west of Drakes Island. Had they maintained their original course, they would have passed within spitting distance of Astute coming out. To be quite frank, if they had received intelligence about the situation, there wasn't much they could have done. SBS teams in Rib's could not possibly take on a nuclear submarine. They were on a training exercise and only carried A10 assault rifles, small arms and stun grenades. They would not have been able to even dent the hull or penetrated the conning tower."

"Thank you for that Brian, I think your boys had a lucky escape."

"Indeed, they did Admiral."

"Now the sit-rep to date, two SBS teams are standing by in Devonport. One of our four man mini-subs is being adapted to be able to spike Astute's propulsion system. Due to the time scale, it will be rudimentary engineering. Basically a large lance made from heavy-duty steel 'H' bar will be welded to the front stiffeners of the mini-sub. The effect will be to pierce the propeller between the blades and wreck the whole works should they engage the main propulsion. Of course, the mini-sub will be written off and the crew rescued by the other mini. The fwd and aft manoeuvring props can be immobilised with steel hawsers that my divers will drape over them, a risky business but we have practised an achievable technique. The whole kit should be ready for loading onto the Sailmaid ('Ocean going dispatch/recovery vessel'), in Devonport, at approximately 06.00 hrs tomorrow. We expect to be in a position to execute the plan by 09.00hrs."

"That's excellent Brian; can this plan work if the sub is on the move?"

"Well Admiral, we estimate anything up to 5 knots will not hinder our attempts. The whole operation depends on stealth and we do believe they would not hear us coming. We would be approaching in our mini-subs from a distance of five miles. As you know, the acoustic tiled mini's we have, give less reflective profile than a tobacco tin. When we conducted trials with H.M.S. Torbay two years ago, we managed to park on the after the end of the submarine without them knowing we had arrived. I have to say they were travelling in a straight line at 4 knots, we assume if Astute, gets under way it will not be. As we know the sub has the 2076 sonar suite, the biggest hydrophone listening devices in the world. It is rumoured it could pick up the QE2 leaving New York harbour while sitting in the Western approaches. If we are discovered before we execute the plan, there's very little chance of success."

"I don't like the sound of that, what you are saying is we have to catch them napping?"

"Yes, Admiral that's exactly right we do."

The brief carried on "If we can cripple the sub then the next phase can be implemented. The engine room hatch will be straddled by a mini-sub and explosive charges placed to blow the strongback hinge. It will take another three or four minutes to get the mini back into position and attempt to get the hatch open. Of course, this will flood the compartment but my divers will gain access and deal with any opposition left alive. Not too sure there would be any, of course, that will include any of our own men in there."

"Mm, an assessed risk we have to take Brian. Given that the 'A' class has the same docking platform as Spartan, what are the chances of it being successful? Moreover, is it assured your people can achieve their goal?"

"Well, Admiral the trials on that sub were not conclusive. The blowing of the hinge has never been tried before but after much deliberation with my team, it's the best option we can come up with, as we cannot expect any help from inboard. It's a high price to pay that your own engine room staff will perish but we have limited options."

"We have considered going in through the torpedo tubes, in trials it has been successful. Getting the bow cap doors to open mechanically is not a problem, but of course, in the compartment, any enemy would know what we were up to. I think they would initiate water shots to eject my men in a very unpleasant way. Also if they have torpedoes loaded, it's a no go? Even if they didn't, to gain access without damage would need the assistance of a crew member. We can blow the inner doors with delayed charges, however with the inrush of seawater all in that compartment friend or foe would be killed. I can't predict how it would affect any ordinance the pirates have stored.

"With shaped charge limpet mines, we could blow small holes anywhere in the hull but this would definitely cause the boats total loss and possibly all on-board. Astute would lay on the bottom with its reactor live and no one to control it."

Commodore Thomas hesitated briefly aware of the gravity of the situation and what he might have to act on. The Admiral rested his clasped hands on his chin and reflected on what had just been proposed.

"Well, I would only want that enacted as a last resort, the reactors integrity had to be of prime concern."

The Chief of Staff looked pensive, far-reaching decisions would have to be made and it fell on his shoulders to instigate them.

"Ayden, how have we got on with the missile threat?"

Commodore Ayden James looked up from his notes. "Well Admiral I have dispatched, four mobile rapiers intercept anti-missile units. Two are now in operation, one on Plymouth breakwater and one on the Rame head peninsular. They have been set up and simulated tests have proved positive, we cannot commit a real test fire until you authorise it, the press would have a field day. I expect within the next twenty-four hours the final two batteries will be operational. One will be on the after deck of the Newton; the other will be on HMS Scott. Effectively, on the surface, we could challenge anything launched from the submarine. I am ninety per cent certain we could take out the cruise missiles, as soon as they leave the water. Fortunately for us, they are relatively slow at exit faze, we know if the warheads are fitted they would be in static mode when blown out of the sky."

The problem is if the enemy is listening and I assume

they are, and then, of course, they will most likely know what we are planning. Our frigates could be used to corral the submarine and use Sea wolf missiles to negate anything launched but due to their shorter range, the sub would be aware of their presence. It's your call Admiral but I feel confident and more at ease with our mobile batteries."

"Yes, Ayden I tend to agree, with the mayhem these madmen have caused already, I am in no doubt they would try and harm our surface ships if they get to close. I think it prudent for the time being to keep them out of torpedo range."

The Admiral turned to Major General Andrew Horswell (S.A.S.).

"Andrew, what do you propose?"

"Well, Admiral we are on the backburner somewhat. I have three teams standing bye, one in the Plymouth Citadel marines barracks and two back at our headquarters in Hereford. They are on an hours' notice to be airlifted to wherever they are required. I have consulted with Barry and he has put fixed-wing and rotary aircraft at my disposal. My men are busy familiarising themselves with the layout of Astute should we need to effect a plan of attack. I am assuming any internal commitment will be handled by the S.B.S. That having been said we are there for back up should we be needed."

"That may well turn out to be the case, Andrew."

"I assume at some time the enemy will have to be ship or shore-bound, that's when we will get them."

"Thank you, Andrew, I really do hope you get the opportunity to take these people out, they are ruthless thugs."

The Major General just grinned; he had been on many operations where death was part of the deal, he still had visions about Sierra Leon. The Welsh Guards were rescued but not until one of Andrew's colleagues, who was also a good friend had been blown up by a rocket-propelled grenade. That was the signal to dispatch as many of the so-called free army as possible. In fact, they were a band of untrained undisciplined sadistic rabble. Andrew remembered the screams of those less fortunate to be on the end of a S.A.S. bullet, knife or phosphorous grenade, not many of the enemy were taken alive. There was never a sleepless night; combat with any enemy was always simple, a matter them or us.

"Admiral," said Rowland Blakelock, "One bit of good news, the Chancellor sanctioned by the Prime Minister has authorised unlimited funds to bring this problem to a conclusion."

"Thanks, Rowland, I have an awful feeling this is going to cost a packet whatever the outcome; I just hope it is in financial and not human terms."

Just then the phone rang.

"Excuse me, gentlemen, this must be important."

The Admiral listened intently to what his adjutant had to say, it was brief and the Admiral did not ask questions.

"Very well, Blake, keep me informed."

He put down the phone and rose from his chair. He paced over to the static map of the world, stood with his hands behind his back and muttered to himself, "Trisonic imaging and hovertrack. Damn and blast."

The British were ahead of any other country with

regard to this development. It was a natural progression to submarine stealth characteristics associated with underwater warfare. America and Russia had been dabbling with it for years. It was developed at the Admiralty underwater research establishment, (AURE). Trisonic imaging was cutting edge technology. The system, when activated on Astute, would triangulate the submarine's position and keep it constant. The hovertrack computer system then engaged, allowed the sub to hover and crawl a few feet above the sea bed or at a certain depth. It would slowly creep to a new destination miles away. An enemy who considered they knew exactly where the sub was would be dumbfounded when the system was switched off. The submarine literally disappeared from their sonar screens. Astute was the only active submarine in service, to have these stealth systems fitted.

The Admiral returned to his desk, sat down and cleared his throat,

"Gentlemen, I have some bad news. Astute has gone."

The people in the room looked at the admiral in disbelief; this situation rendered most of the planning irrelevant. The Admiral regained his composure.

"You will all be wondering how this has happened when effectively the sub was ring-fenced by mobile units and our surface ships. The fact is, Astute carries top-secret evasion devices that when activated allows it to become a ghost submarine. It is extremely complex; even I am not fully conversant with its workings. I do find it hard to believe my submarine crew would engage it willingly."

The Admiral turned a page in his notes and pondered the situation.

"We must establish contact at some time, with all the underwater listening devices we have in the channel, I am hoping she will give her position away." He paused and reflected on the situation. "I anticipate the people who have instigated this heinous crime will be in contact again in the near future. The SBS and SAS teams are to remain on high alert. Long-range transport, air land and sea, will be kept in readiness for men and equipment. As we speak, other units including two submarines are being directed to the search area to try and re-establish contact. We know how far Astute could have travelled and will concentrate on that circle in the box search area. For obvious reasons, I am limiting the size of the surface fleet. If the press gets wind of what's going on, it will become a national scandal."

The professionals around the table did not need to ask questions, they all knew the implications of what they had just been told.

"That's it for now, concentrate on your individual team's involvement and revise your plans accordingly. The fact remains, we will need their expertise at some stage and all must be ready to go at a moment's notice. The next meeting will be convened when considered necessary. In the meantime please feel free to contact me if you feel the need. Any new developments of interest, you will be informed."

As the assembly filed out the Admiral returned to his notes. He had faced much adversity in his naval career and had encountered the prospect of death on more than one occasion. He was responsible for many thousands of lives and billions of pounds of naval hardware. What had made his rapid promotion possible was his ability to second guess situations and act accordingly. He had a major impact during the Falklands War as a junior officer, where his expertise had shone through.

He desperately wanted to know who and what he was up against. He went over the intelligence reports at his disposal and was trying to get into the mind of his enemy. If this all went wrong the Admiral's career was over. That on its own was not his main concern; he had never backed away from a situation and was known for his complete resolve. Most people including the Prime Minister knew Admiral Simon Neilson was probably the only man who could bring this to a successful conclusion.

Captain Channing strolled into the Admirals office.

"Sir, Astute has fired two torpedoes at Triumph; although decoys were implemented, they were not needed. One was inert and the other carried a live warhead it seems they malfunctioned or were deliberately blown up."

"Bloody impossible" spluttered the Admiral, there were no live warheads on Astute." "So, we thought but Triumph's Captain insists it was a full live firing."

"Well if Captain Stephens says it was, then it was. He knows they were initially being targeted directly and the torpedoes were destroyed at source."

"Has Triumph been able to locate Astute at all?"

"Well a brief encounter when they had her location. But otherwise it's a wild goose chase, engaging Trisonic imaging and Hovertrack has been used to great effect."

The Admiral sat back in his chair, "Okay Blake, it's obvious these mad but competent pirates have taken on-board adaptable live warheads, I wonder how many? We cannot risk a British submarine being sunk by another; orders are to hover out of range for the next twenty four hours Passive sonar only."

"Very good Sir, I will convey your orders immediately. I understand Admiral Jennings had instigated that order as soon as the threat was realised."

Captain Blake Channing saluted, turned on his heels and left the room. Bloody hell! He thought wouldn't want to call this one.

The Admiral knew there was very little chance of his submarine or surface units locating the intended quarry. It could be anywhere within a large area of the sea and constantly changing its position. When the stealth mechanisms were engaged, the cunning Red Fox had the upper hand. What on earth were his real intentions was it really only about a ransom or would H.M.S Astute disappear forever along with the brave crew?

Chapter 32

Saturday 17th February 2018
Flat 14 Block 6 Nekrasovka, East Moscow District. 10 a.m.

Alina Petrenko sat at her kitchen table, sipping black coffee. The last few days had been a whirlwind of intrigue and spent emotions. The man she had met and made mad passionate love to was now out of her life. Nadim Babachencko had left an indelible mark on her soul. She thumbed the edge of the jiffy bag, so wanting to open it. Her heart told her to do it; her head told her not to. What was the point? He had gone, and no 'Dear Alina' letter would make up for the loss she felt. She opened the drawer and placed the bag neatly amongst her weekly correspondence. All would be dealt with on Sunday, every week that particular morning was dedicated accordingly. This was a policy adopted by her father. He would always say 'better to get all the good news and bad news together, why ruin six days with worrying about bad news.' Dear papa, she missed him terribly.

Alina mumbled to herself,

"Girl, get on with your life and forget Nadim, I am sure he has already forgotten about you."

The strange thing was she felt no remorse for her fleeting moments of pleasure. Did it really matter, he was gone and no one in her small circle of friends and associates needed to know how wayward she had been? With regard to a stable male companion, Nadim had said. 'There is someone out there who will fulfil your wish and become your soul mate. I will be envious when he comes along.' She would start dating again and find that person to spend the rest of her life with.

Saturday came, and in the morning, she busied herself doing the washing, cleaning and dusting her home. At some stage, she wanted to decorate the main living space. It had not been touched for a number of years and needed refreshing. Putting aside some Rouble each month would allow her the funds to start soon. In the afternoon going to the Mall was her special treat, there was a pair of fashionable tan suede boots that she had kept her eye on for the last two weeks. The original price was far too expensive, but a sale had just started, and they were reduced to half price. Without hesitation, she went into the shop and tried them on. They fitted perfectly, and she purchased them on the spot. Oh well she thought, the decorating will have to wait a bit longer.

A coffee and a slice of sour cream cake rounded the afternoon off nicely. When Alina got home, there was a delicious aroma wafting from the meat dish she had prepared and left in the slow cooker. Kicking off her functional shoes, she put the new boots on and admired them in the mirror. Settling down for the evening with her meal and a bottle of red wine, she suddenly felt very vulnerable and alone. Thoughts of Nadim came flooding back, and the tears started. She wondered how she allowed herself to be manipulated like that. He used me and then left me, she thought, but wow I did enjoy it. The third glass of red wine didn't make her feel any better. After picking at her meal and finishing the wine, it was time to go to bed. "Oh, Nadim I do miss you so, I wish you were here making love to me, I want no other man in my life." With that Alina Alexandra Petrenko cried herself to sleep.

Sunday morning arrived, and it was an effort to get out of bed. She forced herself to do so, showered and dressed. Life had to go on, and there were things to attend to; there was no one to help her with the chores. Her first priority was to deal with the weekly mail. Opening the table draw in the kitchen, she placed the weekly collection on the table. Tearing open the Jiffy bag first, to her surprise, there was just a red silk handkerchief, neatly folded. Alina could smell the Clive Cristian No1, eau de toilette. She raised it to her nose and drank in the intoxicating fragrance.

"Oh, Nadim, you bastard, what am I going to do?" she said.

Crying uncontrollably, she threw the handkerchief across the room. A small key flew out and chinked against the mirror on the wall.

"What the hell." Alina walked over and picked up the key and the handkerchief. Written inside were words that she would treasure forever.

Alina, I will never forget you. You will find secured in a safety deposit box something to treasure. Believe in Ying Yang as I do, take care, Nadim.
Safety deposit box 16876.
The bank address you need to visit is Siret Bank 119 Gavrilova

Street Moscow.

Ask for Mr Victor Savelyev.

Your passphrase is (Never say Never) Memorise the box number and password and burn the handkerchief.

Alina was shaking when she put the contents back in the jiffy bag and put it in the inside pocket of her coat. All her other weekly correspondence could wait. Putting on her warm black boots and long powder blue coat, she left the apartment and walked to the metro. She wanted to go to the park where she had spent time with Nadim. It did not make sense, why all the intrigue, why couldn't he just have enclosed a letter of explanation in the jiffy bag. "My God Nadim you are such a complicated man."

It was a cold crisp morning, and the park was busy. After a week's work, people were taking advantage of the beautiful Sunday morning. She headed for the bench where they had both sat and chatted, to her relief no one was sitting there. Alina took the jiffy bag out of her pocket and removed the handkerchief. She carefully put the key in her handbag. Nadim's eau de toilette was still as strong as ever. She placed it to her lips and kissed it gently, and once again, the tears rolled down her cheeks. Taking dark glasses out of her handbag and putting them on, she raised the hood of her coat over her head. She did not want the people walking by to see her sadness. Reading the words once again, how could she bring herself to destroy the only memento she had?

Alina Petrenko, suddenly she felt very calm, it was like Nadim was reaching out from wherever he was. She wiped away her tears and reread the words. By the time she had got back to the apartment, she had memorised the contents. Placing the handkerchief in a bowl, she set fire to it. The burned essence of Clive Christian eau de toilette lingered in her nostrils. Making herself a cheese and ham sandwich, she poured herself a large glass of red wine and settled down by the T.V, which was as far as she intended to go today. She had the rest of her weekly letters to catch up with and two good films to watch.

Monday the 19th came, and Alina dressed early, the air of excitement overwhelming her. She had decided to call in sick; the trainee receptionist at Dr Comerov's office would have to cope today. Smartly dressed in her office outfit she caught the newly completed Kozhukhovskaya Moscow metro, changing trains once she arrived at the Siret Bank in Gavrilova Street. The bank had just opened, and many people were waiting to transact business.

She had a sudden urge to turn around and leave. Her hands were shaking, what was she doing here? Just then a young lady with an iPad came over and asked if she could help. Alina was nervous; she had never in her life, needed a safety deposit box and didn't know the procedure.

"I would like to see Mr Savelyev with regards to this." She opened the palm of her hand and revealed the key. To the assistant, the key had a special significance; it was colour coded.

"Of course, Madam follow me." They traversed a long corridor adorned with large potted shrubs. Expensive carpet and polished marble tiles were everywhere. Passing individually designed office facades, they all had names on them. Stopping at Victor Savelyev's door, the assistant knocked lightly on it. Alina was aware of a security camera focused above the door. A green light appeared adjacent to it, and the assistant passed a swipe card into a wall-mounted reader. She then entered a six-digit code. The door opened, and they both entered. The first thing that struck Alina was the fact there was no windows, just artificial daylight. The room was large and tastefully decorated. Sat at a desk was a well-built man in a grey suit. He removed his glasses and smiled at Alina.

"Ah welcome, I have been expecting to see you, come and sit down."

Victor Savelyev walked around the desk and shook her hand enthusiastically.

"Thank you, Miss Soskiev that will be all for now. I will call you when we are finished. Can I offer you something to drink?"

Alina was thoughtful, wondering what she was getting into. There was no way out of this room until she was let out; she had heard the door shut with a metallic click when the assistant left.

"Oh yes, coffee please Mr Savelyev no sugar, just milk."

"Please feel at ease, Ms Petrenko. And call me Victor; I am a Director. My specific job is as overseer for special clients who use our bank depositories."

He poured out two cups of coffee, lovingly prepared in bone china cups with the bank's logo on them, placed on gold-rimmed saucers with accompanying silver spoons. He put them on the desk. Alina couldn't help noticing the spotless mini-kitchen at his disposal. It had everything needed to sustain a person or persons for some time. A well-stocked bar was evident behind the wood and glass panelled drinks cabinet. It was evident that he spent an awful lot of time in this enclosure at all times of the day and night.

"I need to ask you some security questions before we can proceed. Do you have your digital identity card with you?" He knew she would have as it was a mandatory requirement for all Russia citizens. They had to be carried by each individual, especially in Moscow. The police had the authority to stop anyone at any time and ask for identity.

"Yes, of course." Alina produced the card from her purse and handed it to him. He took it and read the relevant details on it. Producing an ultraviolet scanner from his desk, he scanned the pass with it.

"Well, I have never seen that done before. Mind you, I have only been asked for it a few times in the past."

"No, the police carry them in their cars but rarely use them unless they suspect something." He paused and sipped his coffee with relish. "The only time I've seen it in operation was in Gorky Park. When challenged, a suspected illegal immigrant produced his pass and much to his annoyance, the policeman had a handheld scanner. Well, the guy did a runner across the park the second it was identified as fake. Two plainclothes officers gave chase, wrestled him to the ground and put him in handcuffs!"

This broke the ice and Alina laughed and relaxed a little. Victor handed the card back to Alina.

"Yes, that's fine, thank you."

You are still at the address of Flat 14, Block 6, Elevatornaya Street, Nekrasovka, and East Moscow District?"

"Yes, I am."

He paused, pushed his glasses to the end of his nose and sipped his coffee.

"Ah! I drink far too much of this stuff; about twelve cups a day. I am now on decaf... I started to get visual migraines until I switched." He sat and studied a large highlighted mural of Gorky Park that stood from floor to ceiling.

"Beautiful, isn't it? I travel all over the world and have never discovered anything to equal our park. In my spare time, I make straight for it whatever the weather."

"It is absolutely stunning; I have never seen a painting so large or life-like. I have fond memories of the park myself." Her mind recalled the few, but wonderful times she had spent there with Nadim

Savelyev pushed his glasses back on. He turned and looked directly at Alicia.

"Now, my special client has instructed me to give you access to a safety deposit box down in the vaults. I have been furnished with information that you have a passphrase given to you by him. Do you have this password?"

She was taken aback by his sudden abruptness, "Yes, I do. It is never say never," she said sternly.

He smiled, "That will do fine, Ms Petrenko. Just a few more issues before we go to the vaults. Do you have your key?"

Alina opened her purse and handed the key to him. He opened his desk drawer and took out a magnifying glass. Handing the key back to her, he went to a large electronic wall safe and entered a six-digit code. The safe opened, and she could see several keys hanging in rows. He selected one on the top row, withdrew it and locked the safe. My God thought Alina. There must be a number engraved on the key. So small, I didn't realise it was there.

He returned to his desk. "Now Ms Petrenko, let me explain how things work."

"Please call me Alina."

"Okay, Alina thank you. I need you to look at some papers." He opened a brown leather-bound file and passed it to her. "My client has set up an account in your name, and also a safety deposit box. I must add I have absolutely no knowledge of its contents."

"Was it set up by a Mr Nadim Babachenko?"

He just smirked. "I am not at liberty to divulge any information regarding any of my clients." He did not have to; his expression told Alina all she needed to know.

"Now your safety deposit box is in the inner sanctum of the vault. You have a platinum key set, which is the highest level of security. My client has paid for a twenty-four month rental in advance. That includes a private booth that allows you thirty minutes to peruse the contents of your box, depositing or removing whatever you need to. After your allotted time slot is up, I will come in, and we will secure your safety deposit box together. Of course, you can request me to come in earlier, by using the intercom. We have found from experience that 30 minutes is more than enough time for clients to conduct business. You have access to the facility once a day, on a daily basis if you require it." "Victor, I'm sure you won't see me that often." He composed himself and looked at the mural again. Alina was spellbound and waited for him to carry on. She knew it was just another chapter in his daily routine, but to her, this scenario was like something out of a thriller film.

"I can tell you in all the twenty-four years I have worked in this post, there has never been a security breach, or loss of box contents, whatsoever. Sometimes clients drop or mislay things, including large Rouble notes. We have a thorough search at the end of each day if we find anything, it will be held securely until a client approaches us. Of course, you are ultimately responsible for the safety of your contents. Is that understood?"

"Yes, of course."

"While I make another coffee, please read the acceptance form applicable to what I have just told you. There is also a form there for you to sign. It's an acknowledgement of the bank rules for an account in your name. You will be given a copy to keep."

"But I don't have an account with this bank."

Victor smiled. "My client provisionally set one up in your name. In your file are a bank debit card and passbook."

Alina opened the book. To her amassment; a deposit of 41,000 Roubles was showing. How much influence did Nadim Babachenko have for goodness sake? Only the director knew that.

"Can I offer you another coffee, my dear?"

"No, thank you, I'm fine."

He allowed her to read the forms in the file without interruption. To his relief, she signed where required. Babachenko had briefed him that she may be reluctant to accept what was on offer. The fact that he was a personal friend of the bank's chairman made it imperative that Alina did conform. Victor returned to his desk and accessed his computer. He typed in a few words, sat back and enjoyed his coffee.

"There! Your account is now live. Welcome to Siret Bank. Your account will be based here, but you can transact business in any of our branches throughout Russia. There is just one other matter about which I must brief you. When we go to the vault, I will direct you to your safe. I will insert this key and unlock the first mechanism in the top slot; you will then enter your key in the lower one and turn it a full turn to the left. This will open the door, and you can take out the inner box. The keys will remain in the safe door for the duration of your visit. Please be aware, if you lose your key, then the whole panel to your consul will have to be replaced. For security reason, we do not keep any replica keys whatsoever. The cost of replacement is currently running at 28,000 Roubles." Jesus thought Alina; 'I nearly threw mine away and had it loose in my purse with my small change.'

"Is there anything you want to ask me concerning what we have discussed" "Well I do find this all a bit overwhelming, to say the least. I don't suppose you will elaborate with regard to the client who has set this up on my behalf?"

Victor Savelyev turned and starred at his treasured mural. He rubbed his chin and sighed. "You know the answer to that, Ms Petrenko."

Victor rose from his chair and drained the coffee cup. He gathered up the papers she had signed, placed them in a folder and locked them in another desk drawer. He walked towards the mural. He took a small electronic device out of his pocket and pointed it at an illuminated panel. To Alina's amazement, the whole mural slid to the side to reveal a lift door.

"This is my private entry to the basement vault, and the only time you will need to use it. Please follow me. I assume you have no guns, knives or drugs in your possession?"

"No, I do not."

"Good, because there is a body scanner and your handbag will be searched. Please do not be alarmed; we have to take all precautions necessary in securing our clients' assets."

The lift was big enough to hold four people but still felt claustrophobic to her. She was shaking, and her knees were like jelly. This might be the world that Nadim Babachenko was at ease with, but it was totally alien and frightening to her. The descent seemed an age, and she did not have any idea how many floors they had traversed. Finally, the lift stopped, and the door opened. Stepping out into a wide corridor, Victor used a zapper again to gain access to the vault. It was much bigger than Alina had imagined. Two armed and rather menacing looking security guards were in attendance. She had no doubt they were ex-military. Immediately they sprang to attention, and both saluted Savelyev.

"Please follow me through the scanner. It has been built for a specific purpose. It is not detrimental to your health. I go through it more than once a day, almost every day. I'm so glad it cannot register the amount of coffee I consume." He smiled.

A female security guard sat at a desk adjacent to the

scanner. A rather large lady, who had a holstered sidearm at her disposal and looked like she knew how to use it, politely asked Alina if she could examine her handbag. It was only a clutch bag, but safety and security rules dictated she had to comply. It took only seconds, and the guard handed it back with a huge grin and a salute.

Victor went towards large opaque bulletproof glass doors and used a different zapper. There it was the vault. Alina's mouth dropped open. From table to head height on three walls, were thousands of individual safe's the size of shoe boxes.

"Impressive isn't it. I am responsible for the higher echelon of depositors, the rest I leave for my minions to deal with. What you see are the deposits of the rich and very rich residents of Moscow. Trillions of Roubles and valuable artefacts are here. The only restrictions to deposits are, of course, size. We have other large vaults all over Russia and abroad if you ever need another facility elsewhere."

He put his glasses on and went straight to where Alina's safety deposit box was. She was impressed; he obviously knew the layout off by heart.

"You have got your key?"

He took his out of his pocket and inserted it into the top recess and turned it a complete turn. Alina did the same and the door opened with a metallic click.

"Right, you can use any booth for your inspection. There is a panic button in each booth. If for any reason you need to use it, my guards will be there in an instant to help. Okay, I will leave you to it. You are the only client in the vault at present."

With that, he turned and disappeared through the glass doors. Alina could not stop shaking; it was all she could manage to lift the box out. Slightly deeper than a shoebox but wider, she carried it to the nearest booth and closed the door. Her curiosity was intense. What on earth did Nadim think was so important and secretive to make her go through all this? It just didn't make sense.

When she lifted the hinged stainless steel lid, the inside was like a miniature Aladdin's cave. There were four jewel cases bearing the supplier's name. On each, imprinted in gold lettering, were the words: Faberge Fine Jeweller. 109 Kheschaya Street, Kiev, Ukraine. The first one contained a white gold rope chain necklace, set with five large pure white diamonds. She lifted it out and admired its absolute beauty. Never in her life had she held such a wondrous work of art. Alina carefully placed it back into the white satin housing. The second box contained a silver bracelet set with surrounding rubies and emeralds. Once again, Alina marvelled at its beauty. Opening the third box was a real surprise. There in all its sparkling glory was a 20-millimetre gemstone. Cut to perfection, all the facets had a diamond-bright glow. It was beautiful "No, it can't be." Alina carefully took the gemstone out and held it in the palm of her hand. Her knowledge of crystals led her to believe it was a poudretteite. One of the rarest and most sort after minerals, she could only guess at its value. In very small quantities, they were mined in a privately owned quarry in Mont Saint Hilaire, Quebec, Canada. Her hand was shaking as she carefully put the gemstone back in the box. The fourth box was smaller. She opened it to reveal a simple gold ring in a small housing. Taking it out, Alina was perplexed.

"What does it mean, Nadim?" To her surprise, it fitted her third finger. She stood there in disbelief, imagining she would wake from this incredible dream at any moment. It was no dream.

A white A3 size envelope contained all the covenants concerning the jewels. The last one stated Alina Alexandra Petrenko was the sole owner of the listed items. Signed and countersigned by the previous owner, Nadim Babachenko. It meant they were hers in their entirety.

"How the hell did he know my middle name?" She said aloud. There were several A4 size manila envelopes. When she took out the contents of one, her mouth dropped open. Inside in used, but crisp notes was a large amount of money. The denominations in one envelope, both large and small, were more than her yearly salary. Written on each envelope was the value of the content. In all, they amounted to 8 million Rouble. There was a crimson silk handkerchief, neatly folded, she instantly recognised Clive Cristian No1. Holding it to her nose, she drank in the heady fragrance and cried uncontrollably she was like a small child lost in an unfamiliar and terrifying world. "Oh Nadim, I love you so much, but you frighten me."

Composing herself, she stuffed the handkerchief into her handbag. At the bottom of the box was a sealed reinforced A4 envelope. Embossed on the front in gold print was the sentence,

NOT TO BE OPENED WITHOUT EXPRESS PERMISSION OF VICTOR SAVELYEV.

Carefully placing the items back in the safety deposit box, she wanted to escape from this tomb as soon as possible. Pressing the intercom, she requested Victor's company. He was there within seconds.

"You are ready to leave now, Ms Petrenko?"

"Yes, I am, thank you."

"Then please carry your box to your safe and we will secure it."

He checked the booth to make sure nothing had been left behind, Alina was perplexed.

"Oh, you would be surprised what people leave behind. My best find was a huge diamond ring, dropped on the floor of her booth; the lady client was very relieved when I handed it back to her."

Alina's safe was locked, and both keys removed. He did a final inspection and was happy that all was secured. He removed a black leather fob from his pocket and handed it to her.

"I think your key would be more secure on this."

"Yes, of course, thank you."

They returned to his office in silence. Victor noticed Alina had been crying. He had seen it so many times before; deposit boxes set up for Russian Mafia or Oligarch's cast-offs. When you have immeasurable wealth, it is easy to dispose of excess baggage and get a younger model. There were plenty available. Strange though, he thought, this young lady seemed different; he had to admit she was one of the prettiest he had seen for some time. It puzzled him; he didn't think Dmitri Sparrov was a Mafia boss or an Oligarch.

"Well, Ms Petrenko, you are now fully conversant

with our system. On your next visit, there is no need to see me. On arrival, you will be escorted by one of our senior members of staff to conduct your business in the vault. You will enter by a different secure system, but the process will be much simpler and quicker. You will have noticed amongst the contents of your safety deposit box a folder with explicit instructions. I can tell you this is a copy of the last will and testament of a certain person. I am the sole non-beneficiary executor of that particular will. It is securely stored in my safe. My instructions were that you should have a copy, the only one. Although it has no relevance in law it needs to be kept safe, it is in the best place keep it there, please. I advise you not to open it until you deem it absolutely necessary. Here is a letter of authority from me to open and read the contents when you see fit to do so."

"But how will I know when it is absolutely necessary?"

He looked directly at her, smiled and said: "Oh, you will know."

If she wasn't confused before, she certainly was now.

"Finally, as a special client, here is my card. If you need any help or advice regarding your account, I am available night or day. Can I offer you the service of our bank limousine to wherever you wish to go?"

Alina thought for a while "No, thank you, I need to get some air."

The Director called in his assistant Miss Soskiev.

"Katya, would you please escort Ms Petrenko to the reception."

"Yes sir, please follow me, madam."

Victor opened his desk drawer and took out another file

and started to read it. Without looking up he said,

"Good luck Alina Alexandra Petrenko. Keep safe."

She shivered at his passing comments, it seemed sinister. This was a very powerful and intelligent man, what did he know that she didn't?

Alina wanted to go back to the security of her apartment. This morning had been the most unnerving experience of her life. What was she to do? It was like her life was not her own anymore. How could she confide in anyone about what had happened? With no explanation from Nadim, was she suddenly a rich woman. Conversely had he made her responsible for the safekeeping of expensive jewels and a large amount of money? God knows where it all came from! Was he really the wealthy industrialist who had made a fortune from his business or just a villain that had involved her with the spoils of his shady dealings?

Chapter 33

Monday 19th February 2018 pm
Flat 14 Block 6 Nekrasovka, East Moscow District.

Inside her little apartment, Alina felt safe and secure. She had hurried home in a daze, once inside she locked the door and pulled the blinds. Still, in shock from her ordeal at the bank she needed to think. Pouring herself large Vodka on ice she curled up on her welcoming sofa. Suddenly realising the gold ring was still on her finger she started shaking uncontrollably. Wanting to tear it off and dispose of it, tears erupted again.

"What have I got into, Alina you have been so silly."

Taking a large slug of Vodka, it burned her throat but calmed her nerves.

"What am I to do?"

Immediately she thought of the authorities, her mother and father had taught her honesty was the best policy.

"But what do I tell them for God's sake." She fingered the ring on her third finger. "No, wait a minute Alina, you have done nothing wrong. The fact is you just had a short affair with a man you know very little about."

Topping up her Vodka she felt calmer, she was stressed and tired and drifted into a deep sleep.

The telephone rang and raised her from her comatose state.

"Oh my God, how long have I been out?"

Glancing at her watch it was nearly five o'clock she had slept for at least three hours. Picking up the phone she recognised the voice straight away. A grouch voice barked out,

"Alina, I thought I had better ring and find out how you are and when you might be coming in."

"Oh! Dr Cherkesov, yes, I am feeling much better and think I will be okay to come in tomorrow. It's just a virus but I have stayed in bed and dosed myself up."

"Glad to hear it, your trainee is not up to the job, this morning was absolute chaos, and I need you back."

"Okay Doctor I will try and make it in tomorrow."

"Let's hope so Alina for both our sakes."

The phone line went dead. Rude old fart she thought. Not for the first time Cherkesov had reminded her of the precarious position she held. On the few occasions she had had time off, he had been less than understanding. In all the time she had worked for him, this was the only the third time she had taken sick leave. On the other occasions, she had been genuinely unwell.

Alina considered she was indispensable and he relied on her totally to make things run smoothly. Over the years, the other employees who had been appointed by Cherkesov had either been fired unceremoniously or walked out, unable to deal with his raging tantrums. She beamed at the prospect of him being in panic mode. He was rude and never appreciated all that she did for him. He may be a great specialist in his field but he needed organising and relied on her for just about everything.

She made herself a strong coffee. The Vodka had temporarily dulled the pain of her predicament, now it was back in her thoughts. She removed the gold band from her finger and placed it on the kitchen table. Suddenly remembering the red silk handkerchief she took it out of her handbag. No don't drink in the intoxication of his cologne. She carefully wrapped the ring in the handkerchief and placed it in the kitchen drawer. Suddenly her head fell into her hands and she began to cry again. "Nadim you have made me an emotional wreck. Wherever you are I hope you get your come upance, I hate you."

The coffee would have to wait; the remaining Vodka was a better option. She was hungry and made herself a lovely cheese and tomato toastie. Her mind wandered back to the amazing meals she had enjoyed with Nadim in fantastic places. Although enjoyable not really her scene, a simple life with someone to love and look after her, was all she craved for.

"Why did he not realise the wealth he has showered on me has complicated my life not enhanced it."

Draining the bottle into a glass of ice and retiring to the lounge, calm returned.

"I will cry no more for that man he has gone; I do not have a need for what is deposited at the bank in my name."

Picking up a magazine she would lose herself for the time being. Alina spent a pleasant evening enjoying fascinating reads and some television. It was midnight before she realised it was time for bed.

As usual, she woke early and showered. Making herself some breakfast she muttered, "Well I suppose I had better go and sort the mess out that the old fool has created."

Alina dressed in her smart working clothes and left for the Metro. To her annoyance, the early morning train she usually caught had been delayed by over an hour. Standing there with all the other commuters, this was frustrating.

"Oh, crap I will be late, Cherkesov will hit the roof."

Taking out her mobile phone she dialled the office, the answerphone cut in and she left the appropriate message.

Finally, she arrived at her office an hour and a half late. Cherkesov was waiting for her with a scowl on his face.

"You're late, not a good start after a day off sick."

"Yes, Doctor the Metro is in chaos this morning. Late trains and some that did not arrive at all. Thought I might not get in, I did ring and leave a message." Begrudgingly, he said, "Well next time get a taxi and I will pay half the fare.

"Where is the other girl then?"

"Oh! Phoned in sick this morning, told her not to bother to come back, totally useless. Out of her depth kept making schoolboy mistakes, some of my clients had to wait over half an hour for their appointment with me. That's not what I pay good money for."

"Well Doctor you did not give her a chance, there is a lot to learn, she's not been here long. I need two assistants." Alina argued, "I cannot run this department on my own." "Yes, yes I know," snapped the irritated Cherkesov. "I have already been on to the agency and another receptionist will be arriving in two days' time. I was here until ten o'clock last evening trying to fathom out what that stupid girl had done. Maybe you can sort this mess out in the meantime."

He pointed to a pile of folders on her desk. He stormed

out shouting,

"I expect to see my first patient in fifteen minutes."

"The ignorant old bastard didn't even ask how I was," mouthed Alina. 'I look forward to the day I can tell him to shove his job.'

And so it was for the next 10 working days. The new assistant secretary was very good and a quick learner. The problem was Cherkesov treated her with contempt, as he had with all the others. He took every opportunity to point out whatever small mistake she made and savoured the grovelling apologies. Alina, you don't need this anymore it's affecting your health she thought to herself. She would look for employment elsewhere even taking a cut in salary. After all, she was now a rich woman (a change of heart maybe) and would subsidise whatever income she could get, with the money from Nadim.

On the 5th March, she took the Metro to work and arrived early. It was a cold crisp morning with the sun low in the sky. Lately, everything had been running smoothly, much to the delight of Cherkesov. He had been quite respectful to Alina of late, maybe, at last, he realised her worth. Yes thought Alina, I actually enjoy coming to work now, probably stay for a while. Arriving at the Medical centre she was amazed to see police cars and an ambulance outside. A Kamov Ka 226 police helicopter was circling overhead.

A cordon had been placed around the main entrance and armed police were funnelling people wanting access to a checkpoint. Alina waited in turn as people spoke in hushed voices wondering what on earth was going on. She presented her pass when requested; the officer studied it for a moment and then nodded to a man in plain clothes. He walked over and pawed over her pass.

"Ah Ms Alina Petrenko, yes?"

"Yes, that's me is there a problem."

The plain-clothed senior Ministry of State Security officer said nothing. He beckoned over a black Mercedes that was there in an instant. Showing his pass, "Ms Petrenko, I am Konstantin Abramov, State Security. We would like you to accompany us to a more convenient place. Alina started shaking.

"Am I in some sort of trouble?" The officer smiled. "No not at all, there has been an accident and we would like you to assist us in our enquiries."

She immediately thought of Nadim.

"Oh my God, is it Nadim Babachenko?"

The officer looked puzzled. "No, all will be explained at my office."

A female police officer jumped out of the car and opened the back door, beckoning Alina to enter.

"But I don't understand, I must let my employer know what's happening, he will be annoyed if I am late."

"That's all been taken care of, please get in the car."

"Do I have any choice?"

She was now in a state of panic and really worried about what was happening. The crowd of onlookers didn't help, some of whom she knew. There were gasps and quiet whispers amongst them.

"We would rather you came willingly but no you do not have a choice; we need to talk to you without delay."

The car journey to Bolshaya Lubyanka square was

conducted in silence. The grey impending building gave Alina the shivers, she started to cry.

"Ms Petrenko, Alina, don't worry, I know this building is somewhat overpowering. Unfortunately, until we move to new premises, this is our headquarters."

The armed guards on the gate recognised the car and its occupants and nodded to the operator in the security hut. The solid armoured round bollards that could stop a tank disappeared into the concrete ramp and the electrically operated barrier rose. The senior guard saluted the car and Abramov returned it. They entered a vast basement car park and drove around to a reserved parking space.

"Please, Ms, follow me."

Accompanied by the female officer who introduced herself as Inna Petrov, (Senior Praporschik) they walked a short distance to a lift. It stopped on the seventh floor. When the doors opened Alina was surprised, for an old building the décor seemed quite refreshing. They passed a few people who were going about their business. They duly acknowledged his presence, as he walked to an office marked Konstantin Abramov, Senior Officer. He swiped a pass card and opened the door.

"Please come in and take a seat, would you like some refreshment"

"Black coffee please, no sugar"

"Would you see to that Inna; I will have my normal tea. Thank you."

She nodded and went to a small anti room, obviously the kitchen.

"Now Alina is it okay to call you by your first name?"

"Yes, off course." She was beginning to relax a little.

"When did you last see Doctor Cherkesov?"

"That would have been Friday evening when I left work at 6.30 pm why?"

"Ms Petrenko, I will ask the questions."

She was taken aback by his sudden sharp tone.

"And were you the last person to leave." "

Yes, the Doctor had some notes to write up for me to deal first thing this morning." Inna arrived with the drinks on a tray and placed them on the desk. Alina's mouth was dry she wished she had asked for water now. Luckily the coffee was not to hot and she savoured its refreshing taste. She was aware that the female police officer was watching her intently.

"I'm afraid Doctor Cherkesov is dead." Alina choked on her coffee and started coughing. Abramov carried on. "It would appear he hung himself sometime over the weekend."

"What? It can't be, this must be some mistake."

Inna went to the kitchen and returned with a bottle of water and gave it to her. Sat with her head in her hands, Alina was in shock.

"Why would he do such a thing? Oh my God, his poor wife and children, have they been told?"

"You don't need to concern yourself with that. I'm afraid the doctor was found this morning by the cleaner."

Alina started to shake and cry again.

"Here drink some water and take some time to compose yourself I need to ask some more questions."

He was completely impassive. She welcomed the water and drank to quench her now raging thirst.

"Did the Doctor appear stressed or anxious at all when you left on Friday?"

Alina thought for a while, wiping away the tears she hesitated.

"Well, the Doctor was always on edge no matter what, it's the way he was. Very good at his job but worried about his patients far too much. Friday was no exception, I told him we needed more staff to cope but he would not listen." Alina's hand went to her mouth. "Oh God forgive me; I can't believe he would do such a thing."

The questioning went on for another half an hour. In that time, she gave Konstantin Abramov all the information she could.

"Well, Ms Petrenko that is all at present, Inna will escort you home and stay with you for a while if you wish her too. Alina just nodded. She was in total shock.

Arriving back at her apartment in the unmarked State Security vehicle, it was all she could do to stumble out of the car. Inna Petrov took her arm and waved the driver away. Inside Alina slumped onto the settee and dozed off. When she came too, it was hard to comprehend the situation; her life had been turned upside down. From the heady heights of a penthouse suite in the hotel, Baltscug to the foreboding interior of the Lubyanka complex was trial enough. The memory of the bank and its vault added yet another chapter to her overwhelming experiences. In the last month, Alina had lived a life beyond her wildest imagination. This latest chapter was just too much, what on earth was Cherkesov thinking when he took his own life.

"Ah Alina, awake at last, I took the liberty of making

some coffee. Would you like one?"

"What time is it?"

Inna looked at her watch "It's nearly 6.30."

"Oh God, sorry I just flaked out. Actually, I want something stronger. There's a bottle of white wine in the fridge, I'll get that."

She went to the kitchen and returned with the wine and two glasses.

"Can I offer you a glass?"

"Would love to, but I've got to go back to the office for a while."

Alina filled her glass and sat back on the couch.

"I still can't take this in, why would the doctor want to do such a thing?"

"Well, that's what we want to find out. Forensics will be at the scene for quite some time."

What she wasn't telling Alina was the fact there was no suicide note left. The medication cabinet had been broken into and expensive powerful drugs had been removed, they could not be found. There was no sign of forced entry to the building; CCTV recordings had been taken away for analysis. To the experienced Konstantin Abramov, there were suspicious circumstances.

"Alina, I have to go, is there anyone you wish to call to come and keep you company?"

"No, I would rather be alone for a while."

"Understood, here is my card if you can think of anything that would help with our enquiries, please contact me immediately, we will be in touch."

"When will I be able to return to work?"

"Well I can't answer that at the moment, it's a crime scene and likely to stay that way for some time."

"What do you mean a crime scene?"

"Suicide is a crime and until the circumstances can be fully determined, then the investigation will continue. It will be up to my boss to close the case, but I imagine you won't be returning to that place for the rest of the working week and probably longer."

"No, of course, I understand, not looking forward to returning anyway but I need the job."

Alina showed the officer to the door. She left with a smile and the door was securely locked. Returning to the comfort of her lounger she enjoyed the refreshing wine. What a day. Tomorrow thought Alina I will return to Gorky Park. Our bench, it's the place I feel nearest to Nadim. Tears began to flow once again she could not help it. I wonder what he is doing? She couldn't get him out of her mind. How can I hate him when he has been so generous to someone he only knew briefly. Is it possible he does love me and is it possible I may see him again? She rushed to the kitchen opened the drawer and took out the handkerchief with the ring in it. Placing it on her third finger she felt close to him once again. Lifting the handkerchief to her nose his cologne was fading. She raised her glass and proposed a toast.

"Nadim Babachenko, if you won't come to me then I will find you."

Chapter 34

Tuesday 27th February 2018 07.00 hrs
Captain's cabin H.M.S.Astute

Captain Robert Southward lay on his bunk somewhat disorientated. It was obvious to him he had been given some sort of controlling drug to keep him quiet. Either in his food or his coffee, the effect was to render him physically incapacitated for a good part of his confinement. Up until the last few days he had spent most of the time just wanting to sleep. Fighting hard to stay awake, he was aware of the comings and goings of Dmitri Sparrov and the guard. There were brief conversations between the two men that just sounded like gobbledygook. At one stage with a slurred speech he asked,

"Are you slowly poisoning me and my crew? Am I going to die?"

Red Fox chuckled, "No Captain that is not the plan, you have been rendered inoperable, and that's all. We are nearing the end of our mission. Soon I and my crew will be leaving this submarine and you will be back in control. The affects you have been experiencing will wear off completely. You have been given just water in the last 48 hours that will speed the process."

With that he left the cabin once more, leaving Robert Southward to ponder his circumstances. He tried to focus his mind on what had happened during the time he had been a captive on his own submarine. He knew they had navigated the channel out of Devonport, passed the breakwater, dived and run for some time. The submarine had then come to rest on the sea bed. Having taken this route on many occasions he could probably have conducted the manoeuvre blindfolded. With the running time until they had become stationary his estimation was they were some 25 miles south west of the Plymouth sound, not a bad guess.

Although all aids had been removed from his cabin, allowing him access to time and motion, he was able to gauge reasonable accurately what was happening. After what he thought was approximately 30 hours, his worst fears were realised. Trisonic imaging and hovertrack had been engaged. Trying hard to monitor the time-lapse, the system had been engaged intermittently for about three hours then switched off. He thought the submarine had first of all been heading westwards and after a day or so had taken and stayed on a northerly course. His reasoning was the sea temperature and the salinity, which affected many aspects of the sub. Any change of temperature had a slight effect on the tuning frequency of the hull. Noises generated would change as the steel hull expanded or contracted accordingly. To the experienced ear, these changes could be quite relevant. It was quite obvious to him that for some time a zigzag course had been adopted. Sometimes the submarine was at flank speed and sometimes almost motionless with only the manoeuvring props fwd. and aft keeping the intended course. What sense could he make of it? In the impossible situation, he was in, the frustration was overwhelming. Not a person to concern himself too much with life's kicks in the teeth, his take on life was, 'if I didn't do it and I can't fix then I will not worry about it.' This had worked very well so far for him but this whole scenario was scary. How was his crew, what would happen to his submarine, what would happen to him?

To Southward, it was now obvious this had been the start of the drug abuse he had been subject to. In the last 24 hours, he had lost all sense of time date or location. Latterly, not eating any food and drinking only water had improved his senses slightly. This had allowed him a slightly better perception of the sub's movements. Trisonic imaging and hovertrack had been in almost constant use, this could only mean two things. They were either hugging the coast or navigating a narrow channel somewhere. Not just that, the sea temperature had obviously risen considerably. He could not figure out what was happening he clenched his fists tightly once again. "My God we could not have been cruising north after all, where the hell can we be? Think man think." He propped himself up and ran his fingers through his hair. His situation was completely hopeless, his life and that of his crew were in the hands of one man Red Fox, would he keep his word or were they all doomed?

The true Captain of Astute was roused from his thoughts with a start, the submarine is motionless, he thought. A lot of movement and voices were apparent. External of the hull he could feel the drumming of powerful diesel engines. The cabin door abruptly slid open and Sparrov entered.

"Well Captain, it is time I took my leave of you and this fine submarine. All demands have been met by your government and most importantly the ransom paid. As I speak my men are busy unloading the last of the equipment we brought on board. Your vessel has been rendered inoperable other than to dive and surface. There are no weapons left on-board other than cutlery in the galley. Ship to shore and satellite communications are now out of action. (By his connivance Mike Grayling had made this possible). The torpedo tubes have been spiked and all computer software encrypted that would allow you to manoeuvre and retaliate once we leave. I can assure you any attempt to put these systems back into action will result in major damage to them. Your officer of the watch has been given orders when instructed to do so dive the submarine to 400 feet and remain there. You can release your S.O.S. buoys and await rescue. The submarine would have already been spotted by American satellite anyway. No doubt ocean-going tugs will be dispatched to tow the submarine back to Gibraltar or home."

What the British Captain didn't understand was this person stood in front of him seemed to be wasting time and not readily making his escape. Would a bullet to the head be his final act of barbarity? The truth was with all that had happened nothing was beyond the realms of possibility. Robert remained surprisingly calm. He had faced many challenges during his naval career but none more alarming than this.

Handcuffed and shackled there was little that could be

done if his time was up he would take it like the professional officer he was.

"So after all this, you and your band are just common thieves."

Sparrov laughed, "Not just common thieves, but very rich thieves. Captain, the challenge to be the best has gone on for centuries. In mother Russia we are not stupid. Some years ago, one of your submarines stole our latest towed array operating system. While in Russian Territorial waters, the 3-inch cables were severed from the stern of our intelligence-gathering ship that was on exercise. It was taken back to your base in Scotland and then flown to America for assessment."

Southward said nothing and just listened with intent. He tried to give the impression he had no knowledge of what Red Fox was talking about.

"Operation Barmaid, I believe. Just making international waters before the theft was discovered was a lucky break for your submarine. What the Captain did not know, was his command could have been despatched to the bottom of the Atlantic by one of our surface ships. Carrying rocket-assisted depth charges; their range and speed would have neutralised and sunk the British sub. The risk of a public outcry was considered too great to execute a plan; the submarine and its crew of 120 were allowed to live. Oh yes, we had her signature from way back, we were well aware of the theft that had been carried out by your Navy."

Captain Robert Southward was stunned into silence. Yes, of course, he knew of operation Barmaid and its unequalled success. What he didn't know and neither did the Admiralty, was how close H.M.S Conqueror came to being destroyed.

"You need to remember we could have sold Astute to a country that would have paid a king's ransom to obtain this cutting edge technology. Under those circumstances, you and your crew's safety could not be guaranteed. As an alternative, contingency plans were made to take the sub to the Feodosiya shipyard in Crimea that has been readied to facilitate the Astute and your crew. Fortunately for you all, your Government have seen fit to comply. So, we really have no need to detain you any longer. It doesn't really matter what you know now, this scenario is coming to an end. I am sure you feel bitter at this outcome but look at the bigger picture. You know Alaska was part of Russia until March 30th 1867. Sold to America for a pittance, that was a big mistake. We know, in the event of a third world war, nuclear missiles targeted at our country will be fired from there. Mother Russia must always be on the defensive and offensive. To balance what the west portrays in public and only reveals in private is a constant battle. Covert operations like this one will always be conducted, this just happens to be the best one yet." Red Fox smiled.

"No matter where you hide, you and your gang of pirates will be hunted down and brought to justice."

A wide grin appeared on Dmitri Sparrov's face. "No Captain, that's not the way it will work. I am sure once your rescue has been enacted; you will immediately be flown back under armed guard to your naval headquarters, along with with your ships log. Of course, I have copied all the relevant pages concerning this adventure. It will make great reading to people who have a vested interested. Your crew will be placed in quarantine in Gibraltar or maybe flown directly home for debriefing. A fresh crew will be on this sub in the very near future and will remain so until the submarine returns to the U.K."

"You seem very sure of yourself, whoever you purport to be."

"Well, I have to say this whole scenario has gone better than expected with very little bloodshed. Believe me, we would have taken whatever action was necessary to bring this to a successful conclusion, I thank you for your co-operation."

"Don't thank me. I absolutely loathe what you and your band of pirates have done; the truth is you gave me no choice. I was not concerned about my own welfare, only of my crew."

"Very noble of you Captain, typically British if I may say so. Your debriefing will reveal some interesting facts. It has already been agreed with your government, there will be no retribution against me or any of my men. I anticipate this agreement will not be kept and some covert operation will be mounted by a third party to try and administer my demise."

It was concerning but Sparrov believed he would be rigorously protected.

"This is a complete embarrassment for the Government your service and the western world in general, the whole incident will be hushed up. For all intents and purposes, you will have been on a training exercise with the Turkish navy and your submarine developed a problem with the reactor. Not serious, but enough to facilitate a tow to Gib for minor repairs. A frigate and a destroyer are on manoeuvres with their navy as we speak, so it's perfectly feasible."

Red Fox's radio sparked into life; it was Ivor Pushkin on the casing.

"We are ready to leave now, Captain."

"Message received, I am on my way, see you topside, over and out."

A lot of equipment had been ditched over the side, of little importance now it made for a swift departure on the fast cruiser. A wry smile crept over Sparrov's face. "Finally, Captain you need to know, the Master at Arms and your officer of the watch, plus one other are the only men at large. All the rest are shackled and in handcuffs but perfectly safe. Your Senior Rate will find the angle grinder and you will be released very soon. Your first officer in the control room has been ordered to dive the submarine when we have left. I expect this to happen within five minutes of our departure." With his guard outside they made ready to leave. "We will be watching and if the sub continues to wallow, rocket-propelled grenades will be fired at your escape hatches and the fin."

Of course, by that time Red Fox intended to be many miles away, the large fast cruiser at their disposal was capable of obtaining 38 knots. With that, he saluted Captain Robert Southward turned and left the cabin, without a second glance. The strange thing was he wanted to return the salute but resisted. Although this man had effectively ruined his naval career, mutual respect had been exchanged. It seemed that Captain (First Rank), Dmitri Sparrov had kept his word and the crew would be safe.

Bob Southward was completely calm, was it the relief of knowing this nightmare was nearly over. Was it the after-effects of the drugs that had kept him in a comatose state for so long? Whatever it was soon his naval training would take over and he would be back in charge, he had to think straight. He was confident all that he had been told, had a consequential element of truth. The shame of losing control of the most important submarine in the British fleet weighed heavily on his shoulders. Surely his commander in chief would never believe he would be a party to what had happened. To encourage and collude in this act of piracy would be a treasonable act, no his conscience was clear and he would be vindicated, at least he hoped so.

Straining every tissue listening intently to what was happening; he tried to gauge what was going on. There was still activity on the casing, then silence. Drumming engines were idling on the port side of the submarine. Within minutes they were sparked into life and he could feel the violent wash of the departing vessel. Whatever it was, it was definitely big powerful and probably fast. Securely shackled and unable to reach the cabin door to open it he reverted to the Mk1 method of communication. Shouting at the top of his voice he summoned any officer or rating within earshot.

He was suddenly aware of the submarine diving. The cabin door flew open and the master at arms entered with an angle grinder and bolt croppers.

"Are you all right, Sir?"

"Yes chief, more importantly how are the crew."

"A bit subdued, total disbelief at what has happened."

A few knocks and bruises metered out from the barbarians

that took over control of the sub. When they needed help with the triso system, they adopted some strong-arm tactics to both the operators. Under the circumstances, they had no option but to comply. I have to say these people whoever they were learned fast. In the days we have been at sea, our crew have in the main been restricted to their bunk spaces. Latterly they have had no input at all in running of the submarine. Who were they, Sir?"

"Jaunty, for the moment that's not important, get these bloody restraints off, please." Aware the ballast tanks were still being blown he reacted instinctively.

"Chief make sure the rest of the men are released and at their stations as soon as possible. Control and Man room personnel first of course."

The instant he was free, he hurriedly made his way to the control room.

"Attention. Captain on the bridge, good to see you, Sir."

Robert Southward returned the Salute. "And it's certainly good to see you, Ray."

In a calm and authoritative voice, he commanded,

"Sit rep please."

"All communications throughout the boat and ship to shore are inoperative. The pirate's somehow shut them down before they left. To all intents and purposed we are a blind and deaf unit. Until the men are back in their compartments, we have no idea what other sabotage has been carried out."

Deceased Mike Grayling had carried out his treacherous acts with impunity. The Captain studied the reactor monitors; he was pleased to see it was at idle state. He hoped they had not tampered with any systems associated with it that would be a serious matter.

"Right, we do it the old fashioned way, when all the men are released set up runners from here to manoeuvring room, main machinery space and torpedo compartments. Is the hydraulic system still functioning?"

"Yes Sir, we can operate watertight doors, all the indications are nothing has been altered. We can switch to handraulic if anything to the contrary shows up. What is apparent though is they have delayed the release of our S.O.S, buoys by an hour. Obviously, to enact their escape, the bastards have thought of everything."

"Okay Ray, I don't have a problem with that, after what we have been through that won't make an awful lot of difference. It will also give me time to get around the sub and see everyone."

"Understood, Sir, we have already logged what we know. Unfortunately, because there was very little conversation and certainly no facial recognition, we don't have much. The barbarians hid their identities to great effect."

Astute hovered at 400 feet, the released sailors went back to what they had been trained for relieved to be still alive. The boat returned to some sort of normality although not able to function as a fighting unit. Just then an enormous explosion reverberated against the hull of the submarine.

"What the hell was that?"

"Certainly not a depth charge, Ray, that explosion came from the surface. Strange, the pirates could be destroying anything they are not taking with them, that's my best guess."

Everyone listened in silence as debris made its way

to the bottom of the sea. Distant gunfire had been heard some minutes earlier followed by the explosion. What no one on-board could possibly know was what had unfolded not far from them. They had witnessed the destruction of the Kirmizi Kayalar along with the deaths of four Turkish fishermen. The shattered remnants of what had been a fishing boat lay more than 1,000 metres on the sea bed.

After all the checks that could be made were made, Robert Southward could relax somewhat. A sense of order had been restored and with his crew, he could do no more than, sit and wait for the rescue. Addressing charge Chief Baker, Bob said,

"I believe tea, coffee and cake all round are in order. Would you communicate with the chef?"

"Indeed, Sir a pleasure to do so."

"Ray, as soon as we start transmitting our locator beacons, I will go to converse with all the other crew. I want to glean as much information about what has gone on before the crap hits the fan. I am going to my cabin you have control."

"I have control, Sir."

The navigating officer waited until the Captain had left and then whispered to Fleet Chief Macdonald,

"God knows what he has been through at the hands of those awful people. The trouble is I think once he gets back home, he has the worst to come yet."

"Absolutely, tough as he is all this will take some getting over."

Back in the confines of his cabin, for the first time, he thought of what he was going to say to Alicia. All that had gone on since he left his base on that fateful day Monday 12th February 2018 would be classified top secret. A professional naval officer or not he was a human being first and foremost. A sense of foreboding came over him and he felt physically sick. Urging a couple of times was all he could manage, the lack of food in the last 48 hours meant there was nothing to bring up. Where had all the years gone, what mistakes had he made? His sense of reasoning had been shot to pieces but still, when he needed to, he fulfilled the role of Captain of H.M.S. Astute. This was especially true in front of his men. He dropped his head in hands and mumbled,

"Is this the start of a nervous breakdown?"

For once in his life, he felt very vulnerable and alone.

There was a knock on the cabin door; he must have nodded off.

"Enter"

It was the runner, a Killick, (leading seaman).

"Sir, from the navigating officer the rescue buoys have been released and have spooled to the surface. It is confirmed they are transmitting."

"Thank you; please relay my order back to stand down the runners. Furthermore, the submarine is to come to action stations until further notice."

"I will relay the information, Sir."

As he intended, Southward spoke in turn to all his men. There wasn't much they could add to what was already known. Everywhere, the pirates had kept their identities to themselves and would only engage in the conversation when necessary. The sparse amount of information he was able to record might be of some help to the powers that be.

His last visit was to the Torpedo stowage compartment. The weapons leading seaman was busy studying the manuals.

"Hello, Sir it's a bit of a mess, trying to figure out just what has been done. I can tell you the hydraulics have been put out of action and the tubes have been interfered with."

"Well, I wouldn't worry about that too much until we get into dry dock."

Suddenly they heard the unmistakable throbbing of diesel engines getting ever nearer.

"I believe our tow trucks have arrived."

The rating laughed.

"That's our Captain, bless him, still has a sense of humour after all that has happened."

"Okay just monitor the situation here until we surface, thank you."

Making his way back to the control room, a sense of foreboding engulfed the Commander. He gave the order to surface and got ready to open the lower fin hatch. When given the nod by the officer of the watch, he exited the compartment and ascended the ladder to open the upper hatch. Climbing onto the small platform a Merlin helicopter flew overhead and circled. Idling close, in all their glory waiting to assist, was the ocean-going tugs Colossus and Hercules. The deck party would make ready the towing cable for the long hall back to safety. Not quite the fitting end expected to an otherwise unblemished career.

For Captain Robert John Southward the next chapter of his life would be challenging to say the least.

Chapter 35

Tuesday 27th February 2018 07.30hrs
Super Cruiser Spring Adventure

As Captain Sparrov stepped out onto the submarine's casing, he knew all was secured. Via the two way radio, Red Fox issued the order to the Executive Officer in Astute's control room to shut all watertight hatches and prepare to dive in exactly five minutes. It was to be taken down to 400 feet and remain there until rescue came. That would be the end of all internal communications, the radio the E.O. Ray Lavis had, would be the only one left on-board. The remainder other than the one the Russian Captain had were disposed of by Ivor Pushkin. It was important Red Fox still had radio communications in case something went wrong with the dive. He carefully made the walk across the gangplank from the submarine to Spring Adventure. In the slight swells of the Aegean Sea, like his men the confinement they had been subjected to, make walking the plank unnerving. Codin was there to assist and make sure his charge didn't end up in the ogin. The gangplank was stowed as they were escorted by a man in camouflage uniform to the bridge. He slung his Kalashnikov over his shoulder and saluted. Ivor Pushkin returned the salute; the escort had to be Spetznaz he thought.

"Hello, Sir, welcome aboard. Great to meet you at last. I am Captain Adrian Rushkov and I have heard a lot about you."

"Thank you Captain all bad I hope?"

"Well I don't know about that, but I do know the powers that be hold you in great esteem. I see you have hitched a lift all the way from the United Kingdom in one of her Majesties great warships."

"Yes indeed, unfortunately, I have to hand it back having been a guest for 3,100 nautical miles; it's a great piece of machinery. I have to say it will be nice for me and my sailors to high tail it back to safety though. Firstly, I want to lay off 300 metres from the submarine until they dive, it should take a matter of a few minutes. What traffic is there around?"

"Very little I'm glad to say, a fishing boat two miles to our Port and a Turkish patrol boat 30 miles distant heading away."

The yacht's tannoy let everybody know they were about to move. The Captain dialled in a speed of 10 knots and the vessel retreated to a safe distance.

"Codin, do you have men stood by with rocket-propelled grenades?"

"Yes Sir, Baskov and Kuzlow are on the stb'd walkway ready to pepper the fin at your instruction, that will make them dive."

Red Fox rubbed his chin, it was imperative the submarine vanished beneath the waves to give them time to escape. "I don't think the British officer would be foolish enough to remain on the surface, he knows exactly what the consequences are if he does."

On the bridge of the fishing boat, Captain Mehmet Abaci watched in amazement as the large cruiser and what he thought to be a Russian submarine appeared to have collided. He barked out an order to his three man crew.

"Hall in and stow the gear immediately."

They had only just shot the drift net so there was very little catch to deal with. As soon as all was stowed the diesel engine was started and they headed for what was thought to be a serious melee. There were no outward signs as to the identity of the Yacht and to the fishing boat's Captain that was confusing.

On the spacious bridge of the 'Spring Adventure', the radio sparked into life. "This is the Kirmizi Kayalar (Red Rocks) to the large stationary vessel, do you need assistance?"

Immediately Captain Rushkov raised his binoculars to look at the approaching menace. His second in command immediately typed the identification number of the fishing boat into the computer search engine. In seconds it came back, Kirmizi Kayalar, Turkish fishing vessel 65 tons, with a crew of four, homeport Imbros, Gokceada. The message was repeated without reaction. Abaci spoke into his mic, "They must be fucking deaf or having one hell of a party on that floating Gin Palace, you would think someone would respond. Anyway, we will mosey over and see if they want to buy some fresh fish."

In his usual calm manner, Red Fox issued orders,

"Maintain radio silence, Codin take two men in the rigid

raider and deal with this nosey intruder. You know what to do, we cannot allow them to give our position away."

Without a word, Ivor Pushkin rushed aft and ordered Michmen Nikolay Popov and Boris Maklasov to get their arms and follow him to the boat.

"Don't forget balaclavas and keep all weapons out of sight until we know what we are dealing with."

The 5.2 metre boat with a single 140 hp engine was launched and underway in record time. Capable of 37 knots it would cover the distance quickly. As they left, the sound of high-pressure air being ejected from ballast tanks was music to the pirate's ears, Codin looked around the submarine was diving.

The rigid raider approached the fishing boat and Ivor Pushkin spoke into the loud hailer.

"Ahoy there, heave to you are being boarded."

Captain Mehmet engaged the autopilot and then appeared on the stb'd bridge wing with a bottle in one hand and a shotgun in the other. He levelled it at the now near idling rigid raider.

"Who the hell are you and what do you want?"

Codin raised the Uday Boa handgun with the collimator laser sight and fired three nine millimetre fragmentation rounds into Mehmet. He slumped back against the bridge wing door and dropped the gun as his head exploded. One of the crew appeared on deck brandishing a large filleting knife. Bad move, Maklasov swung the Kalashnikov rifle around and gave a short burst at the unlucky fisherman, he died instantly. Seeing what had happened the remaining guy on deck, jumped over the port side and began to swim away as fast as he could.

"Get me alongside the boat," ordered Pushkin. It was making about 5 knots so with his backpack he was able to jump aboard with ease.

"Right go and deal with the swimmer and don't bring him back."

Maklasov swung the rigid raider away from the fishing boat and allowed it to drift aft. Clear now he gunned the engine and raced after the hapless man in the water. In seconds he was caught and run down, the propeller gouging great chunks out of him, he was shark bate now. Codin took his backpack off, drew his gun and quickly went to the wheelhouse to disengage the autopilot. On the bridge wing, the mess that was once Ahmed Mehmet lay there. Still clutching the remnants of his bottle of whisky he looked a hapless soul. Pushkin was well aware one of the crew was unaccounted for it was obvious he had to be found and eliminated. There was no sign of the man around the deck area. With gun drawn he stealthily made his way to the obvious place, he was expected to be the engine room.

Gingerly the Russian made his way to where the hatch was open. With his gun at the ready, he made his way down the ladder. Suddenly he had a searing pain in the back of his leg; missing the last few rungs he hit the deck hard. A bear of a man rolled on top of him with the intent of strangulation. With his gun cocked Codin pumped six rounds into his attacker and heaved him off. Blood was now pouring from the wound where he had been stabbed. Taking a medical pack out of a pouch in his jacket he dressed the wound and stemmed the flow. Making a tourniquet with a large rag and a spanner he laid there feeling dizzy. He popped two Morphine tablets that would soon ease the pain.

"Ivor, Ivor are you okay?"

It was Maklasov. "What, oh shit I must have passed out, that twat stabbed me, it will be the last time he uses that filleting knife."

He noticed his leg had been attended to with a clean dressing and a proper tourniquet. What luck, among his other talents the Michman was a trained medic.

"Can you walk?" Ivor Pushkin got to his feet with the aid of Nikolay.

"Did you pick up my backpack with the semtex charges in?"

"Yes, thought you might want to set a couple here."

"Well we are not going to hang about; you will have to deal with them now. It's going to take me a while to get to the raider. Those two five-gallon drums of petrol tip them over and let the fuel drain into the bilges, place one charge there. Put the other one between the diesel fuel tank and the bulkhead. The third one goes in the wheelhouse." The explosives were housed in metal containers that had built-in timers, perfectly safe until primed.

"Once I have got to the deck, set the timers for eight minutes.

Boris Popov helped Codin into the rigid raider while Maklasov set the bombs in the engine room climbed the ladder and secured the hatch. He promptly made his way to the wheel, secured the third explosive and started the engine. He then smartly joined the others in the rigid raider.

"Our Captain must be champing at the bit to get away

and so am I, let's go."

Within five minutes all were safely on-board the Spring Adventure. Ivor Pushkin advised Captain Rushkov of the imminent firework display. Lifting the mic from its cradle he announced to all, the Yacht was about to fast cruise. It set off at pace to the sound of an enormous explosion as the Kirmizi Kayalar blew up. There would be little trace of what had happened, a necessary evil to maintain the secrecy of Red Fox's movements.

Chapter 36

Tuesday 27th February 2018, 8 o'clock in the morning
Penthouse suite, Arlington Hotel, Sandbanks Bournemouth

Alicia Juliet Southward had been lonely and bored. Robert was so wrapped up with the complexities of his naval life that she felt ignored and isolated. His infrequent visits normally ended in an argument of some kind over the most trivial of things. Most recently he had chosen not to come home during his downtime; he just assumed that Alicia would cope as she always had. Even threatening to board a plane and fly off to Australia had made no difference to his attitude to their relationship. Of late he had become very selfish and their marriage was definitely heading for the rocks. So, she did not feel any guilt with the way she had conducted her life for the past 3 months.

Having only two recently contacted good friends in England, their lives were completely different from hers. Both married with children, Alicia felt a bit of an outcast. Of course, she was made welcome whenever they met, especially at their palatial homes. But talk of married life with children bored her silly. Fortunately both her friends had married into money, so their lives were just one long round of having fun, while the kids were in various boarding schools. Alicia was sure that Oceania was having an affair, her husband spent long periods of time in New York and Spain, where he had his business interests. Laura was as mad as a hatter; her attitude to life was the same as when they were at Rhodeen together. Loving her Gin, she certainly drank too much but hay-ho who was Alicia to judge. So why did she envy them so much? God knows what went on behind closed doors. Good friends or not, what went on behind closed doors stayed behind closed doors. Their lives seemed so much more complete than hers; this had to change for her wellbeing.

It had all started so innocently. Having tried the obvious, Gym workouts and a nice social club, it had just left her exhausted and depressed. Going back to Australia seemed the only way out and she had made up her mind that was the way forward. It was Oceania who had suggested joining the tennis club she belonged to. Well, it would be a way of getting Alicia out of what was now a life she hated. With no parents, siblings or children, it was obvious she was lonely and needed to find something to focus on.

"Look just come with me as my guest a couple of time, you never know you might like it, what have you got to lose?"

"Well, actually not a lot I suppose."

"Alicia babe that's the most sensible thing I have heard you say in a long time." Oceania consulted her diary. "How does Thursday morning at ten o'clock suit I will book a 2-hour session?"

"Christ I will be a bit rusty; I haven't played in ages."

"No worries I don't take it too seriously just good

exercise and some fun."

Well, that turned out to be wrong, Oceania was a good player and very competitive. The strange thing was Alicia really enjoyed it and towards the end of the session managed to win a couple of games. That's when she decided to join and book some coaching lessons.

The day after getting her membership, Alicia walked into the reception area and heads turned. In her crisp white pleated skirt and matching top, she certainly cut a dash with the group of male players sat in the adjacent lounge area. Before she had time to ask questions about her lesson, a tennis coach approached her.

"Hello, you must be Alicia, I'm Ben Richards, and I've been expecting you."

"Oh yes, and what have you been expecting?"

"Oh!" For a moment Ben was lost for words. "Certainly not someone who looks like they have just modelled for Vogue magazine."

"Flattery will get you nowhere; I've just come to improve my game that's all."

She flashed her wedding ring and he got the message.

"Of course, forgive me; I understand you want to improve your game, a bit rusty I guess."

"Yes, that will be great, haven't played consistently for quite a while."

"Okay I have booked court nine for an hour, it's nice and quiet there and no one will be watching."

"Well I'm certainly relieved about that, probably won't be able to hit a ball."

This broke the ice and they both laughed.

"Can I carry your sports bag?"

"No, I'm not an invalid, certainly not yet, maybe when we have finished, I might be."

That was three months ago. There lying in Ben's arms Alicia felt safe and loved. The relationship had evolved over a short period that resulted in her ended up in bed in his large Batchelor apartment. Overlooking the estuary of Brown Sea Island in Poole, it seemed perfectly natural to have a sexual relationship with him. She turned over and stroked his long dark hair. He was ten years her junior, although no one would guess, he looked marginally older than she did. His stamina was unyielding and he gave her unimaginable orgasms that she had not enjoyed for a long time. The trouble was Alicia was falling in love with him now and he seemed to be reciprocating.

"Good morning babe, coffee for two, whites no sugar?"

She smiled "Yes Please."

Naked, Ben climbed out of the king-sized bed donned his white robe and disappeared into the kitchen. Why did she not feel guilty, still married, with no intention of hurting Robert was it wrong to be with someone else? Here in her lover's bed, she knew this was a true relationship for only the second time in her life. The first, her marriage was dying a slow and painful death. Divorce seemed the only option; she would confront her husband in the near future, that's if he surfaced anytime soon.

Ben had been brought up by foster parents and had never married. He had made a good career as a gym equipment supplier and tennis coach. A natural sportsman, he could possibly have made it on the professional Tennis circuit, a motorcycle accident causing life-changing injuries had cut that short. A stay in hospital and a long period of convalescence took its toll but he did regain a level of fitness. His million-pound bachelor apartment was his solace in a never-ending round of entertaining rich women who considered him a great coach and easy meat, he wasn't.

Early in the relationship with Alicia, he had confessed to having had encounters with some of the females that requested his professional tutoring. However, since becoming involved with her he had given all that up, much to the frustration of his predatory admirers. Out of a fit of jealousy, one had tried to warn Alicia off; she got short shrift in no uncertain terms. The so-called lady was told to mind her own business and get on with her life, Ben belonged to no one. Alicia had removed her wedding ring and had taken to using her maiden name. Although she had only known this guy for a relatively short time, he had brought happiness into her life. He was so attentive and had even given up the tennis coaching. When not involved with his Buisiness she had his full attention.

He came back into the bedroom with coffee and toast. Jam and marmalade in neat little pots, they were the ones she liked. A single red rose in a crystal stemmed glass adorned the tray.

"What are you doing writing me a Dear John letter?"

"I'm actually writing to Robert asking for a divorce."

"Wow! Are you sure about this?"

"Are you sure you love me like you say you do, especially when we are making love?" He put the tray on the bedside table and took her hand in his. He looked deep into her eyes and whispered,

"I truly love you."

She felt tears welling up and not for the first time but resisted the urge of a proper cry.

"I have never met a woman like you, how the hell your husband has been silly enough to ignore you for so long is beyond my comprehension."

"Oh, it's not all his fault, the service especially the submariner branch expect one hundred per cent commitment. I have lived with it all my life and that's just the way it is. I want a divorce regardless of where our relationship goes."

"Well, believe me, it won't be me who ends it, I have never truly loved anyone before."

That's when Alicia felt the relationship, all be it in the early stages, was not just about the sex. He looked sad,

"As you know, I was brought up by foster parents who did their very best to give me a good education. It's sad to say unfortunately, there wasn't too much love there. Until I got to know you, I didn't really know what love was."

She was a good judge of character and instinctively though their lives would be forever intertwined, at least she hoped they would be. She couldn't help it and started to weep.

"Oh God," chuckled Ben, "do I make you cry?"

"I'm just so happy and am scared it won't last."

"I will ask you just one more time, are you really sure you want to end it with your husband? I have never caused a divorce before and I don't much like the idea of being the third party."

Alicia composed herself and put her left hand around the back of his neck and kissed him hard on the lips. "The deed is done; this letter to Robert goes off today. Come on, quick showers and we can catch the ferry over to Swanage. It's a beautiful day out there, let's take advantage of it."

Would Alicia Juliet Southward (Ne Harris) have felt differently if she had known of her husband Robert John Southward's predicament, during the last 15 days? In that, that period of time so much had happened. For all the people involved death for some and glory for others would be their reward. For the crew of the submarine, their eventual release would be a great relief. There would be an awful lot of guilt and soul searching on the part of people who could and should have prevented the piracy in the first place. Amongst other things, Captain Southward had to consider the possibility of losing his cherished command. Conversely in mother Russia, Captain First class Dmitri Sparrov would be hailed a hero. Alicia Southward had found true happiness, at last, any feeling of guilt and pity would never arise again now. She was not a party to the events that took place on Astute and would never hear of them. At the same time, Alina Alexandra Petrenko had become a rich woman but had lost the love of her life.

With regard to the future, when all the information was gathered and equated, what had taken place would seem beyond comprehension. The people involved including the top echelon, military and civilian would be reminded of their commitment to the Official Secrets Act. For many years to come, the whole sorry saga of a British submarine being pirated away from a top security naval base would be kept from the public domain. To all intents and purposes the unbelievable story of H.M.S.Astute's capture, subsequent revelations of its top-secret stealth technology to a foreign power, and eventual return to the British submarine fleet never happened.

Chapter 37

Tuesday 27th February 2018 10.00 hrs
Super Cruiser *Spring Adventure*

Onboard the fast cruiser the air was electric and spirits were high; it was racing towards what was thought by Captain Lieutenant Ivor Pushkin and the rest of the Russian submariner's, their transfer point. It would lead on to a life of luxury for themselves and their families in a place yet to be revealed. They had just pulled off the most audacious plan ever, stealing a British Nuclear submarine, learning all about the stealth characteristics it encapsulated and then handing it back to the perplexed Captain.

On the bridge of the Yacht travelling at 35 knots across the beautiful waters of the Aegean towards the Dardanelle Straights, Codin turned and looked at Captain first-class, Dimitri Sparrov.

"Sir did we really just hand back a state of the art western nuclear submarine to our enemies?"

"Yes, of course, we did Ivor, we have what we set out to get and a lot more."

"I don't understand Captain; yes, I know we have enough technical information to copy Trisonic imaging and hovertrack and incorporate the stealth technology into our own submarines. But surely the whole kit and caboodle would have been a staggering prize?"

"Yes, it would have been but what would we have done with the British crew?" They would have needed to be disposed of somehow or other. Yes in war we would have treated them as our adversary's and not have hesitated to kill them. But just like us, they have families and I am not and never will be an intentional murderer of innocent people. Of course, blood has been shed including yours, that stab wound could have severed an artery, I'm glad it didn't."

"Yes, me too Sir, the doctor said 10mm to the left and it probably would have been curtains."

They entered the Sea of Marmara and to all the Russian sailors, it was now evident they were heading for the Bosporus Straight and the Black sea. Sat in the co-pilots seat, Red Fox was given the option of taking control of the Spring Adventure, he politely declined.

"Thank you Captain Rushkov but I think I have had enough of being in control, it's never easy no matter what the vessel. It is nice to relax and enjoy the comforts afforded above the waves for a while. Codin, allow the men to enjoy a celebratory beer each but just the one, there is still much to do. Have they all showered and changed clothes as instructed?"

"Yes, Captain every item worn on-board Astute has been sealed in strong weighed canvas bags that are now at various locations on the seabed."

"Good and you are sure no souvenirs have been secreted away?"

"Absolutely Captain, the men know explicitly they

will answer to me if that were to happen. Other than the small arms we have been given here on the Yacht, all other weapons have been disposed of."

They transited the Strait and entered the Black Sea, heading east. Pushkin was eager to find out where their final destination was. He knew all in good time he would be told and instructed to tell the rest. Relief at the thought they were in safe waters was evident by the chorus of Russian folk law songs, heard coming from the lounge. Sparrov's right-hand man knew geographically where they were. As the shape of the coastline appeared, he could not control himself.

"So, Captain it is Georgia."

"Yes indeed, the port of 'Sukhumi' to be precise. The destination for transfer to your new homes in 'Alushta' by Mi-8 'Hip' helicopter I might add. No expense spared for all of you who never questioned my reasoning, I am very proud of all the men, especially you Codin."

"Sir I just did my job, as the rest of the crew did theirs."

"Indeed, Ivor but without all of my hand-picked crew of intrepid sailors this epic journey would never have happened."

When they got too within two miles of the coast the Yacht slowed down to 4 knots. "Right Codin, I want you to assemble the men for the final brief. For your information only, after you all leave I will be staying aboard. We will make for the Feodosiya shipyard to unload our precious cargo of two nuclear warheads and the torpedo explosives we didn't use. They will be transferred to our diesel-electric submarine 'Kronstadt;' it's on a curtesy visit there while conducting sea trials. That will be the final chapter, and then it will be time to relax and enjoy our good fortune."

"Captain if you want me to stay with you for your safety, I am more than willing to do so?"

"Thank you, dear friend, there is no need, the party of Spetznas agents who are guarding the cargo could take on an army. All they know is that it's a very important cargo of high valve. It is better if we part company; our luck has been amazing but no point in tempting providence any longer than necessary. Our enemies will move heaven and earth to try and unearth our shenanigans, what a shame they will be too late." They both laughed.

"I will assemble the men Captain."

Red Fox descended the stairwell from the bridge and walked aft to the lounge. As he entered a tremendous round of clapping and banging on the table ensued. With a grin on his face, he raised his hand and the assembly ceased their raucous welcome. "Gentlemen, fellow sailors we are nearing the end of an adventure the likes of which has never been enacted before. Our enemies in the west have been taught a lesson they will never forget."

With enthusiasm, the Russian sailors cheered there leader.

"Be aware now we are all hunted men, the assurances I have been given as to your safety I consider worthless."

"We have spilt blood and that will not be forgiven or forgotten. You must all be on your guard for the sake of yourselves and your families. You will be flown to your new homes where your loved ones will be there to welcome you all. It has been chosen as the safest place for you all, where a constant vigilance will be paramount. For your own security, I will not be joining you, in time there will be paid assassins out for retribution and my head." He paused, "And finally comrades thank you for your valuable services without which we could not have achieved success, Mother Russia salutes you all."

Captain Lieutenant Ivor Pushkin barked out an order and the men came to attention.

Captain First Rank Dmitri Sparrov took the salute and silently passed along the row of men who would have given their lives for the man they held in awe. Red Fox shook hands with each one knowing this would be the last time he would see them all together. As he turned and marched back the men stood ramrod straight at attention until he left.

"Right men gather your things we dock shortly and head straight for the waiting helicopter," ordered Ivor Pushkin, probably the last one he would be giving to the crew. The mood was strangely sombre; it really was the end of an amazing chapter in all their lives. They were sworn to secrecy and when back with their families could not discuss what had happened during the last few weeks. Sternly reminded that walls have ears, transportation to Siberia was an option none of them relished.

Two Spetznas guards were waiting for Dmitri at the end of the internal walkway. They were trained to take a bullet for the President of Russia if necessary. The one with the Sergeant insignia said,

"Sir you are requested by Captain Rushkov to stay in your cabin until we are safely out to sea."

"Oh yes of course. Sniper?"

"Yes Captain, we don't know how secure this port is. We have created an awful lot of interest with the huge helicopter idling on the football stadium pitch 300mtrs distant."

Red Fox entered the spacious cabin on the stb'd side and drew the blind across the smoked glass window. He would enjoy a glass of whisky from the well-stocked drinks cabinet. Relaxing in the comfortable leather armchair he had time to reflect on how things were. Knowing from the outset his life would never be the same after stealing a British submarine, he had a great deal to come to terms with. Wherever and whenever he went the trained team of bodyguards would be in attendance. Back in Moscow, those privileged enough to know of the success of the operation would be singing his praises. On orders of the President, the Russian hero would be awarded every curtesy and privilege allowable. However, Dmitri Sparrov's freedom to come and go as he had in the past was now a thing of the past. This was certainly evident by the armed guards talking in whispers and shuffling about outside his door.

The noise of the helicopter passing over the Yacht was deafening, a final salute to the great man sat quietly enjoying his drink. With a tinge of sadness, Dmitri raised his glass,

"To absent friends and colleagues."

The powerful Yacht's engines sparked into life and they were on their way. He allowed himself a brief catnap before there was a knock on the door.

"Sir it is safe for you to proceed to the bridge if you wish to do so."

"Thank you; tell Captain Rushkov I will be there presently." Red Fox was deep in thought; perhaps he should have gone ashore with the rest. He would have been flown by charter plane to the safe house set up for him in Moscow. There was no doubt in his mind at least half the crew of the Spring Adventure were Ministry of State Security operatives. Formed from the defunct K.G.B. they could be just as ruthless. The sly old devil Gregor Amatov would have provisioned it that way, he trusted no one. There to oversee the safe return of the two nuclear weapons and the 1280lbs of high explosives secreted in the hold, it was almost full proof. However, until they were safe aboard the 'Kronstadt' Dmitri considered his work was incomplete.

After a while, Red Fox left the cabin to walk forward and ascend the stairs to the bridge. His armed escorts were never more than a few paces from him. One led the way and the others followed close behind. He wanted to challenge them about being so cautious while on-board the Yacht. He realised this would be futile, they were trained to be constantly alert and to react in an instant if they sensed danger. When he got to the bridge he was pleased to see his escorts took up station at the stairwell. "Ah Captain, glad to see you, would you like to join me for breakfast? My pilot can take over."

"Indeed, I would Vlad. The aroma of a cooked breakfast is hard to confine to the galley."

After enjoying a superb meal together, the skipper Vladislav Rushkov was eager to get back to the bridge.

"Would you let me know when we are within 30 minutes of Feodosiya? I want to monitor the transfer of our cargo personally. After that I will be swiftly departing this super vessel, thank you for your hospitality extended to me and my men."

"It has been a pleasure and a privilege to have you all aboard Captain Sparrov."

And so it was at the Crimean shipyard, the cargo was safely transferred to the submarine 'Kronstadt' that sailed immediately for the main Russian naval base of Sevastopol.

Relaxing on his personal plane loaned to him by the President with a glass of Talisker on ice, Red Fox smiled, he considered his work to be complete. As the whisky took effect his mind wandered back to the great times he had had with Alina. Where was she, what was she doing? He considered he had been more than generous for the passion they had enjoyed together. It would make no sense in trying to contact her that would put her life in even more danger. He had made provision to ensure she was safe in her own little world. Ultimately he hoped she would find happiness with a good man that would become her soul mate. Yes, his conscience was clear. He lifted his glass,

"To you Alina Petrenko, you touched my heart."

Chapter 38

Thursday 1st March 2018. 09.00hours
Admiral Nielson's office Northwood Middlesex

Captain Robert Southward was shown into the Admiral's office. He was busy reading a report. He put it down removed his glasses and beckoned the captain over to his large table.

"Sit down Robert, it's good to see you," he beamed. "Coffee?"

Saluting the First Sea Lord he took his seat and opened his pocketbook.

"Thank you, Admiral, I wasn't sure I would get to see you again; I will pass on the coffee thanks."

"No, it's been a rum deal from start to finish, believe me, I quite understand the pressure you have been under during the last three weeks. We should be thankful the final outcome was no more destructive."

"Indeed Admiral."

"Firstly Robert, let me tell you what has happened since Astute was pirated away from Devonport on that fateful day. I know you have had a long debrief with regard to the whole sorry saga, which I have mulled over at some length. However, I am going to let you into some privileged information that you would not have been a party to. What I am about to tell you is top secret and goes no further than this office." The Admiral paused and took a deep breath. "The initial bluff by the pirate leader worked a treat. He was made out to be some rogue ex Russian submarine captain with a grudge. We had to assume he had secured on-board your submarine two nuclear warheads, adaptable to our cruise missiles or torpedoes. We obtained information that they were missing from the Russian nuclear arsenal. At a much later date, this information was rescinded. An abject apology was forthcoming, of course. The explanation was they were deployed on exercise and the paperwork was muddled. A likely story, I don't think. Initially, we knew exactly where you were and made contingency plans. After the submarine literally disappeared because of stealth it was a whole new ball game. Not knowing how far the rogue captain had traversed from the coast of Plymouth was a real headache. The decision was then taken to stop it from reaching international waters. You and your crew and the submarine were deemed expendable, not my decision I might add."

"The government could not risk losing Devonport Royal dockyard and most of the city of Plymouth to an attack. As you well know, the dockyard is the only refit facility we have for out hunter-killer and Trident carrying submarines. We had no idea as to the intentions of the Russian intruders led by, as we found out, a very competent and ruthless captain. To that end, it was decided to negotiate with Red Fox's intermediaries until we could retake or sink Astute."

The Admiral paused and looked at his notes. "I suppose

we should be thankful the stealth technology wasn't sold to China, they have expansionist ideas in the Asian peninsula. As you know their navy is growing all the time and their submarines are good. In fact, their armed forces, in general, are a force to be reckoned with. After all this, we will have to involve the Americans in what we have developed; they are not best pleased with the outcome of this whole escapade. Knowing how they operate it's probable they will take stealth further, look at what they did with the Harrier jump jet. So what it really means is for the time being only us, America and Russia will have Trisonic imaging and Hover track."

The Admiral allowed himself a sigh. "This should never have happened."

"Anyway, after your sub left the English Channel your whereabouts were unknown. We managed a brief encounter when Triumph managed to locate you and an interception was orchestrated. Obviously, you were aware of the two torpedoes loosed at you by your pursuer, one a live warhead, these were considered warning shots." "Yes, Admiral although I was kept in a semi-comatose state, I was well aware of the firings and I was extremely concerned but could do nothing."

"Indeed, anyway the decision was made to break off the attack. Triumph was considered vulnerable with its superior ability your submarine had the upper hand. My surface units were provided with your last known position and considered to be within striking distance. This proved to be not the case." The Admiral paused and looked directly at Captain Southward. "Robert, in the time you were detained in your cabin by those barbarians I can only imagine the trauma you went through." Yes, he had had many flashbacks where he was convinced his life would be extinguished but Red Fox had kept his word. In the main he and his crew had lived to fight another day, but would that chance ever come now? He doubted it. Admiral Neilson could see the captain was in deep thought, and no wonder.

"Anyway your submarine was lost until you entered the straits of Gibraltar. Triso and hovertrack were used to great effect and our efforts to establish contact with all I had at my disposal proved fruitless. We scoured the western approaches and the North Atlantic in the areas deemed most likely to find you, without results, very frustrating. Only three officers on-board Triumph including Admiral Jefferies knew of the stealth devices being engaged assumed to be operated by your coerced crew. We now know the Russians were conversant with its workings, and quickly learned how to operate the system. Ordered to return to Devonport the officers and operators on-board Triumph had been informed there was a malfunction with the active sonar. I had a director and technicians from Thales Sonar visit the sub for some time and verify this. They were informed it was of National Security and the course of action was necessary. Really don't know what my crew thought including the commanding officer, they are not stupid, but we are the secret service and all have been instructed not to discuss what happened."

Captain Robert Southward listened to the Admiral intently; he knew a lot of what he was being told was highly classified.

The Admiral continued,

"The pirate leader was very clever; after passing the straits, he hugged the coast all through the Mediterranean and Aegean seas, knowing we could not execute a plan to halt his progress. To sink a nuclear submarine in that area would have caused an international outcry. We naturally assumed he would make for the black sea through the Bosporus. We had the frigate Norfolk and the destroyer Duncan waiting to intercept. Having the best minds working on this, service and civilian, we were running out of options. The truth is the pirates with a lot of help from God knows where outsmarted us at every turn. The government has lost fourteen billion pounds from the war chest but has been allowed to keep its integrity. Lessons have been learned, we were totally overstretched searching for one submarine, all be it one of our own."

The Navy budget was due to be constricted further, I am sure that will now be rescinded. The new frigate build will be given top priority and two other yards including Appledore Shipbuilders will be given orders to cut steel and fabricate modules for assembly at the Glasgow shipyards. The first eight envisaged will hopefully become a batch of 12. Of course, the build of the first, having been given the name, H.M.S. Glasgow is well underway. If the Defence Minister has anything to do with it, destroyer numbers will also be increased. He will be backed to the hilt by the Navy top brass and other cabinet ministers."

"That is good news, Admiral."

"Robert, we were caught with our trousers down. While we were searching for you, there was no British submarine in the south Atlantic. In fact, all our territories were vulnerable including Gibraltar. I had to make the decisions regarding where our fleet was and I had a lot of sleepless nights over it, I take full responsibility for my actions, it goes with the job. Now we are back to something like normal operations, questions are being asked. The Prime Minister and the cabinet are horrified about the situation we were in. I have been pointing out for years we have been overstretched with our global commitments, with lack of ships and men. Of course, that cuts no ice with the number crunchers in Whitehall."

The Admiral sat back in his chair. "That's the bones of it. Of course both you and I will be retired from the Service forthwith. For some time, you and your men will be under surveillance by MI6. I have vouched for you and your crew's integrity but the powers that be are not totally convinced all is as it seems. After much discussion and investigation, there is doubt over what coercion did or did not take place. I know you will not agree to that possible scenario as your sailors were hand-picked and I totally agree with that. Unfortunately, it has now been taken out of my hands by a higher authority. Have you any questions?"

"Well Admiral, there are many questions I would like to ask, but they seem pointless after what you have just told me. Thank you for making it perfectly clear, I know you have divulged more than you are required to. I suppose I should be grateful to that tyrant Red Fox for sparing my crew. The fact he has cost me my career, I find hard to swallow." "

Yes, I believe the brigand and his pirates will eventually

have cost many people their positions, not to mention lives."

"One other thing when the submarine was diving after the pirates had left; there followed an enormous explosion on the surface. Heavy debris could be heard sinking, what on earth was that?"

The Admiral referred to his notes. "I have scant information about that, I'm afraid. We think they were destroying whatever was of no use to them anymore. It is not our intention to follow that up; I understand the Turkish authorities are investigating, I suggest you forget the incident."

Robert was not convinced but knew better than to push it further. He was sure there was a cover-up and his boss knew exactly what had happened. The truth was, with Turkey being part of N.A.T.O, the authorities had agreed not to investigate further. Indeed the families of the fishermen accepted large financial rewards in exchange for their silence. They had all been coerced to sign agreements to that effect and would be prosecuted if they did not comply.

The Chief of Staff rose from his chair and extended his hand. The Captain grasped the Admiral's hand and reciprocated the handshake.

"Good luck in the future, Robert."

With that, the man who burdened the responsibility turned and left the room. They both knew for security reasons they would never meet again. Blake Channing entered the room.

"Captain your car is ready."

"Thank you, Blake."

Captain Robert Southward picked up his officer's hat

and followed Blake out of the door into a very busy main office. He positioned his cap squarely on his head and ran his fingers along the pristine gold oak leaves, destined to become redundant.

As he walked through the office the naval personnel went about their business. Not one officer or senior rating looked up from their work stations. He knew these were the same people that had sifted over the myriad of information that came in. All relevant aspects would have been relayed to the Admiral since the beginning of Astute's demise. What were they thinking, hero or coward, who knows? Confidently he marched the length of the office and exited through the blast-proof door. Marching on to the main exit he felt very alone. Could he have done more to negate the piracy that had occurred? Certainly the idea of making mechanical noise was an option he considered. This may have resulted in Astute being heard and sunk, but a bullet to the brain would have been his reward. In his comatosed state and for the welfare of his crew he had dismissed the idea anyway. He knew with triso and hovertrack an escape by the submarine would probably have happened regardless. Under the circumstances he was convinced he had made the right decisions, his conscience was clear.

Passing the temporary swipe card he had been issued with to the security officer, he mounted the stairs with a spring in his step. The two armed guards came to attention and saluted, and he reciprocated. He exited the revolving doors into a beautiful spring morning and took a deep intake of breath; it was good to be alive.

Reflecting on the whole of his naval career he had been

a party to some exiting and top-secret events. His private life had suffered immensely as a result of his total commitment. But in truth other than the piracy, he would not have had it any other way. The senior service was in his blood and that now had to change. Maybe just maybe he could salvage something from his marriage. It would turn out to be a forlorn hope.

He whispered to himself,

"Well Robert old boy, what a sorry mess, where the hell do you go from here?"

Printed in Great Britain
by Amazon